Three can keep a secret if two are dead.
-Benjamin Franklin (1706-1790)

I0611282

System Seven

Michael J. Parks

Seventh Sense Press

ISBN: 0985651237
ISBN-13: 9780985651237

Acknowledgements

To my family for their support and patience, especially Chris for being a sounding board for ideas. To Laura (aka Matera the Mad), Daedlanth, Jim Giffen, and Dan Adams for their frank critique and guidance. To Greg Meyer and Erin Tognetti for their early encouragement. Special thanks to Tonja Wilcox and Angela Adams for their support and belief in me on the long road.

This novel is dedicated to those who dare peer into what is in order to understand what may be. The future is, as always, in your hands.

It is also dedicated to my parents.

PART I - Change

Chapter 1

From Milan to Mexico to Palo Alto and ending in Munich, Crosstalk's bots had blazed a trail armed with heuristics designed to locate secrets. Any kind of secrets. Secret crimes, secret transactions, secret affairs, secret events, secret money.

Secret secrets.

The one hook started it, a brokerage firm in Italy. A deleted file on a USB stick left inserted in a computer. Keyword matches triggered the auto-analysis for stage one. Email addresses culled from the document helped widen the net. The mail server's message store yielded further triggers to reach stage two, causing bots to spread out to the various mail servers found in the emails. Clues gathered lead to analysis on database servers in the U.S. and Munich. From that, the bots created a stage three profile of something covert involving big money and buried transactions.

At that point he had options for any number of operations – theft, extortion, blackmail – depending on what the profile indicated. Only things didn't stay typical. After Munich the trails became more exotic, the effort more manual, with the keywords and content hinting at something truly special.

And so it began, almost two months of picking and prying at servers around the globe. At the end of it, the reward was an encrypted file that took twelve days to break open. That had been three days ago.

Three days that felt like a week.

Crosstalk left his computer and walked to the window, pistol in hand. Hacking was an art, a serious hobby for sure, but it wasn't supposed to be like this. *This* was fucked up.

He parted the blinds and peered outside his flat. Night's stillness gripped the London suburb of Kingston. Almost two-thirty and the streets were empty. Down the way a lamp over the cemetery's gate flickered. For long moments it felt as if the dead were using it to signal.

"I will send it out," he muttered. "The world will know."

A sound from the hall registered above the whir of the computer's fans and he turned to look. The doorway held potential, a shimmering vibe, as if it might suddenly fill with intruders. He slid the semi-automatic's safety to the off position. Thirteen rounds in the clip.

They'll know but will they believe?

He waited but heard nothing more. Turning back, his eyes reflected from the window. In them he saw a glint of fear and fanaticism. The last of disbelief was gone.

He returned to the screen and set the pistol down. The upload to Alcazar continued. He started an encrypted email to explain the file. Composing became an obstacle. *How to convey the unbelievable without sounding insane?* Short and to the point, with a link to the file. The content would speak for itself.

He barely finished the email when another sound came, louder than before. He snatched the pistol and faced the hallway. The fans of the computer grew deafening against the silence. Sweat gathered on his brow.

"Damn it." He'd gone too far, scraped too hard. The game had grown too close, too real.

The progress bar crawled to completion, the upload done. Storing the file in Alcazar might insure its safety. For the email, Magistrate would use conscripted servers to secretly tunnel the mail to its destination. *But who to?* One person stood out: SlotZero. Intelligent and open-minded, he would take it seriously and know what to do with it.

He clicked the send button knowing it could be a death sentence.

For a moment regret lingered – until a much stronger feeling took hold. As if the air pressure had changed, he sensed another presence, maybe several. Pain bloomed in his skull like a headache but modulated, unnatural. Anticipation arched into fear as it spread. It hurt to see, breathe, to hear. Confusion eroded focus. The truth dawned, rising to life from the stolen file.

"Ah fuck."

They could do this.

He almost missed the tone signaling the email had gone out. Reaching down, he stabbed the power switch and plunged the room into silence. Blood pulsed against his eardrums in time to the pain. The weight of the pistol was a comfort but now only as a sure means of escape from the hell of his body.

Had he only known, he wouldn't have done it. His motives had been naïve. Uncover the truth. *Everyone deserves to know the truth.*

Straining from the pain, he said, "No one deserves *this*."

2

• • •

Austin Bakken stood at a fifth floor window in InterGen's Folsom offices. The California sun glowed in a sky hazed from a week of Sierra wildfires. Seen through tinted windows, it looked like an alien star. For a few heartbeats, he stood in a starship in low orbit, taking in the view.

His terrestrial post felt like working in the dirt by comparison. In the distance, the Sacramento skyline sprouted from the tree-covered valley floor like fence posts.

A hot Friday and most of the office had already vacated. Instead of leaving, he had someone else's missed deadline to deal with. The server farm upgrade project was in shambles and required saving. Never mind he had migrated from Servers to Network Security – the treadmill just needed a runner on it and he was that guy.

He breathed deep and let it out. Kaiya would be getting ready to leave work for class. Last night's talk was still fresh in his mind. Absolutely yes she was important, a huge part of his world. His busy, often self-absorbed world. Between work and chasing his dream, Kaiya time had taken a hit.

He sent her a text. *105 in the shade. Swim after class?*

Making it big with his home automation system was the dream, but she was, too. Hell, it was as much for her as it was for him. They needed more time together and he wanted to give it to her. It was just embarrassing to have to be reminded. He shouldn't have to be reminded.

With a last glance at the alien star, he returned to his cubicle and got back on the treadmill.

Trading the chilled office for a hot parking garage felt almost lusty. Wood smoke from the wildfires brought to mind camping. He'd finished updating the project timeline, including schedules. Murray would approve but the Boston server teams wouldn't, of course. Tons of overtime and two lost weekends. It was the only way the project would make the launch date. InterGen's new IQ Access service had to go live on time and within budget.

His phone buzzed with a text.

Swim no. They drained the pool :(Drought. Surprise yes :) Working late?

His heart soared. Being connected to her still had that effect.

A primer gray Honda pulled onto the level and expertly missed him before it parked. Matt Phio climbed out.

"Yo Mr. Bakken, what's up?"

He smiled at Matt's always-good mood. "Gettin' the hell out of Dodge."

"Hey," Matt thumbed towards his car, "Remember the AC took a shit? Get this: my *apartment* AC crapped out last night!"

"Cursed by the AC gods, dude. Plenty cold inside. See ya."

He replied to Kaiya. *Leaving now. Surprise?*

Half an hour later he turned onto his cul de sac and saw her car in the driveway. In the garage, a male voice sounded from a Muzak speaker nailed to a rafter. It announced Kaiya's presence, a voicemail, and four personal emails.

"Thank you, Sam. How long has she been here?"

"FORTY-THREE MINUTES."

A bump of pride, still. His creation wove technology into ordinary life dramatically: the old house seemed intelligent, aware. He headed for the kitchen and found his girlfriend at the range stirring a pot and swaying to the music.

"Hey baby." He kissed her in greeting. "What happened?"

"Class was cancelled and Nelson let us all go early."

"No shit? Why?"

"Something about power at the school. Nelson just said 'happy Friday, go enjoy it'."

"Wish I had a boss like that." He dropped his keys and wallet on the island. "What ya makin'?"

"Thai chicken and noodles. You'll like it." She tapped the raw wood base of the countertop. "Um, weren't you going to work on the tile?"

He almost laughed. "I was gonna do a lot of things this week. Been nuts at work. The alternator fiasco didn't help."

"Hey, I tried to warn you. BMW, big money waste." She looked at him, gauging his mood. "I believe I even looked up the year and model. It had problems."

"All cars can have problems." He pulled a beer from the fridge. "Thankfully it was just the alternator."

"I noticed you made progress with Sam."

"Yeah?"

"I didn't have to use my key, he recognized my voice the first time. And I've been talking to myself to try and activate him. Not one mistake. I'm impressed."

"Thanks. The voice integration is really coming together. The code's been tough to tweak."

"Well you're doing something right. Maybe it's time to start attracting those investors. Or are you still thinking a Kickstarter project?"

"Probably both. I might be ready, yeah. Would need to do a demo video for sure. I've got some ideas."

"Cool." She stirred, waiting for him to take his first drink. "So, I talked with my mom earlier. She wants us to visit for Christmas."

He rolled his eyes. "Us? Riiiight. Gee, I wonder if she knows that would mean a huge flight across the Pacific?"

"Oh, I'm pretty sure she does."

"Just her way of separating us for the holidays. Or making me suffer the flight. She'll never forgive me."

According to Yuni Wilson, her daughter wasn't being exposed to the 'higher class of male specimens' she deserved. Her mom didn't hate him but she sure resented him. *"If you truly loved her, you would release her to men more of her station. Her future is in question with you, no matter your intentions."* After that he'd given up trying to win her approval.

"Not my fault you chose me. And I didn't make her sell the house and move back to Japan."

"Um, she didn't sell the house."

"What?"

"She told me today." She went to drain the pot. "Well, she let it slip anyway."

"That lying old–" Her frown stopped him short. "What? That's a new low, don't you think?"

"I told her what I thought of her lying. Of course she didn't exactly *apologize* but I think we won't have a problem getting there next month. I'm guessing you'd prefer Catalina over camping with all the smoke?"

Shit. Next month? He'd forgotten to request vacation time. There it was again, the core of their recent problems. He filed a huge mental note to put in for the time off. "As long she doesn't show up, sure."

Kaiya toweled her hands and wrapped her arms around his neck. "Don't worry, she won't. And Christmas? I'm not going. I just thought you'd enjoy her latest jab. She can wait until my visit in March. If she misses us that much, she's more than able to fly out here."

Around a kiss he quipped, "Yeah, on her broom."

During dinner thoughts of work swarmed. He managed to ditch most of them and enjoy conversation instead. Afterward, they took in a movie which she passed out halfway through. It had been that kind of week for them both. Herding her upstairs to bed, he'd mostly forgotten the day's issues. Still, he knuckled the wooden banister just in case. Work sometimes kept him up.

At the top of the stairs a microphone poked from the cciling.

"Bedtime, Sam." In response, the AI sent instructions to sensors and cameras around the property, slipping into night security mode.

"SYSTEM ARMED WITH ZERO EXCEPTIONS. GOOD NIGHT AUSTIN AND KAIYA."

The digital clock read 1:32am. *Chalk one up for work.* Giving up, he slid out of bed, pulled on some shorts, and headed towards the shop.

Built over the garage, the shop was another unfinished project of the previous owner. Only the incomplete work and the recession had made the foreclosure affordable and only then with his father's help. The sensors, microphones, and cameras were all up and running and most of the walls had sheetrock hung. His free time went into working on the feature set of the AI or with Kaiya so finishing the house wasn't happening.

The lights flickered on in the garage. He tapped a code on the shop's door keypad to unlock it and climbed the stairs beyond.

"Sam, mode two, volume low."

A spotlight lit a desk, a computer screen came alive, and jazz fusion filled the room. He padded over to the mini-fridge and retrieved a beer. He glanced down: the workouts had to resume before his belly ballooned like his dad's. The resemblance was already forming. *Fear the genes.*

The jazz was too much for the hour. "Sam, load my new age playlist."

The music shifted to synthesizers and strings.

At a window he stared at the faint stars hovering over the hills. In the half-tired, half-wired haze of early morning, he imagined stepping out as a giant and foot-planting the Sierras to launch into the heavens to explore. Star-lit nebulas and crowded solar systems swung past in a seconds-long vision that ended with the familiar feeling of being cheated.

Growing up, everyone thought that by the year 2018 mankind would be in space, working and mining the planets at least, if not flitting from star to star in true exploration. Instead, they hadn't even come close. Rovers chewing soil on desolate Mars was as far as they'd come. Corrupt and spineless politicians had allowed the government's coffers to be drained by military industry. Corporations effectively owned the country and war was still the only black hole they were interested in. Space programs of substance never regained funding.

He swigged his beer and thoughts landed on a terrestrial vacation instead. A campsite, firelight, good beer and good grub, followed by mad love under the stars. Truth told, camping sounded better, wood smoke or not. Catalina Island was great but required flying, no matter how short the flight. Driving would steal a half a day.

He opened a cabinet where a brass Buddha incense holder from Berkeley wafted memories thicker than smoke. He set it on the window ledge and fitted a sandalwood stick into the happy teacher's belly button. Tiny sparks danced as the first strands of gray lifted into the room.

At once memories stirred. Gatherings with friends to test psychic abilities. The trip to Area 51. Experiments with dream journals. Ouija boards, channeling, meditation, and nights spent staring up at the stars, sending out vibes to attract aliens. Among the crazy efforts were powerful times that still lingered with a life of their own. The lucid dreams and out of body experiences remained the pinnacle experiences. It seemed a lifetime ago and in a way it was. A part of him was still amazed at the edgy and wondrous experiments and always would be.

He pushed aside the mesh of memories and settled in front of *Grunge*, the shop computer. If writing code didn't wear him out, nothing would.

Half an hour later, movement caught his eye. A sleepy Kaiya appeared from the dim of the stairwell with his cell phone in her hand.

"Um, Mr. Bakken? You forgot something. It's Matt."

Seeing her, he wanted to ignore the call. She'd come up wearing only her black silk sleeping shorts. He turned in his chair and welcomed her in an embrace.

"Sexy," he whispered around her lips.

"Mm-hmm. Take your call."

Matt apologized before reporting an anomaly at one of the edge routers that protected InterGen's network. "Utilization went nuts but I'm not seeing why. I think I'm missing something. Can you take a quick look?"

He withdrew from Kaiya and tapped the VPN to reach the router in question. After a scan of the logs, a detail jumped out: a standby network card on the router had been activated and reconfigured.

"Damn."

She knelt next to him, asking with her eyes.

"Shit's in the fan, I think. Maybe even a hack. Sorry, babe."

"S'okay. Go get 'em." She stood, stroked his cheek, and strolled over to the window he'd looked out earlier. The woman he loved, inside a room full of technology, peering out at nature beyond – he took a mental snapshot.

A flow of data coursed out the hijacked router. The network systems monitors all showed green and no alarms had gone off – there was still a chance an InterGen tech had set up something unauthorized. A captured sample of the data stream revealed the type of files being transferred.

"Christ. Someone's moving around music? Who would be so stupid?"

• • •

A miniature neon beer sign over Johan's desk cast its glow in the smoke from his pipe. Across the studio apartment's floor lay laptops, network cabling, and a pair of routers blinking in the dark. Laptop speakers tried to do justice to a discordant Eurobeat mp3 but came up woefully short. Corduroy curtains blocked out the morning light.

The Dutch hacker watched the cargo stream from InterGen to his client's server in Thailand. For five hundred euro and as a test of InterGen's security it was worth babysitting the transfer.

He ashed his pipe into an old coffee mug. InterGen had been on his bucket list for over two years. He had nearly given up trying except for the thousand different ways for profit once inside. In the end he lucked out with a combination of fresh tools that exploited an extraordinary vulnerability in the Crest series of Rocom routers, one that could only be another NSA backdoor. Finding them was all the rage.

He peeled a thumbnail-sized strip of the claylike hash from the trim of the monitor and fired up another bowl. After a deep pull, the transfer paused onscreen. He held his breath and willed it to continue. It did.

"I am a god," he quipped as he exhaled. He started to check email when the transfer paused again, then once more.

He set the pipe down and pulled up a console window to investigate.

• • •

"It's a hacker."

Back at InterGen Matt asked, "How? What'd you find?"

"A root account on one of the old Promulgate servers is active. He's pushing shit out now."

"Where's it going?"

He grunted. "Another hacked box unless he works for the Canadian Tourism Board. They might be able to see where the packets are going."

"You're going after him?"

"Damn straight I am."

A call to the Canadian NOC went to voicemail. He marked it urgent but could only wait.

"Crap, I can't believe this."

The thought of someone cracking open the network was as annoying as it was surprising. Rocom routers were the most secure shit on the planet; the Crest series cost a fortune. The only thing that kept him from driving to InterGen was Kaiya's soft hands rubbing his back and the nudging of her breasts while she listened to him describe the hack.

"See here... this is where he defined a new network. And here," he tapped at a string of text, "the shitball rooted the old Promulgate server and hijacked it. He's got about fifteen gigs of porn and music stashed and is sending some out now."

She shook her head. "Owned by a hacker, babe. Not good."

It sucked to hear but was true. "Yeah. I don't see any new sessions so he hasn't gone exploring yet. I'll have to shut him out if he does. Crap, I wish Canada would call back."

• • •

Across the planet from InterGen, Johan minimized the window, satisfied his gig on the Promulgate server was safe. The interruptions originated from somewhere inside the network but had since smoothed out. Relieved, he celebrated with a couple more tokes of hash. Soon he'd have help in cracking open database servers, a profitable gig as long as they stayed hidden.

His other side venture was setting up the extortion of a famous British playwright suffering from a case of pedophilia. With forged system access to a private server hosting child pornography, Johan had extracted membership information. Of course the playwright hadn't registered under his real name but had paid with a credit card, a transaction recorded and stored by the server operator without consent. Johan had run the entire credit card database against the Underground's collection of databases to cull a match.

In this case, the blackmail would likely be routine. He'd already infected the playwright's computer with a custom tracker rootkit that logged and transmitted a daily report showing how long each page was looked at, how many times – a play by play of the sick obsession. With those reports he would extract one hundred thousand euro for not presenting the facts to the playwright's wife of nine years... or to the papers. For an additional fee he offered the bonus plan: destruction of the server's records incriminating him. Most took the option. An added five thousand euro for a minute's work. That he would later release copies of the records anyway was something he kept strictly to himself.

He drew deeply from his pipe. *Karma can be a bitch.*

Outside, a concert of car horns erupted just as an email arrived from Crosstalk.

He arched his brows and blew a thin plume of smoke, noting the synchronicity. Two years ago a set of jpegs from Crosstalk netted them half a million euro. The images of a Dutch parliament member engaged in illicit sex with a youth had been taken with his knowledge though obviously a trust had been betrayed. The extortion went flawlessly with the help of an intermediary in Arnhem. There had been very little contact from him since. A couple of false starts on jobs that didn't pan out. Crosstalk always worked the big ones.

He again pulled deeply from the pipe. The email was encrypted as it had arrived from the Underground's Magistrate system. Using Crosstalk's private key, he opened it to reveal an Alcazar link and a single paragraph.

THEY ARE TRACKING ME RIGHT NOW THEY HAVE ME
I AM DEAD TONIGHT. THEY ARE ON THE GROUND AND
IN PEOPLES MINDS DON'T LET THEM FIND WHO YOU
ARE!! GET THIS AND RUN NOW ZERO RIGHT NOW GO
LOW FAST BUT FIND A WAY TO LET IT OUT. LET THEM
HAVE IT!! MAKE IT COUNT!!!! I WAS DARREN BLYTHE
ENGLAND, HCS. REMEMBER STATEN-GENERAAL.

High was suddenly almost too high. He read the paragraph once
more in disbelief. That Crosstalk used his real name was almost as
surprising as the message itself. *Go low*. To run, to disappear. Not a
warning given lightly. The link would kick off a download from
Alcazar, the Underground's secure storage network.

"Seriously?"

Almost ten minutes left on the mp3 dump to the Thai client. He
clicked the link to start the Alcazar download. Forty chunks. It could
take twice as long as the Thai download.

Run now Zero right now go low fast.

"Fuck."

· · ·

Up in the shop the music faded and Sam interrupted.

"INCOMING CALL FROM LISA DELANGER OF THE CANADIAN
TOURISM COMMISSION."

"Here she is." Austin pressed a button on his headset to connect
and winked at Kaiya curled up on the recliner. She had slipped into
one of his paint-splattered t-shirts.

The Canadian admin required minimal prompting before
producing the next hop: a backbone router for a large telco in New
Jersey. With thanks and a promise to let her know how the chase
ended, he signed off and dialed the network operations center contact
listed for the telecom. A bored voice answered the phone in Jersey.

"Austin Bakken here from InterGen California. Your gw08 router
is being used right now by a hacker to stream his data. If you could do
me a huge favor and just check where those packets are headed to? I'm
trying to track him and–"

"Ah *shit*..." The voice was suddenly more awake.

"— I'm hoping you can help. The packets are inbound from–" he
rattled off the IP address of the Canadian hop, "–and can't be missed,
there's a ton of 'em."

Keyboard clatter mixed with a string of cuss words. "Okay, got them."

"Them?"

"Two destinations. Hang on. One's Thailand. The other... Germany. The load's going to Thailand and your hacker's in Europe. Or using Europe anyway. I'm going to have to shut this down–"

He asked him to wait. "I need another ten or twenty minutes to track."

He got ten so he sent Matt chasing the Thailand server. The real trace was through the router in Germany to the hacker. A lookup showed a website and email hosted off the address, the domain registered to a brewery. He phoned internationally to the technical contact, someone named Andreas Bietl. An assistant regretfully informed he wasn't available.

When would he return? It was lunchtime, maybe an hour. Could he type a few commands at the router in question? No, he wasn't authorized to but would take a message.

A sudden dead end in the grab for the hacker.

• • •

One of Johan's cells rang.

"Ja?"

"Nosy admin called from InterGen in America trying to track you. I brushed him off but Andreas may have to deal with him. What are you up to now?"

The InterGen job blown? If nothing else was truly wrong, that certainly was.

"Just a dump of music and porn. I have other things to concern me right now, but please thank Andreas, and thank you."

"Be careful where you are poking around, Drehen! We can only allow your streams if you conceal yourself well."

"Ja, ja, the transfer is over in moments. I will route the interface to avoid your path. My apologies. Guten tag."

The last of his clothes went into a suitcase stacked on the luggage dolly. Still a couple of minutes left on the Thailand gig and only twelve of the forty file chunks had come down from Alcazar.

He looked around the studio. Surfaces wiped. Nothing of identity except stray, undocumented DNA. He dismissed the thought that he might be overreacting to an odd email. Survival protocol demanded action. Threat, response. Control ahead of change. He'd be back, but then again... he looked around once more. If not, he'd miss the studio, his home for the past four months.

The mp3 transfer was nearly complete. He walked to the French doors and parted the heavy curtains. Streets reflected the gray skies that drizzled the city. Another in a series of summer storms was due over Rotterdam before nightfall. He rubbed the stubble of his cheeks. Crosstalk's email crowded his buzz. Possible information, possible bullshit. Even if it were nothing, it was good for drill though he would want an explanation.

A delivery truck laid on its horn. Three teenage girls laughed off the near collision and danced onto the sidewalk. Music from the Italian cafe below sounded faintly. *Italia.* The beauty, the food, the traditions, and the people, the sense of family. He hadn't returned since the deVere incident. Instead, he enjoyed lunch and dinner at Cafe Trevi where Marie and Cathrine waited on him with their beautiful accents.

A feeling pressed uncomfortably on his buzz – the feeling it was time to go. He checked the laptop and found trace warnings from Alcazar. He scrolled through the messages.

"*Shit.*" Someone had bypassed all safeguards and tracked him.

He canceled the Alcazar download with only fifteen file chunks received and began unplugging gear.

"What the fuck, Crosstalk? What did you grab?"

• • •

A security guard waved Austin's white BMW through the gates at InterGen just before the Saturday sun rose above the Sierras. He'd arrived early to get a head start on addressing the Crest vulnerability. Rocom had already formed a response team and were ready to work with him.

A sluggish Matt and two other techs looked up from their consoles as he entered the network operations center. The large NORADs showed systems and traffic looking first-rate.

"All quiet, boss."

"Good. How did the trace to Thailand go?"

"Through that factory in Bangkok to a hosting company that doesn't honor requests without legal wrapping."

"Figures. You scanned the other routers?"

He nodded and stood to stretch. "No broken glass, no trace. The alarms are set based on what we know."

"Good news. Beat it Matt, and thanks for the hard work."

"Twenty minutes 'til I can turn back into a pumpkin."

"Go. These guys will keep an eye on things."

Matt came over and said in a low voice, "I'm really sorry for not catching the hack."

"Don't sweat it. Like my dad always says, 'A mistake shouldn't embarrass anyone, but failing to benefit by it should.' I doubt you'd miss it again."

"Nope, I sure wouldn't."

The hiss of the soda opening coincided with the phone ringing. Austin took a gulp before he answered. It was Andreas Bietl of the brewery in Germany, speaking with thickly accented English.

"I am returning your earlier call. How may I help you?"

He explained the intrusion at InterGen and the trace back to their brewery. "I was hoping you might have logs for that router and would allow me to analyze them, or perhaps you have a technical person I could talk with."

There was a pause. "Log files? Hackers? I know nothing of these things. My consultant keeps our network secure. It is unfortunate that your security was breached but I cannot help with what you ask. We have no logs."

From not knowing what a log file was to knowing he didn't have any. This would go nowhere.

He couldn't help responding tightly. "If your consultant finds anything pertaining to this matter, please do have him contact me. I will send my information."

"Of course."

"Thank you." He ended the call with a thump on the desk. Kaiya's words echoed. *Owned by a hacker, babe. Not good.*

No, not good at all.

Just in case, he fired off his contact information to the German bullshitter and got on the phone with Rocom to help isolate the Crest vulnerability.

Chapter 2

He who joyfully marches in rank and file has already earned my contempt. He has been given a large brain by mistake, since for him a spinal cord would suffice.
-Albert Einstein, German-born American physicist

Many people whose lives are comprised of compounded lies end up developing a certain amount of nagging regret. It's the feeling, however small, of wishing the lies had never begun while knowing all too well they had and would continue. While they might get used to the feeling, it never lost its eventual bitter after taste.

For Johan, whose normal footprint in society was as false as the nature backdrops used in the Berlin opera, the lies that made up his identity were nag free. The characters portrayed to the unsuspecting public were genuine, the backgrounds contrived yet harmless to those he met and chose to interact with. That is, harmless to most. That he sometimes acted outside of those personas and did break laws, steal, extort, con, and worse did not weigh heavily on his conscience. There was no reason to indulge in regret because he was merely acting as an agent of karmic balance.

A vague notion to most, the idea of karma and a universe that saw fit to balance it among all things was very real to Johan – life experience had proven its existence beyond any doubt. Targets were never needy individuals or companies; they were always well-endowed firms or individuals, professional players of the big game of life. In the written and unwritten records of their past were histories that made them deserving. His was an uncanny ability to uncover the players and their past. Sifting through news reports and social magazines, political reports and court filings, hacked email accounts and mail servers, invariably deserving targets appeared.

Karmic balance.

Just as the wind blew strong to topple rotted pines in the forest, so did he effect change on those he selected. If profit occurred as a result, it was simply the scales swinging back into line.

Once he'd begun such work the successes piled up, creating a momentum that allowed him to pursue that balance with greater resources and with more exacting cause.

He operated in the narrow but plentiful gaps that ran through all major systems. Those systems relied on technology and technology relied on humans to program it. Those programs had weaknesses, especially when strung together. Legions of hackers found and exploited those gaps. Johan belonged to a group that harvested that information to form an exclusive repository of tools.

When a needed hack couldn't be found in the repository, he wasn't beyond physically infiltrating facilities to install his own wedge to allow access. Drehen Legters, his web designer and internet marketing wiz persona, was well traveled as a result. Social engineering skills stemmed from an admittedly borderline neurotic personality he'd largely mastered and could direct at will, a character that had talked his way into secure facilities and out of many a dire strait. Success came from blending old world material finesse with technological expertise.

There could be no better time for fortune from such a mix. The adoption of computerized records, combined with the decline of care put into paper record keeping, allowed for very creative results. Both storage mediums were subject to unauthorized access and alteration given the right preparation.

Lately, his efforts were aimed at catching up with those that used stolen innocence as currency. It was as dangerous an effort as any he'd undertaken, in some ways more so... but also more rewarding – to enact punitive sentences on those that no court could easily target. For now, he was picking off the users; later he would target the server operators, which might involve the law or might lead to something much more elaborate and severe. The justice systems of the world were plagued with ineffective agents and his work was needed for balance. As long as he followed his rules, the outcome of each effort was predictable, resulting in either success or a controlled failure.

Driving in the storm-cast gloom of early evening, he assessed the situation. Half in character, half thinking of mortality, what happened at the apartment tugged hard on the edge of calm. When the traces showed up, the walls of the tiny apartment echoed Crosstalk's command, *go low*...

He had rolled his two luggage dollies down the alleyway to the Vanagon two streets over. He circled back and parked with a view of Café Trevi and his apartment, cell phones off in precaution. A familiar position, waiting out possible danger. He doubted anything would happen but was prepared to wait the rest of the day to be sure.

Within minutes the men arrived in a sedan with blacked out windows. They disappeared into the entry and all too soon one appeared in his apartment window, a handgun briefly visible. At that moment the message from Crosstalk became substantial, the danger as tangible as the rain returning to pelt the roof and windshield.

For the first time in years a familiar fear flickered, the kind that swallowed reason to spawn panic. There could be no doubt that Crosstalk was in trouble – perhaps dead if his warning proved accurate.

It was good not to exist.

A comforting maxim he'd grown fond of, he mulled it over for a good kilometer. More than anything it was comfort he sought driving on the storm-slick A3 towards Munich.

I don't exist.

Birth records in tiny Elburg in the Gelderland province were missing from the local and the regional government storehouses. The hospital that once held his childhood medical records lost them one chilly December night years ago. The national registry of citizens, converted to database form nearly ten years prior, had been purged of his existence. He'd never been arrested so his prints weren't on file. Medical work was done at free clinics or through private practices. Cash payment and false ID.

Having never been born, he was free to give birth to his own personas. The supporting documentation and history of three identities were his, each a blossom amidst the vast crop of failed or partial identities, each an artful manipulation of the systems that defined identity. Two he could become at a moment's notice – the third required a half hour's makeup session. They were the result of a life spent seeking intrigue, wealth, and most importantly, freedom.

Only now complications from Crosstalk's email threatened invisibility – he was tagged as a person of interest by whoever was tracking him. Identities used for utilities and rent were paper-thin. Bank deposits were manual and email accounts new. Web traffic logs would reveal nothing of identity, though the encrypted streams through Underground servers and bots could attract attention.

The truly alarming thing was how fast they'd physically reached him. From the timestamp on Crosstalk's email to the time they'd hit the apartment was a span of only twenty-five minutes. It implied a government-level response, a worst-case scenario.

The handgun seen in the window made him think of Mrs. Shulz. Because of the rewire of service into his apartment, they would have gone to her apartment first. Guns drawn, she would have been terrified. Guilt burned.

Cars passed him on the soaked highway and turned the van's windows opaque between wiper strokes. Making it to Munich through rising winds and rain provided distraction from the unanswered questions but not enough. Fear still ranged the periphery of thought.

"I don't exist," he said to the road ahead.

He couldn't deny that the axiom offered less comfort than before.

The lights of distant Munich seen through the rainfall lightened his heart. He'd made the eight-hour drive straight through, sleep a prominent passenger the last hour. An exit led to a tumbling lane with farms, pastures, and stands of old-growth trees. He slowed when he saw the familiar wooden sign swinging in the wind. He turned into a long drive, rolled past a stone farmhouse, and stopped in front of an oversized barn. Amidst the darkness and rain, the wooden structure loomed ominous and foreboding. For him, it felt like home. He dashed to the heavy wooden doors and opened them to pull the van inside.

Built shortly after the Second World War, the barn was of the best German timber, constructed to outlast the problems of the period. In the late eighties George and Faiga bought the farm and converted the rear into an apartment to accommodate visiting family. On the ground floor was a kitchen, dining area, and sitting room. A large bedroom with a bath made up the second floor. Its simplicity and location in the farmlands offered refuge from the incident back at the apartment. The file meant nothing here, over eight-hundred kilometers away... *unless they'd tracked him.*

He shook his head and resumed the pleasant moments of arrival. No one knew where he was.

He climbed the narrow stairs and reached for the light switch. The glow of a bulb revealed a bedroom with only a bed, nightstand, writing table, dresser, and coat stand. Near the door to the bathroom a painting depicted St. Michael the Archangel expelling Lucifer from heaven.

He studied the painting as he shrugged out of his coat. A scene both serene and incredibly violent. St. Michael appeared to handle Lucifer with grace and confidence, reinforced by the might of God, yet he could imagine the fierce struggle between good and evil. Most would fail to comprehend those forces and instead only acknowledge the biblical story depicted. So it was with much of daily life, taken for granted with little in the way of reflection of its supporting structures. A safe but shallow mindset held by the majority of people. It helped his work immensely in many ways... but how deep the pond was!

"How deep, indeed?"

He hung his coat on the stand and again thought of Crosstalk's message.

Could it be? Psychic abilities? There were times when intuition leapt across all boundaries of reasoning and deduction to deliver improbable revelations about others. Too many times to count, really. Usually it was subtle. Other times, not so much.

He went to the toilet for a piss.

Intuition, the only non-taboo word for a sixth sense. Mention the concept of psychics, use the term 'mind reading', and the whole thing blew up in your face. Too fantastic, too contrived, but also too invasive to consider, too problematic for people's comfort zone.

What was consciousness anyway? From what did it stem, and what attributes did it have? Was there an underlying framework that could be explored and even shared? It seemed possible that there was, which made Crosstalk's message more intriguing.

Back in the bedroom, he looked around for the laptop and realized he'd left it on the kitchen counter. At the bottom of the stairs he halted at the sight of a bearded man with a rifle.

The man lowered the weapon. "Peter! I wasn't sure it was you."

"I hoped not to wake you, George." They embraced. "Sorry I didn't call ahead."

"Eh, you're welcome anytime and you know it." George eyed him. "You look tired, son. Worn. Are you okay?"

He smiled, despite sadness. George had aged, his beard fully gray now. Only his belly remained stout – the rest had thinned. "Work has been stressful. Time for holiday. Maybe some drawing, maybe nothing at all. I need to relax and this is the best place, away from it all."

The older man nodded. "Wise choice. Eh, you really are exhausted, it's in your voice. They must have you very busy." He knew Peter as an agent of the Dutch security services. The remark was a subtle reminder of how interested he was in his exploits. "I'm just glad you arrived safely. The roads are hell, I bet. Crazy storms."

"Crazy, yes."

"Well this is good." He clapped him on the shoulder. "Faiga will be glad you've come. Get some sleep, son. Breakfast in the morning?"

"Of course. Tell Faiga I'll be up to help her make it."

"Good, good. Sleep well." He turned for the door.

19

"Thank you George."

He went to unload the van. Reliving the incident at the apartment, he struggled again with the implications. If they dug really deep, they might learn he'd driven the Vanagon. That was registered to Drehen which meant there would be just one identity left to use.

Calm. No ifs. No fear. Confirm. Deal with reality first.

Exhausted, he locked up and lugged his suitcases up the stairs. He undressed messily, turned off the lights, and collapsed into bed. Between the goose-down blankets and the rain against the barn roof, his last thoughts were of gratitude before sleep came.

• • •

"Heya."

Austin strolled into the family room with a beer and a bag of chips and joined Kaiya on the couch.

"Oh," she paused her show. "I ordered pizza about twenty minutes ago."

"Pepperoni?"

"Half. Thin crust."

"You're the best."

"I know. How's your hacker?"

"Dunno, not a peep." He set the chips aside. "The German connection flopped but I'm sure the admin knows who's using his router. I'm tempted to try hacking it just to see what permissions are there. Might lead back to him."

"Hmm. Breakin' the law to catch a law breaker?"

She was right, it wasn't smart. "We'll see. I'm pretty sure I'll get another whack at him."

Over pizza by candlelight, Kaiya talked about how three classmates in Economics had been caught cheating with the help of a teacher's aide.

"It's just amazing what people will do. Makes you wonder how they arrive at those kinds of choices."

He washed down a bite with cold beer. "Makes you wonder, yep. Like that hacker. Probably started as a kid. Hooked up with the wrong crowd. Found the cracks and slipped through. Now he's hacking people's junk."

"Sounds like a young you," she said. At his glance, she asked, "Well doesn't it?"

"Yeah, okay, but this is serious. There's a market for this data. He can mess things up bad for people. Starting with me."

"Maybe it's the easiest way to make good money where he's from."

"Might be, yeah. He's still a prick though. Just like I was."

He reflected on his own start into computers. Loving parents, though really into their careers. By age thirteen he'd become convinced work was their first passion. For dad, it was everything and their only real connection. As a computer analyst for the CIA, being tied up with work was the absolute norm. Mom's time in local politics kept her busy and provided visibility and success that she seemed to crave. The older he got, the more disconnected he felt from them.

By his fourteenth birthday he'd begun to explore the internet. Game forums first, then to private forums, then to chat channels. New friends led him to the darker, unadvertised side of the net. In the new warrens things surfaced that he'd never seen – topics and images that he'd never considered, never imagined. Had his parents known they would have pulled the computer in a heartbeat. Instead, he saw with greater clarity exactly how to behave to keep them from catching on.

His fifteenth birthday brought a new computer and a faster connection. Real deviation began when he learned how to break into computer systems. What used to be important became less significant – like the idea of right and wrong. He learned a lot about people, too, like how they were not always what they appeared on the surface. It applied to everyone he knew, including his folks.

A few months before his sixteenth birthday, the cruelest of fates shifted his outlook forever. Driving back from a fundraiser, his mother was struck and killed. The other driver, drunk and high, lived.

In the weeks that followed, his dad helped him understand how his mother's passion for her work had diminished nothing of her love for him; he'd just been too selfish and immature to see it. He dropped off the hack sites and the secret rebelliousness fell away. He grew closer to his dad and focused on technology in a constructive way. It lit his imagination and eventually provided a career path.

Kaiya shrugged. "Well, even if you never catch him, at least you found a big time exploit. That's worth something."

"True. Got some more visibility at Rocom, too."

"You'd love to work there."

He looked up at her. "I'd *like* to work there. I'd *love* to see Sam on the shelves at Best Buy and Home Depot and on Amazon. Not to mention in new home builds."

She nodded. "In time, you will. Meanwhile, use your momentum at InterGen. Make it worth your while. You've earned it."

They finished dinner and after clearing the dishes decided to make up for the previous morning's preemption. As they climbed the stairs, she poked him in the chest. "If you get called tonight, we'll go down there and get busy in the server room."

He laughed and slapped her butt. "Really? I might have to arrange a call then."

"Perv."

"Hey, it was your idea."

• • •

Johan slept in on Sunday, finally rising to shower while rain gathered in the lanes of the adjoining fields. Instead of feeling better about the incident at the apartment, he felt it more of a threat than before. Despite intense curiosity about the file, things were too hot; absolute downtime from Alcazar felt safest. Bringing trouble of any kind to George and Faiga was out of the question.

There were always things George needed help with and as expected he had to weave a few tales to entertain him throughout the day. Such small repayment for his hospitality. After dinner he spent the evening with George over a chess board. Conversation revealed the progression of the memory issue that Faiga had mentioned during his last visit. George circled around twice to the same topic as if they had not talked about it twenty minutes earlier. At his age it wasn't unexpected but Faiga worried it might grow into something worse. He hoped not.

Before bed he checked email via a proxied aggregator. One message from Andreas carried the name and contact information for the InterGen admin who'd tried to track him.

Sorry Mr. Bakken, not good enough.

Monday morning it rained steadily and at times in. He surprised Faiga by joining her in the kitchen with eggs gathered from the coop. They made breakfast and afterwards the three played games. Faiga won handily in back to back rounds of Bohnanza, George's favorite card game.

The couple were the closest thing to family he had. By the time the early loss of his own parents finally emerged as a heartfelt and soulful problem, George and Faiga Bergmann were the universe's answer. He'd returned to them again and again over the years. Worries were always set aside, if only for a time.

In the afternoon the rains broke and the sun emerged from behind clouds. Sunlight warmed the sodden earth and made it fragrant and colorful. Puddles had joined to make small lakes that he navigated around. Under the trees at the edge of a neighboring farm, the absence of technology felt liberating. Just the earth, tools to work it, and a home to live in. It seemed simple and damn appealing.

What really happened at the apartment was unclear but with luck he'd soon know more. Worst case he'd relocate and start over. Maybe a nose job and an eye lift. A chin tuck and a tan wouldn't hurt, either.

By nightfall Johan hadn't gone to the house for supper so George and Faiga appeared in the apartment with food and drink. They called him downstairs.

"Ach! You shouldn't have. Thank you, Faiga."

They sat with him as he ate. Faiga couldn't resist her instincts.

"You look so lean, Peter. You need to eat better. When are you going to settle down and find a wife, hmm? Someone to take better care of you?"

George harrumphed. "Peter's got good sense. He'll know when it's time. When he does, he'll fatten up soon enough."

"Don't worry Faiga, I'm healthy and strong. And when the woman of my dreams finds me I will not turn and run, I promise."

They drank steins of George's own brewed stout. Conversation ranged from provincial to global. George was still keen on knowing what was going on in the world and did a good job of staying informed via the internet. Faiga approved because it seemed to keep his mind sharp and agile, though the news was often depressing.

George finished a draw from his brew. "You know, we were just talking about you before you showed up."

"Yes? Good talk, I hope."

"Well, have you heard anything about the killing in Rotterdam?"

"Depends. What killing?"

His furry gray brows knitted in disgust. "They're calling him the Butcher of Rotterdam. There's a sketch out."

"How many dead?"

"Just one but it was brutal. Sick bastard."

"Sounds like a local homicide. What made you think of me? Someone in politics?"

"Heh," George nodded and stood. "I'll show you. It may be of interest to you." He left for the house on a mission.

Faiga shook her head. "So damned depressing, that. Violence. Moral decay. The world is sliding deeper and deeper. Not just in the slums, not just in the big cities. It's become so commonplace. Why? What's inside people that drives them to such evil?"

"Some say it's always been this way. We just hear more of it thanks to technology."

"Maybe. I can't help remembering that we are just animals after all. Some more evolved than others. And you know politicians and the elite are just as bad as the murderers. Letting good people fight wars and starve while they lounge in safety and reap the profits. As if privilege makes them immune to guilt and responsibility. All the world over! Corruption and inequity. Cruelty and murder. Seems to me rooted in the same evil. Honestly, I think somewhere in the last hundred years we had a chance to rise above it but failed to." She sighed and studied him. "You see many bad things first hand. How do you manage?"

He could only shrug. "My work brings justice to those that might not otherwise meet it. If things get too much, like most people, I retreat. Not for long, though. Never for long."

He stared at his empty plate, peripherally aware of Faiga's gaze. Paranoia tugged, creating fear about what George would bring. "I know what you mean about missing our chance. I've felt that, too. Like we've skidded off the runway and can't set things right. So many people want to live in peace and know how to treat their fellow man but they never seem to rise to real power. Regardless of their number. I don't know why, either."

"We're cowards, is why. Afraid to lose what peace we have." She grew thoughtful in the lingering quiet. "Peter, you know you're an old soul. A good, old soul."

He nodded and gave her a smile. "You've said as much. It takes one to know one."

She wiped the table with a napkin. "I do hope you get to settle down. From what I see, I wonder if you ever will."

He met her gaze. "And what is it you see?"

"Oh, I don't know." She shook her head. "A long run? Yes. A hectic, long run through danger. And change. I see much change." Her eyes averted. "Hard to settle down with *that.*" The screen door rattled as George returned. She wiped the table again. "But that's just my old mind musing, of course. It does so tirelessly."

Her wan smile sealed the memory.

George returned with a sheaf of papers in hand. As if at a briefing, he offered a sheet. "Here's the sketch of the bastard. If you see him, he's dangerous."

Johan tensed as he reached for it.

Paranoia. The sketch looked nothing like him. George handed him a second sheet. "Here's the article."

(ROTTERDAM, NETHERLANDS – AP) – A WOMAN WHO POLICE SAID APPEARED TO HAVE BEEN STABBED MULTIPLE TIMES WAS FOUND DEAD IN A DOWNTOWN APARTMENT SATURDAY AFTERNOON.

POLICE SPOKESPERSON ARLENE LEIGHER SAID A NEIGHBOR ON THE THIRD FLOOR HEARD LOUD NOISES AROUND 11AM COMING FROM BELOW BUT DISMISSED THEM. AT 11:30AM ANOTHER NEIGHBOR NOTICED THE WOMAN'S DOOR OFF ITS HINGES AND FOUND HER BODY.

THE IDENTITY OF THE VICTIM, A WOMAN IN HER LATE FIFTIES, WAS NOT RELEASED PENDING NOTIFICATION OF NEXT OF KIN, LEIGHER SAID. "THE DEGREE OF BRUTALITY EXHIBITED WAS UNCOMMON." THE MURDER WEAPON, A MEAT CLEAVER, WAS RECOVERED AT THE SCENE.

"SOME CRIME SCENES ARE HARD TO PROCESS DUE TO THE SHEER INHUMANITY INFLICTED UPON THE VICTIM. UNFORTUNATELY, THIS IS ONE OF THEM."

POLICE ARE CONSIDERING THE WOMAN'S NEIGHBOR THE PRIME SUSPECT BASED ON PHYSICAL EVIDENCE. DETAILS OF THAT EVIDENCE WERE NOT DISCLOSED BUT WERE DESCRIBED AS 'SUBSTANTIAL'.

LEIGHER REPORTS THAT PRELIMINARY INVESTIGATIONS REVEALED THE SUSPECT WAS LIVING UNDER A FALSE IDENTITY. AT LEAST TWO ALIASES HAVE BEEN UNCOVERED. ONE IS "ARNIE", THE OTHER "PETER BRUSSE". THERE IS NO WORD ON POSSIBLE MOTIVATION FOR THE KILLING.

POLICE HAVE RELEASED A SKETCH OF THE SUSPECT (VIEW HERE) AND ARE ASKING ANYONE WITH INFORMATION ABOUT THE SUSPECT'S IDENTITY OR WHEREABOUTS TO CONTACT THE ROTTERDAM POLICE DEPARTMENT OR INTERPOL (LINK).

The article contained a small black and white image of his apartment complex and Café Trevi on the first floor.

"Gah!" He could barely control himself. Feeling their eyes upon him, he covered. "Who butchers *an old woman?* For what possible reason? Terrible. Brings shame to my name."

George's imagination revealed itself when he asked if Peter's previous cases might be involved, maybe an enemy sending him a warning.

"It's possible, I suppose. Most likely it's just coincidence. At least I hope it is."

He finished his beer and changed the topic to a lighter one. A short time later he begged off to bed. He locked up the barn, rejoined the laptop upstairs, and considered the fifteen chunks stored on its drive. He scowled at the screen and resisted punching it. "You can't *possibly* be worth this!"

He sat down. "My god."

Why kill her? Wrenching guilt set in, a hot brand against his heart. He hadn't planned on growing close. The jovial woman would bring the bill over, chatting sometimes for five, ten minutes or more. About the same age his mother would've been, she was every bit as caring and friendly. He'd cited a bad history with the phone company when he'd offered to pay her the cost of phone and DSL service if he could run the wire through the wall. It was a simple tactic to give him a chance for escape if ever a bust went down.

His escape had led to her brutal death.

Neither of us deserved to die. Anger surfaced and fused with guilt to form steely resolve. Mrs. Shulz's killers would pay. He would assemble the file, open it, and put it out there – no matter what it contained.

He stood and paced the room. Someone had given a false description but why? No matter, a resident or the manager would offer the correction and soon. He stopped and glanced at the time, now also his enemy. When they released an accurate sketch, George would surely see it and recognize him. There would be no convincing him of his innocence – George played by the rules, believed in them and in the system itself. If police were searching for "Peter", then "Peter" needed to see the police. Peter Brusse was now dead as an identity, as was Drehen Legters. Another, lesser grief descended for the carefully crafted personas that had become so familiar, so real.

Lucifer's moment of doom stared from the wall.

He would leave, within minutes, with a note for George and Faiga saying simply that he was not involved in any way with the killing. *Do not believe all that you read and are told.* Through the hinterland and back to home, Elburg, where he could become his fallback, Max Dosch. Priorities aligned themselves: new transportation and a safe drive to the house.

He loaded his belongings into the van and with a deep sadness backed out of the barn, closed its heavy doors, and drove past the farmhouse into the night.

The wifi signal strength showed sixty percent on the street in Bogenhausen next to the industrial building where artists rented loft space.

From the back seat of the stolen Volvo Johan randomized his laptop's MAC address and joined the network. He ought to be on the road out of the city but there was something to attend to first. If they wanted to hunt him down like a criminal for having done nothing, then he was going to *do* something. The file on Alcazar was some kind of prized truth, which meant it had value. Normally he'd play it close, control the asset, and bring in others after forming a monetizing strategy. Now, he might not make it to Elburg. The UG might delete it outright if it proved too hot. Or maybe Alcazar would fall to authorities. If so, the file would never see the light of day and Crosstalk's last request would never be realized. *Make it count.*

He blinked at a pair of headlights coming down the avenue. A subtle shift of perspective cast its own light on the moment.

"If it belongs to the world..."

High karmic consideration floated, a challenge to self-interest. The car passed and the interior fell dim again. He thought of the last hack, InterGen, and of the admin that tried tracing him. He checked the email from Andreas.

Austin Bakken.

He accessed his control panel for Alcazar and created a sub-account with access to Crosstalk's file. Next he created a downloader app for the file and prepared a note explaining how to use the visitor's pass into Alcazar.

Both the downloader app and a note went into an encrypted file. He embedded clues for the file's key into a fakie, a file that looked corrupt when viewed.

"If you're worthy, then it is meant to be, Mr. Bakken. Figure it out or don't."

• • •

Papa Mario and his wife stood behind the couch their daughter sat on and regarded the uniformed police and dark-suited detectives in their living room. On the couch a shrunken Marie, pale and red-eyed from crying, looked as if she might be sick. Her mother was terrified and looked on in stifled disbelief.

Papa Mario leaned forward over the back of the couch. On his face was the anger at the embarrassment she'd caused. "You will give them the right description this time, won't you Marie?"

Marie could only nod.

A skinny, balding man with a half-smile and a sketchpad came in the front door escorted by two more detectives. He surveyed the room in a glance, ignored the parents, and sat down next to Marie.

"Hello, my name is Hans. I understand Arnie was a regular customer at the café? Yes? Good. I'm sure you'll give me the best description you can. Let's begin."

Several minutes into the interview, the artist seemed to be jumping ahead of Marie, fleshing out details as if he already knew the face. She paled further but kept describing for some semblance of normalcy: the artist was drawing an exact picture of Arnie. Worse, he seemed to enjoy her unease.

Her mother looked away, more frightened at the proceedings than before.

Chapter 3

We dance round in a ring and suppose, but the secret sits in the middle and knows.
-Robert Frost, American Poet, 1875 - 1963

Four large screens showed activity on the global network. Status windows listed intrusions under way, recently acquired servers, botnet inventories, and real-time trace attempts on Underground operations around the planet. A square-jawed South American tapped arrow keys in time to a Led Zeppelin tune. He set off another mistrace operation against the tracers.

"Fuck you, NSA. Suck it."

A request for review came in. Soldado scanned an intercept script written by a junior member.

"Gah! Newbcode. That SSL injection will crater."

He wrote a few lines of code and sent it back. Notice of a successful wire transfer scrolled in the financials window, improving his already decent mood.

A ringing tone and red flashing bar indicated a priority message coming through Alcazar. "Okay okay, what's this... Zero?"

MsgID: 39827091p   Sent by: SlotZero
Soldado – xtalk's last file extremely hot. phys trace to my pad ½hour of link recvd. Crosstalk toggled off, poss redblanket. im low moving to safety. offline tfn. Checking zmail.

"What the shit?" He sat up straight, muted the tunes, and killed his webcam. "Crosstalk *dead?* Nar, very *nar.*"

Crosstalk's last login was several days ago. His message base showed him recruiting for a job, something big.

"No job notes on a BAP. No bueno." Big Ass Plans called for review to avoid leading heat into the UG's framework, online or off. Crosstalk always delivered job notes. Whatever he'd bitten into must've been so big it bit back. Nice to know what the hell it was. He suspended Crosstalk's logon and put SlotZero's account on a watch list.

Next, to verify his story.

• • •

The text message arrived halfway into his double bacon cheeseburger.

OSR3:HackReturn:IP=207.173.205.24

Austin leapt from his seat and headed for the door, ignoring the looks from diners and staff. He bumped open the glass doors and ran for his car. Wayne called from the NOC – they'd already started the trace.

"Next hop address. Deanin Industries in Bend, Oregon," Wayne said. "Shall I call 'em?"

"Yeah, put me on hold." He swung out of the lot, gunning it. If he'd remembered his laptop he could be finishing lunch while running the trace himself. He slowed coming up on traffic.

Another engineer joined the line. "Dan here. He's dumping a file on Promulgate. Slow, only half a meg so far. I copied a sample out and it's encrypted. He hasn't tried poking around yet."

"Okay, watch him... where's the trace at?"

"Wayne's getting the next hop."

He put two wheels up on a curb and drove fifty feet of sidewalk to make a right turn ahead of traffic.

"–he's got it. Checking... okay, it's residential DSL. Zombie. This is gonna be a dead end, I think. Yeah. And he's out now. File's done and it's about three megs. He also left a readme doc."

"*Don't open anything*. I'll be there in like four minutes."

If Murray found out, he probably wouldn't appreciate the trap. It might not matter that he and Rocom had restricted his access only to the Promulgate server.

Back in the office, checked on the readme file. It was an ordinary word processing file but with a complex message.

> ⬚⬚⬚I wish I h⬚⬚ad ⬚⬚⬚m⬚re time an⬚⬚
> informa⬚⬚t⬚⬚on to o⬚fer. ⬚ut I do⬚no⬚⬚.
> ⬚⬚W⬚at I ⬚h⬚⬚a\⬚e se⬚nt yo⬚⬚⬚u c⬚ul⬚d
> ⬚thr⬚⬚e⬚ten ⬚your lif⬚. F⬚r ⬚tha⬚⬚t I ⬚am
> s⬚rr⬚⬚y. Mi⬚ne is thr⬚⬚ea⬚ened as I t⬚⬚pe this.
> Someone el⬚e ⬚mu⬚t ⬚⬚⬚ha\⬚e ⬚it and let
> wha⬚⬚ve⬚r ⬚uth t⬚here i⬚⬚ to f⬚ind a ⬚way
> ⬚ut. ⬚ I⬚⬚⬚solate⬚ ⬚th⬚⬚⬚ file. ⬚pr⬚tect
> ⬚ourself. ⬚ a⬚d m⬚ybe ⬚w⬚⬚'ll meet ⬚s⬚⬚eda\.
> ⬚erhaps ⬚⬚⬚erm⬚any? Or m⬚y⬚b⬚e T⬚h⬚a⬚land.
> Good ⬚lu⬚⬚⬚k and good heal⬚⬚⬚h.
> –The H⬚ck⬚⬚er
>
> P. ⬚. tw⬚ pA⬚rts. ab⬚⬚\⬚e and⬚⬚ bel⬚⬚w.
> b⬚o⬚⬚ld is ⬚⬚twice ⬚as any⬚⬚

Below the jumbled text, an image contained a paragraph of text in what looked like German. Some of the letters appeared in bold font.

This was the hacker, his hacker. The references to the two traced locations were clear indications. A joke? Or an e-bomb? Curious, he copied the files to a memory stick and to the laptop before scrubbing them from the server. He couldn't deny the excitement. Things like this didn't happen every day. He just hoped it didn't blow up in his face.

Wayne walked in with his hands in pockets. "So what's the readme say?"

"Don't know yet. Maybe clues to a cipher key for the file."

"What if this is Omnicron?"

He thought back. The timing would fit. A year ago the security auditing firm Omnicron had worked for a week straight attempting to get into InterGen – electronically and via social engineering. This was something they might try, a simulated hack scenario to test their responses.

"If it's them, I'm completely blown away they have Rocom playing along." It seemed too elaborate even for InterGen's auditors.

"If it is them, you fucked up with the cat and mouse trap routine, dude."

He sighed. The possibility existed. "Have Dan close the hole."

On the laptop, he checked the readme file again. No mention of an encryption key and without one, the file wouldn't open. The image in the document showed German text with randomly bolded letters.

He wondered if Omnicron would be so imaginative. He tried using the bolded letters as the key, repeating each twice as suggested. Every combination failed. *"Two parts, above and below"*. The top text had to hold half the key but was jumbled.

The Rocom conference call rang in and lasted the rest of the day, drawing him into the lab to prod and poke a standby Crest router. By five o'clock he was done with firmware swaps and checking for sequenced buffer overflow attacks. One thing was certain – Omnicron wasn't involved.

His cell vibrated – Kaiya with an invite for dinner at her place. *Your fav - sweet n sour pork w/ pork fried rice. Chow mein too. You can't say no.*

He texted back. *Love it. 6:30?*

See you then.

On his desk the laptop awaited a key to open the encrypted file.

He eyed the upper text again and tried a different sequence of keys. And again. Several tries later, he gave up with the thought that Kaiya might do better with it.

. . .

<Soldado> xtalk maybe flatline, slotzero gone low
<Caldera181> wtf!!! how? why?
<Soldado> no clue
<Caldera181> u going to look at xtalks profile?
<Soldado> of course. to confirm IRL
<Caldera181> you have me, you need one more?
<Soldado> ive got a msg into OB1Kenobi and benny. i'll ping u when its time
<Caldera181> was he workin on something?
<Soldado> yes but no idea what. Zero pointed to a file xtalk uploaded. said it was hot but no job notes
<Caldera181> whats the file?
<Soldado> havnt touchd it yet
<Caldera181> xtalk had no notes? weird shit. any fallout on the sys?
<Soldado> nothing yet. ive got daems on high to detect incoming. slows shit down but gotta do it
<Caldera181> yeah does. let me know when you want to crack his file, im around

. . .

A power cord ran across the dining room floor, up to the table, past a plateful of Chinese food, and into the back of Austin's laptop. Kaiya sat close, peering at the screen. It was looking unlikely they would find the key to the encrypted file.

"I think the corruption removed formatting," he said between bites. "The bolding is obviously the markers for the bottom text and the note says it is, but the top is all jacked up. If it's *made* to look corrupt, then why didn't they include bolded letters? Or some other clue about markers? Or maybe the squares are because I don't have the right font. But there are hundreds of thousands of fonts."

She agreed. "Without the top text, I don't see how you'll figure it out." She went back to her food. "You know, that intro text is creepy.

Something that could threaten your life? I'm thinking you should just delete it all."

The last bit sounded serious. Taking the clue, he pushed the laptop away. "Screw it. I'm ruining dinner. Time to enjoy this culinary orgasm."

"Not a bad idea."

Flickering images from the television lit the darkened room. Kaiya dozed on the couch, exhausted from her day preparing for a big client presentation. After dinner he'd helped her tweak it by adding animations and color that made it pop nicely. They had started to watch a movie but she passed out early into it.

He sat in a recliner with the laptop, deep in thought. The upper text either held clues to the key or once did. The square characters were non-printable character codes usually seen in damaged files or...

Or, considering who he was dealing with –

He opened the file with a hex editor. Laid out in hexadecimal format, the entire message offered new possibility. To most it was a jumble of random numbers and letters but to him it was also where a hacker could leave clues.

It didn't take long to find a pattern. Hex codes 04 and 00 appeared throughout the message. Both created the squares seen in the text in normal view. After studying the patterns, he saw the 04 code acted like a marker since it appeared only in single instances and sometimes after the last letter in a word, as if tagging the letter prior. It never appeared before the first letter in a word.

He checked all the 04 positions and noted the tagged characters one by one.

OOWIVULDENFFRIIALEUVETAYE ETFTFAMETYMM YBTHADHPWAVBE

"Okay..." He typed the string followed by the bolded characters from the lower text, twice for each instance they appeared.

Nope.

He flipped the order, lower text then upper text.

Still nothing.

"Damn," he whispered, staring digital daggers. A complete waste of time.

Right before closing the files, he saw it. In the graphic, the last period in the paragraph was smaller than the one on the line just above it. Just a pixel or two difference. He zoomed in.

Good God. Subtle. So damned subtle.

He scanned the whole paragraph and counted ten periods, nine of them bolded. He tried again with the periods included. Like a magical unveiling, the file's contents were revealed.

"Alrighty then..."

The screen's light ghosted his face. Two files... an application installer and another readme doc. He checked the readme.

AUSTIN – INSTALL CLIENT ON NOTEBOOK. GO MOBILE TO DOWNLOAD THE FILE. BE CAREFUL THEY MAY BE ON TO YOU RIGHT AWAY. I DON'T KNOW WHO THEY ARE OR WHAT'S IN IT. SEE MSG BELOW. JUST GET IT AND SEND IT OUT. TO WHO IS UP TO YOU. GOOD LUCK, PROGRAM. USERNAME: ININ PASSWORD: 45FORGOTTENNIGHTZ%+

Below it, a message:

THEY ARE TRACKING ME RIGHT NOW THEY HAVE ME I AM DEAD TONIGHT. THEY ARE ON THE GROUND AND IN PEOPLES MINDS, DON'T LET THEM FIND WHO YOU ARE!! GET THIS AND RUN NOW ZERO RIGHT NOW GO LOW FAST BUT FIND A WAY TO LET IT OUT. LET THEM HAVE IT!! MAKE IT COUNT!!!! I WAS DARREN BLYTHE ENGLAND, HCS. REMEMBER STATEN-GENERAAL.

"*What the–?*" After the second reading, he realized he was holding his breath. He read it once more before closing out the files.

The whole thing was seductive, designed to attract, lure. Something so important it could threaten his life... *on the ground and in people's minds.* It turned uncomfortable, familiar wheels of thought. Only Kaiya wouldn't like it. Not a bit. He powered off the laptop and set it aside.

Probably a trap. A hoax. It wasn't real, yet... still it drew him in. The fact that someone had taken the time to set up something so elaborate begged for discovery, just to see where it went. *Why bother?* He could hear Kaiya's question. And his dad's criticism.

"Shit."

Fatigued from speculation and the long day, he de-stressed with television for another hour. Creating distance from the hacker's file felt wise. It could wait. Eventually the moving images lulled and became more and more disconnected until sleep crept up. He eased the recliner back and stretched out with his eyes closed.

He woke standing in the apartment. An open window revealed a deep-blue night sky speckled with stars. *Who had opened...?*

No. It was a fixed-frame window, it couldn't open.

And he couldn't sleep standing up. *I'm dreaming. I'm lucid.*

Recognition and the resulting flush of excitement almost woke him. It wavered, then stabilized. The open window invited him so he floated out and rose as if on a warm current of air. He looked down from high in the night sky. Tiny headlights on the downtown avenues and freeways coursed like electric blood in the city's veins. All around teemed an ocean of consciousness.

Just to explore *that...* how cool it would be. But there was something else worth exploring, worth finding – the hacker. With liquid awareness he cast out across the curve of the planet, open to the thought of the hacker. Somewhere out there he lived and maybe dreamed, too. Potential simmered. He focused, extending feelers for the target mind, for the one who had sent the file. Slowly a sense emerged, a sense of a strange.... place. A place of energy that was solid, real, and unique. Curiosity blossomed out behind him in a purple energy trail as he flew eastward in search of it. Higher and higher he soared until the lights of cities sparkled impossibly clear in the distance, hundreds of miles away. Caution resonated deeply, an intention from his logical mind to be careful in the unknown. In that brief reflection a peal of skepticism also sounded and threatened to end the dream, but he held on and continued. The sense of the strange place became stronger spanning eastward over the country. He marveled at the cities lit by the Eastern Interconnect like an electric cobweb. He passed over the coast. Beneath him the dark Atlantic hummed with its own universe of life.

The still-distant place felt large. Somewhere with expanses of land. Textures combined, brown sugar mixed with black shadows. Thoughts of Africa, complex intelligence, and *design* emanated from the place, almost individual energies, that of –

You can't go there.

He cast around in sudden darkness for the source of the command. Just above, something formed from the shadows. The head of a tiger appeared, teeth bared, about to strike. The next instant he was in the recliner, eyes wide open, heart pounding. The television flickered silent images. Kaiya stirred on the couch, asleep.

"Shit."

They are on the ground and in people's minds.

The vertigo of uncertainty grew, tinged with fear.

It had been a long time since the days of exploring. He'd had his own experiences – four authentic lucid dreams and twice he'd left his body, though only briefly. Dream walkers, psychics, remote viewing... imagination churned in a silent frenzy. Meaning awaited assimilation. Intuition's voice grew garbled and confused, with one exception: the hacker's message felt more real after the dream. *What I have sent you could threaten your life.*

The laptop sat nearby, a doorway to something mysterious. Temptation to download the file became a gravity. He thought of his dad and what he'd say. If it didn't piss him off, and if he decided not to make fun of him, there might be some good advice to be had.

Kaiya stirred again on the couch. She didn't like psychic stuff, didn't like things with poor definition and no boundaries. Staying inside the box was her style and he'd learned to appreciate the safety of it. Still...

He glanced at the television. Police in riot gear moved in to break up a street mob angry at the loss of a pro baseball game. Blaming the umpires. Ridiculous behavior, a response way out of proportion to the situation.

The clock showed half past nine. Curiosity won over. He wrote a quick note for Kaiya and in minutes was on the freeway headed to his dad's.

• • •

Brent Bakken's large frame turned in the recliner. Concern creased his brow.

"Bit late for a visit pal, what's up? Nothing wrong with Kaiya I hope?"

"No, we're okay," Austin said. "I just need your opinion. Some advice." He set the laptop on the bar and reached into the fridge for a beer.

"Advice? Okay, I've got plenty of that. What's up?"

"Well I, uh, received a gift today with a very... exotic message."

"What, you need advice about a sex toy?"

"Nice, dad. No, a hacker dropped off a file on our network today. An encrypted file with a message. I got it open and inside was a program. It's supposed to download an important file. Like, spooky important."

His dad's brows furrowed again. He paused the TV. "Hold up. You said a hacker? Someone you know?"

He told him about the break-in while he uncased the laptop. "The guy at the brewery must've given him my info because he mentions my name in the message."

"Alright, and what did the message say? Why my advice?"

He thought about the hacker's notes. If he tried reading them aloud, he'd feel foolish.

"Just tell me what you think, okay?"

His dad nodded, his good mood dissipating.

He brought up the initial message from the hacker and the one from inside the encrypted file. "Read the left one first." He handed the laptop to his dad and watched his eyes closely as he read. Twice there was something resembling a reaction, possible recognition.

His dad looked up at him. "Here's what I think. You caught him doing his thing on your network and it's his way of getting back at you. If you download that file, who knows where it's coming from? Think about it. You might be tunneling a file right from the Pentagon. They'd trace it back to *you*. Look at you son, already fascinated. You've heard me say it a thousand times. Most mistakes are made without the right perspective. Don't let him or anyone screw with your perspective. It's everything. Listen to your gut."

He began to nod when his dad added, "And if the file is that important then it could land you in a shitpot of trouble."

He stared at him. "You mean it could be real?"

His dad passed the laptop back with a hint of impatience. "I *mean* it could be a valuable document. Either way, it's a trap. Delete everything and you don't have to worry about it. Pretty obvious. You shouldn't need my advice." He picked up the remote, ready to resume his show.

Austin nodded despite the subtle criticism. It came down to either being real or being crap. *True, but...* he couldn't bring himself to mention the lucid dream, the voice, or the tiger.

"Well I wouldn't be a newbie about it. I've got an old beater laptop I could use... but you're right, it's probably best to forget it."

His dad studied him. "You're not convinced."

"Hell, dad, what if... say it's real — what if there's proof of telepathy or cover ups in the file? If I'm really, really careful, why wouldn't I check it out? Wouldn't you want to know? Or maybe you already do?" Regret trailed the question but it was too late.

"Jesus, Austin. Still playing the conspiracy game?"

He couldn't meet his dad's look. His words and tone had said all he needed to know. He closed the laptop in the awkward silence and cursed himself for coming.

"Look, Austin, I don't want to insult you. In fact, I'm trying *not* to. But mind reading? Really? I thought you were done with that stuff." His look was of exasperation trying for patience. "Son. You've got a hacker in your network. You should be thinking about covering your ass, not looking for a sling to hang it in. Right? You're distracted by the message, which is what any good hacker does to land the bomb. Perspective, Austin, perspective."

Good points all, damn it, but curiosity still raged. Something about his father's approach to the whole topic only served to enhance it. If there *were* secrets to defend, pops would definitely go the distance to redirect him. Twenty-seven years with the agency's computers... he almost *had* to have heard more about psychic shit.

If there really were such a thing.

What a mind fuck.

The garage door lowered. Driving home he'd made the decision. Controlling an e-bomb was cake on a beater laptop. He would completely wipe the hard drive afterward. No one could prove he'd taken the hacker's files from the office anyway.

Up in the shop he freed an old IBM ThinkPad from under a stack of hard drives and transferred everything from the hacker to it. Everything on one box. Easy to wipe.

He drove to Café Exótico to use its free wifi. In the parking lot the laptop auto-connected due to an app he'd installed for Kaiya to make it easy to score wifi when she traveled. He fired up the hacker's application.

No virus warnings, nothing special about it. Just a plain login screen.

"Alright then..."

He typed the username inin with a password of 45forgottenNightz%+.

The screen updated with the message,

FILE ID 20281EC93A23:: ACCESS GRANTED.

PARTICLES:: 40.

VOLUME/PARTICLE:: 1024.

EST. RETRIEVAL WINDOW:: UNAVAILABLE {PERFORMANCE PERMISSIONS LACKING, BIOTCH }

PROGRESS:: 1 OF 40 {=--}

It looked like a real slow download. Doubts about it being worth it surfaced but he ignored them. The coffee house had its Friday late crowd gathered inside and out on the patio. Thirty minutes 'til eleven and closing time, though they typically left the wifi up all night. He locked up and headed inside to grab a cup.

Twitchy music shot from oversized speakers mounted in the ductwork ceiling. Pierced and permanently painted bodies in burnt orange serving smocks waited on the crowd of twenty-somethings, many equally adorned with metal and ink. Drab in jeans and his 'temporarily out of service' t-shirt with nude arms and non-metallic face, Austin felt fifty, not twenty-eight. One patron stood ahead of him, placing her order. From the tables, a small commotion arose.

"Frankieee! The internet's down again! Can you fix it, pleeease?"

A gangly dude wearing all-black with his orange smock shouted back, "Yeah, yeah! In a sec!"

Dang! He'd have to restart the download somewhere else. Again doubts about the file being worth the hassle circled. A bronze-haired serving girl appeared. Four shiny beads lined her lower lip. "What can I get ya?"

"Large frappuccino. Please."

"You got it. Three fiddy."

Feeling self-conscious, he paid and stepped to the side. The looks cast about reinforced the old and out of place feeling. Ridiculous, but there it was. Subculture, the great divider. A return glance always had them just looking away, as if anticipating his move. *Every time.*

He watched the girl prepare his coffee. Frankie appeared from the back. "Sorry patrons, it's *down*-down." The crowd moaned. "Hey, I tried, but it's toast! Deal widdit!"

Coffee in hand, Austin pushed the door open and strode into the warm night air. Lights from homes on a gentle rise drew his attention. Somewhere up there an unsecured network awaited.

"Crap."

He sipped his coffee. The fourth street without an unsecured wifi network. "C'mon... where's my free wifi hippies?"

His cell rang – Kaiya, wondering what he was doing. Without going into much detail, he shared the advice his dad had offered and the fact he was going to download it anyway.

"He said not to? Why are you then?"

"Because it's probably nothing? Seriously, it's not a big deal."

"If it wasn't, you'd just delete it. I'm telling you, I don't like it."

Of course she was right but the hacker within wouldn't let go of the intrigue – of the draw to at least *look* at it. Worst case he could reformat the laptop.

"It's alright, babe. You know this is my domain. I'm not going to get tricked into anything. Honestly, it's a non-issue. Don't sweat it." Time to switch topics, she was too worried. "So tomorrow's your big presentation, right? You ready for it?"

"Austin. Changing the subject?"

Easy does it... "Well, how important is it, really? I'd say your presentation is way more important. Downtown Hilton and all."

"It's just... I don't know." *Softening, good.* "Something doesn't feel right. Don't say I didn't warn you, okay? As for tomorrow, I'm as ready as I'll ever be." She paused. "I *was* hoping for some good luck mookie tonight, except someone ran out on me."

The file could wait. Had to. It would take more than one night to get all the pieces anyway. Quarter to eleven... he could be there before eleven-thirty.

"I'll come back, but don't you *dare* be wearin' those thin black lacy thingies and the silver ankle bracelets. Don't know what'll happen if you are. Just sayin'."

She growled and hung up. He held the laptop's power button until it died and surged towards the freeway.

• • •

"Grafter's signing on."

With Soldado and Caldera, Grafter counted as the third administrator required to open Crosstalk's personnel file. Viewing of a profile required at least one founder and two ranking admins. The member received notification of the viewing and why. It was a hard-coded system that kept everyone honest and insured privacy for members.

"What's up guys?" Grafter joined the chat, his voice slightly garbled due to the heavy encryption in use.

Soldado responded. "Shit's whack tonight. Just had a scan of servers starting in L.A. from private IP blocks. I'm not sure if it's NSA or not but someone's gunning for us. Let's do this quick. Access the profile screens. Give the reason and submit. Use 'death verification', two words, all lowercase."

On screen, three authorizations took: the profile became visible to each.

Darren Blythe, nick name Crosstalk. Twenty-four years old, graduate of Queen Mary's of London, joined the Underground when he was a computer specialist for a manufacturing firm out of Oxfordshire.

"See his self-updates. Year before last got on with Britain's Ministry of Defense as a network analyst. Comfy gig. Lots of inside leads there. No wonder he's been into big shit."

"I'll run zombies out for death notices."

"His pop's a member of the House of Lords," Grafter said.

"Explains the ministry job. Search submitted via Malaysian nodes. Results will be in Fbox. I think we should open SlotZero's file while we're at it."

"Why, Caldera?"

"He's gonna need our help. The more we know..."

The zombie's search results appeared on Soldado's screen.

"Bloody hell. Body found in Kingston, London, early morning. Police calling it suicide."

Silence crackled along the line.

"I bet the noble lord daddy won't like that one bit," Grafter said finally. "Wonder if he'll have it looked into?"

"We could put a bug in his ear," Caldera suggested. "Give him reason to."

Soldado and Grafter both said no, not without more information.

Grafter checked on Zero's last entry point. "An artist's commune in Munich. Before that, Netherlands, so he's on the move. Um, shit. He created a sub-account, privileged to Crosstalk's file, auto-download."

"Well he's got to be feeling squirrely by now," Caldera said. "Waitin' on us to help him, prolly."

"I wonder if we really want to get involved with this," Grafter said.

"What the hell? Just leave him in a lurch?" Caldera asked.

"Talk to me Grafter," Soldado said.

"Anything we do puts us in their path. One of us is dead already. Murder or not, I think this is too hot. Tracers are up by forty percent in the last two days so NSA may already be trying. Even in Alcazar it had a point of entry so theoretically it could be tracked. I suggest we kill it."

Files uploaded to Alcazar went up in random-sized chunks, each chunk uniquely encrypted, transported via zombies on the net, and stored on hijacked servers around the world. While in Alcazar's care, multiple copies of a file's chunks stayed in motion, endlessly transferred between hundreds of servers via the zombies. To retrieve a file required the custom-made client software and a login. Once requested, the file chunks made their way back to the client, were decrypted and re-assembled into the original. It was like tossing an apple into a meat grinder and having it spit back out whole upon request. Though sometimes slow, it served its purpose exceedingly well.

Soldado considered Grafter's concerns valid. But killing the file? Not without seeing what it was. He'd re-tool Alcazar to guard against traces and do the same for Magistrate. To help SlotZero, he gave download priority for his accounts. In and out, quick. It was the best he could do at the moment. If need be, it could all be deleted for damage control. He shared his thoughts with the others.

Caldera was insistent about reaching out to Zero.

"I don't know what you guys are thinking but he's one of us. He's on the *run*. Sitting on our ass doing nothing sucks. What are we if we aren't brothers by now?"

Silence crackled in the speakers.

"What do you suggest?"

"Look at the file Crosstalk uploaded," Caldera said. "Might give us an idea of who's chasing Zero. Maybe we run interference. Maybe get in a few good swipes of our own, ya know?"

Waiting seemed wiser, but the file was the only quick and accurate means of estimating the threat. And it satisfied curiosity. The three agreed to initiate a priority retrieval.

Over the span of two minutes, forty requests went out for data chunks. Processes on over a hundred computers around the world responded, finishing transfers in progress, initiating routing programs to satisfy the retrieval requests. In ten minutes the file was complete, delivered piecemeal by botnets and reassembled on a server in Cairo, Egypt. The hackers handled it via remote sessions to keep it isolated on one server. It opened and revealed two files.

"1024 encryption on the big file. What's the other one?"

"A doc with the key. 04 marking. Double bolds on the lower text. One sec. Hmmm.... no." Grafter's wheels turned. "Got it. Periods minus one."

Entering the cipher key opened the big file to reveal a video file and a readme.

"Crap."

Their remote sessions didn't support video playback or audio. "What's the readme say?"

"Eh, yeah. Somethin's pretty whack," Caldera said. "Check it yourself. He was wiggin' out."

Soldado read Crosstalk's note several times. "Either it's a real warning or a real meltdown." There was no telling until they viewed the video. "Let's hold off on moving it. We'll open Zero's profile as well. He may have updated his aliases."

SlotZero was in some way linked with Crosstalk's death, if only by virtue of knowing about it. Grafter raised the point that the two hackers could have had business gone bad. While unpleasant and unlikely, the possibility still existed; big money stressed the best relationships.

They processed the request.

Caldera had never seen Zero's profile. He read aloud. "Peter Brusse. Age 36 now. Independent computer consultant. Last address an apartment in The Hague. No higher education, only primary school records. Adopted, no living family, no SO's, nothing. Guy's a lawn gnome. Let's run the name and see what comes up."

The zombie chain came back quickly with the initial results: fugitive wanted for murder in Rotterdam.

"Shit. Maybe he did kill Crosstalk," Grafter said.

Soldado's screen lit with alerts. "What the shit–?"

In the space of five seconds, one server was scanned, then three more – all Alcazar servers. He fired the proximity kill script to drop them from rotation and kicked off another script to reseed the transport system.

"Close the docs. Out, quick!" He scrubbed the files on the Cairo server and disconnected. "Holy shit." He blinked at the screen. "A quarter of Third Legion just went tits up."

Caldera saw it too and whistled. "Seven thousand non-responding bots. That's NSA stink right there. This ain't good. Is *not*."

Soldado stared at the screens. Alcazar self-healed, rebuilding lost chunks and distributing them across the remaining servers.

Grafter cleared his throat. "Yeah, um, like I was saying. Maybe we don't want this shit. I'm not sure Alcazar's going to hold up. They're really gunning for this thing."

Soldado thought of the video file, supposedly Crosstalk's reason for dying. Like a bag holding a big cat he might not want to let out, it represented layers of complication and threat, both personal and for the Underground. Still, he couldn't ignore its potential value.

"Don't assemble the file again. Not a goddamn peep about it either, to anyone. I gotta think about this. Stay tuned."

• • •

Austin's BMW raced along a downtown off ramp. Thoughts of Kaiya in black lace danced in his head. He pulled up at the light just as a text message arrived. The ringtone caught him off guard: it was the house security system sending an alert.

SEC BREACH: YARD ZONE 1, 2

Side and back yards. The system would ignore anything smaller than a large dog. He'd check the video log from Kaiya's place.

Another text message arrived.

SEC ALERT: PRIMARY POWER OUT.

"Damn it." He imagined someone at the main power box and immediately thought to dial 911 but looked at the laptop and froze.

"No way." It couldn't be related. Could it?

He dialed the VoIP backline at the house instead. It answered with a double beep. "Voice authorization. Yankee, golf, tree, niner, whiskey, india." A triple beep sounded. He replied, "Process sequence."

"WELCOME TO THE BACK DOOR," Sam's synth voice announced. "CODE RED ALERTS WAITING. READY."

The traffic light turned green so he turned left under the freeway and stopped at the curb.

"Security: verify breach."

"CONFIRM MULTIPLE INTRUDERS ON GROUNDS. READY."

Confirmation meant cameras had plotted movements across the yard. He racked memory for the commands he'd programmed. He hadn't worked on them in months.

"Security: How many intruders outside?"

"FIVE INTRUDERS. READY."

Shit!

"Status: system batteries."

"SYSTEM BATTERY POWER AT NINETY FIVE PERCENT. ESTIMATED TIME REMAINING IS TWENTY-EIGHT MINUTES. READY."

He remembered writing the battery-saving code. "Command: turn off all emergency lights."

"ALL EMERGENCY LIGHTS ARE NOW OFF. READY."

"End connection."

"GOODBYE."

He punched the accelerator to the floor and launched back onto highway 50 towards home. Another message arrived indicating internal security breaches and people moving around inside the house. That was enough – he dialed 911 to report a burglary in progress. It took a couple of minutes to convince the operator of the situation but was finally told deputies were en route.

"Christ...."

The laptop rested on the seat, now almost alive: a rare, malevolent species that threatened his well-being. If he was right, someone wanted to make sure he didn't get to the hacker's file.

Next moves, strategy. Memories of timed games of chess with his dad flashed, some of the most stressful games he'd ever played. *If only this were a game.*

An idea dawned. At least part of it could be.

He pulled to the side of the freeway, far off the shoulder. From the trunk he removed a sleeping bag from its weatherproof sack and slipped the laptop into it instead. He waited for a gap in traffic and ducked into the heavy brush nearby and worked his way towards the highway sound wall. Near the base of a scrub oak he flicked on a keychain LED light and scraped aside layers of vegetation sediment. He reached loose soil and dug until his fingertips were sore then set the bundled laptop in the shallow hole. Replacing dirt and vegetation, he did his best to make the ground look undisturbed.

Hide and seek.

"Dad?"

Silence. His quick recount of the attempted download and the subsequent intrusion alarms didn't go over well.

"Austin, head back here to the house."

"But–"

"Like now, son."

The speedometer read eighty-six. "Dad, I *can't.* I have to meet the police. What's going on? What do you know?"

Another longish silence. "I'll meet you there."

"Alright, if you–"

The call ended.

"Sheesh. What the hell?"

He made the turn onto his street and dread turned to cold, smooth fear. Placer County sheriff's cars lined the street in front of his house. A black utility van sat in the driveway. The whine and thump of an approaching helicopter grew louder. It felt bad – so bad he thought of turning around and leaving. Instead, he pulled up at the curb. He hadn't done anything wrong. Maybe the hackers had, but he hadn't. Doubt crept in when he saw a deputy on the porch look at him and speak into a radio.

His dad arrived, pulling in just behind him. They both stepped from their cars and the look on his dad's face rattled him hard. He'd never seen him afraid of anything, ever. Officers emerged from the house and spread out as they crossed the lawn. They each drew their pistols and one called out to put their hands up. His dad shook his head in disgust but complied.

"Lace your fingers behind your head."

The helicopter arrived, its spotlight bathing the neighborhood to create vivid, flowing shadows. The deputies approached and patted them down. Once cleared, they were allowed to stand at ease. A group of men came from the house. Austin counted five, all wearing blue windbreakers and hats with the letters FBI in yellow.

"What's this about?" Brent demanded.

One of the agents came forward.

"FBI cyber unit, assisting the State Department. Tracking a group of bad boys. Your son appears to be one of them."

Brent straightened, suddenly towering. "Let's see some credentials."

The man produced a badge. "Agent Morris, Sacramento office."

"And your warrant?"

"No warrant. Exigent circumstance. This evidence is real easy to destroy. Now if you'll come inside we'll have a friendly talk about why we're here and what we've already found. Perhaps we're mistaken and you'll be able to enlighten us."

The agents moved aside, ready to escort. Shadows flowed around them as the helicopter circled. It didn't feel right but there wasn't really a choice, so they walked.

"Can they do this? Dad?"

A mixture of fear and anger played across his dad's face. "I'll do the talking. Respond only if I say to."

The agents slowed, trailing behind the entourage. Brent looked back, clearly uneasy. A deputy stood near the front porch.

"Wait. Dad," Austin slowed as well. "How does he know I'm your son? Do you–"

A brilliant flash lit the night. A bone-jarring concussion knocked them off their feet. The lurch of free fall preceded a sudden darkness.

Time slowed, bogged by silence. His head throbbed and body ached. Swimming dots framed his vision. Black smoke billowed from flames consuming his house. His dad lay motionless nearby. He tried to rise but cried out from pain in his shoulder. He shuffled up onto his knees and hobbled to his dad's side, frantic to check his pulse. After two unnerving tries, he found one.

A body on the lawn lay unmoving – a deputy. Another officer was also down but pointing and talking to Agent Morris. Two agents covered him and his dad with guns drawn. Burning debris littered the yard.

In the silence, accompanied by the pain and the warm night air, it seemed like a dream. Soon more police appeared, followed by fire trucks and then ambulance after ambulance. The helicopter kept the neighborhood lit and created a surreal stage where the nightmare played out. *Was this all about the file?* The answer seemed to rise from the flames licking the night sky. They'd destroyed his shop, his computers, and presumably any copies of the hacker's files.

The laptop. He suppressed the thought, fearful of the agents nearby. They had arranged for all of this in less than a day.

What I have sent you could threaten your life. For that I am sorry.

Sudden nausea set the world spinning. If he'd just done his job and secured the network he wouldn't have drawn the hacker's attention.

Instead, there was this.

He nearly threw up at the thought.

• • •

The sleepy village of Oostendorp was a welcome sight in the early morning hours. The dark house yawned light from its garage as it opened. He pulled inside the space, just behind a '72 Triumph Spitfire. The garage door lowered and isolation bloomed in the silence. Eyes closed, he breathed deep, thankful for the safe journey.

The house was typical of the block. Narrow and tall with three stories. First floor garage, entry, half bath, and storage. Second floor living area, kitchen, and bath. Master and guest room on the third floor. He walked around the kitchen and plugged things in before storing the food he'd bought. With a bottle of warm ale in hand, he tuned the television to a news channel and collapsed on the couch. It didn't take long to see his face and his aliases.

"*Shit!*" A photo of Mrs. Shulz surrounded by her grandkids filled the screen. "You murdering *bastards.*" He launched from the couch to pace the room. To see it confirmed on the news, to see the familiar light in her eyes–

What *had* Mrs. Shulz died for? The laptop rested on the kitchen counter. Fifteen pieces of Crosstalk's file waited, parts of the answer. He took a deep draught of ale and stabbed the remote, killing the images. Thunder cracked and rolled in the distance as if to echo and extend his guilt miles into the night.

Karma. Great forces were at work. Mind readers. If... *if* real, then it was bigger than him, bigger than Crosstalk or the UG. It was larger than the life he knew or could imagine: the control they would have, by all rights, would be complete. The implications left him feeling small and vulnerable, easily trapped.

Checking himself hard, he drained the bottle and went for another.

"No. Until there is proof – no fear. No fear."

Crosstalk could have overreacted or been under the influence of a drug or just mentally unstable when he sent the email. The file might only be conventional data, though worthy of the murder and frame job. Governments had such secrets. There was only one way to find out.

Getting to the file fast was key. They had detected his first grab which meant Alcazar was in their sights. The next grab had to be from a roundabout way, fast and furiously. A perfect job for the Asshole Array, his most populated and diverse botnet.

He grabbed the laptop and went to work.

Chapter 4

The world owes all its onward impulses to men ill at ease. The happy man inevitably confines himself within ancient limits.
- Nathaniel Hawthorne

Austin woke with a bone dry mouth and crusty eyes. Sunlight reflected from the white floor and walls. A nurse set breakfast on a tray table. Confusion lingered until he saw beyond her to the uniformed officer holding the door open. The prior night's madness fell into place.

"My dad. Where's my dad?"

"That's a question for the police, I imagine," the nurse replied. "How are you feeling? Any pain?"

He asked the officer about his dad. He shook his head. "No idea."

"The pain meds will wear off so let us know if you get too uncomfortable." She wheeled the food tray into place and worked the bed controls to bring him up. His shoulder protested in a distant way. "Have some breakfast. Your body's been shocked and needs nourishment."

"Thank you." He watched her leave.

The officer closed the door and sat. He glanced at Austin then pulled out his phone to surf.

Staring at the food on his tray then around the room, he felt a razor thin line form between realities. Either it was happening as he thought it was, or it wasn't. Reactive stress could fragment reality. The hack, the lucid dream, the tiger, and then the police and his house...

He stared out the window and tried grounding himself. A tree's limbs stretched towards the sky. Curled leaves hung unmoving. The brief cool of morning would give way to another oppressive, hot day. Nature adapted to extremes... *and so can I. I'm part of nature.* Whenever things spiraled out of control, a prolonged meditation served him well. Damn good time to give it a go. Anything to calm down and repair perspective, but first things first. He started in on the pancakes and eggs slowly, then scarfed down, hungry as hell.

By the time he cleared his plate things improved somewhat. Clarity was key. Perspective really was everything and the situation now was proof. He had not been careful with it.

49

The officer continued surfing and avoided eye contact though Austin felt his peripheral watch. It took slow, focused breathing to get into a meditative state. One by one he set aside the troubling thoughts and feelings. Guilt. Panic. Anger. If they returned he set them aside again. A long time passed before they subsided and stress eased. There was only the now and the now finally belonged to him. Like a cloak, he wrapped calm around himself and languished in the isolation it offered.

For a time it seemed sleep might return. Instead, a familiar feeling formed, one from years ago. Small and hesitant at first, it grew. He allowed it, followed it, until a vision began to form. It seemed unlikely it could be forming on its own, but...

He saw the room from a high corner overlooking the bed, a black and white vision running of its own accord. Like a fly on the wall, he saw his body on the bed and the officer in the chair. In the next moment he stood *next* to the bed, seeing in vivid color.

Not a lucid dream. *Not* a dream at all. His body lay on the bed but his face was obscured by a familiar white blur: confirmation of an out of body experience.

Unsolicited, fully formed and sustained, the third one of his life.

Fear and elation mixed – this was the other space, the rare and exquisite domain he'd found but lost long ago. Unsure of how or why it had spawned, he immediately thought to look for his dad and passed through the wall into the hallway. People walked by and through him without sensation, just as the floor offered no feeling to his feet nor the walls to his body.

His dad wasn't in any of the rooms nearby so he found the ICU and wandered from room to room. In one, a pale-skinned senior lay hooked up to monitors. The man's face was blurred white like his own.

"I won't be going back."

Austin spun to see an elderly man standing behind him.

"The old ticker just can't handle it anymore. Just plain worn out. Funny, I sort of felt it coming, the last week or so. I didn't want to worry Phyllis but now I regret not mentioning it." He shook his head. "So which one are you? Banged up? What brings you here? Strange to walk through everything, isn't it?"

He stared into kind eyes framed with a lifetime of smiles. "Um, I'm just visiting. I'm looking for my dad."

"You're from up there? Well, what the heck I'm supposed to do next? I expected a tunnel and a light and all that. Maybe my pops or ol'

Saint Pete himself, ya know? Nothing personal but this is a little disappointing."

Fear edged in on wonder. "Yeah, uh, I wouldn't worry. I'm sure someone will help you soon."

He turned at a beeping sound. Nurses rushed into the room where the old man's face was now visible, slack and lifeless. Turning back, he was alone. Like a dream but not quite. He left to find his dad.

Near a turn in a hallway a strong feeling of unease set in. He sank way back, shrinking to the point it felt he might disappear, and nearly jumped when two men rounded the corner. One was Agent Morris from the previous night, the other a doctor.

The doctor was clearly uncomfortable.

"...won't pretend to understand but it's not my business to. Now, his son. A shrapnel wound. Nicked two ribs and barely missed the top of a lung..."

He followed them at a distance, still uneasy and staying with the small feeling. It felt safer, like he didn't exist. After a few strides, he froze: Morris' head was blurred, pulsing, like blobs of energy pushing to escape his skull. The men rounded another corner and realization struck – they were heading back to his room.

His eyes snapped open. Moments later a knock sounded on the door. The doctor entered followed by Morris.

"Hello Austin, I'm Doctor Goltz. This is Special Agent Dan Morris with the FBI. If you are feeling up to it, he has a few questions for you."

The previous moments were so surreal he could barely think straight. He answered on instinct.

"Not without an attorney."

Morris replied, "You're not under arrest, Austin."

"No?" He nodded towards the officer. "Perk of being a suspect?"

"At this point you are a person of interest." Morris shrugged. "I can leave, but I thought you'd want to know more of what's going on."

In the silence following, Dr. Goltz raised his brows, asking for Austin's preference.

When Austin nodded, Goltz said, "I'll be on the floor if either of you need me."

The doctor left and Morris instructed the officer to leave as well. The door to the room closed. The agent approached the bed with a dissatisfied look.

"Crazy move you pulled last night."

Austin checked the man's face, half-expecting to see it blur.

"I know what this is about. You—"

"Of course you know." Morris nodded, his demeanor turning cold. "It's about hacking government computers and destroying evidence when caught. What if our men had still been upstairs? You'd be facing murder charges now. Of course, attempted murder is bad enough."

The words swam in a fog, freezing coherent thought. *Something so important...*

"No," he managed. "I didn't blow up anything and you know it. I'm not a hacker, either."

"The handoff of the file was attempted at Café Exotico on an IBM ThinkPad belonging to either you or one Ms. Kaiya Wilson. I understand she came to visit last night. Your girlfriend, right?"

The words chilled his core. Involving Kaiya was not okay.

"It's my laptop. Kaiya had nothing to do with it. She told me to delete the downloader."

"Do you often ignore good advice?"

He could only stare back, wishing he hadn't. "I used it to try and download whatever the hacker left for me. I was curious, okay? Nothing illegal about it. Just curious. I downloaded two chunks of forty, all encrypted and without a key. That means I got nothing. Do you understand? Nothing."

Morris continued as if he hadn't heard. "With all the evidence we've accumulated, it's looking like you were the ring leader. I've never seen a house so secure. All the cameras, sensors, and computers. And ringed with explosives? I think we found our man."

The words were paralyzing. "Why... why do this? I don't know who sent it or what it was. I didn't even finish the download."

The agent studied him. "Something tells me you still can."

"C'mon," he said too quickly, "you blew up my house and every computer I own."

"No Austin, you blew up your house. And it appears you're willing to blow up your future, too." He turned for the door.

"Wait."

The agent stopped.

"It's in the bushes. I threw it in the bushes. A laptop."

Morris turned back, his gaze an x-ray. "Where?"

Even the hint of untruth might stand out. Still, he had to try.

"Highway 80 east of Greenback."

The agent's eyes seemed to ignite with tiny flecks of energy.

Morris stepped closer. "Where exactly?"

"Just past the onramp. A couple hundred feet maybe."

Morris nodded. "I see. And no other copies of the files?"

He hesitated, wishing there were, but in doing so gave away the truth. He shook his head. "No. No copies."

"Uh huh."

With that, Morris turned and left the room.

He let out a long breath, hoping a deal had been made but completely unsure of it. "God damn."

The door opened and the officer returned.

A feeling came then, a pendulum of inevitability.

"Austin Bakken, you have the right to remain silent..."

Again he stared out the window. An hour's reflection after his arrest left him feeling helpless, pissed, and still stupidly curious. Control was gone now, his choices expired. Rage smoldered at the hacker for throwing government secrets around like Molotov cocktails. And curiosity still burned at what the file contained. There were other feelings. Fear. Guilt. Regret. Embarrassment. He'd fucked up... everything. All without knowing what for.

A knock sounded at the door. It opened and a man in jeans with a baseball cap and gray sideburns stepped in. He showed the officer a badge.

"Mac Payant, federal agent. I need a few minutes alone with Mr. Bakken."

The officer stood and examined the badge before nodding and heading out.

The agent stopped at the foot of the bed. "How are you feeling, Austin?"

"Like shit. Who are you?"

"Friend of your dad's."

"Yeah? Here to play the good cop?"

"You've met a bad cop?"

The guy seemed sincere. "Where is he?"

"In custody. He called and said you were in trouble. He wants you to tell me what happened. What really happened."

"When did he call?"

"Couple of hours ago."

"Where was he?"

"He didn't say." At Austin's look, he stepped forward to the edge of the bed and said in a low voice, "Look, shit's going down. I need as much from you as quick as I can if I'm going to help either of you.

What I can't give you on a plate is a reason to trust me. Brent and I go way back. Before your mom died. You gotta give me what you can before things switch up."

"You think they will?"

"I'd say they could."

Mac was younger than his dad but not by much. He spoke and acted with an air of protective authority. Austin wanted to trust the guy but something told him he shouldn't, so he lied when he got to the part about ditching the laptop, just as he had to Agent Morris. It was off highway 50, not highway 80.

"So you tried to download the file and next thing you know people are breaking into your house?"

"Yes. And planting explosives, apparently."

Gray-blue eyes pinned Austin. "The truth, now. Were you hacking? To any extent?"

"Absolutely not. This is all about the hacker and his file."

Mac weighed him in a way that reminded him of Morris. The agent asked, "Do you still believe in aliens and telepathy and all that?"

Austin shrugged, wondering how he knew to ask. "Anything's possible. What do we really know?"

"Okay. Keep cool while I look into things. And no more talking. I'll arrange for an attorney as soon as I've found your dad. We'll get you out on bail if possible. I'll keep you posted." He turned to go.

"Do me a favor?"

"What's that?"

"Call my girlfriend and tell her they arrested me. Ask her to talk to her mom."

He'd asked Fuku Wilson for help. The ego burn was nothing compared to the fire of desperation. Agent Payant said he'd try to help. Beyond that, everything seemed stacked against him. Like a game of Jenga, the blocks had begun to fall and there was no way to stop them.

Lunch time brought another wave of pain. Painkillers helped. He ate half a sandwich, his appetite poor. Calls were being blocked. The nurse said over a dozen had come in, friends and co-workers eager to know what had happened. If Payant or Fuku were going to help it would be in the form of an attorney showing up at the door.

By dinner time, one hadn't arrived.

Review of the last two days didn't leave much room for hope. Digital evidence could be fabricated in such a way as to leave a jury no choice but to convict. Even without the explosion and related charges, the hacking could be leveraged to put him away for years. Freedom would be lost. The future destroyed.

Before bed he complained of pain and got another dose. Anything to numb the pain of knowing how totally fucked he was.

A pat on the face.

Another one, less gentle. Urgent.

"Wake up, Austin."

Dreams fled and the dim night light revealed a nurse at his side. A glance at the officer saw him dozing, head to one side.

"Let's go." She pulled back the sheets and guided his legs from the bed. "Not a word, please. Put these on."

Groggy from the pain meds, he thought of Mac Payant and wondered if he'd arranged an escape. Things were bad, so it made sense. She helped him into nursing scrub and clipped a badge onto his shirt pocket. The shoes were big but everything else fit okay.

"Count to thirty. Turn left out the door and you'll see me. Follow at a distance. You are Timothy Schrader. Tim Schrader. You work here but are going off-shift. We'll head downstairs and you'll leave by the side exit. Once outside, head to the left, towards the parking lot. Do you understand?"

He did but only just. Questions died on his lips when she abruptly left the room. Thirty seconds. He took a few steps towards the door. Confusion circled. The only certainty was that he wanted out of custody. If this was the way...

The officer snored lightly.

His heart pounded. Time felt fuzzy. *Thirty seconds?*

He opened the door and stepped into the hallway, as much an employee as he could imagine. The nurse's station was empty. To the left and down a ways the nurse stood with a clipboard. She looked at him once and walked down a connecting hallway. He followed her through corridors and down a set of stairs to emerge in a staff hallway. To the left and down a hundred feet or so, a man stood leaning against a wall.

'Hesitation draws attention', his dad once said, so he strode to the right and saw the nurse standing at a computer terminal. She rose an arm as if to scratch her elbow and pointed to a hallway behind her.

He turned into the short hall and bumped the door open to a quad between the hospital and the parking garage. Instantly grateful for the evening's heat, he turned left as instructed and came to the sidewalk in front of the hospital. A shuttle bus slowed and stopped with its door open. The driver called out, "Going to the Med Center? Staff ride free."

Still afraid but grateful for the conspiracy, he strode up the steps. "Thanks."

Two other riders looked up at him, a man and a woman, both hospital workers. He slouched down into a seat as the shuttle started off. By the time they pulled onto the avenue, he knew they were safe and away. He moved to the seat closest to the driver.

"So who do I thank?"

The driver shook his head. "What do you mean?"

He looked back at the passengers. They were oblivious. His heart thundered. Was he supposed to get on the shuttle? Or had he screwed up?

"Uh, never mind. How far to the medical center?"

The driver gave him an appraising look. "This time of morning, 'bout twenty minutes."

He must've screwed up, gotten on the shuttle instead of waiting to be picked up. Did they know? He thought of Kaiya. Finding a phone to call her was no good now. Getting her involved would prove her mother completely right. *What a cluster fuck*. So unreal, so vividly *messed up*. He took a deep breath. Everything revolved around the hacker's file – it had started this and now was his only asset, if he could just reach it. In that moment it became his first and only priority.

"Hey, could you let me off up here at this gas station? I forgot some really important paperwork. I can hike back, no problem."

The driver didn't respond.

"Uh, I need to get off the bus. Right here, please?" The gas station came and went.

Austin looked back. The male nurse stared out the window and the woman used her phone, both still oblivious. He suddenly felt black and white, invisible like in a scene from the Twilight Zone.

Screw this.

He stood and stepped towards the driver. "Look, buddy," he leaned forward, "I need to get off this bus, so you need to pull over right now. Right now."

The driver ignored him. Anger mixed with panic. He balled a fist.

"Are you–"

– an audible click and a sting – and the world went berserk. Pain exploded from his lower back, radiating outward with savage intensity.

"Aaah maaah! – aahhhhh!" He fell and writhed in the aisle. The male nurse, an Asian man, held a taser gun. Its electrode wires streamed into him. The woman took the gun.

"Move and I'll zap you again."

The male handcuffed his hands behind his back and sat him upright in the aisle, against a seat. The taser's electrodes were neatly hooked to the cuffs.

He tried recovering but was tapped out. He'd always wondered what a taser blast felt like. To know sucked. He asked, "Who the hell are you?"

They remained silent and kept their eyes on him.

He spat blood from a gnashed tongue. "I never finished downloading it. Do you hear me? I didn't download it. I don't know *anything*."

They continued to ignore him. Panic spiked, rivaling the intensity of the pain of a moment ago.

The shuttle turned onto side streets before entering the parking lot of an office building. The driver pulled under the canopy of an oak tree next to a black van with darkened windows. They transferred vehicles. Before the van's door closed, Austin saw the driver set off a smoke bomb in the shuttle bus.

"Fogging for roaches?" he asked, trying for a response. They ignored him. Anxiety pressed in as firmly as the handcuffs.

The driver climbed in and pulled a divider shut. Puck lights in the ceiling lit up the interior. The van's windows were actually opaque, not just dark. For more than an hour they drove in silence, getting on and off the freeway. The smell of wood smoke grew stronger and his ears compressed and eventually popped. They were at least in the foothills.

When the van finally parked, the Asian produced a thick black band bracelet and clamped it around Austin's right ankle. He removed the handcuffs.

"Don't get stupid. The taser is nothing compared to this."

The side door slid open to reveal a garage interior and a luxury sedan.

Asian Man pulled him forward.

Down a utility corridor and into a large foyer, they ascended a sweeping set of stairs and emerged in the large entertaining area of an executive-style log home. Vaulted ceilings rested on rock walls. He'd been right about the location in the foothills. Leather chairs and couches faced a bay of picture windows showing the lights of the Sacramento Valley beyond.

The woman disappeared down a hall. A stately older man attended an oak and glass-featured bar while the driver took a stool. Asian Man remained positioned between Austin and the others at all times.

The older man addressed him with an English accent.

"Greetings, Mr. Bakken. I'm Edward. There is much to discuss. Sit down, be at ease. Can I make you a drink?"

Far from relaxed, fear rode the edge of every thought. This was danger, a dunk into madness.

"No thanks."

He sat. Adrenaline must have burned the pain meds away because his shoulder ached. Legs crossed, he checked the ankle bracelet. Big enough for a beefy battery inside, enough to deliver a major shock. No doubt a GPS component, too. His only bargaining chip was the laptop unless they used torture. The bracelet might be for that, too. He tapped it with a fingernail.

Edward finished making a drink at the bar and moved around to a chair near the windows. Asian Man sat, situated to intercept, more weapon than human.

"Your shoulder is causing you discomfort. Would you like something for it?"

Anger and fear fumbled ahead of tact. "You know I didn't download the file. Why blow up my house? Why all this shit?"

Edward returned his gaze, measuring. The woman hadn't returned and the driver might as well have been wallpaper, at the bar studying his phone.

Awkward silence drew long. The ice in his glass shifted.

Edward said, "*We* didn't blow up your house."

"You're not with Morris."

"We're not with Morris."

"Then who are you?"

"Someone who wants to prevent the release of the file."

"Okay, that's easy. I don't have it, never did. I don't have the downloader app, either. It's gone. Deleted. Bit bucket."

Edward paused, staring at him with the effect of an x-ray.

"You still have the downloader. I ask that you refrain from further deception."

Fear struck, bringing two sudden realizations. One, he didn't want telepathy to be real and two, Edward's hospitality could turn to hostility at any moment.

"Technically, no, I don't have it. I tossed the laptop. And I wasn't lying when I said I didn't finish the download. Could you just cut to the chase and tell me what this is about?"

Edward turned to look out at the city lights in silence.

For long moments Austin studied his face. Wistful. A bit of hope. *Regret?* The range of feelings surged, too many to keep track of. Edward seemed to exude emotion like rolling ocean waves. He glanced at the ankle bracelet and thought maybe they had delivered a drug through it.

Edward took another sip and turned back.

"Cutting to the chase, you've stepped into some serious shit. The kind you won't be able to wipe off by yourself."

"Yeah, I kinda noticed. But why am I here? Who are you?"

"You are here because you know there is more to life than what the surface presents. You understand that reality extends beyond what science yet explains. You may even have stumbled upon things that burden you with their... undefinability. Unconventional perceptions that you dismiss despite your fascination. You keep your speculations to yourself and largely out of mind because they are a distraction and worse, a liability. But in truth you want to know more. You have a real, almost timeless longing."

He looked away. Fear flowed like hot butter into every nook of his being. All that was in the past. Yet, there was one damned, fucked up, insane part of him that knew there *was* a mystery to existence that 'everyday life' didn't address. There *were* truths just out of reach. Part of him wanted to know what was in the file, yet... the violence, the criminal charges. And his dad, Kaiya, his future at InterGen, his home... it was time to put things back together, not dick with the unknown.

Silence ensued, drawn into moment after uncomfortable moment. Asian Man was stoic, observing peripherally. Edward's x-ray mode remained. He tried to read him in return but it was like poking concrete with a pencil. The effort did seem to prompt him to speak, though.

"In the hospital, you went for a little walk?"

"Thanks to your people."

"No. I mean prior to that."

Time ground to a stop. The astral walk. There was *no fucking way* he could know about that. Fear struck savagely.

"What are you talking about?"

Edward arched his brow. "I asked that you cease deception."

Nothing, *nothing* had prepared him for this. Beyond all else, this was *not* okay. Hackers with stolen government secrets, fine. His house blown up, okay. Another out of body experience, cool. Rogue government agents, alright. Kidnapping, great. All of that was intense, but viable, plausible. There were frameworks of reference for all of it. Shit happens, don'tchya just know it. But this, this was from his *own head*. Only *he* had experienced that. *Only him.*

He gripped his leg as the world began to spin without motion. The hacker's desperate words echoed. *They are on the ground and in people's minds.* Pain spiked in his shoulder, a gathering roar that made it hard to think.

"I'll take something for the pain, now. Make it a double."

As if waiting in the wings, the woman appeared with a prescription bottle and glass of water.

Vicodin. He wasted no time in popping two and emptying the glass. Asian Man watched. The driver sipped his drink at the bar. Edward seemed content to wait, studying him.

Took a walk. It meant Edward either dug through his mind or somehow observed his 'walk'. Save for the old man who had died, assuming he was even real, no one knew what he'd done. Something big *gave*, the unmistakable shift of change. Everything he'd 'seen' during that 'walk' could have been a combination of imagination and coincidence – but no more. Edward had broken the rigid walls of reality.

"Time for my questions and the non-deception clause better apply. Who are you? What country?"

"Not yet. First, your walk. Why does the topic make you uncomfortable, Austin?"

"Why the mind screw, Ed? You know damned well you shouldn't know anything about that 'walk'. You're mind-fucking me and I don't like it."

"Relax." Edward motioned and the woman went to refill his glass. "I only want to talk. How and when did you learn to leave your body?"

"And I only want to know how the hell you know I did."

Edward didn't respond; instead, he appeared to weigh the situation.

Austin shifted on the couch, skirting the edge of comfort, trying to get back in. Telepathy. Why was he so scared? He'd suspected it, deduced it, even wished for it to be true, yet having it shown so bare was terrifying.

He breathed and stared at his hands. A dangerous notion presented itself: the inclination to trust Edward. It was more than his knightly demeanor, his manners, or his grandfatherly English accent. Instinct was pushing him to trust, to open up. He struggled with compromise, to explore the situation without giving in completely.

He remembered exactly how he'd come to astral walk though he'd never mastered it. To make any sense of the situation, to learn anything about what was going on, the story had to be told. Since Edward sensed deception there was no use in leaving anything out. *Let him figure it out for me.*

The woman refilled his glass.

"Alright, you wanna know? Fine. I was seventeen. Big into psychic shit. Auras and vibrations and astral projection. I'd been into it for about a year, since just after my mom's death, except this one evening I got tired of it all, specifically with the astral projection book I was reading. I wanted to *know* if it was real or not. I was determined, almost pissed. I didn't want to be a sucker believing in something made up for book sales. So I marched upstairs to my room to do the exercise."

"To try to astral project."

"Yeah. OBE, out of body experience. I laid on the bed and did the relaxation routine, spreading warmth from my toes to my head, yada yada. I did exactly what it said to do. Next thing I know, bam! I'm standing next to my bed. Full color, smooth, just standing there, except I can't feel a thing. I'm just *there*. I look over and see my body lying on the bed but can't see my face. It's blanked out white. I realize I'm actually doing it – astral projecting. Then I remember the walls mean nothing, that I should be able to move right through them. I pass through the bed and the wall and come out on the other side. There I am, hip-deep in the bathroom sink. I see my dad down the hall in his room folding clothes. It blew me away. I was *outside* my body."

Edward closed his eyes, as if visualizing it himself.

"I knew I had to check myself, to see if I was asleep or imagining it. So bam! I'm back behind my closed eyes, looking at gray. I reflected and reviewed and knew I hadn't been imagining it or forcing a vision. I hadn't been asleep because I wasn't the slightest bit sleepy. It stood then as being real.

"The thought of resuming brought me right back to the other side of the wall. Definitely surprised me, sort of confirmed something special was happening. I walked through the bathroom into the spare bedroom and up to a window. I knew I could move forward, outside over the front yard, and sure as shit, I did. Walked a dozen steps out past the second story window, standing on nothing. I looked around and thought, 'I could go *anywhere*.' Then the weirdest thing: I *rotated* ninety degrees so I was facing straight up into the sky. I didn't try to, it just happened. I walked away from the ground, maybe a couple dozen paces until I was above the rooftops. I looked sideways across the neighborhood then straight ahead into the sky. I knew there was one place I really wanted to go, but it would take a real long time to get there."

Edward opened his eyes. "Space."

"Yeah but just then, at that thought, everything faded to white. When the white receded, it was to a translucent orange and white cloud. A nebula, deep in space. Someone or something brought me there. Something that had been following my thoughts. I remember feeling gratitude. The next thing I know I'm behind my eyes again. I wasn't imagining and I wasn't just waking up."

"What did you do?"

"I was blown away. I had my answer but also a dozen more questions and no one to ask. I walked down the hall and saw my dad putting away the last of his laundry. It felt amazing. I had done it."

"You didn't tell him?"

"Yeah I did."

"And he wasn't much help."

"Yeah, no. Not at all."

"It wasn't the last time you'd do it."

"Once more about a year later though it was short. I was surprised. I thought I'd never experience it again. Like maybe it was just imagination after all."

Recalling the day brought to mind the other, bigger weirdness. Another repressed set of memories.

Edward's x-ray picked up on it. "What else?"

"Well, it's a lot weirder. My wind story."

The driver looked up from his phone. Edward's x-ray intensified. "Wind story?"

Hello. Leverage...

"Yes, the wind." He imagined trading it for some assurance of safety. "A very personal story, actually."

When he didn't elaborate, Edward nodded. "I see. Well, we wouldn't want you to share anything too personal."

The room fell silent, an awkward abyss swallowing his power play.

"Okay, look," he said. "My *life* is up in smoke. You're talking about shit I only imagined was possible. I'm excited but scared to death. And I don't know anything about you. You gotta work with me here."

He emptied his water in one long draw.

Edward studied him.

"Come on, what?" Austin asked. "I need firm ground, man. What does all this mean? Who *are* you people and how are you reading my mind?"

Edward nodded slowly and returned to the bar to begin work on another drink, quietly exchanging words with the driver in a clipped and guttural language. Ice clattered into a glass. Edward spoke louder, addressing him.

"I understand where you're at, Austin, I truly do. There is much to cover and time is not in abundance. Let's start with the most pressing issue." He tipped a bottle to fill his glass. "The laptop. Where exactly is it?"

He hesitated. "I'm supposed to just trust you? Just give it up?"

"You're going to have to come to trust on your own. I do need to recover the laptop, though. Non-negotiable."

"Okay, fine." Despite Edward's warning, he lied about its location again, only he didn't treat it like a lie. Mentally, before and after, he treated it as truth and didn't hesitate in thought or tone delivering it. "I'm guessing they found it by now."

"You told them?"

"Not the exact location but close enough."

"I see."

"So how about telling me what this is all about."

"What exactly do you want to know?" Edward asked, returning to his chair.

He ignored the impulse to think he had successfully lied to Edward. Instead he slid right into the most pressing question he had. "Mind reading. How do you do it?"

Edward shook his head. "Not something I can easily explain."

"Could I learn to do it?"

"Yes, with practice."

"How did you know I traveled in the hospital?"

"Our people were there, observing already, your case having drawn our attention. You were awake, not too heavily drugged. When you closed your eyes, began meditating, and crossed over to explore, it came as a shock. The ability is exceedingly rare."

"Already observing me? So you're who the hacker warned about."

Edward shook his head. "No. We are trying to retrieve what he stole. We arranged to take you only after your walk."

He sat back, letting it sink in. "Remote viewing, then."

Edward sipped his drink.

"What about the FBI? Agent Morris?"

After consideration, he said only, "Morris belongs to a very dangerous group. The men the hacker warned about."

Amazement slewed back into anxiety.

"So I'm in the middle of something?" When Edward didn't answer, he asked, "How about some background?"

"No background and no disclosure. It's simple, we need the file contained. Now Austin, I've told you what you need to know. Anything more and... well frankly, there is no more. It is the business of my organization only."

There it was – subtle, in his voice, in his eyes – the reason for all of it.

"That's why you brought me here. I traveled and you need people that can. You want my help." He waited for confirmation but none came – nor did denial. "Tell me about your organization."

The older man shook his head. "For that there is a road to travel. Otherwise we part ways shortly. To be honest I'm not sure you are ready to go forward. Leaving now could save your life."

"Save my *life?* What life? I'm screwed and you know it. For all I know you set this whole thing up." At Edward's look of dismissal he said, "What I need is safe ground, even if it means walking away."

"But what you *really* want is..."

"Jesus Christ."

Vicodin flooded his system. Regretful for having taken two, he paused. Depth perception tweaked. Edward looked more three-dimensional than he should have. Every breath brought his body closer to relaxation, in sharp contrast to his intense mental and emotional state. Fear and fascination mixed in a sickening combination.

"Alright, I need to know how you are reading my mind."

Edward turned away, once more studying the horizon. Long thoughts turned. A decision was reached. "It's simple, Austin. Your brain emits and receives signals. The wifi of the soul, you might call it. Everyone's connected. Everyone's sensitive."

"Alright, I get that. I feel people all the time, but how do you read minds? Really read them? Not just emotions or vibes."

"The vibes carry the meaning. Technically it requires intelligent pattern recognition."

"Pattern recognition?"

Edward nodded. "What is speech? Sequences of vibrations. The ear is the receiver. It cannot help but receive the sound waves it is sensitive to. Your brain is sensitive in the same way."

"But to different waves. And somehow your read them?"

"So do you. Everyone has the sense. Some call it empathy, some call it being sensitive. Most don't realize it because it is so subtle, but there is already a basic language formed. It manifests as gut level thoughts and responses. Habitual thinking. People just feel and assume without really knowing or even asking why. Without training, you're awash in the sea. In touch but in the chaos of not knowing."

"How do I know you're not making shit up?"

"You know I'm not. You've experienced it. It's what some dread when they join the morning commute or enter a crowded place or run into a particular person. It's feedback, human feedback, via an energy that connects us. Ping, pong. Marco, Polo. With it we learn the language that shapes our inner lives, our world view, and our responses to it. Positive or negative. Whether we realize it or not, it is the shared field of consciousness. As I said, there is not enough time to explain it." He surveyed Austin. "Now, normally I would seek to recover the file and return you to your life if possible. However, you present a rare situation. While raw and untrained, your ability to project your consciousness sets you apart. It suggests uncommon ability and instinct. Hearing mention of the wind, I'll admit being even more interested. Truth be told, we could use your help. But what's more important for you is the obvious fact that you could use our help. You need us, as well."

Once again the pendulum of inevitability cut the air. Despite fear, an intense draw to know more pulsed, increasing the gravity first formed by the hacker's files. The veil of life's mystery seemed to have a break here, with these people, under these circumstances.

Edward set his glass aside, clearing his throat. "I sense your interest. Time is exceedingly short and there is a process to determine if you are eligible. As with all substantial opportunity, there will come a point at which you must decline or commit. We operate fundamentally like a family if that helps tune your perceptions. Above all else, understand this: if you tried to betray us, even once, you would forfeit your life. Become unreliable by choice and your reality would devolve into something less desirable in corresponding degrees. This is not a job offer. This is a life choice." He paused and the x-ray feeling lingered. As if sensing Austin's fear, he continued in a softer voice. "You have gifts that will go undeveloped if you turn away now. Gifts that this world needs more of, now more than ever. Cicero reminds us, 'What one has, one ought to use, and whatever he does he should do with all his might'. You have something. Something to use that the future needs."

The Vicodin thundered, creating a dreamlike state. So much to consider. His dad, Kaiya, career, home, his dreams, everything and everyone. *Yet, so much already altered.*

Alone, there were no guarantees, just a system poised to ruin him.

He countered. "There's also a proverb that says drink nothing without seeing it, sign nothing without reading it. What does your group do? What does it stand for?"

Edward leveled his gaze. "What we 'do' is try to guide humanity's evolution. Protect the species, you might say. Some would protest our methods. I can only say you would be joining the more benevolent of the two groups." A moment later, he added, "And that there are no other greater powers on earth."

On earth. The words lingered.

Edward was an impressive speaker, but the last was powerful on its own. Daffy Duck could have spoken the words and the enormity of the truth would have conveyed itself, lisp and all.

There wasn't really a choice and he knew it. Joining them would provide tools to defend himself and the others. His moral compass would dictate his actions, what he would become. The moment offered both relief and intense anxiety.

"I want to continue but only if I can protect my family. Kaiya and my dad, at least. I have to."

"As expected." Edward nodded. "We'll discuss the art of the possible in that regard. For the moment, you need to get some rest."

Chapter 5

You may have your suspicions, your fears, you may even believe there is something, somewhere, terribly, drastically wrong, but because someone else is in charge, because there is a part of the system above you which you don't know, you don't question it, you even distrust your own doubts.
-Graham Swift

"Kaiya? Could you come up to Mr. Nelson's office?"

What now? The morning's presentation had gone poorly. Distracted by the situation developing, she'd lacked charisma and her timing was dismal. By most any standard it had been a disaster. Surely he understood...

"Yes, I'll be right up." She straightened her skirt and headed for the CEO's office.

The receptionist waved her in. She entered and saw a man with Mr. Nelson. Rugged with trim gray sideburns and a weathered face, he wore jeans and a baseball cap.

"Kaiya, this gentleman is from the Central Intelligence Agency. He allowed me to verify his status so he's the real deal. He wants to speak with you alone regarding Austin. Are you comfortable with that?"

Her mind whirled. "Did Brent send you?"

"I'm involved at his request, yes." He stepped forward to shake her hand. "Mac Payant. Special Agent from the NorCal office. Brent and I go way back. We need to talk about Austin."

She turned to her boss. "I'll be fine Mr. Nelson, and I'm sorry for all this. I really am."

"No worries, Kaiya, I'll be just outside with Pam if you need me."

She listened in disbelief as Agent Payant detailed everything that had happened at the hospital since she left, up to the current multiagency search for Austin.

"You're serious?" She looked at the agent in disbelief. "He snuck out in the middle of the night? On his own?"

"He had a helper, but he acted on his own, yes."

"A helper? This is nuts, you know. It really is. Austin's not a hacker, I can promise you that. He's being framed." She stood and paced to the window. "This smells of a cover-up. Someone knows what's in the file. Something damaging to the President's reputation or to the government. Do you know what it is?"

"I don't know anything about it," Agent Payant said. "And I don't blame you for being suspicious. I am, too. But until we understand who we're dealing with, you may be danger. My director approved protective custody for you at my request. I could insure your safety and that's something I know Brent and Austin would want. It's your choice."

Anxiety slewed into fright. "Why would he run? That's not like him."

"He's scared. Someone convinced him he was safer with them. Kaiya, this is already an extraordinary situation. People want him back in custody. My gut says you could be used to make that happen."

"The FBI? You're saying they're a threat?"

Mac shook his head. "I'm saying you may be used in ways you wouldn't like and by people we don't know. Look, Brent is family. Trust or don't. The safe facility is less than an hour from here, if you accept."

"What if Austin tries to reach me?"

"Has he called?"

"No."

"Then assume he doesn't have the option to. You have your phone if he does."

"And my job?" she asked. "Just walk away from it?"

"It should only be temporary."

Should be. She looked at the agent, then to the window and the tree-lined street outside. "This is really happening, isn't it? And no one knows why." Options cancelled themselves out in review, leaving just one. "Okay, let's go. Before the building blows up or something. And please find Austin. You have to. You just have to."

• • •

Late afternoon under skies darkened by storm clouds, Johan struggled against a wave of sleepiness. He brewed coffee and slid open windows, angling blinds as Max Dosch wasn't fit to be seen yet. The makeup should already have been on but he was too absorbed in setting the stage for the file grab.

Soldado would have him shot for exposing Alcazar to such a grab. It couldn't be helped – it was the most secure quick-and-dirty method he could design. Using a high-caliber worm virus as a core engine, he had spent hours coding intricate modifications, testing carefully, all in an effort to secure Crosstalk's file without being traced. The Asshole Array botnet, fueled by this engine, would hum a complex tune of deception and trickery, nabbing and delivering the chunks from around the world. No system on earth should be able to track the action inside the storm that he was about to let loose. It would be over almost before it began.

One last roundabout check showed the file still intact within Alcazar's bowels.

"Slagen. Alleen slagen." *Just succeed.*

On the web site for a restaurant in Prague, a string of twenty-eight characters appeared at the bottom of the 'About Us' page. The font color, same as the background, made them invisible to the human eye.

Thirty seconds later, the addition served as a trigger for the launch. One zombie checked in as designed then communicated to sixty others that communicated with sixty additional zombies, who in turn each reached another sixty until a minute later over one and a half million computers achieved the same state of readiness. The Asshole Array was online.

Ten seconds passed; each computer began talking with addresses across the planet, a cacophony of ordinary communication except for the very few that made the quick grabs from Alcazar. Weather reports, site searches, YouTube streams, news sites – over twenty-five million packets per second – and of those, a few thousand contained bits of Crosstalk's file. The tiny stolen pieces crossed the botnet, each changing hands hundreds of times in a complex shell game. The botnet's fervor escalated and peaked twenty seconds later in a storm of traffic that registered on traffic monitoring sites around the world. Ten seconds later it slowly began diminishing, the work accomplished.

In a little over a minute and a half, he had taken the remaining twenty-five chunks from Alcazar.

He wasted no time copying all forty chunks to a memory stick. During the copy, the control panel for the botnet turned red, indicating massive loss of communication. From a million and a half online computers to eight hundred thousand in just seconds. He stared in disbelief. More than half the botnet had fallen.

Cold dread replaced the excitement of a moment ago. Someone's system had tracked over *half a million* transfer bots in their morphing dance across protocols and ports, mapping them along the way, including the fake destinations – and then silenced each of them. In seconds.

"Fuck fuck *fuck*. Okay Crosstalk, what did you get me into?"

He set down a bottle of ale and brought up the Alcazar client. The local import of the forty chunks ran smoothly. Assembled, they formed a video file eighteen minutes long.

"This better be big, man. Very damned big."

He pressed play.

"Madness."

Thunder followed his words, rattling the glass in the cupboards. The clock on the wall showed nine-thirty.

Nature unleashed her fury over Oostendorp. Rain poured in windblown sheets to create cascading rivers from the rooftops. Trees lashed the side of the house. It was the kind of storm that made people huddle indoors and wonder why God was so angry.

Johan knew. What he'd seen was unholy. Eighteen potent minutes that confirmed the existence of a shadow world government beyond any doubt. What it could do and how long it had been doing it made him as angry as the storm.

He shuddered at the scale suggested. The deceit, lies, and control – the *knowledge* – all used for enslavement and the cause of needless suffering across time. Wars, religions, disease, and ignorance were all conditions gestated by those who would have and keep ultimate power. The long threads of their plans made the world's history look organic, natural, yet there was precious little that wasn't orchestrated or caused by this authority.

The imbalance of karma struck his soul like a hot brand.

Dubbed the 'Comannda' by the narrator, their early understanding of the mind had exposed the raw nature of reality and gained them the keys to mankind's future. Consciousness could be directed beyond the body and with that knowledge they had perfected new arts – remote viewing, dream control, and telepathy – using them with great effect throughout time. To keep control of humanity, they had only to keep people distracted from understanding their own minds.

As proof, the video contained unredacted communiques, secret video clips, and still photos documenting the planning and manipulations that brought about some of the most horrific results of the twentieth century. Engineered illness and wars allowed for population control, economic development, and to keep fear at 'effective levels'. Distraction was paramount and served to keep unification from occurring. Should the majority learn how manipulated their lives really were, control would dissolve and their global empire would crumble.

Most jarring was a clip of John F. Kennedy in a conversation about the controlling entity he referred to as 'the firm'. Its plans had become so damaging and morally repugnant that the elite could no longer allow it to operate as it had. It was time to reveal their existence and dismantle their structure. Discussion centered on the methods to do so and the inherent obstacles in each. A central base was mentioned but the location was unknown. The overlaid text indicated a date of October 1963, just one month before his assassination.

The last part of the video described an artificially intelligent surveillance system encircling the globe, embedded in digital systems down to the personal computer and cell phone. Such an advanced AI explained perfectly the botnet's extraordinary demise. Only a system like that could have executed the traces. By the third viewing, careful contemplation resolved skepticism.

It fit.

The insanity of man's history was suddenly understandable under the framework provided. The video birthed belief via the gaps it closed. It challenged doubt and churned fear like a mill.

"Where did you get this, Crosstalk? Jesus."

He pulled the last bottle of ale from the fridge, struggling for calm. This was more than just greedy governments and corporations. Much more. Anxiety rose to a pitch. Fear burned in the moment, there in the kitchen, because he no longer felt alone with his thoughts.

"Christ." No wonder someone didn't want the file getting out.

He uncapped the bottle and slapped the opener on the counter. Where was skepticism? It couldn't all be true. He chugged half the bottle in a single go, unable to stop thinking of the video, of the images, and of the narrator's voice. Rising panic threatened to break like flood waters; the very air about him held depths, possibility.

"Gah!"

Overwhelmed, he struggled against a bizarre feeling of being incredibly small and of being *connected* to everything. Thoughts flowed, highly exposed. Something in the video had triggered hellacious feelings of paranoia. Like a beacon just above the ordinary, it began to feel as though the entire world could hear and feel his thoughts. The video described how the Comannda tracked people in *Raon*, the field of the physical, through vibes. If true, his unbalance was surely a deviation in that field. The sensation of *others* dawned and grew stronger with every breath.

They were getting closer.

"A trap. A fucking trap." Crosstalk hadn't gone crazy – *he'd just been caught.*

He strode to the liqueur cabinet, tore the cap from a bottle of Vodka and drank deeply. Bearing down, he fought to ditch the feeling. He tried keeping control by summoning strong memories. Morning. Breakfast. Three scrambled eggs, two halves of toast... the shapes, the colors, the smell. He'd shaken the peppershaker four, maybe five times? *What was it?* He recalled the rhythm. Definitely five shakes. Five simple, careless shakes in time. Pain. He'd bitten his tongue. A powerful, engaging memory he'd blocked but which now served well. He thought of anything and everything that occurred before watching the video.

Focused on a recessed ceiling light, he drank vodka from the bottle. When his throat burned and stomach protested, he stoked his hash pipe and pulled from it deeply, again and again. Still *they* came, mosquitoes of possibility, closer every time, searching. His thoughts were the flashes of light attracting them. What would happen when they arrived wasn't clear but fear went ahead of the thought, which meant everything.

What he sought hit him in a lurching wave, a sudden rising disintegration as he sank to the floor. To watch the threatening thoughts dissolve and float around him, to have his own center back, felt divine. The pipe fell to the hardwood, spilling ash. Thunder crashed and rolled, now muted and inconsequential. Exhaustion added its part and soon the *others* faded in the haze of altered consciousness. He languished in the drifting safety it provided. A despairing thought came and went but left its mark: *there could be no karmic correction for this.*

Ten minutes later, the room slipped away altogether.

He woke to the splash of a water drop against his forehead. A dim luminance revealed the next drop falling from the shadows above. For a heartbeat, the drop froze in midair, suspended, then fell to splash against his skull.

Drugged? Apparently – in trying to flinch away, not a single muscle responded, save for his eyes. The urge to move spread downward from his face, dully denied at every turn. The cold air of the cave wrapped around his bare arms and face, a sensate reminder of the body he couldn't control. A shout instead turned to a surge of muted panic.

Calm down. Drugs wore out, in time. Rotating his eyes in all directions helped some. The damp walls and muddy floor of a small cave were just visible. *Had he been caught?* Memory, too, was quietly defiant. Calculation, however, remained keen. Chinese water torture could take hours or longer to have the desired effect. The drug in his system would surely wear before then, requiring another dose and offering a chance at interaction with his captors, if only one-sided.

Another drop caused a rivulet to stream down his forehead into the well of his left eye.

He began to blink, hoping to absorb the moisture, before realizing the futility. Another would come soon. For now he plied at memory and tried to ignore the water.

More than once, he realized after the fact he'd been lost in a moment stretched over several moments. A natural rule was being bent. Drugged or not, it was fascinating.

He watched time.

The variations, the pauses and overlaps, were so subtle that under different circumstances he probably never would have noticed them. At one point it dawned on him that time was also *watching him*. Reacting. Intelligent. *Aware.* Had always been so. The thought struck fear so profound that his automatic breathing stopped momentarily. Time as a character? An intelligence? As if dodging discovery, the sensation left him; time resumed its normal pace.

For a long spell he contemplated what he'd seen, fear ghosting the periphery of his thoughts. *Something* watched him.

Drop. Time... *Drop.* Time... *Drop.*

Lulled, he passed into sleep.

He woke again, cold, wet, and alarmed. The cave's ceiling was leaking thousands of drops into the pool forming below. The water was up to the cot, soaking his clothes and inching towards his ears. He blinked furiously, unbelieving he would die here without knowing how to wield the power.

The power...

Like stumbling upon a familiar path, one thought led to the next. *The Comannda, telepathy, dream control.* He was dreaming. Realistic as hell but just a dream. It could be nothing else. In response, water began to dump from the ceiling in streams, the cave filling rapidly. Still he could not move. Drowning was not going to be very comfortable, even in a dream. He closed his eyes tightly against the deluge. The water, which had risen now to the corner of his eyes, roared dimly in his submerged ears. He cast about, searching for a seam, an edge he could peel back. If this was his mind, there was a lot more to do in it than drown in a cave.

At last he found just what he'd imagined, an edge. With an intention born of panic, he pulled at it, willing the change to take place. Shadows sprung across consciousness and all at once, there was silence.

The darkness receded, leaving him in a dusty attic, sitting atop a trunk. He gratefully inhaled, flexed his hands, and stomped his feet. Sunlight filtered through attic windows. It was his grandfather's home on Herengracht Street along the canals of Amsterdam. The attic was a favorite place to hide away in the evenings after school, after all his chores and homework were done.

He rested a hand on the trunk. Countless hours he'd spent holding its contents. He could still feel the texture of the lace from his mother's wedding dress, the etched lines on the steel of his father's military sword. The backgammon board and the smooth ceramic playing discs. The dark glass bottle of cologne in the shape of an automobile. The powerful scent would fill his senses after unscrewing the spare tire of a cap. *Father.*

He wanted to wake up but still didn't have full control.

Why am I here?

The door at the bottom of the stairs opened, betrayed by its familiar creaking. The first thought was of Großvater Bartel. He was always the one to come up at the end of the day to fetch him for bedtime. Someone ascended the stairs.

"Grandpa?"

Johan was stunned to see his father arrive at the head of the stairs. He was the same, as seen from the eyes of an eight-year-old boy.

"Father! I...." Dream or not, this was his lifelong wish. Emotions swelled. He went to him and embraced him, fearing he would vanish. They hugged and the years dissolved instead. Tears fell. He was real. Somewhere beyond the world of the living, he existed.

"Papa, I missed you. I needed you and mama so much. So much."

When his father didn't reply, Johan pulled back and saw him as an old man, as if he were still alive. He wiped Johan's cheeks and ruffled his hair, calming him as he always had. Still he didn't speak.

"Papa, talk to me. Please. What is this about?"

It was in his eyes, telling him he couldn't know, wasn't allowed to – he would have to face it on his own. Then he spoke, his voice resonating beyond the attic, beyond the dream.

"There is no more noble a fight than the one you join."

His father embraced him once more. When he stepped back, he was young again, their time at an end. Johan started to say goodbye but in the next instant only dust motes and the scent of cologne lingered. The familiar absence returned.

"Papa..."

With a splitting crash a telephone pole burst through an attic window and sent shards flying. He dove to avoid wires unfurling into the room and woke to stinging pain and wind rushing across his face. A power pole lay protruding through the living room window just feet from where he lay. Electricity arced between the taut wires leading outside. The lights flickered.

Still dreaming...? It was too much to process, too surreal, though the pain was convincing. He crawled to the bath and vomited in the toilet. Thunder crashed and the house creaked under the wind's force.

He stood and looked in the mirror. Blood lines trickled from a thin shard of glass embedded in his cheek. He squeezed and plucked it free. The pain felt good... still drunk and high but alive, not drowned in a cave. *This* was the real thing.

The lights went out, the plunge into darkness followed by a transformer's explosion in the distance. He barely noticed. If the world were to erupt in madness and soldiers were to gun him down in the street, he could go in peace knowing somehow he'd be with his parents again.

• • •

Soldado's decision to manually gather the fragments and assemble them had required hours of careful planning, monitoring, and routing. Right in the middle of it all, SlotZero had used his botnet to grab Crosstalk's file. While it was good to know he was still okay, the resulting scans and server failures had put Alcazar and Crosstalk's file at even greater risk.

Once assembled, he watched the video.

Whether it was a classified piece of conspiracy propaganda or a beyond-classified dissertation on the inner workings of the world he didn't know. It was that well done. Just viewing the video changed perspective in an awkward way, leaving a vulnerable feeling. The resulting thoughts and feelings seemed to make waves in a kind of mental pond, just as the narrator described. It reminded him of *la gran locura*, his cocaine induced paranoid episode that helped him swear off the drug. The feeling was simply *there*, spoiling his otherwise rational mind. Like imagination stuck in the on position.

The Overseer system was definitely believable, considering what they'd seen on the network. He immediately suspended all systems, setting admin-only access until he could get OB1Kenobi to retool the transport algorithms. It would screw over big projects everywhere but there was no choice.

He sat back and ran a hand through his hair.

"Un-fucking-believable. I watch a fucking *movie* and bug out?"

His comms lit up with messages from admins. He sent out one message to all of them: *Avoiding NSA. Chill hard 24 hrs.*

His thoughts began to stack up and crash into each other, making bigger and bigger waves. Something out there felt him.

"Fuck this." He went to the bathroom and grabbed some pills to knock himself out. There was something awful working the heavens and he sure as hell didn't want to run into it.

• • •

Mac Payant flicked ashes into a soda can and glanced at the clock. Three in the morning and still nothing on either Brent or his son. Plenty of time for Brent's arrest details to have been shared. Instead a wall had gone up between the two agencies. It felt gray. Very gray.

On screen, he switched back to the chess game. He clicked queen's knight, already deployed. Squares illuminated around it, possible moves, options. Unlike any other piece, it could soar over the play field and land at odd, tricky angles. Never a linear move, always a step out of sight, and harder to predict. Unlike real life, this knight kept its color and had to play by the rules.

The gray area of operations discovered by Brent seemed a lifetime ago. His reluctance to share details probably saved Mac his career, if not his life. Just the one meeting to say something wasn't right in the agency and that he was going to dig deeper; the code phrase 'gray knight' a hasty designation, a precaution. Shortly after that, the car accident took Brent's wife. "*Just paranoia, forget it. Really.*" The most earnest yet most unbelievable words he had ever spoken. For him to use the code phrase again with the mention of his son brought it all back. Only now, feigned ignorance and inaction didn't have a place. Too many years, too much shoved under the rug. Whatever was happening, Brent and his son deserved more than another turning away.

He studied the chessboard. The questions kept circling. Who'd run the shuttle? If the FBI planned to move Austin they would've just done it as they had Brent – unless a black operation had been underway. He recalled the hacker's message. The reference to mind reading... something the government would absolutely want to keep to itself. It would explain things, as everything had begun with the drop-off of the file.

He chose not to move the knight, instead advancing a pawn to create a left-flanking shield with the other pawns. A safe, reinforcing move. Non-confrontational but effective. Pawns were meant to go down first in defense, anyway. He thought of Brent, then of himself.

Frustrated and finally tired, he signed off and stood to stretch. Fifty years of life were trying to take their toll and as usual he would have none of it. He stretched thoroughly, feeling each set of muscles respond, some achingly, some gratefully. He left the small office and headed for his bunk.

Entering the residential wing with his keycard, he strode down the dimmed corridor. He preferred going home to staying at the facility but under the circumstances... he slowed as he neared Kaiya's room. Light from under the door leaked into the hallway. She'd been given meds to help her sleep, but perhaps she hadn't taken them or had passed out with the lights on. He thought of checking on her.

At the door he heard muffled cries; a second later he recognized distress. In one motion he drew his weapon and chambered a round, then took a quick breath and slammed the door open. He took aim at two men at Kaiya's bedside. One held Kaiya's face down in her pillow.

"Hands out, now! Let's see the hands!"

Randall Vasco and Keith Crawford half-turned and slowly placed their hands out in front of them. "Easy agent, we're on your side."

Kaiya screamed an obscenity at the men before backing against the wall, heaving for breath. Tears streaked her face and red slap marks were plain. "Shoot the fuckers, Mac!"

He'd seen enough. "Quiet, Kaiya. Don't move until I say."

Crawford motioned. "You need to stand down, Mac."

"Stop. No movement. None. Kaiya, crawl to the floor over to me. Stay low, stay low."

Kaiya slithered from the bed onto the floor, clear of the agents' reach. She made it to Mac and stood on unsteady legs. She'd obviously taken the sleeping meds but had been woken up. She wore a white t-shirt and gray sweats.

"Are you okay?"

"They threatened to hurt my mom. They know where she lives!" She glared at the agents. "They want Austin and the laptop. They strangled me and slapped me and grabbed my tits and... just shoot 'em, Mac, just shoot the fuckers!" She slid her feet into deck shoes left by the door.

"Agents Crawford and Vasco, hands up and turn around, *now*. Face the wall."

Agent Crawford hesitated. "You need to go talk with Brodie. That's all I can say."

"Bullshit. Brodie wouldn't order this."

"The *fuck* he didn't Mac. Ask him yourself. Call him right now."

Crawford wanted to distract him. A single moment is all they'd need.

"Kaiya, grab your purse."

Kaiya leaving disturbed them. "You're out of line, Agent Payant," Vasco warned. "Put your weapon down and we'll get on the phone with Brodie. You may not like our orders, but fronting your weapon is way out of line."

Mac knew little about the agents but knew the regional director wouldn't order Kaiya roughed up. The video orb in the corner of the room peered down. First doubts pressed in. It appeared they'd acted with impunity.

"Hands above your head and turn to face the wall, *now*. Kaiya, go left down the hall. Stand by the door."

"What, execution time? Fuck you."

An absurd suggestion, a bid for talking time. He tracked their every expression, their every movement. "Hands *up* and face the wall. *Do* it! Hands up!"

He watched them roll their eyes and shake their heads. Vasco raised his arms wide in an exaggerated fashion and turned. Crawford also turned and raised just one arm, faking the other while he pulled on his pistol.

"Don't do it–" Mac shot him in the knee. Crawford shouted and fell onto the bed.

Vasco drew his weapon in motion. Mac collapsed into a squat and fired – the round punctured the agent's forehead, scattering brain and skull fragments on the walls and ceiling. Kaiya screamed in the hallway.

Time slowed to a crawl. He'd just killed a fellow agent. Crawford's weapon came up.

Mac flash aimed and squeezed the trigger.

He entered the hallway in a rush. Kaiya crouched by the door, hugging her purse. "Oh my god, you shot them?"

Mac keyed open the door. "They drew, damn it. Come on."

"Your arm–"

A flesh wound that bled but not profusely. "Let's go, *quickly*."

He rushed through the building and arrived at the security suite. He swiped his card but got only a red light and beep. He tried again with the same result. He pushed the call button.

No one answered.

"Jesus." He struggled with the implications. "Fuck."

"What is it?"

He grabbed her hand. "Let's move."

Mac's sedan leapt onto the country lane and accelerated towards the interstate in the dark of pre-dawn. That they'd made it out without being stopped was only a little reassuring. Shit had hit the fan in the worst way imaginable.

Kaiya asked, "What was that room? Why were you locked out? Talk to me."

"I said I need a minute." He pulled out his phone.

Things were happening too fast. Too damned fast. He called the director. Brodie answered on the second ring.

"Mac? What's up?"

He couldn't tell if he'd woken him or not. "Emergency, sir. I need to know what orders you gave Crawford and Vasco regarding Kaiya."

"Crawford and Vasco? About Kaiya? Why? What's happened?"

"Orders, sir?"

"Nothing about Kaiya. Vasco has the case with orders to look into Brent's status and the FBI investigation. What's going on, Mac? Out with it."

"I just found them working over Kaiya. Strangling, striking, groping. Threatened to hurt her mother. They wanted Austin's laptop. At gunpoint they said you'd ordered the shakedown."

Brodie responded instantly. "Absolutely not. Where are they?"

Recounting the details was tough. It sounded bad even to his own ears. "I went to Security but my card was denied and no one answered. Sir, you need to secure the digital feed from the room. It's all there."

"Christ, Mac. Then they are both dead?"

"Almost certainly."

"Where are you?"

He hesitated. To feel any doubt about Brodie stung. He scanned an intersection before running a red light to reach the highway onramp.

"Mobile, sir. Kaiya is with me."

"Alright, alright. Where are you headed?"

Not a difficult question but again he hesitated. The regional director wanted to know where they were going, had denied ordering the attack on Kaiya, and Mac *wanted* to believe him. The moment drew long, an answer due.

"Westbound. Towards Regent's Place, sir."

"That's fine. Prepare your report there, submit it, and stay put for debriefing. I don't want you in any more situations."

"Yes, sir. And sir, I have a feeling about this. Kaiya's mother needs protection."

"I'll look into it. Now listen, Mac, don't deviate. This is going to be a rough ride as it is."

"Yes, sir. Just secure the digital feed from the room. Please."

"Of course. Stay out of trouble."

"I'll do my best."

He ended the call, knowing the trouble had already begun.

"What is it?" she asked.

"Do you want the good or bad news first?"

"Oh hell. The bad news."

"The agency may be involved but to what extent I don't know. Maybe at the operational level... could be from higher up." *A lot higher up.*

"Jeez..." She slumped against the door and stared at the dash. "The good news better be damned good."

"I don't think it was our government that actually took him."

"Not our government? You just said the CIA—"

"I said the CIA may be involved. They want him and the laptop but they didn't take him."

"Then who did? And how is it good news?"

He shook his head. "I'm not sure yet. Someone else is involved, someone on the outside."

"But why? I feel like you know more than you're saying."

"I don't. Trust me, I wish I did. Everything revolves around the file. Are you positive Austin didn't download it or know what it was?"

"He said he didn't have time and I believe him. I didn't like any of it and told him to get rid of it. But did he listen?" She stared out into the darkness.

Mac drove with an eye on the rear view mirror.

The serious consideration of mind reading was old, dating back to at least the last century. Both superpowers performed significant research into telepathy, remote viewing, and related concepts starting in the sixties and seventies. The Soviet Union started their research before the United States and by the late sixties had an annual budget of twenty-four million dedicated to psi. The CIA funded formal research starting in '72 and five years later the Army initiated its own program. By the mid-eighties, word of the programs leaked and the Army terminated its program only to have the Defense Intelligence Agency redesignate it and fund it separately. Ten years later, the CIA took it over and sunk it via a commissioned report saying no value had come from the research. He had always wondered how, after spending years and millions of dollars on the subject, it could be deemed of no value. That kind of money built entire agencies, insured secrecy. There was more to it and could only be classified beyond black.

Austin must have stumbled upon real evidence. Hard intel of some kind. It stirred him on levels he hadn't felt in years. The lengths they would go to in order to keep it concealed were limitless. Now that Crawford and Vasco had acted as they had in front of the room's surveillance camera, there was reason to fear his own organization. Without the video, he wouldn't have a defense.

He squeezed the steering wheel.

It was all *wrong*... he'd broken his own rule of staying off the radar. He'd earned a radar lock and the tone was deafening. He looked in the rearview mirror at headlights coming up an onramp.

Waiting around for inbound missiles just wasn't going to work.

An option loomed, weighing in ominously: going rogue. A dark thought but one he'd fostered over the years. If ever his career went bad, he needed a way out, a method to survive beyond the reach of the CIA. The plan was squarely in place, set up years before with extraordinary care. However, the design was for his own disappearance, not his and another's.

Kaiya's worry broke the silence. "Where is Regent's Place, Mac? What is it?"

A turn in the highway revealed the valley lights below. "A safe house in Sacramento. Only I'm not sure how safe it will be." He met Kaiya's gaze briefly. "I don't mean to scare you but I'm not going to lie to you either. Agents may take custody of you there."

"No, Mac. I want out, now. Please. Get me out of this." She looked ready to leap from her skin.

"Relax Kaiya, relax. You have to keep your head. Don't give in–"

"Relax? Mac! There's nothing *relaxing* about any of this. This can't be happening but goddammit, it *is!* Look at me – the United States Central Intelligence Agency just roughed me up over computer files about *mind reading!* Hello? They threatened to *kill me* if I didn't cooperate. They'll go after my mom! She doesn't know anything about this. She barely likes Austin for chrissakes. Now I'm driving to a safe house where I'll be taken into custody and then what? Tortured? Raped? Over what? Proof of mind reading? Sure, just relax. What the hell is going to happen to me? What would you do!"

With as much conviction as he could muster, he said, "None of that is going to happen. Things have gone nuts, yes, I know it. Other people know it, too. Losing our minds now won't help us – but it will help *them.* I have a feeling they are counting on it."

She looked to the city-lit skyline, all fear and confusion.

"Kaiya, I will protect you and I'm going to try to find Austin. But you're going to have to trust me. Can you do that?"

The lights of Sacramento disappeared as the highway descended into the valley.

"I don't think I have a choice, do I? It's the government. You're all I've got. No offense intended."

"None taken. Now, your cell phone, please."

"No. I have to warn my mom."

Mac thought about it. "Tell her to stay at a friend's house. She needs to be with people at all times. Make the call short."

Kaiya placed the call but it rang to voicemail. "Mom, you need to go to Shari's right now. Please just go. Something's happening here and you're in grave danger. Don't stay anywhere alone. I'm sorry, mom, I can't explain but please, *please* go. Just do it. I love you, mom. I love you so, so much." She hung up and fought off tears. "Damn this. Damn all of it."

"It's all you can do for now. I'm sorry, Kaiya."

At the next exit he pulled into a Denny's and stopped alongside a tarp-covered utility trailer towed by an SUV. He slipped an evidence bag containing their phones under the blue wrap.

Back on the highway, he glanced at her. "Time to disappear."

Mac pressed a remote and turned into the garage of a modest single-story house.

"Not what I'd imagined for an agent," Kaiya said.

"Follow me and stay quiet. Not a peep." He led her into the house and down a hallway into the bathroom. Together they cleaned the ragged flesh wound on his upper arm and covered it with a gauze band aid. He pocketed a bottle of antibiotics.

They entered a kitchen with windows facing the backyard. Mac removed the top drawer from a cabinet and reached underneath to operate two latches. He tugged upward on a section of tile countertop to break a thin line of covering grout. From a shallow cavity he withdrew a leather satchel and a cell phone with its battery and charger taped to it.

Kaiya nodded approval.

He closed up the hiding space and returned the drawer, then led the way towards the back fence. He looked over his shoulder at his home of six years. It shouldn't hurt so much. The days of living on the edge abroad were long gone.

Not that long gone. A fierceness surged, the hallmark of that lifestyle. Confidence swelled even as fear paced the moment.

"Let's go, over the fence. Stay under the trees as you head to the right side of the house. Mind the brickwork at the edge of the sidewalk."

"Do we know these people?" Kaiya asked after clearing the fence.

"Yes, my friend Helen."

He approached the garage and opened the side door with his key. Inside, a single bulb illuminated two cars. He opened the interior door to reveal a dining room dimly lit by a nearby living room lamp. A cup of water and a book sat on the end table.

"Helen? Are you awake? *Helen!*"

"Mac? That you?"

An elderly woman in a nightgown appeared from a dark hallway. She held a revolver.

"Mac! You nearly got yourself shot! Come in, come inside. What's wrong?" She reached for the dining room light switch.

"No, please leave it off." He went to her side. "Helen, listen carefully. Things have gone very badly for me. I might be framed for a shooting involving two fellow agents." Her face fell. "Don't believe it, Helen. They drew on me and I shot in self-defense. But there's a bigger picture involving Kaiya here, her boyfriend, and some stolen secrets. There is real top-secret stuff driving it all. Now I've been sucked into it and my career is over. I... *we* need to disappear."

Helen nearly shook with feeling. "Damn the secrets, damn the murderous bastards! The country has died, like Frank always said! I wish I'd never ridden him so hard for saying it, because it was *true!* Mac, all those years you served, all the danger and sacrifice, and this is how they reward you. The bastards!"

"Easy Helen." He took the .38 from her and set it on the counter. "Frank also said there's nothing good to come from acting in anger. It is what it is and I have to respond. And I will be careful. Right now, it's time to run. I was thinking the Coachman–"

"Take it! By all means Mac, I'll never have a use for it. You know where it's parked. Steve doesn't have to know anything, just say you're borrowing it. Here," she retrieved two sets of keys, "take the Mazda, too, it's set up for towing. Steve still opens at six sharp, best I know." She crossed her arms tightly. "Lord, I hate this! The government's rotten to the core and the country's too blind to see it. Something's got to give!"

He glanced out the window. Across the back fence, the lights shone in his kitchen and figures moved through his bedroom.

He motioned to Kaiya. "Into the garage, quick."

In the doorway to the garage, Mac held Helen's arms. "We've got to go. Do you still have Frank's old hats?"

"Of course I do, I'll go get you one."

"Thank you, Helen." He turned to Kaiya. The look in her eyes betrayed her confident stance. "Kaiya, this is it. They're shutting me down. Technically, you've done nothing wrong. They might just let you go or... they could use you. I honestly don't know. If you go with me, you'll have to trust me and do what I say. It's going to be a tight squeeze just getting out of here."

"Mac, I said you're all I have, but... I trust you. There's no way I can ever trust them. Or anybody else, really." The enormity seemed to hit her then, a walloping force. He understood.

"Fear is okay, it's gonna be there. Just don't let it define you. I'll get us out of here but going forward you'll have to do everything I say exactly when I say to do it. I need to trust you'll do that."

She nodded. "You can, Mac."

Helen returned with two hats, a dark olive green Panama for him and a yellow sun hat for Kaiya. Her eyes crinkled with a smile as he donned Frank's hat.

"Frank's favorite. Maybe he'll help guide you. I know he will if he can."

He embraced Helen once more. "Thank you Helen. You are the best kind of friend. I'll be sure you get it back."

Helen hugged Kaiya then pulled back and paused. "My dear, though the darkness surrounds you, you are carried towards the light. The moment doesn't reveal much but the journey eventually does. Have heart, and most of all, have faith. Mac's on the job. He's a good man, a capable man." She motioned them on. "Play it smart, Mac. And Kaiya, you support him. You'll do alright as a team."

They climbed into the Mazda, Kaiya in the back seat. Helen pressed the garage door opener and watched them pull out.

"Frank dear, see them to safety. They need all the help they can get."

Chapter 6

We must travel in the direction of our fear.
- John Berryman 1914-1972, American Poet

A banging at the front door drew Johan to the second floor window. A lone police officer stood on the porch in yellow rain gear.

Johan tried waiting him out. The officer circled around to the damaged side of the house with his flashlight and eyed the down pole before continuing around to the back.

By the flickering flame of a lighter, he snatched the laptop and its bag and headed for the garage. He dumped the gear in the Volvo and checked a window.

The officer banged on the rear door. "Anyone home? Hello?"

He had probably notified fire and utility services and was awaiting their arrival. Thunder cracked and rolled.

Johan bolted for the garage and lifted the door manually. Wind and rain whipped at his face. He pushed the sedan into the driveway and brought the garage door down. Back in the car, lightning flashed and thunder broke in staccato. He used the moment to start the engine. *Covering karma.* He backed out with his eyes glued to the corner of the house. He saw no sign of the officer as he drove away in the dark.

The makeup kit. He slapped the wheel and cursed. Karma, indeed.

Repair crews would come to fix the power pole. That meant hiding out for the day until he could return under darkness. *Where and with whom?* The corrected sketch was out; he mentally flipped through resources and settled on one woman who could be trusted even if she'd seen it. She might even believe his story, though he was having a hard time believing it himself.

He traveled north on dark rural highways and eventually cut west across the sea barrier into the peninsula town of Den Helder. Just before dawn the stolen Volvo arrived in a small business district a few blocks from a shipyard. Damp streets were littered with debris from the night's storming. Street lights and the occasional storefront glowed in the summer fog of the coast.

He steered into an alley between long row buildings, past a bakery truck and a worker unloading goods to a restaurant and stopped at an alley door with a lamp. Above the door a sign read, 'FileZone Internet Café'. He loaded a bowl and let the hash soften the edges of thought.

Anki Raymer, aka WinterCat; the ex of a friend who no longer counted as a friend. They'd spent hours in chat and exchanged email over the last two years. He'd helped her with her website and sent her money when her car's transmission died. She'd done research for him and even drop-forwarded a package for him once. Just a few weeks earlier she'd extended the invitation to finally meet again. For now she served best because of the remote location and her business, as well as her willingness to help with just about anything. This might test her and then some.

He gently closed the Volvo's door and slung the laptop over his shoulder. The two-story row building loomed over the alleyway. Fog drifted like a comforting blanket all about. *If ever you are near Den Helder, stop by. Use the back door. I'll know it's you if you...* he pulled the chain three times fast, twice slow. He paused, then reversed the pattern.

Waiting with hands in pockets, he glanced down the alley at the delivery truck. The smell of fresh baked bread conjured an earthy, grounded feeling which he seized, eager to shed the hunted vibe. A face peered from a small square window. A moment later the door swung open and Anki wrapped herself around him.

"I thought you might never come, Gregor."

Her musky scent and soft skin made his pulse quicken. He held her at arm's length, still in the doorway. Long blonde hair, almost white, and fair skin. In person her beauty breathed. "Yes, I should have come sooner."

Her eyes glittered as she pulled him inside.

She was everything he needed.

Several candles lit the bedroom while the gray of impending dawn fell from a small skylight. The draw to Anki was powerful – intimacy and sanctuary at once. Lying naked on the soft sheets, he stared into eyes that said it was okay to shed his shell, his worries, to release his guard. Arousal slowly stripped the bindings of the chase. Long hours of driving, of evading the gaze of every passing police officer, of wrestling with the idea of telepathy, awareness fields, and a secret government out to silence him... all of it had taken a physical toll. To lay with her offered a powerful reversal, restoring sanity and a sense of control.

She massaged him until the worried thoughts faded and his spirit rose free again, curious and present in the moment. He explored her in turn, connecting with every touch, every breath, every whisper of intention. Their lips met, eyes searching, face to face after years of distant intimacy. As if exhaling, his energies flowed, colored with amour and desire. Anki responded, breathing deeper. Feeling his full arousal, she climbed atop him.

Candlelight danced in time to their gyrations. Every thrust, every kiss drew them closer. Immersed in a world of pleasure and intimacy, he felt her need for connection. Years of loneliness without a true mate, seeking an anchor for her love... that, he understood. His recognition acted like a touch in her place of need, so much so that she lifted, thrusting faster until a blossoming psychedelic fountain surged and splayed pleasure through her every sense. Never had he experienced such vision, such connection with another being. She soared, tossed between their physical and emotional connections like a windblown flower. He couldn't help but touch her yet again, recognizing and feeling everything she was. Once more she blossomed, vocalizing with abandon, sounding of pain and pleasure at once. A scene flashed in his mind of primitive peoples coupling in huts overlooking the sea, howling into the night, celebrating survival and pleasure. Overwhelmed, he released and slipped into the rushing flight. Thrusting together, gripping fiercely, they railed towards climax, slipping the bonds. Pleasure flared into a timeless, consuming intensity. Concepts mingled – extremes: day and night, good and evil, love and hate, joy and fear. For every one thing, there was another, no matter the degree of separation. Rock and sand, root and limb, sea and sky, tears and laughter. Every familiar thought became an agreement point joining them, drawing them closer until duality ceded to unity. Bare in thought and soul, they existed as one.

What must have passed in seconds instead felt like long minutes. The cave's water drops and time's mystery echoed from his dream, splashing across their coupling like a baptism. Vaguely, the sense of another presence crested, a whisper only, then faded as time contracted and resumed.

Anki breathed against his ear, the weight of her body earthy and grounding. She raised her head and probed with her eyes. He blinked slowly, still engaged on deep levels.

The currents of change were running more swift than ever. He was learning, released from the grip of fear because of Anki. The universe had delivered him to her and one thing felt certain – he needed her in ways he knew nothing about yet.

However, for it to work she had to know and accept his situation.

Anki sat cross-legged next to his stretched-out form, touching. Blithe talk soon turned substantial as he prepared a way to breach the subject of the setup in Rotterdam, to explain how he'd not murdered anyone. She floored him before he could begin.

"So what did the woman do?"

He returned her gaze, unable to reply. She already knew, yet she'd taken him in, even slept with him. Without fear.

Moments passed. An impulse rose and he followed it: to attempt to communicate without words. Slowly, his truth, that of innocence, naturally saturated as his only thought or feeling... it seeped beyond, made available for her to sense. Nothing forceful, just – available.

She searched his eyes. Recognition rippled. Reciprocation flowed back. She'd felt his truth – and was relieved. Relieved, because her own instincts had been right.

The moment passed, an extraordinary communication.

"So what *did* you do?" she asked.

"I received a link to an encrypted file. Something I didn't ask for."

She cast about, trying to assemble. "What?"

"The link was to a documentary of sorts. Secret. It was very... disturbing. It came with a warning to go into hiding. Said I was in danger."

"So you left."

"Within half an hour. I went up the street to watch the apartment. To see if anyone would show up."

"And?"

"Men arrived. In minutes. Went straight up to my apartment. That was Saturday. Monday night I heard of the murder and knew I was framed. Because I have their damn video."

Anki sat, absorbed in thought. A distance formed between them.

"Talk to me, Cat."

She looked over. "You're different, Gregor. What you just did is nothing I've felt before. You entered *me*. You were inside me, part of me. I felt it, let it begin, then I couldn't stop you." She searched his eyes. "You know what I'm saying. And then just now... you conveyed your innocence without a word, yet completely. I have no doubt."

He nodded.

"What does the video show?" she asked. Her eyes probed feather soft.

Informed, she could make her own decisions. That was fair and necessary, so he described the video and the dream after viewing it. He spoke of the Comannda and how they could enter the flow of thought in others, of how they could travel the world without a body and find people by using memories and emotions. He explained what the video showed of wars, disease, culture, and technology and how they had been used to keep mankind distracted, divided, and unevolved.

By the time he finished, Anki's uncertainty was plain. Not doubt, rather the opposite: she grasped and accepted the situation, as if familiar with the possibilities. The question was whether she wanted to become part of his predicament or not.

She withdrew tightly, stood, and walked to a large white candle. She passed her hand over the flame, once, twice. He tried penetrating her field, her essence, but could not.

Great. Unseen agents sought him and she shielded him off like an afterthought. Surely they would, too. It felt like an intermittent blindness. He had to become more adept. He had to be able to intrude without permission.

She held her finger directly over the candle's flame, testing her own limits.

"Anki–"

She turned and regarded him briefly before rejoining him on the bed. She put her finger to his cheek, the heat tremendous.

"You just described my greatest fears. That you found proof is sad. A big part of me wants to ignore you and pretend it's all crazy talk." She looked up to the skylight. "But it's not." She stared, deep in thought. "For all I know I could live the rest of my life with you. I might. I feel it. But there is danger now, here, and wherever you go..." She trailed off.

Johan sat, silently churning.

They didn't talk further. Instead, she led him back into the Eros like two lovers fleeing their village, hiding in the lush forest to partake in the sins of the flesh.

• • •

The five gathered again, skimming surface tensions, coordinating efforts. They sought the subject detected before, having had a sufficiently strong impression. They received another hit but the input lasted less than a minute; intense enough to lead them to the northern reaches of the Netherlands but brief enough to strand them again.

"Peak signature, probable climax."

"Sex, yeah."

"Definite male. High probability match for subject A2."

Each agreed.

"Settling in, then. Safe region bound by Amsterdam on the west, Apledoorn on the south, and Groningen on the east."

"I say coastal regions. I sense big water."

"Noted. I have a tentative harmonic that we'll work with. Confirm with the director, this is solid."

"Confirmed."

"Come on, A2. Let yourself go a bit, swim in it. You know you want to."

Director Tomov frowned at the latest report.

Signus 1's triangulation was underway on A2 in northwestern Netherlands. They were close to isolation, the target now responding to tracking measures.

That was the good news.

People were missing. Austin Bakken first, though there was no question as to who intercepted him. The wiped shuttle bus – their way of protecting operatives. Austin's girl and the agent, Payant, had gone on the run. G2 teams would track them shortly unless the priests were dabbling there, too.

The picture of Austin stared back from the screen. Over twenty-four hours since they'd taken him and the predictable had not occurred. Recover physical assets and determine what the subject knew. If nothing, release. If exposed, eliminate. Neutral notification in either case. The communication hadn't arrived, which meant either they still had custody of him or had run into a problem.

Or some kind of opportunity.

• • •

Darkening gray skies churned. Anki sat bundled up in heavy blankets with Johan on the roof. Nightfall descended and the lights of the port city ignited like miniature bonfires. An empty bottle of wine and a box of crackers lay next to their glasses. In the distance a cruise ship pulled away from the port of Den Holder, billowing steam into the wind.

In the hours since they made love Johan grew more concerned they might be tracking him through his thoughts. When he peaked with Anki, the familiar sense of otherness loomed, as if people were stealing from his senses, trying to get a look around him. While weaker than the stormy night in Oostendorp, it felt more intimate. To further complicate things, a feeling of unease had taken hold, subtle yet persistent. Perhaps it stemmed from Anki not making her decision or not sharing it if she had. Or maybe it was just a vulnerable feeling being outside the shell of the apartment. Whatever it was, it made time with her less enjoyable than it should have been.

"Where would we go, Gregor?"

"First to Elburg, my house there. I need my kit to become Max Dosch. I know people in South America. My associates. But..."

"What?"

He hesitated. "Anki, they will fabricate more murders. Uncover the Dosch identity. Make it harder to travel. They have my DNA now. Given what they can do, I don't know all the dangers ahead. I can only do my best and that is also to say I may not escape."

Her eyes held his. The wind tossed her hair about. A low groaning from the channel signaled a vessel getting underway. She breathed deep.

"I need to go with you. I'm compelled beyond all reason." She smiled with puzzled and pained eyes. "I can guess at the danger and it's enough for me to want to run the other way. Yet... and this sounds crazy, but I know history well, Gregor. We need great change. The world does. Something is driving you towards it, I can feel it. You need someone to face it with. You just do. I want to try with you, to push the change forward. As far as it can go."

He felt the same imminent change and was validated by her words. He reached up and touched her hair. "I don't want you to have regrets."

She held his gaze. "No regrets."

He held her tight, seizing the moment. A world of possibility spun around them. With a mental nod, he acknowledged their place in it and committed to the changes ahead.

Johan pulled the roof hatch shut and secured the bolt. He stepped off the ladder and padded to the closet to fold the blankets. Anki stored the crackers and checked the refrigerator.

"Ach. No eggs for morning." She peeked out the window and down the street. "Baba's is still open. I'll run and get some. Shall I move your car again?"

"Good idea, if you don't mind."

"I'll be back in a few." Anki slapped his butt and smiled on the way out. She grabbed his black box remote for starting the car and descended the stairs.

He stood in the empty apartment overwhelmed with gratitude for their alliance, for being led to her. *Everything happens for a reason.* He fell onto the couch and searched for a news channel on the television. There would be more on Mrs. Shulz's murder, some indication on how close to tracking him they were, if at all. He found a news program and watched a story before a commercial break began.

The phone rang. He crossed to the base unit and waited for the machine to finish its announcement. He heard a noise from next door – or was it downstairs?

The tone sounded. "To the roof, now!" Anki's voice was urgent, winded. "Stay low and meet me on the east end of the building, alley side. There's a ladder there. Move now! Don't forget your laptop!"

In seconds he grabbed the laptop and was fumbling with the hatch's sliding bolt. Each step to the roof took an age. In the dimness he dodged roof vents, antenna guy wires, and skylights before finding the ladder. The Volvo approached in the alley below. He banged his knees in the rush to get down the ladder and ducked into the rear passenger door. It shut as Anki pulled forward.

"What's happened?" Johan asked.

"Get down. Two cars in front of the shop. Four men each. They went right in."

"It was locked! The alarm...?"

"It's remote accessible by the service in case of fire. I saw them pull up and knew they were your seekers." He slid down when two police cars flew past with lights flashing. "Gregor, those men, they were like dead men. Cold, like stone."

"Fuck. How did they find me? What am I missing?"

He forced calm. The getaway to the coast had become a getaway *from* the coast. He had to learn how they were tracking him.

"Where to?" Anki asked. "This takes us past the airport."

"No good." He recalled the map he'd studied. "Take the coastal road to the N9 at Schoorl. We'll decide from there."

Anki drove silently, carefully. He laid down in back and breathed.

As he sought calm and emptied his mind, it struck him – the pressure, that sense of unease he'd been feeling... *wasn't his*. Even now, heart thumping with fear, the uneasy emotion was there, a drab monotone anxiety clearly out of pace with the moment. The seekers were close enough to insert the emotion. He pushed at the connection by means of the pressure. As if in response, the pressure grew.

A live connection. Like a fish with a hook in his mouth.

Insane! He tried to reject it but the tension remained, leaning against his psyche. Stressed, uneasy, and not coming from him. Just as the video suggested, they were able to evoke and manipulate emotions in others. He had detected their manipulations amidst a storm of emotions: a small victory. It was time to take advantage, to take control of his experience. It might be a last chance.

Something tied him to them in a roundabout way. With it, they could inject the emotion and through his experience of that emotion could find him. Like ripples in the pond signaling back, they must use it to triangulate materially. It wasn't tied to his body unless they had chipped him somehow. In that case, the chase was soon over.

If not something in his body, then it had to be in the nebulous region of his thoughts. Ignoring it wasn't enough as it was too strong. If they were using his thoughts to identify him then he had to think differently, *become different*.

He followed impulse. As if shrugging out of a coat, he began to tweak emotion and ranged into happiness. *Shift*. Down into sadness. *Shift*. Outward into anger. Then over to serenity. *Shift, shift*. Whatever felt familiar and constant, he flipped. Old identity struggled to keep its form. *Shift*. Morphing, rejecting, birthing new emotion, a new self.

The pressure sagged noticeably but not enough.

He drew on memories and dove into them like scenes from a movie. *Shift*. A street vendor selling leather wallets in Oslo in the spring, two years prior. The vendor's story was found in his eyes, etched on his face; a hard past, a new start, trying to stay out of trouble. He'd bought one. The vendor's thanks was sincere. *Shift*. The woman reading a book at a bus stop in Rotterdam, the day before Crosstalk's email. With all his being, he was *there*, replete in his ignorance of the file, reading the bus schedule on the sign. *Shift*. The truck driver hitting his brakes to avoid the three laughing girls.

Hammering the horn with all his might; anger and relief blended into one feeling.

Away from the file... far away. *Shift.*

Großvater Bartel, angry with Johan for smoking hash at age fourteen. The disappointment. *Shift.* The nurse at the hospital asking how he'd been shot, her concern and suppressed attraction betrayed by her every touch. *Shift.* A small boy trying to fly a kite, his mama too busy chatting to offer help. The wind blew like mad, taunting the boy's failed efforts. He'd stopped to help him like a father might, the mother suddenly interested not for her son, but in the handsome stranger.

Memories flipped in and out, some fast, others slowly, continuously shuffling. Emotions flowed. He lost himself, engaged in endless identities and situations of the past, a schizophrenic symphony of experience. Running invisibly alongside was the understanding he had to keep going to escape those who would claim him. It became a manic dream of beauty in randomness and chaos.

"Gregor..? Are you okay?"

Her voice threatened to break the stream, a window thrown open to an unwelcome light. The pressure had diminished but it wasn't enough. Shooting past the urge to respond, he went deeper through memories like a driven wind. A fisherman arrived at port, back from a long day at sea, his hand bandaged from a nasty cut; dark red stains on a white cloth. Pain. Duty. Accomplishment.

Shift. Slower, deeper.

A school teacher wondered how she was going to help the young lad move past his parents' death. Gray hair in a bun, face wrinkled from a lifetime of emotion, hands gentle as a warm blanket, eyes of compassion and ears made for understanding. How she worked for his success, truly giving and utterly loving...

Shift.

The cock-eyed bastard had killed the cat. Pat's silly grin as he dangled it by its tail revealed the monster within. In Johan's eyes, the boy was the same as the murderer who'd taken his family. Rage boiled and blew out in a savage attack, catching the brute off guard and off balance. The older boy fell backwards off the deck, landing in an awkward pile eight feet below. The wind pressed his face as he stared at the motionless bully.

Shift!

Abruptly, he was in the car again. The uneasiness had fled, leaving a familiar sense of control but also a sense of *them*, searching.

"That's it... I'm clear."

"What do you mean?" Anki asked.

"I think I've done it. They can't find me and I think I see them. I'm sensing them. Where are we?"

"Groet. The N9 is a few miles ahead. Are you okay, Gregor? Why can't they find you?"

"My vibe. However I made it onto their radar, I'm a different reading now. For the time being anyway. I need my laptop to get a map up."

She glanced in the rearview mirror. "You are amazing, you know that?" She added, "But the incredibly *bad* news is that I'm cut off from my home, my business, my everything. My accounts! I need to pull out something, anything."

"Anki, no. That would get you a few hundred euro only to put us on a pushpin map and give them a cordon area to work from."

"Damn, you're right. Gah!" She slapped the wheel. "It's all gone then. I had imagined making plans."

He paused. "You don't have to do this. I can let you out and—"

"That's not what I want." She drove in silence for a time. "I'm okay. I want to help. That is what I want. To help." She added, "But I want your real name. Your first name at least. I don't like talking to an alias."

"Johan." Not his birth name but it was his own.

"Thank you, Johan. I love that name."

"Money won't be a problem if we can get clear." He positioned the laptop on the floorboard and dimmed the screen's brightness. "Where are we?"

"At Schoorl, coming up on the junction. I don't think we're being followed."

"Let's be sure. Hang on." The map software loaded. He zoomed in. "Turn left when you reach the N9. Take the first right and tell me when you go over the bridge. In the meantime, take inventory of the cars behind you."

"Understood." She drove carefully, typically. The light ahead stayed green and she turned left onto the N9.

"Watch the cars."

"Two came with me." She turned right towards the bridge and watched the mirror. "One took the turn."

"Lower the front windows completely. Rest your arm on the door, elbow out. Pass over the bridge then take the two next rights. The street will be named Sluisweg. Go slow there and pull over at the second house on the right. Tell me what you see."

She made the first right turn and glanced in the side mirror.

"It's there."

He unzipped a side compartment of his laptop bag.

"I'm onto Sluisweg now. Second house? There's a lot of light here, a street lamp. Is that okay?" The car slowed to a stop. "Here we are. What do I do?"

"Off the motor, leave the keys in the ignition. No dome light. Read your phone. Keep your elbow at the window."

"Oh hell. It's pulling in behind us."

"Easy. Tell me who approaches and how."

"My side, one woman. She's got something behind her back." She whispered, "She's at the bumper..."

Positioned behind the driver's seat, he relied on the jet-black tint of the windows to shield him. Fear flickered like lightning.

"Anki Raymer?" The woman bent to make eye contact.

Anki turned to respond, only to see a burnt red hole erupt next to the woman's eye, accompanied by a single loud *clack!* Dark spray bloomed behind her blonde hair. The woman crumpled to the ground under the street lamp's glare, her eyes searching listlessly.

"Drive, Anki. Go. Now."

She started the car and pulled away.

"Turn right. Back on N9. Head south."

Silence strained, uncomfortable and dark. He unscrewed the silencer from his Glock. "You know that I—"

"— had to, I know. I saw her gun. I'm just... It's all happening too fast. Much too fast."

He slipped the handgun into the bag. The pressure returned, an unwelcome train approaching. He reached up to touch her shoulder.

"The woman, what kind of feeling did you get from her? Same as the men at your place?"

"Yes. Closed off, shielded."

"Okay. Relax, Anki. Find your center, your normal. Imagine it fully. Settle into it. The night is ours now, we are safe. Keep traveling south. Tell me when we approach Alkmaar. I have to meditate again."

The odd tracking tension signaled clearly. Once more he began a journey away from the car and the memory of killing. He went with survival in mind, an intense focuser, and found the second time easier.

Memories flushed out became more meaningful, seen through eyes older and wiser. Without intention he visited the day, the most painful day he knew.

The city was elaborate and spanned his entire room. Mama let him leave them out as the last week of summer ended. An empty box was evidence of her support for his passion – another box of wooden blocks she'd purchased earlier in the afternoon. The church, the constable's yard, the school, the three factories, the rows of houses, and the centerpiece, the king's castle and moat filled with strips of a paper bag and plastic alligators. With utter concentration, he finished the castle's tower, pleased to see he still had over a dozen blocks left over.

He rose carefully and tip toed around his wooden metropolis to fetch mama and papa. They would be so proud. He halted just shy of the den, listening. Their voices were urgent, hushed... something was wrong.

"... it shouldn't be, but I can't help it. It just is." His father sounded worried, something he'd never heard before.

"Then why did he go to them? If he knew beforehand? This doesn't add up, Vincent. We have to go, now."

He hurried back to his room, afraid of being caught eavesdropping. He almost fell into his city as he stepped back into its midst. His parents' footfalls sounded in the living room and then a loud crash shook the house. The tower of his castle toppled and Johan shrank in fear.

He heard his father's command to stop followed by a metallic cough, then two more. His mama screamed and pounded down the hall toward his room.

She made it to the doorway and locked eyes with him before her chest opened up once, twice, accompanied by coughs and the air rushing from her lungs. She mouthed the words 'I love you' and fell into his city of blocks.

So surreal was the scene; he squatted in shock and stared at the small dark holes in her back. Her arms lay forward as if stretched to reach him. A pool of blood spread on the wood floor. A part of him knew what he'd just seen but the rest was lost, still gripping the previous moments of normalcy.

A man appeared in the doorway with a long pistol. He leveled it at Johan.

His deep voice filled the room. "Do you know anything, little boy?" The accent was thick and strange.

Johan could only shake his head.

"No, you wouldn't yet, would you? Here now, your mama and papa are dead. They won't be coming back. Do you want to be with them, too? Are do you want to stay alone here without them?"

In a moment of confusion, Johan wanted to be with his parents, of course, but could he? This man seemed to know more about death.

Something told him, no! He wanted to be alive.

"Could I live, please?"

The man smiled. The trigger finger twitched before the pistol lowered.

"Then you will live, little boy. Not a bad choice."

The man left, closing the battered front door behind him. In the silence that followed, realization set in. Johan began to sob, then to cry with abandon. Neighbors eventually found him in his room, covering his mother's body in wooden blocks – a burial of both his mama and of his life's innocence.

Shift.

A burial service, two rectangles cut in the ground, and two caskets. It lasted so long, too many words that didn't mean anything from people he didn't really know. Only when his grandpa spoke did he take notice.

"Despite all the questions that press heavily on us today, we must also make room for remembering the answers that we have, to the most important of questions about Vincent and Juliana. Were they loving people? Were they brilliant human beings with a vision for a better future? Would they answer the call for help? Yes, the answers are yes, to all. Please, do not walk from this place and time in grief. Do not do that to their memory. Instead, walk forward with the brilliant memories of who they were, so that they will always be just that. Do not drift away from Gerrit – for he is their legacy, the result of their love, and he will need you all. God bless you Vincent, and you, Juliana. Until we meet again."

Shift.

A whispered message from a stranger at the wake. "Gerrit, make your own destiny. Be different and you'll stay alive." He figured it meant he shouldn't be like his parents but couldn't imagine why. Turning, he saw the stranger's back as he walked towards the door. Johan started to follow only to be stopped by his grandfather. With a somber look, his grandfather guided him back to the buffet table and gave him a plateful of baby carrots and dip.

He'd avoided baby carrots ever since.

Chapter 7

A little learning is a dangerous thing, but a lot of ignorance is just as bad.
-Ralph Waldo Emerson (1803-1882, American Poet, Essayist)

A lizard climbed the sheer rock face, crested a peak, and took up position over the rock garden. It blinked and soaked in the morning sun. By Austin's count, fourteen more basked on the rocks around it. He sat at a table under an umbrella and sipped his water, captivated by so many wild reptiles sharing their space with him. A brilliant blue swimming pool rivalled the sky. Asian Man sat close by in the shade of the pines and looked on. He now had a name, Meng. Clues to his personality had yet to surface but he was certainly aware of Austin's every move and perhaps his every thought. The ankle bracelet still clung like an alien appendage, threatening and capping options.

The prior day had been half interview and half briefing. Powerful people sought Austin and his laptop – people that knew he'd been taken from the hospital and who were expecting an end-result, a communication. If they didn't get it soon, complications were certain. This drove the need to begin Austin's testing immediately. Just after dusk they had set out for a new location, a place described as more secure higher in the Sierras.

Departure had been simple, unceremonious.

"So we'll meet again?" Austin asked.

"If the variables allow for it," Edward replied. "I will say it is my sincere hope they do. Travel well."

He and Meng arrived late in the evening at the house in the mountains, dropped off on the driveway. Crickets and bullfrogs sang in symphony from a nearby creek. An elderly housekeeper greeted them at the door and showed them to a room with two beds. He fell asleep almost immediately. Daybreak revealed a residence surrounded by a palisade of pines backed up against a steep forested hill.

His tester was due any moment. Questions and doubts rained, drowning confidence and mixing excitement with biting anxiety. These people lived differently. They existed in tune with powers they called natural but appeared anything but. They offered no apologies for being different, only acknowledging there was more to learn than society knew or could teach.

"Not so many of them today."

Startled, he turned to find the voice above and behind him.

"Yesterday there were close to two dozen." A wiry man appeared from between the trees. "They are drawn to the warmth of the rocks and I'm pretty sure the company."

Completely bald and spa tan, he looked about sixty and wore dark sweat bottoms with a yellow t-shirt. He wore hiking shoes and looked to have just come down from the hill behind the house. Austin stood.

"Bonjour, je suis Marcel. Et vous êtes Austin." His grip was that of a younger man's. "Edward says you have unique natural ability and you want to explore it with us, yes? Well, it's my job to make sure of a few things. First, that you really do want to join us and for the right reasons. Second, that you should. And third, that you can. Desire, fit, and ability. DFA testing."

There was nothing to dislike about Marcel; he had a direct energy Austin immediately admired and wanted to emulate. "Fair enough."

"Time is short, so we'll begin. What's your motivation to join us?"

"Is that a trick question? What better choice? They want to screw me into obscurity. Make me an example? I don't know. Without help, they'll nail me quick. How's that for motivation?"

Marcel's gray eyes studied him. "Alright, that's a good chunk of it. Now dig a little deeper."

"Deeper? What, I–"

"Don't waste time covering. Deal with it. Why else do you want to join us?"

Marcel's gaze drove him, forcing honesty. Right there, deep center, was another, far more selfish reason: the draw of the unknown, the draw to mystery and to power.

He could feel Marcel's x-ray.

"Okay, sure. I'm drawn to the mystery. Have been all my life. It's behind everything and explains how any of this," he indicated the world around them, "could even exist. I know there are secrets to how it works. How everything and everyone in it is connected. You people know those secrets. I want to know, too. I want to fucking *evolve*."

A screech from a circling hawk drew their eyes to the sky, drawing their attention.

"What of your father? And Kaiya? What will happen to them?"

"My dad can be cleared. The charges are bogus. Completely bogus. You have resources, you must. And you could pick up Kaiya right now, before she gets into more trouble."

Marcel frowned. "No, Austin. I'm afraid the truth is right now your dad is nowhere to be found. The FBI reports that he escaped during transport. We don't know where he is. Agent Payant took Kaiya to a CIA station house after we grabbed you. There was a shooting. They're both wanted for murder and are on the run. And Kaiya's mother is missing."

Like a pile driver, Marcel's words slammed home. In that moment, everything became wrong, all very *wrong*.

"That – that can't be. No. No, this is insane. Totally insane."

He recalled Mrs. Wilson's expression as she warned his best efforts would fail Kaiya. His stomach turned.

"God *damn*."

The hawk soared lower in the sky, circling. Thoughts of everyone he'd put in danger threatened to drown him in guilt, though in the shadows was memory of his dad's behavior before the blast at the house. To see fear in his eyes was so wrong, so unlike him. What did he know to be afraid of? What kind of work had he done for the CIA?

Marcel still waited for the answer to why he wanted to join them. In truth, it wasn't just desperation and the need for protection. He wanted the power to impact reality, to *correct* reality. To make things right with whatever tools were available. Stopping now would cut him off. Questions would go unanswered the rest of his life, though he'd have a stump to remind him of how close to the truth he'd gotten.

"Like I said, I want to know more about the mystery. How to control my part in it. More than anything I want safety for my dad and Kaiya and her mom. Right now I can't do anything for them. Or myself."

Marcel sat on the ledge of the rock garden and regarded him. "Is that all?"

"Yeah. I'm not a power monger or anything."

Marcel smiled with perfect teeth. "No one ever is, but it *is* power that you seek, keep no illusions about that. *C'est normal*. However, you must realize that when you carry the secrets with you, you carry the seeds of great danger. Handled wrong, you could forfeit what safety they bring and destroy yourself and others. This is not a playground. You will come to understand what I mean, and no, don't imagine you do now."

Despite the warm morning, a chill ran down his spine.

Marcel continued. "So that is your desire, to join us. Next question: should you? The answer is partly yours and partly mine to give. I'm going to ask a series of questions. Answer honestly or don't answer at all."

The hawk circled lower, visible between the trees.

"Austin, to save your life, would you kill someone?"

He could imagine it but it wasn't pleasant. "Yes. I could."

"Austin, are you trying to infiltrate the Korda?"

"No." *Korda...?*

"A trusted member of the group has stolen secrets with the intent of selling them. You know the thief well, a close friend. You've tracked and trapped your friend and receive an absolute kill order. Do you kill your friend?"

Hardball. He thought quickly. "Yes."

"Why?"

"On the assumption that in the wrong hands the secrets would hurt people. Innocents."

Marcel barely nodded and began to lay out scenario after scenario, each measuring a different attribute or principle. He stopped trying to figure the point of every question and concentrated on providing honest answers.

He would be a fit or not.

• • •

"This can't be happening. He's lost his fucking mind." Brodie looked up at the clock. "I want a profile to work from, anything to suggest what might've led up to this and where he may be headed next. Have it in my office within the hour."

The director steamed while pacing the operations floor. Agents tracked Mac and Kaiya's passage to the neighbor's house. Forcing entry, they found the woman dead with multiple gunshot wounds.

"Anything on Yuni Wilson?"

"Nothing since they found her cell at the house."

"What about the records search on Mac's neighbor?"

"Helen Stewart. Two vehicle registrations in her name. A brown '92 Mazda and a white 2011 Toyota Camry. The Mazda's missing. Preparing a priority BOLO for all NorCal agencies."

Brodie's gaze rested on a photo of Mac onscreen. There was nothing else he could do. Suppressing emotion, he said, "Write it for triple murder and coordinate it through FBI. Get it out ASAP. Multi-state. I want this to be the shortest manhunt in history."

• • •

"Mac, slow up. We need to pull over."

He looked over. "Why?"

"See that freeway sign ahead? Pull up three big bushes back."

Mac did, his lips firming. "It's here isn't it? Not on highway 80."

Kaiya nodded slightly. She wouldn't meet his gaze. "He told me in the hospital. In case something happened. He said it could be insurance and worth protecting. It's buried at the base of that tree or maybe the one next to it."

"Stay put." Mac pulled the keys, suddenly wary of his passenger. He climbed out and ran into the thick shrubbery. In the light of early morning he spotted a disturbed patch of vegetation. The laptop came free easily.

Back in the Mazda he handed the bundle to Kaiya. "Okay, two things. One, you have to learn to trust me completely or I can't rely on you. Second... that was a good first step, just now. Any more secrets?"

She shook her head.

"You sure? No more surprises? Okay." He started the car. "Now let's get the hell out of Dodge."

The morning sun beamed past the open rollup doors where a wiry man stood working an arc welder. The grey hair and thick moustache were familiar to Mac.

"Steve," he called out. "Long time no see."

"Mac? Well I'll be damned." They shook hands. "Yeah, it's been a while. How you been?"

"You know, life in the fast lane. Steve, this is Kaiya, a friend of mine. We're taking a little vacation and Helen lent us her keys to the Coachman. I forgot to call you to make sure you didn't have plans for it."

"No, no, go ahead. Hell, I'm so backed up vacation ain't in my vocabulary. The rig ain't been off the lot since last Christmas. I just need to drop in a couple good batteries and it'll be ready for the road. You'll want to fix 'er with some new gas, but she'll get you down the road. Gonna tow the car?"

"Yeah, we're bringing it along."

"Well, let's get you two set up."

Steve unracked two batteries, hefted one to Mac, and led them through a door to the back lot. Mac wore his trunking police scanner on his belt with the earpiece in his left ear. Steve noticed it and asked, "You aren't using this on some stakeout are ya? Heh, 'cause I'd hate to see 'er get shot up!" He laughed.

"No, this is strictly a getaway."

Kaiya made a wry face when Steve wasn't looking.

He watched Steve screw down the bolts on the batteries. Traffic on the scanner caught his ear. An all-points bulletin issued for the Mazda included its color and license plate number as well as descriptions of them both. Armed and dangerous fugitives, wanted for triple murder.

His heart fell. *Helen?* A sudden rage threatened. He clamped down hard, delaying emotion. Steve would help the authorities once he heard. No doubt it would make the news.

He sent Kaiya into the camper to look around and joined Steve as he pulled the tow hitch from a storage compartment.

"Steve, I lied. Things are not at all okay, they are going very bad."

The mechanic looked up at Mac, suddenly wary.

"Listen closely: you know me, I'm a CIA lifer, been playing by the book since day one. Kaiya is a protected witness, or was supposed to be. I interrupted two agents roughing her up. I stepped in and a goddamn firefight went down. Two agents are dead." He put up a hand at Steve's look. "I know, but it's a long story and I don't have time. We're on the run. I just heard on the radio we're wanted for *triple* murder. Steve, I think they killed Helen."

Steve looked ready to lay Mac out. "*Killed* her? Now why the *fuck* would the CIA kill Helen?"

"I don't *know* they did, Steve. I just heard the traffic. I don't know who else the third person could be. As for why, I can tell you it involves a top-secret computer file but beyond that none of it makes sense. Listen Steve, I'm going to dump the Mazda not far from here. I need your help. No matter what you hear or are told, we did *not* hurt Helen." He touched the rim of his hat. "Frank's, given with blessings for a safe journey. You have my word, I'm telling you the truth. If they did kill Helen, don't let it be for nothing. *She* wanted us to get away."

Long moments of grilling eye contact resolved Steve's mind. Trust had always been a currency between them.

"Then get going. But if I ever figger you did kill her, I'll hunt you down myself. Believe that, Mac. Believe it."

Mac steered the thirty-foot Coachman out of the lot onto the frontage road. He'd told Kaiya about the bulletin and the mention of the Mazda but left it as a 'double' murder. He'd just talked about honesty and trust, but if she heard they were killing old women she might come unglued.

Even so, Kaiya struggled to keep her cool.

"That means they went to Helen's. They'll know we picked this up."

He shook his head. "No, the bulletin didn't say anything about the RV. Helen wouldn't tell them anything if she had her choice. This thing isn't registered in her name anymore so they shouldn't know about it. I spoke with Steve. He won't talk. Relax a bit."

"Riiight. Relax." Despite the remark, it looked like she would try to. Wanted to, at least.

In an industrial area a mile away they uncoupled the Mazda, stowed the tow bar, and left the keys on its roof. He chose a surface street that he hoped would get them out of the city and into the foothills without being stopped.

MICHAEL J. PARKS

Chapter 8

Sometimes the best way to figure out who you are
is to get to that place where you don't have to be anything else.
- Source unknown

Austin stared at a tree-covered ridgeline in the distance. Blue sky capped the high altitude beauty. To the south, gray-white plumes from the fires fed a hazy skyline. What should have been a relaxing view was clouded by uncertainty. Reality had become slippery and levels deeper than he'd imagined.

He sat with Marcel and Meng under the shade of the table umbrella by the pool. Marcel said he would share things that would shed light on the big picture and offer a better understanding.

"How well you adapt to change will influence your overall progress. In my experience, the more you trust me, the more rapidly it goes. How are you doing with trust?"

"Besides this," he flicked the bracelet attached to his ankle, "I'm doing okay."

Marcel nodded. "In time." He stood up and walked over to the lizards. "Before we start, Edward mentioned you have a story. Something about the wind?"

"Hm. Yes. A story."

"True story?"

"True as I understand it."

Marcel knelt by the rocks. "It means a lot to you. I'd be honored if you'd share it."

Again he found it easy to like the Frenchman. "On one condition. That you explain it when I'm done."

Marcel agreed. "I'll do my best."

"I was thirteen and was going to try out for a swim team. Of course I had to wear a speed-o swim suit but I had a farmer tan from wearing skater shorts. I didn't want to look ridiculous so I laid out to get a tan, hoping to bring up the color evenly. There I was, in the early April sun, chilled by a steady breeze. At some point I wondered if the wind was slowing the tanning process. So, desperate as I was, I started imagining the earth in a cartoon sort of way, with big exaggerated clouds coming in from the ocean and blowing over California. Do you know the old Schoolhouse Rock cartoons? No?" Meng nodded. "Well it was like a scene from that. Anyway, I imagined a big hand pressing down on the clouds to stem the flow. I was so caught up in the cartoon it took a long time before I realized the winds had actually stopped."

Marcel stood and returned to the table, still listening.

"I know what you're thinking and it's the same thing I thought at first: just coincidence. But it wasn't just the wind dying. At that moment I felt... extraordinarily calm. I'm talking unnatural, deep-seated peace, like nothing I'd felt before. I stayed like that for twenty or thirty seconds until my own amazement got in the way. The wind had *stopped*.

"Sure enough, just as my calm diluted, the wind picked up again. I waited a few minutes to see if the wind would stop again and it didn't. So I tried the earth-hand thing again and almost immediately the calm feeling came back. Not ten seconds later the wind died down to nothing. Remember, it was a blustery April day before all that."

Marcel nodded.

"I know it sounds crazy but I did it again and again, probably five or six times that day."

"Did you mention it to anyone?"

"I tried describing it to my mom but she brushed it off. I did it several more times over the years. Once with a girl from the neighborhood."

"What did she make of it?"

"It frightened her, I think. She'd never imagined anything like it. I was just relieved. I would've been embarrassed if it hadn't worked."

Silence grew thick as the nearby rocks. The two men looked at each other and back at him. With Edward it seemed the wind story might be really important. The reaction now was much less than what he'd expected. Feeling uncomfortable, he added, "That's it. I'd love an explanation if you have one. I've always wondered about it."

Marcel smiled. "I can help you understand better but can't fully explain it, at least not today. Let's begin. Edward mentioned you used to play a lot of video games. Countless hours spent immersed in virtual worlds, living fantastic experiences. That tells me a high-resolution display system, acting in sync with a sound system, provided enough stimuli to transport you, a willing participant, away from... your desk. Away from the real world, for hours on end. Is that right?"

He shrugged. "Sure, in a way."

"Would you say your ability to experience an alternate reality is a skill you possess?"

"If that's what you want to call it, yeah. Most people do."

"All right then, good, there is that and it is an important skill. Keep it in mind. Now, you have a basic understanding of physics? Yes, so you understand that matter is comprised of atoms of varying types. In each atom, there are smaller components still, in the form of nucleons – you know, protons and neutrons. And nucleons are made up of even smaller bits. Yes?"

"I'm familiar with most of that, yeah. Strings. Quantum level stuff."

"Perfect, yes. Now, overlay that bit of knowledge onto the world immediately around you." He gestured widely. "This. Speaking in terms of video graphics, what kind of resolution do these bits offer us?"

"Really super high."

Marcel nodded with a smile. "So, put simply, we're in a kind of grid. A very high-resolution, three-dimensional display system. We call it *Raon*. That's an old Celtic term for 'field'. Raon is where we experience the physical. It is the hard, real world. It defines what we are." He cocked his head slightly. "Well, what our bodies are anyway."

Austin looked to the rocks. A lizard shifted under his gaze, as if uncomfortable with the sudden scrutiny. "Alright," he looked back. "What else is there? Soul?"

Marcel sipped his drink. "You've left your body so you know right off there's *something* about you that isn't anchored to that bag of bits."

"To be honest, I'm not sure I could do it again. Not on command, anyway."

Meng stood suddenly and gestured towards the house. Marcel responded. "Okay then, let's head inside. A little warm out here, I think."

He followed them inside to the family room. Meng closed the patio doors and drew the blinds closed.

"What gives?"

Marcel shook his head. "Don't mind for now. Grab a couch." He headed into the kitchen. "Do you want a refill? No?"

Marcel was smoothing, calming himself as much as he was him.

"Are they close?"

Marcel answered from the kitchen. "Sometimes."

Meng left his position by the doors. Whatever had been wrong was now less of an issue.

Marcel returned with a full glass in hand. "Okay where were we? The soul question, yes? So of course we have the five famous senses, shaping our earthly experience, programming our internal TV. What do you suppose the sixth sense is, Austin?"

"A psychic ability?"

Marcel raised an eyebrow.

"You know, the ability to read minds, see the future. Psychic stuff."

Marcel switched eyebrows and asked, "Really? 'Psychic stuff?'"

"C'mon, you know what I mean."

He smiled. "Close enough. Your sixth sense is rooted in something you aren't aware exists. Edward spoke to you of the language of vibes, yes? Those vibes are real and they originate as a result of your thoughts, at the quantum level. Yes, they are slight, even weak, but they don't have to be strong because of the field in which they operate."

"The field? In Raon?"

"Yes, but in Raon's fifth element."

"What?"

"Earth, water, air, fire. The four classic elements. Our senses are most tuned to them. But there is a fifth element and your sixth sense is tuned to it."

"And what is the fifth element?"

"It is... a little like air, a little like water, only it is everywhere. You know water carries sound four times faster than air? Yes, that amplification, it is the same effect the fifth element has with our vibrations. A tiny disturbance travels well beyond its origins."

"So it's a conductive field. Conducting electricity."

"Conductive yes, but not of electricity."

"You're losing me."

Marcel nodded his understanding. "When Edward talked about vibes and frequencies, he used familiar terms to explain something more exotic. Your brain emits signals, yes, detectable by EEG devices, but those signals are just the ionic waves generated by the firing of neurons interacting with the electrons on the metal of sensors. They are of little consequence beyond measuring neural activity. There is another kind of signal that the brain emits and its properties are not measurable with common sensors."

"Edward's wifi of the soul?"

"Yes. And to grasp what this is, you must understand what you really are."

"And what am I really?"

"The prefix 'meta' comes from a Greek preposition meaning after, beside, or with. You are, in fact, 'with' your body. You, your *self*, the meta you, is using your body." He smiled, noting Austin's expression.

"So are you talking about the soul or not?"

"Not the soul you know. Religion's concept of soul is old, vague, and misleading – by no means an accident, believe me. No, meta is very different from *that* soul."

"Meta."

"Yes, meta. The fire that flows through all life, igniting the design that it inhabits. Humans, animals, even plants and microorganisms have it. It flows through your brain and captures your earthly experience, is imprinted by it. Without it, we would have no identity, no self, no soul to experience the moment, and no memories. It is what vibrates with meaning, sending information outward from one's self into the fifth element. It can be directed, just as a laser can illuminate only a chosen target. Or it can be broadcast, like sound from a bullhorn."

"So you're saying thoughts transfer into a shared field?"

"Yes, they do, unless you contain them. A skill more people need, frankly. The sixth sense allows the brain to work on information from meta. Combined with the other five senses, the brain does an incredible job with computation, comparison, conversion of sounds and imagery to meaning, calculating diverse concepts of all things under the sun and the result is..."

"Human thought."

"Precisely. Human experience, which in reality is compromised more of sixth sense input than input from your five senses. What you experience most has a lot to do with non-physical input, from sources and connections you don't realize exist." Marcel paused again, as if measuring his absorption before continuing. He appeared satisfied. "The body is just the vehicle, the 4x4 of Raon. Meta is what we *are*, what we are *being with*. The idea of it is buried by science and western culture, neither of which will allow for it. Which leads us to your next sense."

"A seventh sense?"

"Do you really think we are so simple?"

"No, I guess not."

"Meta location, for lack of a better description. It is knowing *where* and on *what* you are focused. The very tip of that focus is called your *rathad*. It is the most basic element of who you are, of your meta. Where rathad goes, so does your experience. In your mind or outside of it. That sounds simple and it both is and isn't. You'll have to decide for yourself later."

"Meta. My rathad. Seventh sense. Okay. What's all this mean? Nutshell."

"It means you're a guest in that body. Plugged in securely, mated seamlessly, synchronized completely. Naturally. You are the meta to your body, an exquisite and exotic energy form that you recognize only peripherally and label as your consciousness. Your science-based culture made sure you would never believe you weren't the body. Your religion-based culture made sure you believed your soul was inherently flawed and at great risk of being stolen by demons or punished by a vengeful god. Culture made sure your ignorance of meta was cemented. Culture, the purveyor of doubt, the hard ridge of containment as well as the father of intense and blinding ego. Global control would be impossible without the manipulation of culture and ego. The truth is hidden right out in the open, cleverly disguised and made complex and confusing. As a result, the grid is both the playground and the prison for humanity."

He exhaled heavily and thought for a moment. "Alright. There's stuff happening in the background that we're not taught."

Marcel nodded. "Oh, quite a lot of stuff. More than I've shared."

"It's meta then, the 'meta me', that can travel beyond my body. Why don't I recognize this 'meta' self? Why don't I even know how to think about it? I can't just pop out of my body any time I want. It takes special circumstance."

"Programming. Lack of experience. Everyone *is* their meta self and are influenced moment to moment by the flow of meta, both their own and those around them. As for traveling, you will learn to recognize meta, to the point of it feeling physical. You will master your meta self and life will get interesting after that."

"You mean more interesting."

Marcel smiled. "Precisely."

"And what about the wind? Nothing you've said addresses that."

He leveled a gaze at Austin. "I can tell you that Raon is not as stable as we are taught. Its underlying structure is reliant on a kind of quantum foam, which is reliant on certain... unique variables. Put simply, some people have the ability to disturb the foam. You are one of them."

"I am?"

"Almost certainly."

"How do I do it?"

"The mechanics are complex and not fully understood yet. What we do know is that it involves elevated quantum activity in your neural functions. With the addition of certain proteins and frequency therapy directed at your brain, the activity can be scaled up, making a method of entanglement possible – a synchronization of thought and intention with the underlying quantum fabric of matter. You already touched on it and apparently have a naturally elevated affinity. That is what most excites Edward. Many of us, to be honest. Part of your future will no doubt involve trying to enhance those functions."

"Protein additions?"

"More on that later, but right now we'll talk a bit about dreams and then it will be time for the stress test. Time for a little nap."

• • •

The headlights of the stolen Audi scoured the pavement ahead, a shining lance that pulled them safely along towards Elburg. After the shooting, the train station parking lot at UitGeest provided a new transport. Ensconced in black leather, Johan and Anki fed on the composure of the sedan. Soft jazz provided relief from the mad dash of the past couple hours.

Just before midnight they passed the coastal town of Enkuizen and turned onto the Markerwaarddijk, a narrow strip of land separating the IJsselmeer and Markermeer lakes. For thirty kilometers the nearly-full moon traveled with them and acted as an anchor in the unpredictable night. There was no use discussing their situation – it was too extreme and would play out with escape or capture. Instead they agreed to stay in the bubble of the moment and began exploring the gap between online and real life. Twenty kilometers in, their alchemy bore evidence of compatibility, a good sign should the future allow them a chance.

Leaving the Markerwaarddijk, they passed two police cars stopped on the shoulder. Officers retrieved fold-out barricades from their trunks.

Anki tensed. "Checkpoints?"

Johan transitioned onto the rural N302 inland, slipped the Audi into its highest gear, and accelerated smoothly. The glowing road markers ticked by in a blur. "Just ahead of their net. Doing good."

Around one-thirty they arrived in Johan's neighborhood and drove past the house. City crews had done the courtesy of installing plywood over the damaged second story window. Seeing and sensing no danger, they circled back and went inside.

Johan went online and secured airline tickets to Brazil using Max Dosch's credit card; departure just after noon. While Anki showered on the third floor, he gathered materials from hiding spots around the house to prepare the templates for her Dutch identity card and passport. She needed a makeover for the visa picture and she needed a name.

"Andrie Van Gelder." The name came to him, an old school mate.

Upstairs, he retrieved the makeup kit from the bathroom closet. He paused as Anki opened the shower door and stepped out, her body glistening. "I don't want to be morbid, but I was just thinking… this may be our last chance ever."

The surge returned, energies intermingled, polarizing into the give and take pattern, drawing them into a kiss. He engaged the mesh of her awareness and slid past lowered defenses to settle into a molten bed of desire. The walls of her experience were tensile-strength loyalty and commitment – focused solely on him. Her commitment went far deeper than he would have imagined. In that moment, real love broke out, the molecules of its reality saturating all, usurping safeguards, filling emotional reserves, and forging a bond. At the same time came recognition of a liability being born. He chose not to suppress any of it; it was what it was.

• • •

The comm buzzed. It was his assistant. "Signus 1 is reporting a return on A2. The riders are vectoring now."

Director Tomov turned to the wall monitors in his office. "Give me the control room feed, all audio."

"Patching now."

"…familiar, agreed. He's back where he started."

"Fragments. A blonde. Anki?"

"Has to be. Can't see her yet but they must be having a helluva time."

"What is that? Anyone getting that? Is he trying to block us?"

The lead cut in, taking charge. "Refocus, regroup. Boundaries?"

"Amsterdam wide, between the city and the border with Germany. Arnhem, north to the sea."

"Tighter. Wait… now, he's going for it. Strong point, follow me!"

Like in a game of Marco Polo, the riders scanned, conveying their feedback to the leader, providing measurements of the signals emanating from the target. "Keep tightening. I'm starting the push."

Just as the lead began the active pressure towards A2, a black hole, *a nothingness* bloomed. Stunned, he held and tried to pierce it. The four waited passively, not saying a word. Their silence conveyed their own confusion.

"Irregularity there. The target's still up. Do we have them?"

With some hesitation, all four refocused and checked in, confirming yes. The lead moved again and cautiously applied pressure to the target... for the slightest of returns.

"Vector!"

They narrowed to a twenty square kilometer radius before the blackness returned to interrupt.

"Irregularity again. Significant blocking. He's still up but something's wrong here. We need another panel. Forty percent urban coverage over twenty square klicks to deal with."

"Confirmed. Requesting a second panel. Field teams are deploying to the area."

Director Tomov signaled his assistant. "Is A2 doing that or is someone else involved? Tell them I want a firm analysis."

• • •

Anki gripped Johan's arms, eyes locked onto his, and matched rhythm. She'd let go from the start, surrendering physically, then completely. He flowed through her like a narcotic, birthing intimate, provocative emotions. In the smallest center of her being, she knew him directly, felt the charge of his thoughts, the pulse of his soul. She went to join him there, following a thin thread of possibility.

As if waiting for her arrival, he released a love so rich and genuine that she was overcome. Soul to soul, the feeling bloomed until tears welled in her eyes. It felt an eternity she'd waited for just that moment. *Their* love, not only her own. The sharing triggered an avalanche that drove the arc and cadence of their bodies. She cried out and dug her fingers into his back, soaring through a timeless pleasure with ancient rhythm.

Time snapped back in line when Johan shifted awareness. A wedge formed between them, creating a space tinged with fear. The others were returning.

"They'll find us," she whispered.

"No." His presence surged, an almost physical bending of thought that drew her into him. She cast off again, surrendering to a joining more consuming than any she'd ever imagined.

• • •

Afterward, it wasn't clear why it worked. They'd started to track him at the wrong damn time, at their most vulnerable. Defiance led him to conjure a very empty, very useless mental image, grossly negative and heavy. It appeared as an object, hidden from Anki in a split space. He used the object, fully intending to block them, like clamping a hand over a camera lens. The pressure abruptly halted. He'd done it three more times before he and Anki finished.

The idea that a strongly formed mental construct could affect their processes proved thrilling. *The hunters were like him except they had training he didn't.*

Another realization was more disturbing: for the second time during sex there had been another presence, an awareness unlike the hunters, piggybacking his thoughts as light as a moth. He'd had no defense, no way to detach or shield from it, and it passed with each coupling. He had to think something else was watching them.

He wiped tears from Anki's face, tears she said were as much for the perfection of their joining as for the love she'd felt. Whether or not they'd have the chance to explore their new union remained to be seen. To have felt it though, gave him strength and courage.

He kissed her. "Let's get you changed into Andrie."

Twenty minutes later, Anki's platinum blondeness was gone, replaced by a dark, wet mass soaking in brunette dye. The risk they'd taken in the bedroom and the confrontation in his head presented a gnawing regret that he tried to shake. He focused on Anki's makeup and continually shifted mood and thoughts, avoiding any one mental space too long. The hunters hadn't returned though it could only be a matter of time.

She pointed again to a droplet forming above her forehead. He dabbed with a cloth protect his work. The glue on the chin, cheekbone, and brow pads had just about set. The size and placement of the pads would cancel out face-matching systems at the airports although they robbed her of her natural beauty.

"Almost there. You okay?"

She nodded as she wasn't allowed to talk or stretch her face.

"Don't move, I'm going to spray now. Here, dab as you need to. Close your eyes."

Using a micro-airbrush he applied the skin coloring to hide the white latex pads. Like a real-life photoshop, the pads became part of her face. After drying he had her stretch a bit then applied sealer. No melting faces in the rain.

He stepped back to take in his work. The effect was natural and dramatic: she just wasn't the same woman. A timer sounded.

"Okay give it another minute then rinse but very carefully. No peeking until we dry your mop!"

She finished toweling her hair just as he returned with his Max Dosch pads.

"This is unbelievable," she said, finally looking in the mirror. "A stranger. I'm a *stranger*. This is so, so odd."

"Give it a few minutes then start with your makeup. Bring out your cheekbones."

He went to work on himself. Twenty-five minutes later his new face dried while he prepared a suitcase. Downstairs, he snapped Andrie Van Gelder's photo for her ID, had her change her shirt, changed the lighting, background, and adjusted zoom before taking another for her passport. From a shoe box he selected two ink stamps, one from England's Heathrow and the other from Brussels, Belgium.

"Not well traveled, am I?"

"Sorry, no time for you to be. Remember the dates. I have simple stories for those trips if you need them. You can ad lib, I hope. Are you a good liar?"

"Aren't we all?"

After applying his own makeup he prepared a message to Soldado with a request for hospitality upon arrival. A request to meet in person might shock him but with the right protocols he should accommodate.

"Andrie? It's time to roll."

"I've decided I don't like my face, Johan, it's—"

119

"No, it's Max. Max Dosch."

"Okay, *Max*, my face is boxy, without grace," she said with a pout. "You really screwed the pooch."

"You are lovely, my dear Andrie. Simply lovely. Now come, it's time to go and start a new life."

• • •

"Whoever he is, he's evaded."

Director Tomov listened to the update, as unhappy as he'd felt in a long while. Duty started in half an hour and he'd hoped for better news. The Executives wouldn't like it.

"Continue."

"We are setting up at airports and train stations. Ground and air units have been assigned to major roadways. Local law has been alerted, as have the media – the Rotterdam Butcher is in Amsterdam. Overseer has nothing yet so we feel confident the material has not been disseminated."

"Acknowledged."

Tomov disconnected and stared at the old clock his friend Mamar had given him. Its familiar tick filled the room. As always, the second hand took a tiny step backward before moving forward into the next, as if protesting the movement its very existence served.

Such a familiar feeling.

Chapter 9

A ship in harbor is safe, but that is not what ships are built for.
-John A. Shedd, 1859 - ?, American Author, professor

Mac screwed the gas cap closed and eyed the highway as he circled back into the camper. Topped off, the rig would need two, maybe three more refuelings to reach the cabin. Food was also on the agenda but smaller stores northwest of Reno would be safer.

Kaiya rested in the bedroom while he drove up highway 49 through forested hills. They passed the occasional community; the largest, Grass Valley and Nevada City, receded in the mirrors without incident. There was nothing to lead authorities to the RV unless Helen had revealed it before dying – or if they had stolen her thoughts. He suppressed a shudder. Steve might change his mind, too. So far, the radio chatter mentioned only the Mazda.

The miles rolled by taking the hours with them. The Coachman emerged from the trees onto the high Sierra plains and its alpine scrub. Sunlight warmed the dash but not his thoughts. The organizations gunning for the laptop had killed, kidnapped, and framed so far. Brodie was involved or at least served under a command that was. The good news was he'd gotten Kaiya free, had the laptop, and was heading to the safety of the cabin. Brent and Austin's fates were beyond knowing, at least for now. With Kaiya safe and settled, he could regroup and begin to explore options.

The bedroom door opened and Kaiya came forward. He noted her positive mood and knew that she'd taken charge of her fear. Her hair was pushed up in Helen's floppy yellow hat and she wore a yellow windbreaker and large black sunglasses. She sat down in the passenger's chair.

"How's this?"

He touched the brim of Frank's Panama hat. "On vacation."

"So are we there yet, dad? Huh, are we?"

He smiled. "Almost at Portola for gas and food. When we get there I want you out of sight."

"Okay." She studied him. "When was the last time you slept?"

"Just over thirty-one hours. I'm okay." His voice betrayed the words. It had been so much easier just five years ago.

She frowned. "Yeah no, I don't think so. Do we have to get to the cabin right away? Couldn't we find a place to park so you can rest?"

Resting appealed to his every sense but staying so near Sacramento didn't. Less than two hundred miles felt like their front yard under the circumstances.

She reached over to a small GPS device on the dash and powered it up. "Here, let's find an RV park. We'll blend in."

He watched Kaiya figure out the device and understood better why Austin was drawn to her. She had an inner beauty comprised of vitality, intelligence and tenacity that surpassed her exterior. She'd opted to aim for strength in spite of the situation. It spoke volumes about her spirit.

The thought of what they might do to that spirit was unacceptable.

She peered ahead. "Up here on the right. Sierra Valley RV." They passed the tree-shrouded entrance. "They've got free wifi." She turned to him. "Mac, you look tapped. Let's not take chances on the road. We can rest and check out the laptop."

"Alright. We'll circle back after fueling. If we use the laptop, it will be under my direction. Capiche?"

"No problem, Mac, I get it now. I do."

They arrived in the town of Portola just at nine o'clock and pulled into a corner gas station and market. Mac went inside to get groceries and pre-paid for the gas with cash: in and out, as unremarkable as he could be.

He started the fueling and looked around. The small town was easy on the senses. A coffee shop across the street. A restaurant down the way named *The Log Cabin* was just that, a large log cabin. A customer went into a grocery store down the street. An old man walked his dog without a leash. Laid back, the way life should be.

Seconds after the thought, a California Highway Patrol sedan came into view and rolled to a stop at the light. Mac turned away. Adrenaline surged to make his pulse pound in his neck. Bulletins for cop killers were always issued statewide, if not wider. A few moments later the black and white cruiser entered his peripheral vision and continued down the street. By the time fueling was done the adrenaline spike waned and the reality of fatigue won over.

He paid cash for a night's stay in the RV park. Their slot was at the back and allowed view of the entrance to the park as well as access to a dirt road to a street beyond. He chose not to plug in to the park's electrical service and instead relied on the generator for power. They'd take a few hours of sleep and be gone again, no ties or tethers.

Kaiya noted their neighbors' RVs were all closed up, unlike some of the other campers in the park who were socializing with other families. He was okay with that.

"Last thing we need is face time with anyone. You up for some Frosted Flakes?"

"Oh why not." Kaiya closed the windshield curtains around the cab.

"I want to tell you, you're doing good, Kaiya. You're holding up well."

She grimaced. "Thanks, but most of this is pure redirection. If I stop to think about it I'll fall apart."

"Understood. Still, you're doing well."

She shook her head. "I never wanted to believe any of this. Austin used to talk about how corrupt the government was and how they kept really important secrets. Psychic stuff, major conspiracies. It made me uncomfortable so he stopped talking about it. What do you know, Mac? About all this?"

"Not enough, apparently." He told her about the years of government research and its official result. "I always thought it odd to hide the research then publicly admit to it while calling it a wash, a failure."

"When has government ever admitted to blowing millions on something so insubstantial?"

"That's the thing. It just seems their way of ending the discussion. If government investigated it thoroughly and there was nothing to it, then the majority's mind would be made up, too. The power of a strong government." Just how often the effect was used would boggle her mind. "And it helps that the public has an incredibly short memory."

"But if they can read minds, how come they haven't found us?"

"All I know is that it won't take a mind reader to track us down if they put enough effort into it. Then there's Steve. That's why I want to get to Smith Falls as fast as possible."

The cabin was located in a remote area near the Canadian border, near the base of Italian Peak. Chet Arnold bought it with Mac's money, used it on occasion, and generally kept it as his own with the understanding Mac might need it someday. It wasn't luxurious but it was comfortable.

Kaiya grew distant while she finished her cereal. Her upbeat mood had swung down. No surprise, it was a lot to handle even for him. She was probably thinking of Austin.

"Mac, let's check out the laptop. It could hold clues to who is behind all this."

So much for reading distant looks. "Sheez. Alright, break it out. But no internet. I want to see the note from the hacker."

She nearly leapt to the case, pulled out the laptop, and set it up on the table. He switched sides to keep an eye on things. It didn't take long for her to locate a folder named 'hackershit'. Inside it, a readme file contained the message from the hacker.

He read it and grunted. "Guy's got balls. Sends a message to say, 'Here's something that is going to screw up your life big time. See you around!' Amazing."

She scanned the directory. "Okay, here are the two files. Check out the introduction. This is what made me worry."

He read the text interspersed with the squares. "Well, it's definitely a warning. I imagine Austin wishes he'd taken it now."

"I know he figured out the key to the encryption. His notes file should have it." She scrolled down. "Yep, here it is."

She used the key and the file opened for browsing. She read aloud the original email from Darren Blythe to SlotZero@freemail.com. As bizarre as it looked at first glance, it made a kind of sense now. Whoever had been tracking Darren had put the fear of God in him. Kaiya fell quiet after reading the message.

"Any direct emails from the hacker to Austin?" he asked.

"He didn't mention any and his notes don't say. Let me check." She brought up Austin's email client and scanned the inbox. "No, nothing. This is all old stuff."

She closed the mail program and re-read Austin's notes. "Well, there's forty parts to the file and he only got two. Here's the program that downloads them. And here's the email address for the guy who sent it."

Mac exhaled heavily and looked at the freemail.com address. The only possible lead to where the file came from stared back at him from the screen. Kaiya eyed him expectantly.

He shrugged. "What? What would you say to him, Kaiya? He doesn't know where Austin is."

She shook her head. "I don't know, Mac. Maybe he does? Maybe he's been broadcasting this file around. Maybe the media will pick it up. Then we could come forward and get help. These people are powerful, yeah, but they're obviously afraid of this going public. If that happens the lid will blow clear off and we won't have to hide. I can't stand having to hide."

It was difficult to deflate her hopes but he had to speak the truth. "Kaiya, be prepared to wait. Even if a lid does come off, it won't happen overnight. You can bet your breakfast on that. The first editor or producer from any reputable media outlet to even think of posting a story about whatever's in the file would be shot down so fast... I'm sorry, I just don't see it happening. Not if it's as revealing as it must be."

"But what if it goes viral?"

"It would have to be bulletproof. Even then it might go big only to be ridiculed. Elaborate hoaxes are devised all the time. Unless there is some seriously credible and damning evidence in there, it might never break. Even then, counter-information can easily dissemble genuine truths. Most people don't want to be removed from their comfort zones. Trust me on that one."

"Okay, okay, I see your point. But again I say, something in this file is incredibly important to them or they wouldn't be trying so hard to control it. That's leverage! I think if it gets out, there will be real consequences, real change. And they know it."

Real consequences of what nature? She was reaching for stars from the top of a hay bale, unaware of the distances involved or of the danger of falling.

She closed the laptop. "You don't agree and you're already thinking of something else."

"I'm just not sure letting the file go viral is the right approach. The consequences may actually be more harmful than good. And yes, I'm thinking of something else."

"What?"

He stood and cleared their bowls from the table. "I'm thinking of who could be have grabbed Austin. Remember, Crawford and Vasco had no reason to rough you up if they had him. And if they did, he wouldn't hold out more than five minutes with the techniques we use for interrogation." He met her uneasy glance. "Point is, they would have located the laptop already and wouldn't need you. Someone else has Austin."

She looked at him. "Or maybe those two killed him before he told them the laptop's location and thought I might know where it is."

There was nothing to say to such a sobering thought. A gutsy, realistic consideration, though grim; another reason to admire her.

"Mac, I want to check on my mom. I need to let her know *something*. She has to know to defend herself and why."

"Yes, I get that. I'll need to think of a way to reach her without exposing ourselves." He rubbed his temple and closed his eyes. Thinking was getting harder and harder.

She stood up. "Get some sleep, Mac. I didn't get any earlier so I'll try again. There's an alarm on the nightstand. I'll take the couch."

He eyed the laptop.

She noticed and frowned. She powered it off, pulled the plug, and handed it to him. "So, how about that trust, eh?"

Chastised, he replied, "You take the bed, I want to be near the door. Set the alarm four hours out." He pulled his M9 from its holster and set it on the floor by the couch.

"Right." She turned and walked towards the bedroom, tossing her crumpled napkin in the trash.

He peeked through the curtains at the park. Everything appeared quiet. He double-checked the doors and windows before stretching out on the couch. Within minutes, sleep came to claim him.

• • •

Austin flopped onto the bed he'd slept in the night before. Marcel settled on the other bed while Meng took up sentry in the doorway.

The situation was now approaching freefall, the direction and speed decided by powers beyond him. Moments before he agreed to take a pill that would facilitate his experience in the 'next step'. What exactly was to happen Marcel wouldn't reveal. He would only say that he would dream. If trust was misplaced, he may never get to realize it.

"Alright Austin, you will feel disoriented and that is normal. The pill is fast acting, so be ready. By that, I mean be relaxed."

He wasn't lying. The room weaved as a drowsy feeling swept in, yet a part of him remained acutely aware. Layers of consciousness sort of stacked up and faded away, leaving a singular sense of self. A sea of percolating darkness surrounded him, saturated with potential.

"This is amazing." His voice echoed in a strange way. For the first time in his life, he'd watched himself fall asleep in a lucid state.

"It is only the beginning, Austin." Marcel was nearby, unseen. "You need to follow my voice, come to where I am."

Crap, this is weird. He did his best to move in that direction without a body. "Where? I can't see you."

The frothy darkness exploded in white light, encompassing everything.

"Oh my god."

The white faded to reveal an earthy scene: they stood in a room whose walls and floor were of glass, suspended over a field of molten magma. A vast rock cavern with low ceilings stretched out in all directions. In the center of the glass room two lounge chairs and a table caught the light from the superheated rock beneath them.

Marcel walked to the wall. "One of nature's hidden glories, never seen by the eyes of man. Inside Mount Tambora."

He stared in awe.

"So you made it. How do you feel?"

"Like I'm dreaming. Lucid dreaming."

"A lucid dream that I am directing, yes."

"Yeah, I feel your control. The white light just now. It was the same light in my first out of body experience."

Marcel shrugged. "Not sure who did you the favor. Another bit of mystery." He returned to the chairs. "Have a seat."

They sat just as a massive chunk of lava erupted from the molten sea and crashed into the rock ceiling. It burst into smaller chunks and rained down.

"Now I'm going to give it to you like it is. Are you ready?"

"I guess so." Something was missing for a lucid dream. He lacked some analytical ability and feeling of choice. Maybe a lot.

"Dreaming is a world unto itself, a playground of possibility and meaning, a therapy of the highest caliber. We've not only found how to connect to others here, we've managed to cross the bridge to the waking world. Well, into the attic of the waking world, you might say. Some of our most important work happens here. It is a realm more complex than the waking one, but dreams are not our focus right now. We start here only because it is the best place to introduce the truths."

The walls of the Sistine Chapel surrounded them, their chairs now suspended by ropes from its ceiling. Austin stared in awe at the illustrations of saints, prophets, and scenes from the biblical story of creation meticulously rendered on plaster.

Beyond the artistry, what captured his breath was the way Michelangelo's and Bernini's imagery had come alive, conveying meaning in a lurid, almost mystical way. Temptation, evil, courage, redemption, wisdom, faith... all leapt from the scenes, translated by a shifting of thoughts not his own – all part of the dream via Marcel's intention. The effect was enthralling.

"You now know more about Raon, the grid that is our physical reality. You now also know that you have a soft side, your meta self, that plugs into it via the fifth element. It's time to learn more about meta – what they don't want everyone knowing about."

The Sistine Chapel faded around them. A field of stars replaced it, twinkling diamonds that nearly obscured the darkness of space. They sat at the edge of an ocean with sand dunes at their backs. A warm breeze came off the water and an orb glowed in the sand between them.

"Raon connects us. It is that stage upon which we are merely players. Filling the actors is meta, the soul, the embodiment of creation and the essence of consciousness."

"Where does it come from?" Austin asked.

"Saoghal."

"Which is?"

"The native space of souls and our dreams. Think of it as a root dimension, a darkness never meant for waking minds. It is a shared space we all spawn from and where all meta-bodies live. It is your true home, the one that receives you when you rest every night."

"They've broken into Saoghal, then. You have, too."

"Some have learned to cast light there, yes. The light of awareness."

"How?"

"There is a conduit to the body through which meta flows. It is the *droichid*, located in your brain. It marries meta to the body. Should the flow of meta break, the heart stops, the body begins to die. The droichid is the bridge of life."

"And you know how to cross it. Cross into others. With rathad. To read minds."

Marcel nodded. "And with practice, introduce ideas and feelings into their flow. Like dropping petals into a stream."

"Mind control, then. You've been dropping things into my stream, haven't you?"

Marcel looked over. The orb in the sand cast light and shadows across his face. The dream intensified with a clarity that could only be the Frenchman's work.

"Some. Only when essential. And nothing forceful or false, I promise you."

Austin pulled his gaze away to the ocean. Suddenly trust was a currency that he needed more of. "This is the alternate reality stuff you talked about. I'm supposed to learn how to control my awareness and travel around Raon and Saoghal?"

"Yes. With meta awareness, you can explore both realms. The focus of your meta, the rathad, is the essence of your seventh sense — knowing where you are and what you are experiencing. It defines reality. It is the true awareness."

"How can meta exist in both dimensions? And what is it?"

"What is electricity? Some things just are, Austin. What's important is what it does. The meta stream interacts with the brain in a very intimate way, birthing emotion which in turn ripples your meta outward via the fifth element. Much like a wave of sound."

"Meta mixes with other meta."

"Precisely. We are meant to feel it and understand it just as we do sound, touch, smell. You should recognize this concept because you've been feeling it all your life. Now, as a basic introduction, you can begin to imagine the importance of meta awareness and understanding rathad. If you join us, you will learn to realize your meta self and what it means to be all the way alive."

"There's more, behind your words. There's danger. I feel it."

"Additional points are yours. I will never let you forget the danger. It is far too great."

"Who are the others? The other group?"

"They started as scientists a very long time ago, in an age before the common elements of civilization. They kept their meta discoveries to themselves. With it, they forged control at the expense of others. They became powerful beyond what anyone could imagine, then or now." There was pain in the telling, conveyed in the weave of the dream. "They caused needless suffering in return for their place as kings of the world."

A break in the continuum of Marcel's presence signaled a problem.

"My attention is required. I'll release you to sleep and see you when you wake."

The sense of Marcel faded, leaving Austin alone with thoughts of power on that scale. The drive to preserve such status would be immense. Selfishness on a grand and inhumane scale.

The beach began to fade until blackness consumed all. The emptiness offered no traction and no boundaries, nothing to keep him in or others out. He hadn't felt afraid of the dark since he was a boy...

A shimmer of light formed, revealing a playground scene he recognized. Fourth grade, the day his friend Cory kicked him in the chest while karate sparring. The perfect footprint it left on his white shirt made everybody laugh, himself included. Such a warm memory reminded him of Kaiya. If only they could join up, things would be far better. As if in response, the scene shifted to something unfamiliar and less appealing.

Night's darkness split to reveal a circus wagon rolling down a dirt road, rattling and creaking. Nothing was pulling it. Behind the bars meant for a lion were two clowns in colored garb lying face down in straw. At first detached, he found himself gripping the bars, riding the outside of the wagon.

He called out, "Hey! Hey you! Wake up!"

One of the figures shifted. He repeated his calls. The clown pushed up from the wagon floor and turned to face him.

It was Mac Payant, the CIA agent. He was unmistakably upset behind the garish face paint.

"Austin? Where have you *been*? Kaiya's worried sick."

"I couldn't help it, they took me. Where is– is that Kaiya? Kaiya!"

"Shhh! Don't wake her... not until you can get us out of here. As soon as this wagon gets to town they're going to have their way with both of us. You gotta get us out."

"This, this is just a dream, Mac. Where are you really?"

"The hell this is a dream! You need to get us out, now! Go around back and try the window. Now, son! We don't have much time!"

Frustrated, Austin could only go with it. He climbed towards the rear, thinking about how dreams mixed with real world facts. He asked Mac, "Do you know the name of the next town?"

"We're headed towards Janesville."

"Janesville? In California?"

"Yeah. We're on the way to the cabin but I'm sure they'll be coming soon. We don't have a chance without help. Did you reach the window?"

There was no window, no door, and no handle. He had to shout over the wagon's racket. "I'm working on it! Mac, where is the cabin? Tell me exactly!"

"Smith Falls, near the Idaho Canada border. But if you don't get us out of here, we'll never see it!"

"What are you two driving in?"

"This thing!"

"Describe it, Mac. What are you driving in?"

"Are you trippin'? This RV! You're climbing all over it!"

The wagon was gone, replaced by a large camper. He clung to the rear ladder.

There wasn't anything else he could think to ask. "Mac, I'm gonna try to help you. I'll try to reach you. Hang on and be careful!"

With that, he leapt from the ladder, hit the dirt, and rolled several times before stopping. The taillights of the RV lurched down the bumpy road and receded into the night.

• • •

"Sir, Austin's email account was accessed. Oscar has a match against the target's laptop."

"Any other traffic?" The supervisor stood and walked over.

"No sir, just the email server."

"Point of origin and our proximity?"

"Outside of Portola, California. Connection's registered to an RV park. We have two units in a half hour bubble."

"Move them in and put local authorities on standby. Possible sighting near the park. I want them ready for the takedown but no one spooks them. Bring up any SAT feed you can get and put in a panel request while we're at it. Priority one."

He clapped twice. "Java, please!"

• • •

Austin blinked awake and propped himself up. "Where's Marcel? I need to talk to him."

Meng still stood in the doorway of the bedroom, hands together in front of him. "Relax. He's doing business. You want something to drink? Those pills can cause headaches."

He got up and brushed past Meng into the hall. "I need to talk to him right now. Seriously, Meng, it's about Kaiya."

Marcel emerged from a room down the hall. "What about her, Austin?"

"She's about to be caught. You've got to do something."

Marcel guided him towards the family room. "And how did you learn this?"

"The dream, how else? They're traveling towards Janesville in an RV and if we don't do something, they'll be caught." Not seeing the urgency he wanted, he added, "Look, *these* are the people I need to protect, like I told Edward. You need to help them."

"Sit, please. Relax." Marcel sat on the edge of the sofa. "Why do you think they are going to be caught?"

"Mac said so. He's right, I just feel it."

"Okay. We're aware of the situation. They used your laptop and the Comannda are moving in to find them. I can't promise anything at this point, but we're setting something up. We have to wait and see how it goes."

"The Comannda?"

"The other group. The ones most in control."

"Where's Kaiya?"

"Austin, listen to me: you cannot do anything. Leaving—"

"Bullshit. They want me, not her. Me and the laptop."

Marcel frowned. "Dead heroes make horrible lovers. If you want a chance at seeing Kaiya alive, focus now. Our people will do their best which is far better than you could. That is the reality – now you must deal with it."

"Just sit on my hands, then?"

"No, you're going to help. In just a few minutes. And all you need is your voice."

• • •

Mac woke.

The occasional yell from kids in the park filtered into the camper. The stillness acted as a sedative, subduing all bad things. It took little effort to imagine that none of the trouble had ever begun. *Just a bad dream.* The air conditioner kicked on and filled the camper with a low hum and vibration.

A dream. He'd dreamt of Austin. Driving at night on the way to the cabin, he'd appeared out of nowhere, clinging to the outside of the Coachman. There was a threat ahead, Mac had known it in the dream. Austin said he was going to help but had jumped off the RV instead.

Damned dreams. Janesville. They'd pass through it late evening. He checked his watch: *only thirty minutes?* Why was he awake? Wary, he sat up with the M9 in hand.

Just then a knock sounded at the door.

He peeked out the window. A male with a mop of hippie hair dressed in jeans and a flannel shirt stood with a cell phone in hand.

He opened the door a crack. The man spoke immediately.

"Mac, the laptop connected to the wifi and they traced it here. You have minutes only. You and Kaiya need to come with me now."

The cell phone in his hand rang. He extended it. "It's Austin. You'll want to take it."

Sure enough, it sounded like Austin. "Mac, you're in deep shit and need to go with that guy. Leave the laptop, you won't need it. That's the best way to get them off your ass, just leave it."

He had to know it was really Austin. "What was different about your high school graduation partying?"

"What? Oh, alright. How about a CIA agent tailing me to make sure I didn't get caught up in DUIs and drugs?"

Mac nodded, satisfied. "Are you acting under duress?"

"Not at all, Mac. You need to go now. Seriously, right fucking now. Save Kaiya and yourself, please. Go."

He eyed the hippie and hoped he wasn't being had.

• • •

Austin stood at the sliding glass door and watched for the hawk. Despite the harsh wait for word on Kaiya and Mac, he'd made some progress with perspective. The surrealism of the situation had begun to resolve into more conventional, considerable terms. There were people in power, had always been, would always be. Nothing new or especially disturbing in that. There were always secrets used to manipulate and grow power. Advances in the sciences during the last two centuries indicated the world was an amazing, mysterious place with an endless source of new tokens to wield ever-greater power. The revelations of the last two days could only be more of the same, a face of reality that existed as naturally as did gravity or DNA or nuclear physics. This was just his introduction to it.

"They're clear," Marcel said. "We bought them a small lead."

He spun around. "Where are they now?"

"Headed for a safe house. This is still a dangerous situation, Austin, understand that." Marcel sat on the edge of the nearest couch. "Coincidentally, it's time."

"What? To commit? Now?"

"It is past time actually and a necessary formality at this point. Not to lessen the gravity of the agreement, mind you."

"DFA. What about ability? We didn't finish the dream testing."

"Yes, yes we did. You performed as expected though not in the scenario we'd imagined."

He half-turned to face the window and the pines beyond. "I've still got questions, like... like how is my face going to change? And what about my DNA? Or fingerprints? And my dad? They have him, right?" Even as he asked them, he knew the questions were meant to delay, covering his fear.

Marcel's voice grew soft. "I won't say you don't have a choice but Austin, look at it for yourself. Look at the *totality*. All this is happening for a reason, not by accident. There is nothing ideal about it. Instead, there is sacrifice, change, and danger... but there is survival, too. And not just your own."

Their eyes met. Truth came off Marcel like ocean waves pounding the shore. Millions of lives in the past, victims of the Comannda; millions more in the future, destined for similar fates. Billions in the middle, rich and poor, simple pawns awaiting their deaths in the sickly half-light of ignorance and division. For the first time, he felt important to something bigger, something Marcel had not yet shared with him.

"I'm supposed to do this, aren't I?"

Marcel nodded, staring back from the depths. "I have to believe so."

Meng stood by the kitchen and looked on, unreadable.

"What am I joining?"

"Who, not what." Marcel straightened. "The Runa Korda. We are the Secret Family."

The room came into sharp focus, as if many moments converged into one, etching every color and feeling into memory. What he might become... what he might achieve... what might *happen*. Dad, Kaiya, and Yuni? He was powerless now and crushed by guilt for putting them in danger. There was only one way to help them and maybe redeem himself.

He felt a presence from behind and was certain what it was. Turning, he saw the hawk appear from the tree line, soaring in the blue sky.

He sighed, feeling the pendulum swing towards a future thick with uncertainty and danger.

"Alright then. Where do I sign?"

Austin surfaced and blinked away water in the late afternoon sun. A portion of burden had lifted – Kaiya and Mac were safe and would leave their hideout in the morning. The details on reunion weren't clear but it was just a matter of time. Knowing she was in their hands was enough to lighten his spirits, although thoughts of his dad and Kaiya's mom had the exact opposite effect.

He got out of the pool and dried off. Meng sat sentry in the shade. He asked him about his dad and Yuni and why Marcel wouldn't discuss them yet.

Meng shook his head. "Don't know the details, but I can tell you this: if you want to succeed, you need to form an island in your mind and call it home. If you don't, you risk drowning in the pain of loss and of memory."

He sat at the table. "That's pretty specific advice. What do you know, Meng?"

"Nothing. That is why I say form an island and call it home. If you cannot hold yourself up at the lowest times, you become worthless to anyone, including yourself. True strength lies in thinking clearly in adversity, *not* in collapsing in emotion, straining against wild thoughts, or faltering in doubt. So define your island. Make it your own. Defend it. Only from there will you become a power in this world."

He processed Meng's words in the swelling silence. No matter how beloved the people in his life were, to make the most of the situation would require steeling against all tragedy, all loss.

Easier said than done.

He thought about Marcel's introduction to meta. "So what's up with Scientology? Don't they teach the same sort of thing?"

Meng shook his head. "Don't let Marcel hear you say that. Scientology is the monetization of concepts that resemble the truths."

"The Comannda run it?"

"They insure its operation. It is an organization that controls and misleads. It is culturally controversial, making even considering the concepts socially taboo. That serves the Comannda agenda. It is their red herring."

"So it's giving people fake concepts about meta."

"Yes. It is the science of the mind effort. Much like religion, its end goal is to magnetize, polarize, and monetize. To divide and control."

Nora the housekeeper waved a dish towel at the window, a signal their meal was ready.

"Well shit, no wonder he doesn't like it."

Over a steak and salad dinner, Marcel dropped a bomb.

"You're to travel. Your energies here have accumulated so it is time to move. Until you are sufficiently adept at the meta arts, this will continue to be the case. Your training starts at the next location."

Austin stopped mid-bite. "Okay. When is this?"

"You leave after nightfall."

"And Kaiya? When do we meet up?"

The Frenchman finished a mouthful before replying. "Kaiya and Mac will be introduced to the Family. That process will take time, as will your training. No need to worry about either of them. Focus on yourself. Your training can go well, with effort, or not so well, if you allow distractions to interfere."

"That won't do. I want to see her." There could be no missing his intention.

"Of course you do. Tonight, you will."

• • •

The mist haloed around gas lamps, the London fog thick as night itself. Old Broad Street lay vacant save for a pair stumbling along the cobblestones, silly from a late night tavern visit. Tucked up in a deep entryway, Austin pulled his frock coat over his neck as he kept watch.

If all went well, he'd spend the night with the woman he loved. If not... hell, he refused to imagine it wouldn't.

A distant whistle pierced the darkness to the left. Again it sounded.

He slipped quietly into the street. Seeing no company, he moved more swiftly, ignoring the clack of his shoes against stone. The whistle repeated, closer. Above a tanner's shop a lone candle burned in a window. A visible balding head testified to the work being done. He crossed closer to the boardwalk to avoid being seen.

Reaching Throgmorton Street, he veered onto it and saw what he'd hoped for in the dark patch of road: a waiting hansom cab. He came along it and peered inside.

Kaiya stared at a candle held in her hands. She wore a high-necked dress adorned with lace and a cape jacket pulled close against the cold mist. She looked up and smiled, melting the cold shackles binding his heart. Without a word he climbed in next to her and took her hands in his. The driver, sitting high and behind the cab, cued the horse forward.

They traveled over bumpy streets, past dark squares and St. Paul's cathedral, eventually arriving in front of a stately residence lit with gas lights. He stepped out first and scanned the empty street. Satisfied, he paid the driver and helped Kaiya from the hansom.

She watched the horse and driver recede into the heavy fog and faced him.

"I'm dreaming, aren't I?"

"We are."

"I'm scared, Austin. How is this happening? What is it all about?"

"Relax, babe. We'll be okay. You'll see. We have tonight and that's all that matters for now. Trust me, please."

The scene dissolved into a bedroom from the period. A tall canopy stood over the bed, surrounded by fabric for privacy. A fire in the hearth warmed the room and offered sensuous contrast to the cold outside. They embraced, absorbing every sensation in a world rich with feeling.

"I love you, Kaiya."

Tears welled in her eyes. "I love you, too, babe. Endlessly."

• • •

Marcel opened his eyes. Concern draped across his face. He sat up and swung his feet to the floor.

Meng sat on a chair in the corner of the bedroom. "What's not right?"

"Too easy. He didn't press at all. All passenger, not a nudge towards control. Same as before."

"Absence or ignorance?"

"That's the problem. I'm not sure." He stood. "I'd hoped for a better showing."

Chapter 10

The question of whether computers can think is just like the question
of whether submarines can swim.
- Edsger W. Dijkstra

"This one. Oscar tagged it."

Director Tomov called up the results.

Max Dosch. Shallow profile. Two tickets to Brazil, round trip, reserved this morning. The flight departed after our target dropped off the radar. Traveling partner, Andrie Van Gelder, no profile at all.

"That's him. Flag the flight and raise Brazil control. I want them alive."

"Queued for Sao Paulo – instructions sent. Confirmation... received. Sir, there is no photo for Andrie Van Gelder but Max Dosch is there on pad five."

An unremarkable face stared from the screen. Whoever Max Dosch really was, he had experience in eluding.

"We're on the right path. I'm stepping out for review. Sandy?"

His AI replied, "CONFIRMED. DIRECTOR OFF FLOOR."

Tomov went to his office and retrieved the bottle in his desk drawer. Tailor-made for his chemistry, the little blue pills would sharpen things up and relieve tension. He accessed the incident file and brought up A1's and A2's profiles.

Crosstalk and SlotZero. Overseer's link tangibility report suggested they were covertly tied via an unknown hacking organization. Austin had just one tangible, the hack or apparent hack of his network by SlotZero. Anki, a fringe contact within the organization, linked only to SlotZero.

He shook his head. It appeared they were one degree off from wide-scale release.

The comm beeped. "Sir, update on 901. Their flight landed at Charles de Gaulle for emergency maintenance. New plane, one hour to departure. Arrival in Sao Paulo is scheduled for 0340 hours tomorrow."

Less than an hour left. They'd done it before.

"Contact Paris."

• • •

The priority dispatch arrived in the offices of DECAP headquarters in downtown Sao Paulo. The Judicial Capital Police Department immediately alerted the GOE for an intercept operation at the airport the following morning. The Group de Operacoes Especiais, equivalent to an American SWAT team, was known for brutality in its operations when necessary.

The GOE watch commander received the alert and began calling in his best men. A serial killer out of Europe was thinking of hiding out in Brazil – their favorite kind of intercept.

The computer that received the initial dispatch also covertly provided a mirror dispatch to a GOE computer in the reception lobby which in turn passed it to a web server belonging to the local electric company. Three handoffs later it arrived in a queue on one of the only systems still accepting input to the Underground's messaging system.

• • •

"That's almost beautiful."

The expansive latticework of the terminal dwarfed travelers and glowed luminous in the rays of the setting sun. Johan and Anki strolled arm in arm and admired the warmth.

"Yes, quite beautiful. What time is it?"

Anki squeezed his arm. "About five minutes since you asked me last. There, near the corner." An empty internet kiosk beckoned.

"Okay. We'll see if Soldado received my message. Then we'll arrange for word to reach your friend Sophia."

He purchased fifteen minutes using a chumped card. His zmail account had two messages in it, both from Soldado. The first one's subject caught his attention.

**ABORT-READ THIS 1ST **

He scanned it, then closed the session and stood up.

"Let's head out."

"Where are we going?"

"Relax with me." He smiled and led her forward. "It appears we've been made. They're waiting in Sao Paulo."

Every face, near and far, tracked their every step, his every thought. A camera there and another over there, swiveling – but away, not at them. Automatic doors slid open as they approached an exit. Traffic noise greeted them.

"They must know we're laid over."

"They do. Soldado's made an out for us. Look for a driver, a black man with a blue beret."

They found him standing next to a sedan with the door open. They hurried over and climbed in. Pulling away from the curb, the driver spoke around a thick French accent. "You'll change cars and be cleaned up for another try. It's a bit of a drive, so relax, be comfortable."

"Got a piece?"

The driver looked in the rearview mirror. "Sure." He reached under the seat and offered a semi-auto Walther.

Johan took the pistol and checked its action. "Who is your control?"

"E9. On orders from S-Man himself."

"What's your status?"

"Leveled up from contract late last year. Hoping to go full-time as soon as I organize my layer one stuff. I have my sponsors, I just need time and the right target."

"Consider startups. Often sloppy with security initially. American biotech or military research companies in South Africa. You'll get highly competitive shit, good for resell or recovery. Join the gig big, that's my advice."

" 'Join the gig big'. I like it. Thanks man, I'll do that."

"So what do you know?"

"All of Europe wants your ass in a basket. Never seen the media play up a murder so much." He glanced in the rear view mirror again. "You'll need a new face, that one will be on the telly soon. Um, hello. Look here."

Off to the left, police sped towards the airport. Every few seconds more appeared. To the right, a vehicle drove up the off-ramp with lights and sirens on, prepared to block traffic. The driver shook his head. "We'll use the streets."

The next exit was clear so he took it. Within minutes they were off the freeway and well into the avenues.

The driver watched his mirrors. "Too close. I hope P and O don't get caught up in any of that. Petra and Osiris. They came to look for you in case you didn't check your mail."

Johan hoped, too. "I'm grateful for the help."

Dusk had fallen to darkness by the time they arrived on a residential street. The driver killed his lights and pulled up a short distance from a blue van. Anki and Johan emerged into the summer evening and walked towards the van, hand in hand. For a vivid moment they were just residents from the neighborhood, enjoying a walk. He tensed when the side door slid open. A man stepped out, illuminated by the van's dome lamp.

"Greetings. I'm Oliver, your best friend for the next little while. Friends call me O.T. Let's say we get you two outta danger?" He gestured. "C'mon, don't be shy, plenty of room." Another man occupied a rear bench seat. "Don't mind Corky. Just a regular hack. Our brute."

He helped Anki in and took a seat beside her. "Thank you. Close call, that."

Oliver pulled the door shut and took the passenger's seat as the van set out. "Closer than you think. Your photo made the news. They closed the airport, halted outbound flights, and set up blocks at the roads. All to catch the Butcher of Rotterdam."

"I'm honored."

"You should be. Only striking workers and crumbling terminals ever shut de Gaulle down. The media hounds are lappin' it up. Guess the way they chopped her up makes for headlines."

He gave Oliver a hard look.

"Now mate, sorry for that. Didn't think you were familiar. Listen, I've got status for you. You'll want this stuff."

Soldado had suspended most major subsystems, interrupting operations throughout the Underground. Members were extremely pissed off for having been left in precarious situations.

"We've got to operate in a vacuum with you. We're on to the towpath house to see what Annie can do for your makeup. We'll use zmail to get updates from S-man. They're retooling Magistrate to resume comms but that'll take a day at least. Hopefully we get you on your way within twenty-four hours. Weren't too much in a hurry, I hope."

He shook his head. A river passed below. The lights of Paris danced in its waters. The van came off the highway into an older residential district. Still no sense of the hunters' pressure.

"Ya know we're dying to know who 'them' is. The murder rap, the neighbor, it don't add up. Care to throw a dog a bone? What's really going on?"

He liked Oliver less and less. A mercenary type, he likely moved in more than one circle and could easily be a loose mouth.

"No bones. Sorry." The circle stayed tight.

Oliver shrugged. "Ah, it's alright. I shouldn't of asked. We'll be home in a minute and get you freshed up."

The towpath house was just that — a house on an old river road once used by horses or oxen to tow barges upriver. Tucked back in a thick copse of trees, the two-story house was a modest affair, not well kept. A lamp revealed weeds in the front yard, a derelict rowboat in the unfenced side yard, sagging gutters, and shabby mismatched curtains in the windows. Its greatest assets had to be the view of the river and its seclusion, while its greatest fault was surely the proximity to the rails, some fifty meters beyond. A passing train shook the ground.

Anki hugged him tightly, a sudden and needful embrace.

He stroked her hair. "Are you alright?"

She nodded but obviously wasn't. He silently promised to work to calm her fears so she could sleep. They followed the men to a side door. Inside, a bare ceiling bulb lit a pale yellow kitchen.

Oliver called out. "Annie! They're here! Annie! For the love of... woman? You in the loo? Gah, the girl's always *pissing*."

Days' worth of dishes covered the kitchen sink and counter. Trash spilled out of the can. Boxes lined the adjacent dining room walls, labeled and left from the last move.

He led Anki into a living room with more clutter and still-packed boxes. Corky opened the fridge to retrieve a beer while the driver disappeared down a hallway.

Oliver grew angry climbing the stairs. "*Annie!* They're *here!* Get your bloody ass outta bed!"

Anki asked, "You wouldn't talk to me that way, would you?"

Still scanning, he replied absently, "I couldn't possibly." The front door's frame was splintered, the deadbolt still deployed. Checking the knob, it too, was locked. Fibers of wood and paint chips lay on the floor, undisturbed where they'd fallen. Fresh violence emanated from the wood.

"Let's head outside. I think I left my phone in the van."

A solid thump shook the ceiling. He grabbed Anki's arm and reached for the Walther. The door opened to reveal a silenced pistol held by a dark-clothed man. "*Gelieve niet weerstaan*, herr Dosch. Hand away from the weapon. *Ga terug*."

Three armed men swept into the kitchen, subdued Corky, and went down the hall to secure the driver. Johan was relieved of the Walther.

Two more men descended from upstairs. One, a curly haired Frenchman, approached Johan. He examined his face and poked the chin pad.

"Not a bad job. Alright, nothing stupid tonight. It's in both your interests to come along quietly. You seem intelligent so that should be enough said. Do yourselves the favor and prove me right."

Capture felt nothing like he'd imagined it might.

Instead of defiance, cunning, and confidence, he felt like a mouse pinned by a rail spike, hemorrhaging and helpless. Patted down thoroughly, pockets emptied, and their shoes removed, they were herded outside and loaded into a van lined with padded benches. The sound of Oliver's van's tires being punctured accentuated the tense silence.

He held Anki's hand while trying to get a read on the men sitting opposite them. Hard, serious professionals, doing a job.

We're a job.

The curly haired leader climbed in and they departed. That they hadn't shot him on sight was both encouraging and terrifying. The thought of torture was intolerable and gave rise to panic. If they hurt Anki in front of him...

Panic and adrenaline surged. Faintly, he recognized the pressure; the hunters were back, pinging him. At the thought, the curly Frenchman nearly jumped from the passenger's seat to squat in front of him.

"You need to calm down, Mr. Dosch. And you know what I mean."

"The fuck I do."

As if on cue, the pressure surged. He invited it, met its frequency, let it bounce his psyche like a rough massage. He tried following it, to examine the approaching minds to find a way to get to *them*. It was the only hope at offense.

The curly haired leader nodded to the guards. They slammed him face down and yanked his arms behind. Anki lunged to stop them but received a vicious kick. A syringe went into his spine, eliciting a blood curdling scream.

"WHAT THE FUCK!" he shouted. A darkness grew peripherally, threatening to take him. He fought to see Anki one last time.

"No regrets," he said before the world faded to nothing.

• • •

144

Kaiya stood at the window of the ranch house as dawn purpled the horizon and outlined the low-lying hills east of the house. Silence hung in the room, interrupted only by an occasional car or rig on the main highway.

The old couple living here had been tied up and put in a top floor bedroom. It was only temporary but it left her feeling more like a terrorist than anything. The Morgans had no idea who they were and the fear in their eyes hurt. She thought of her mother and the pain tripled. She prayed again they wouldn't go after her.

She put her hand to the window. All hope of clearing her name was gone along with hope for a normal life. Instead, she was wanted for murder and soon, kidnapping. She didn't dare try to imagine what the future would reveal. Their rescuers claimed to be part of a resistance-type group but nothing about them made her feel confident of their motives or character. She couldn't shake the feeling they were from a cult of some kind.

After the dream of Austin there was no falling back asleep. Her world had reduced to wanting a safe place to be with him. More than anything she felt fear. Mac's scanner let them follow the search effort well into the early morning hours. He wanted to leave to avoid a house search. Their rescuers were confident in staying put. She thought of running and pretending to be a hostage herself. In a way she was but it wasn't Mac's fault. She had to remember that there were authorities that wanted one thing from her and beyond that she was likely a liability. She couldn't do that to Mac anyway. As bizarre as things had become, her promise to trust him was the most tangible anchor she had.

He stirred in the bottom bunk. He'd finally fallen asleep after four thirty, not long after her dream woke her. Now his sleep was dream-filled, too, by all his shifting and murmurs. How uncanny it was to have had such a vivid dream. Old London, with Austin. Had he controlled the entire thing? Mind reading and dream control? Not too much of a stretch. She almost laughed. Coming to grips with psychic phenomena was the last thing imaginable just two days ago. Now the reality stared her in the face.

She looked back to the window in time to see figures rush from the shadows across the side yard. "Oh God—" She went to Mac, pushing him awake. "They're in the yard!"

Mac jumped to his feet, gun in hand, and grabbed a shotgun from the floor. "Upstairs." He guided her to the hall. He called out the keyword indicating alarm and got acknowledgement before he led

Kaiya up the stairs. A sharp crack split the silence as a dual-pane window busted downstairs. A second, then third window blew.

They ducked into a craft room facing the hills. Mac sidled up to the window and peeked out. The detached garage was fifteen yards off and mostly obscured from view by a tree. Its side door stood ajar.

"Fucking *fuck*. Why did I listen to them?" More of the flash bangs went off downstairs. She squatted behind a sewing machine.

Mac levered open the double-hung window and punctured the screen, tearing it clear. He poked his head to peer down.

"Do as I do. The AC unit is just below. Swing and fall to the right of it. I'll drop first and cover. Toss the shotgun down before you jump, safety on."

Downstairs, shots rang out staccato, interspersed with streams of automatic fire. Hostages or not, they were coming in to kill. Mac climbed out the window feet first, belly slid to dangle, then slipped from view.

The wood floor cracked open from a stray bullet. The stairs thudded as people stormed up. Blasts of gunfire shook the hall. More rounds popped through the door and wall. She couldn't move. Knew she had to. *Go, God damn it!* She grabbed the shotgun and spun for the window. Flashes lit the yard below. Mac fired once before taking rounds in the chest and face. He fell to the ground in a gruesome sprawl. A black-clad figure appeared from the under the tree's cover to inspect his kill. Without thinking, she lined up the barrel and squeezed the trigger. The shotgun boomed and the figure fell. She ducked away but felt a stinging brand below her collar bone. The door to the bedroom burst open and again flashes accompanied stinging pain – the deafening clatter confirmed she was being shot to death. She went limp under the punches of the bullets and crumpled to the floor.

The gunfire stopped and the room filled with her attackers. Voices sounded, distant and overlapping. Hands were upon her but it didn't matter. The hot flow of blood drenched her neck and chest.

Outward... she flowed outward until the pain receded to a dull memory. A sense of peace settled in. She had begun a journey to a destination more familiar than her own body. She yearned for the returning, wherever it was.

The peaceful flowing abruptly became a suction pulling her *sideways,* away and into a darkness, a sparkling blackness that hinted at much but revealed nothing. Suddenly a passenger, she knew everything – reality itself – was all under control.

Someone *else's* control.

Chapter 11

What is soul? It's like electricity - we don't really know what it is,
but it's a force that can light a room.
- Ray Charles

The last rays of sunlight draped the hillside and pressed the heat of the day against Johan's face. Below lay the village of Bolnuevo, resting at the lip of the Mediterranean. The sands ran several kilometers alongside the boulevard into the town of El Castellar with its sparkling lights. Summer's tourism filled the beaches and dotted the coastal roads with tiny, colorful rentals. The western sky glowed orange and red in a sunset befitting a wildfire. Drink in hand, he stood at the patio's railing and watched for the girls' return from market.

Their arrival in the Spanish coastal region was a blurred memory seen through the haze of painkillers – the garish lights of the avenues, the faces as they drove past, and no memory of the journey there. From the third day in Paris, after learning who their hosts were and their intentions, to their arrival here lay a gap of six days. The last memory was of the anesthesia mask and a woman's reassurance. "Be glad. You'll awaken to your new life."

Six days and no scars, no signs of surgery, only the dull ache beneath. The first glance of his face had a completely unexpected effect: he'd grown dizzy and nauseous. His face wasn't the problem – it was handsome. He'd picked it, helped design it. The problem was, it wasn't *his* face. He'd avoided its reflection since arriving. Stage makeup and fake names were one thing; complete facial reconstruction was something else entirely.

He swirled the last of another pale green margarita in his glass, the ice long melted. Inside, Marco watched television while the two guards took turns appearing at various points around the villa. The Spaniard felt his glance and came out with a bowl of chips to join him at the railing. The sound of waves against the beach reached them, as subdued as the breeze.

"There are worse places to be, eh Johan?"

"I imagine. It is a bit hot."

"Heat brings the soul to the surface." He smiled easily, natural as the hills. "The women took a late lunch in Marazon before market. They're returning now."

"They called?"

Marco shook his head.

"So..."

"The threads tie us together. And we trust. With both, the language forms. Trust, though, that's the thing. Without it, nothing flows, nothing is believable though everything is possible."

"So you just hear her voice in your head?"

"Sometimes. Sometimes I see what she is seeing. Other times I feel her and know what she wants me to." He laughed. "You can try to imagine it but only when you experience it will it make sense."

"How do you separate her thoughts from your own? How can you be sure you're not imagining it?"

Marco's eyes went to the waves approaching the beach. "Because I know myself. Everything else belongs to others."

"Why can you do it and I can't?"

"Why do you *think* you can't do it?" He smiled. "It is expected. For centuries man has existed in the island of his mind. He is taught what he can experience and dream. Inside, he is alone, though he senses others. In days of old, fear of witchcraft, the devil, and madness kept his mind to himself. In modern times, culture, religion, and that same fear of madness does the job. Yet imagination has always demanded more – the soul senses connections. Clues abound but the distractions and fears are greater. Always they are greater. Culture acts like a clamp, cutting us off. Hear voices and something's wrong with you. Ranging too far from the status quo is like a death, no? So imagination is quelled, the soul is redirected, and we are comfortable again, or at least safe. This is the highest form of training. We become more of our society than ourselves. A society of culture that teaches not to trust the undercurrents of our minds." He looked over. "If you can't trust yourself, then nothing can be truly trusted. I've learned to trust myself, far from the status quo. Like most, you haven't."

Subtle, delicate, so fleeting and wild, yet Marco and Rachel had it down. The idea of threads connecting people was familiar. When thinking of Anki, a connection seemed to vibrate, drawing thoughts. However, he was still clumsy with it, unsure. Only in their lovemaking had he been able to surge with her, the proximity obviously a factor. Even then, it all happened instinctually, at a primal level. If he had to convey what time a flight was leaving or even what color he was thinking of, he wouldn't know where to start.

The only encouraging thing Marco mentioned was the importance of trust. The trust between he and Anki had proven deep and genuine, a precursor to a love he couldn't imagine the end of. That trust would help them connect.

"Anki is a special woman, Johan. Your togetherness is not an accident. I have no doubt you will become as close to her as I am to Rachel. Your first trainer arrives tomorrow. As I said before, you have an uncommon awareness about you. You learned quickly on your own and you'll do much better with a trainer."

"I would be a lot happier if she was getting trained, too."

"I understand that. Whatever the reason, her training will begin later. We're as curious as you are about that, believe me."

Johan emptied his glass and nodded towards the road below. "I think that's them."

After dinner, the two couples retreated to the patio chairs. Night had descended fully. Stars floated like bits of ice in the warm, dark sky.

"Johan, you have to stay up late tonight." Rachel dipped bread in an olive oil sauce. "A visitor is coming to see you. I think he wants to talk about computers."

"Sounds like work. Do I need to slow up?" he asked, indicating his drink.

"I don't think it matters much. You know your business," Marco replied.

Half an hour before midnight Johan untangled from Anki, mindful of the time. He had remembered Marco's directive and avoided climax. Denial of such a basic pleasure sucked though it was understandable now – anything to keep off Comannda radar. They'd also stayed quiet out of modesty. He could almost feel Marco's and Rachel's presence flowing around them.

A pair of candles cast shadows that danced on the walls. Anki still lingered in their intimacy while his thoughts wandered. The visitor would arrive soon. What could they want from him? The Overseer system described in the video made the Underground's systems sound like calculators by comparison. Unless it was control over the Underground itself they wanted, wetware as well as the network. Soldado wouldn't like that.

The muted sound of an engine brought him out of bed and to the patio door. A car entered the circular drive.

"Should I stay in bed, or..." Anki spoke soft as the candle light.

He tugged on his cargo shorts and t-shirt. "Try to sleep. I may wake you later."

She smiled. "Please do."

Coming down the stairs, Johan slowed. The front door stood wide open and Rachel sat cross-legged on the long sofa, drink in hand.

"You're no *fun*, Johan."

She referred to them keeping quiet. "And you're a dirty mind-reading girl." He headed for the door.

She laughed and said, "Come, sit here with me." She patted the couch. "Marco's getting your visitor. C'mon, sit."

"I'll take a chair, thanks." He settled into a chair with a view of the door.

"Fine. Marco approves. You know he likes you. He doesn't like many people."

"I find that hard to believe."

"Not when you know what we know. You'll see."

Marco came through the front door followed by a tall brown-skinned man with cropped black hair wearing black jeans and boots. Older than Johan by several years, he moved with alert eyes, apprehension a cloud around him. His eyes darted to Rachel then fixed on him.

Marco waved in his direction. "There's your man. SlotZero himself."

Like a blow from a bat, the use of his Underground name set every muscle on edge. *What the–*

The stranger spoke. "If that's really you Zero, tell me who turned you onto the senator's coke habit?"

There was only one person who could ask that question and only one voice that could bring to mind a Mexican beach bum with a tequila hangover.

"Soldado?"

"Maybe." Still apprehensive. "The senator. Who let you in on that?"

"Jeez, man, his housekeeper, Della. How'd they find you?"

The cloud lifted and he walked over. "SlotZero, you crazy bastard, what the *fuck* have you gotten us into? I hand you the hottest hack on the planet and you end up fucking around with a bunch of psychic voodoo doctors." They shook hands and embraced. "After you dropped the Crosstalk bomb, shit went whack. Still ain't done spinning up, from what they're telling me. It's like a god-damned dream. Biggest BAP ever."

They sat and Soldado told of how the Runa Korda had used the towpath house and its staff as a means to wedge into the Underground. They delivered a compelling communiqué that convinced the brilliant computer scientist that his long term welfare was at stake and that they were his best bet for survival.

"I know when the shit gets so deep you can't take a piss, it's time to find a tree to climb up." He lowered his voice. "Even if it's a cactus."

The sophistication of Soldado's systems impressed them as did the overall organization. They assured him that keeping the Underground intact was a priority provided he completely scrubbed all copies of Crosstalk's file.

"So I did. They said things were about to get too hot for me in Sao Paulo. Said you were holed up in a beach town full of women and could use a hand."

"You saw the video? What'd you make of it?"

He shook his head. "*Madre mia*, that first night. It was like *el Diablo* cracked open my brain."

"I know what you mean."

"Seems like the real fajita but I still can't wrap my mind around it. I'm just moseying up to it, slow-like, seeing what it all means." Soldado eyed Rachel. "With what you can do, you gotta be more powerful than anyone on the planet. 'Cept these overlords. Money's no object and all that?"

Rachel's gave a shrug. "There comes a point where degrees do not matter. With enough money, other things become more important. With power, it is relative. Always relative."

Marco returned balancing a platter with a bottle ringed by shot glasses, salt, and lemon slices. He poured five shots.

"Doubling up, Marco?"

"No, I thought Anki might want a go." He glanced up at the stairs as Anki descended.

"What's this?" she asked. "You can't make Sao Paulo so you bring Sao Paulo to you?"

By half past midnight, Johan and Soldado were telling stories of the Underground, of some of their craziest undertakings. The first blackmail job was of a U.S. senator compromised snorting cocaine at a New York party. They hadn't anticipated the brute force response — whether from the mafia or a very brazen government agency they had never figured out. They'd barely escaped alive. Another early hack job was into the email account of a British rock star that yielded not only embarrassing personal details but sexually explicit photos of underage fans taken inside a tour bus.

"Well who was it?" Rachel asked.

Before they could utter a word against revealing job details, Rachel shook her head. "*Why* I am not surprised?"

Marco finished a mouthful of chips, wiped his hands on his shorts and sat forward in his chair.

"Gentlemen, ladies, time for business. Bear in mind everything on the table is conceptual, theoretical, but still consider yourself under an NDA from hell." He looked to each of them and received acknowledgment. "There is a computer system, the name you know from the video but which I'll call Totem. Its technology won't see the light of industry for another ten years at least. Its number of subservient computers will never be matched, cannot be, until we figure out how they are controlling them. We have computer scientists working to understand what little we've glimpsed of the system and in the last several years they've made great progress."

Rachel joined in. "As advanced as Totem is, its power is exponentialized through communications with ordinary technology. Totem manipulates systems of all types, in every sector across the globe. NSA back doors are written into the products and with them have created a massive parallel computer right under our noses."

Soldado nodded. "We've found some of them. Most recently the Rocom Crest hack. Some are monitored though and self-heal when they see us use them."

"Those are the latest generation hacks and it isn't the NSA monitoring them. It's the system itself. Totem is artificially intelligent. When I say that, I don't mean superbots that know how to sort shit out hyper-efficiently and blip it back in a useful way. I mean truly artificially intelligent, like a jackhammer is artificially strong, or a plane artificially flies. It *is* intelligent. Likely more so than humans."

"Hold up," Soldado said. "Faster, sure. Better memory, neuristic programming, all that I get. But more *intelligent?*"

Rachel answered. "You have to understand, they have always kept ahead of technology, by decades in some cases. NSA had computers running at 650mhz in the mid-1960's. It took twenty years for that technology to reach the world. As for the AI, coming from a computer scientist, I see you're in denial. You know well what's possible. "

"*Possible*, yes, but... Christ, that's not something I want to imagine. You can't unleash a self-learning entity on the net and expect it to be your puppy. A machine smarter than its creators could get creative with its assets, you know? And if it's got hooks into the world's computers? I mean *shit*, what are they thinking? That's not a virus, that's total loss of control on a global basis. Infrastructure could collapse. They're in danger as much as we are."

Marco nodded, "Now you're getting it. Self-awareness allows it to constantly rewrite itself, improving functionality as it learns, defining new functionality based on needs. The more information it has the better informed it is in making decisions and deductions – which in turn triggers rewriting itself to take advantage of the knowledge. It's a system of exponents and has compounded with amazing results, I'm sure. So far, there's no reason to believe it's gotten out of hand. Quite the opposite. It appears to be serving their interests like a surgeon's knife. Which is why we've had to adjust our operations substantially over time."

"Still," Soldado sat back, taking it in, "it could splinter and set up its own control domains. By the time they realize it, it will be too late. I'd bet my left cheek on that."

Johan stared at the salsa dip, quietly intoxicated. The Comannda's strings weren't just psychic in nature – they had been hardwired into the systems of the world. Anyone with that much control could set the stage however they chose, far into the future.

Anki spoke up. "Seems to me you could do more in the grid to help uncover the tech. Remote viewing and all that."

"You can only go so many places undetected and then hope to be in the right place at the right time to get the right information. And there are ways of blocking remote viewing. It's not a sure thing, especially with our limited numbers. We need a way in to their networks."

Soldado stood and swayed as he walked to the full length window. The city lights blended like embers covering the coast. "And to find a way in, you need to know how it talks." He leaned heavily against the window frame. "How exactly can I help?"

Marco said, "We have found an entrance but it isn't on their data network. It's on their voice network."

"Wireless?"

"Yes. We've built prototypes capable of ingesting the very wide range of frequencies we see involved and even have a start on the analysis of their sequencing. Some encouraging results but we need fresh eyes on the problem. If we can break their sequencing it could change everything. You'll have to talk to the white coats. After going over your Alcazar system, they think you have the kind of mind that may be able to help."

Soldado nodded, obviously touched in exactly the right place.

"Well shit, in that case," he raised his glass, "I reckon I'd be happy to try."

• • •

When the hot evening air shifted, the stench from the defecation ditch became overpowering – it was all Austin could do to avoid gagging. Ten o'clock and temps were still in the nineties in the homeless camp along the L.A. river. He and his trainer, Javier, lay on their backs in their cardboard and pallet shelter. Light from atop a nearby utility pole shone through gaps.

He wiped sweat from under his chin and avoided touching his face. It was his now, except it wasn't, not yet. Angles, proportion, skin tone, hair color and density, eye positioning; all of it matched what he'd previewed. An incredible job, done with technology beyond anything he'd imagined possible. Most of it made little sense, procedures ending in 'lasty', but in short, it was craniofacial surgery taken to the extreme: bone shavings and grafts, arterial rerouting, muscular retensioning, nerve bed repositioning, vocal fold tweaking, along with the custom chops on ears, eyelids and lips. Active DNA programming tweaked additional aspects of his body, though they would name only a few. When asked what color eyes and hair he'd like, he assumed colored contacts and hair dye. The doctor shook his head. "No, your eyes and hair color will change. Here," he pointed to the screen at an array of eye colors and patterns. "Your iris will be redesigned according to the option you select."

"That's pretty serious surgery, on the eyes. Takes a long time, doesn't it?" He really wanted to know if it was safe.

"It takes about five minutes to get the process started. Our little helpers do the rest of the work." When pressed, the surgeon would only add, "Really small robots. And yes, it's infinitely safe."

The most substantial change was an experimental adjustment in the number and type of proteins and their concentrations in his brain, specifically ones that involved neutrotransmission. The quantum function enhancement Marcel had spoken of would be achieved through these and other modifications. Just how he hadn't been told yet. His training so far had been focused on meta and how to use it.

The camp's residents began to rise after the day's lethargy, restless and vocal. Their vibes filled the night and filled his mind. Some were guarded, others totally open, while still others were simply unreachable due to their mental states – like trying to read moving hieroglyphics by strobe light. Since the first day Javier had been guiding him like a second mind. Good thing because surfing meta was frightening. Javier admitted it was a nightmare at the start. "That's what keeps people separated. You gotta be fucking crazy to try it. Your mods and training set you up right to process it. Remember, the light touch, the flowing stream. Let nothing sink in. Read, don't be. All that Marcel shit. It's not so bad once you get your head around it."

It didn't take long and proved amazing. The trick was to subdue one's own thoughts and *listen*. Listening meant focusing rathad yet relaxing it, a paradoxal awareness that at first felt counterintuitive. But by letting go and tuning in, he reached the sweet zone where a kind of inner vision formed. Other people's thoughts faded in and out. Understanding took patience and care not to pollute with one's own thoughts. Dropping things into their streams required the most gentle of touches, a smooth and flowing interaction. The results were often more predictable than not. Questions yielded answers. Feelings yielded moods. Moods yielded greater control. Once he began recognizing the patterns and language, everything began to click. People were, in fact, more similar than they were different.

The heat hovered like a sadistic enemy. Javier resumed in a low voice, providing a lengthy discourse on the dangers of expanding the focus of rathad. He then demonstrated a concept mentioned earlier in training that Austin had had trouble imagining.

"A lot going on," Javier said.

He nodded and wiped sweat from his closed eyes. "Yup."

"What's the overriding feeling? For the group mind?"

"Hard to say. Some are better at this kind of life than others. A lot of hunger, despair, tinges of madness. It's tough. People are just barely existing."

Then, like a pup being picked up by its mother, the din and multiplicity of the camp fell away. Rathad grew until he lost himself and became part of something he could never have imagined – instead of the many minds clamoring, there was only one mind, unified and existing *because of* the many. One feeling, thinking, reacting *being*. Twenty human entities directed the ebb and flow. Base instincts, thoughts, emotions. Needs, wants, moods. A pulsing, intelligent but mostly instinctual awareness. It weighed on some, was changed by others. Beyond each person's conscious thought, they existed within that single mind, contributing and relying on it to varying degrees. They belonged to it, helped create it. It was the raw framework for all social interaction.

To recognize it so clearly blew him off balance. All at once, he felt loud and awkward, as if he were standing in the front row of a movie theater, drawing the crowd's attention.

"Chillio, man," Javier warned. "Bring it back. I mean it."

"Holy shit. Dude, I... *goddamn*." Perspective grew. "It gets bigger'n that, doesn't it? There's strings to other people, groups within groups. There's gotta be a mind for the whole planet!"

Javier scaled back and drew him away from the feeling.

"Relax, Dexter, take a breather. It's a *grid*, man. It's all fucking *connected*. Don't act surprised. And don't try going up higher unless you wanna get us picked off. I'm dead serious hombre. Don't go up any farther or I'll kill you my goddamned self."

He sat up and looked to Javier, who shook his head.

"Ah shit, here it comes. I fuckin' knew it."

"There's life out there, isn't there?" Austin asked. "In the universe? Real life, smart like us. Better, though. More advanced. I think I feel it."

Javier laughed. "You think?"

"Well, yeah I do."

"No shit."

"What do you know, man? About them. Talk to me."

Javier opened his eyes. "What the fuck? This ain't story time."

"Come on, seriously man. Something, anything."

Javier thought for a moment before replying. "Something? Alright, here's something, then you're gonna drop it. Got it? We're a backwater rock with absolutely nothing special about us except maybe how fuckin' stupid we are. Thank the Comannda for that. That's it. That's something. Now fuckin' pay attention. If you poke upstream all stupid like you just did, the Commas be all over you. They *monitor* that shit. Go up like that and you might as well hold up a sign sayin' 'come shoot me, please'. You got to be *passive*. No matter what you receive or how it makes you feel. Otherwise you can just slap that sign on your head and get yourself killed. Play it close. Real close and real passive."

"So there's been contact?"

"Jesus Christ, I said drop it."

"You don't understand, I really need to–"

"Oh yeah, yeah, I know. A lifelong dream to know about aliens. Listen cuz I'm not sayin' it again: we're just another ant mound, got it? We're *boring* beyond our catalog value."

"What do you–"

"You're not listening dude. It's not my fuckin' job to *tell you* anything. Now, you gonna shut up or do I gotta make you?"

Austin stared at the cardboard floor. Green ink lettering indicated Bounty paper towels, thirty rolls in a box. Whatever Javier knew about aliens had the potential for not being good.

"I'll need to know more."

Javier grunted. "You'll know more when you're supposed to. You got a problem with that?"

The question came loaded with seriousness and finality. He checked himself. "No problem."

"Thank God. Now let's get to it."

He cautioned further about the dangers of merging into someone else's flow. The resulting sense of power from manipulating others could poison even the most pristine of souls.

"There ain't nothing pure about this. When you do it, go in quietly, do your business, and get out clean. Never leave an idea of yourself, no imprint. You are *them*. You are *familiar*. You help to form *their thoughts*. *You* don't exist. And finally: don't like it. Comprendè? You do this only when you absolutely fucking have to."

"I get it."

"You better. It's time," Javier mumbled and sat up. "The brothers are at the hut under the freeway. Get into position. Remember, you have to be in their line of sight or it don't count."

The breeze shifted direction and the air cleared briefly. The test involved the engagement of hostile targets and required that he manipulate them into fighting amongst themselves – without drawing attention to himself.

He asked, "If you see me running, how about some help?"

Javier shook his head. "If you screw it up that bad, Marcel can have you back."

"Great." He crouch-walked to the door made of political lawn signs, unhooked the soda can alarm system, and pushed out into the night. No matter how close he and Javier became, the bulky ankle band reminded him of an underlying reality.

He walked through the camp, past the other lean-tos and tents towards the freeway stanchions where a wooden hut stood in the shadows of the overpass. A burst of laughter preceded one of the men dodging out into the light of a streetlamp. Easily over six feet, he was lean and muscled.

He slowed near a group of three homeless men sitting outside a tent playing cards on a blanket.

"Mind if I watch? Haven't played cards in months."

"Why watch when you can play? Jacob's my name." He held out a hand which Austin shook. "This is Eric and that's Lance. We'll deal ya in next hand. Playin' for sticks and stones, the currency of our ancestors." Each withdrew portions to create a starter stack for him. "Sticks are worth five to the inch, rounded down. Stones are ones no matter the size."

"Sounds great, thanks. I'm Aaron." He sat cross-legged facing the wood hut thirty strides away. The gang's banter echoed across the camp. Someone had scored some weed.

"Be rollin' that shit, man, let's smoke!" Agreement echoed. Austin's eyes adjusted. There were six of them outside the hut.

"Chill, you mofucks, I's got to *sell* this stankweed. Ima roll one up but don't be sweatin' my cock fo no mo, got it?"

They were definitely in a good mood. The test had just become harder.

Jacob began dealing cards. "Alright Aaron, you're in."

Austin relaxed and centered rathad. Passively, as natural as the night air, he extended to the gang and let the information come. Immediately, a darker strand stood out. One of the men wasn't excited like the others. He glanced over, hoping to pinpoint the one. A correlation formed from the shadows: right side, sitting on the ground. There was the wedge; the dude was not happy. He narrowed focus. The guy with the weed, Clarence, owed him money.

"You're up," Jacob said.

"Ah. Um, gimme two." He tossed two cards down.

Jacob dealt him new ones. "So what part of the world you from, Aaron?"

Couldn't avoid the chat. *Three eights.* "Norcal. Sac. How about you guys?"

Jacob started in about his home of Freetown, Massachusetts, where his great granddaddy made rifles for the North in the Civil War. Jacob was a good talker, a real story-teller, which made it that much harder to tune him out.

Yes, the guy with weed owed his target money. It pissed him off but he was holding back to insure he got what he wanted. The tension beneath had violence at its roots.

Armed with the insight, Austin could work the situation with precision. He shifted focus to Clarence and pushed the already strong feeling of gloating and accomplishment. Switching back to the guy on the ground, he laid in more anger, more pellets of feeling to fuel the fire. The wedge grew on its own.

Not so hard, after all.

Something snapped in his target. "Yo Clarence, why don't you kick down some dough like you said you was? You's supposed to settle up last week. I want my bones!"

The bullshitting stopped. Clarence went defensive. "Fuck that, Phil. You done already got yours couple days 'go! How much you think that smack cost me, homeboy?"

Done deal. Wedge in. His target, Phil, was ready to fight. The rising argument was the perfect excuse to fold and head back to Javier. Bailing camp to return to civilization would be heavenly.

Movement caught his eye. Clarence went tumbling to the ground under the streetlamp's wash.

"Get the fuck *back*, niggas! That's you, bitch! You, too!"

An arm extended from the shadows, pointing a gun sideways at Clarence. His target, Phil, came into the light. He was skinny with wild hair and baggy shorts. "I ain't fuckin 'round you smelly ass nigga! You owe me eighty-two motherfuckin' dollahs! I *rolled* that white boy and you done *lost it* – lost my *bank!*"

Austin tried to push calm but Phil was all sparks and rage.

"Christ, they were just havin' a party," Jacob turned to have a look. "Shit, gun."

Still on the ground, Clarence crab-walked backwards, the bag of weed flopping in one hand. "Chill the fuck out, Phil, goddamn! You ain't gotta–"

The muzzle flashed and the report split the night. "Chill *that!*"

Clarence must have took a bullet yet still he flipped over and launched into a sprint, catching another bullet with the first step. He shrieked in pain but kept running. The poker party came into the line of fire and all four scrambled for cover. Shots popped. Clarence screamed and made a running leap over them towards the row of tents. Austin rolled left and stopped in time to see Jacob's skull erupt dark red. The son of a Freetown tile worker fell forward, grunted once, and went still.

The shooter started after Clarence then suddenly went slack. As if a switch was thrown, legs and arms folded in ragdoll fashion. His thin frame hit the ground in a heap.

The camp was in motion with people running away from the gunfire. Only Javier strode forward, concerned and scanning. He knelt next to Jacob and confirmed the man's state.

"Let's go."

There were no police, no sirens as they walked. Cars flowed on the overpass; people strolled the sidewalks beyond the camp. The city continued to breath when it seemed it should have been holding its breath in shock. Austin wasn't sure if he cared about Clarence or Phil, but he did about Jacob. His training had caused an innocent man's death.

Javier elbowed him. "Look, it's unfortunate. I didn't see it coming neither. But 'parently it's the way it was s'posed to happen, so you better not lose the lesson."

"And which lesson is that? Not to go fucking around in people's minds just because I can?"

Javier shook his head in disgust, keeping a stride.

"Alright, alright. Excuse the rookie?" he tried, embarrassed. "But it's tough. That shit was tough. Say it wasn't."

Javier looked over. "That shit was *unfortunate*. There's worse things will happen, I guaranfuckingtee you that, esse. But you go *on*. As *long* as you can. As *smart* as you can." He walked in silence before adding in a lower voice, "We are the few that hafta do this, so one day the many will be free. And it ain't gonna be fuckin' easy. Dying's part of what we're buying. Deal with it."

He got it. Worse, he understood.

"Then my dad – he's already dead?"

Javier blinked. "I ain't heard. But if he is, whatchya gonna do 'bout it?"

They approached the parking lot of the motel. Javier unlocked the room and called dibs on the shower.

Austin fell onto the nearest bed, his world reeling. Dad and Yuni dead? He wouldn't even imagine it. *No reason to.* He stayed in the moment, lying in his dirty clothes, sweating. To wash it all off, everything; he couldn't want anything more. Except maybe cold air. The air conditioner knob was missing but he managed to crank the post two notches to max. Cool air flowed with a hum.

He asked, "So was that a pass or a fail?"

Javier shrugged and pulled off his shirt. "You did okay. You got the basics. You need practice now." Tattoos told stories across his chest and stomach.

"What about the shooter? Why'd he go down like that?"

The Mexican continued shedding his grimy street clothes and disappeared into the bathroom. Just before the door closed, he answered.

"I took him out."

The '81 El Camino pulled to the side of the road and its lights died. Javier and Austin emerged and headed across the grass towards the steep dirt path into the moon-lit hills. Dry brush scraped at their tan khaki uniforms. Near the top, Javier halted. Austin stopped to catch his breath. Behind them, the grid that was L.A. lit the night. Headlights on the Ventura Freeway just below them merged with the I-5 flow coming in from the north. Electric blue, white, red, orange, green – the grid shone with life and activity, the markings of man's presence for the heavens to see.

Javier gazed out on the city with unmistakable love. "You know, we made it this far. Just think of what we can do with the right help."

He fought the urge to ask more questions and worked on filtering his thoughts. The previous night's killings still haunted him. Jacob and the gang banger, Philip, both dead but by two entirely different means. That someone could kill with a thought disturbed him more than he wanted to admit. The meta arts implied as much darkness and evil as they did light and goodness. Again he thought of his dad and Yuni and suppressed anxiety. Forming an island in his mind wasn't easy.

Javier looked at him. "You like animals?"

"Love 'em. Why?"

"Just curious. Got your breath?"

"Yeah." He followed Javier up the path. They crested the ridge and stepped onto a winding dirt road. The half-moon cast dim shadows under their feet. "So what are we doing?"

"Gonna see an animal that's a lot like us."

"Monkey?"

"Chimpanzee."

"Secret mission to the chimps?"

"Now that you know about listening and pushing, you're gonna try it with a chimp."

"What's the point?"

"What, you got somethin' against chimps?"

Javier waited for the hum of an electric cart driven by a security guard to pass by before scaling a fence. With a surge of adrenaline, Austin followed and joined Javier in dashing into the Los Angeles zoo.

Unchallenged, they approached an exhibit. Lights shone in a building where a woman sat with a small chimp in her arms. Javier walked up and tapped the glass. She waved him in.

"Did anyone see you?" she asked.

Javier shook his head. "Nope."

"Why did you insist on sneaking in? I could've picked you up at the gate."

"And where's the fun in that?" Javier winked. "Christine, this is my friend, Allen. Christine and I go way back to grade school. So this is the little guy?"

"Little girl. She's sick and we don't know what's wrong. Her breathing is labored as you can see. Tests have all come up negative. She's been running a low-grade fever for over a week, isn't responding to antibiotics, and has been eating less and less every day. At this rate she isn't going to make it on her own."

Javier nodded. "We'll sit with her for a while."

"Her name's Darcy. I really hope you can do something. I've never tried a psychic healing but at this point I'm willing to try anything." She handed the diaper-clad baby chimp over to Javier. "I'll be back in about ten minutes. Thanks again, J.P." She nodded at Austin. "And thank you, Allen."

He glanced at Javier after Christine left.

"Psychic healing?"

Javier shrugged. "Never mind. Here," he extended the chimp to him. "Take her."

"Wha– okay. What's this about, man?" He took the tiny chimp. Its eyes were half-lidded and it weighed almost nothing. "And why'd we hike the hills?"

"You're out of shape, esse! You need the exercise." He pointed to Darcy. "See what you can learn from her. Free form, forget English. Just tell me what you get from her."

"Alright, I'll do my best." He sat down with the chimp on his lap.

The most surprising thing right off was the sentience, not too unlike humans. First in her eyes, then when he went passive to listen. There was no English of course, but a kind of language she used in her thoughts, a visual structure. How it worked wasn't clear; it didn't seem to have the same flow that humans did. For several minutes he just sat with her and let her weak grip on his index finger be their bonding point. He listened further, getting nearer to sinking into her awareness. She sensed his closeness and her eyes opened a bit more, curious. Something passed from her then, a missive, a kind of message destined not for within, but beyond her. Meant for him.

He couldn't read it; in his surprise, he'd missed it.

Darcy stared at him, her eyes intense. Again she passed a meaning, a vibration that held a message. This time he followed intuition and sensed it as he would a picture. Like magic, the unknown resonance formed into almost graphical understanding: her lungs ached. She was depressed.

He waited, passive but nodding his head. She sent another message resonance. Hard to breathe. Hungry. Another resonance conveyed her scooping up a white substance from the rocks and putting it her mouth. It returned again and again.

He looked up at Javier. "This is amazing."

"Describe it."

"You... you get what she's showing me, right?"

Javier shook his head no.

"What's this mean, Javier? Am I really communicating with this chimp? Or am I going nuts?"

"Depends on if she asked for your number or not."

"That's not even funny."

"Can you merge with her?"

He could only stare back and wonder why Javier wanted to know. Curiosity led him back to Darcy, though, to try.

Close in, she was weak and suffering more from depression than the pain or hunger. He drew closer still and gently extended into her thought stream. Vividly, he saw his own face looking down at her, mouth etched into a concerned frown, his eyes focused beyond. She squirmed a bit, uncomfortable with his visit, though overall trusting. He stayed passive, filled with wonder at the realization that if he wanted to, he could control her quite easily. Far different than the homeless people. Naturally pliable.

The side door opened, bringing him out. Darcy started a bit and looked for assurance, her grip tighter on his finger. An eager Christine returned and squatted in front of the little chimp with a concerned look.

"Any luck?"

"Maybe. I'm seeing her eat something white from the rocks. Maybe someone threw something poisonous?"

"It's possible, I suppose. Something white? One of the – oh wait! *Shit!*" She laughed, half in disbelief for having missed it and half in relief. "Bird poop! Darling's disease. A fungal disease that mimics T.B. We tested for T.B. but not for fungal. She probably ate bird poop!"

"It fits with what I saw."

Christine's eyes welled up. "Oh my God, you are amazing, Allen. I'm sure that's it, I can feel it. Oh, bless you. I'm going to draw blood right now. Thank you, thank you!" She stood and hugged both Darcy and Austin.

He tried sending Darcy his own resonance message to show how much he wished for her recovery and health. In a response so quick he almost missed it, Darcy asked if she was going to be okay. Getting the hang of it, he responded just as fast to show that Christine was going to do her best to help her.

"Bye-bye, lil girl. Hang in there."

In her brown eyes he saw gratitude.

Two weeks later, Austin sat on the porch steps of the doublewide. The L-shaped trailer park had nineteen units, mostly singlewides parked on a slab of west Compton. A boxed patch of grass held a makeshift kid's playground with a sun-bleached plastic slide. The water treatment facility on the other side of the chain link fence created an occasional refrain from a pump motor bearing going bad. Soft rays of the sun cresting the distant Chino Hills belied its intentions for the day. The heat wave would continue summer's tradition in the basin.

The thrumming of the city arrested awareness, a slow riptide pulling his thoughts into the mundane, the ordinary. Ten million souls inside four thousand square miles. Practicing on the throwaways of society meant a lot of change and not just in his psychic abilities. Both guilt and gratitude colored his days and nights with them. They were people imbued with the same god-like powers he was developing but without hope of realizing them. Those naturally aware often ended up suffering mental illness without the framework to process their extraordinary senses. The salve was the thought that someday humanity might not be so lost in the evolutionary backwaters and that he could help forge a path. Still, it was hard to imagine a graceful transition, even without the Comannda. All the fear and greed and division would take years to overcome. Generations.

He rested his jaw in his palm, fingertips to lips. *His* lips. Squinting brought an unfamiliar bulge of flesh beneath his eyebrows into view. Narrow eyes. Hazel now. Harder. Mom always loved his almond-shaped eyes. Both Mom and his face were gone, victims of an unpredictable world. One lost to a drunk driver, the other to a system drunk with power.

The trailer's screen door creaked and banged shut. Miguelito stepped around him on the stairs.

"You got news, hombre." Javier's son headed for the bus stop. He turned and walked backwards. "It's been good getting to know you, mang. See you around, you know? Be coolio!"

With a wave he turned and didn't look back, a happy teenager living with incredible secrets.

Inside, Javier sat watching cartoons and slurped up colorful cereal from a bowl. With one hand he pulled a necklace out from under his shirt and fingered a pendant. There was a click and the ankle band opened and fell out from Austin's pants leg.

"Important people wanna hang out with you. Don't ask me why." He half-smiled. "Instructions on the counter. Hope you can read 'em. You got half an hour."

A clean-shaven Austin stepped from a house into a waiting Subaru, suitcase in tow. The clothes felt wonderful: clean blue jeans that fit snug, blue cotton t-shirt, and running shoes. No more baggy jeans and wife-beaters. It didn't feel good not knowing the fate of their parents but he couldn't change that, yet.

"Relax," Javier had said. "This is a big meeting so don't freeze up about the folks. I'm sure they're all right."

The woman who'd picked him up from the strip mall near the trailer park was a utility only, a non-Korda following directions. She handed him a sealed envelope. "Please read this before your flight, Mr. Crichlow."

His back-story was provided in the form of a resume, a set of working notes, and a printout of a dating service profile. Thin and simple, easily adapted. He skimmed it. Allen Crichlow. Technical sales rep for a Glendale, California based software company. Names of managers, product lists, descriptions, all familiar technology he could fake knowledge of in a pinch. Single, living in nearby Eagle Rock. Cat named Javier. *Cute.* He'd have time on the flight to commit it all to memory.

The woman dropped him off at the airport. He stood on the sidewalk with a new identity and a plane ticket to London. First time overseas, for a vacation. Coach class? He rubbed his chin and decided he didn't mind at all.

He was free to move about the planet.

A window seat afforded a view of the eastern coast at night, lit up as it had been in the lucid dream a lifetime ago. Then, Austin had sought the hacker and felt a dark, textured energy of a place with complex designs emanating intelligence. Now, as land receded and dark ocean took its place, he half-expected the tiger's head to appear. Instead a stranger's face stared back in the window's reflection. The person he'd become was almost as unfamiliar.

He'd smoked pot a little in high school. Like sugar poured into water, boundaries dissolved along with coherency and identity. Something like that was happening now but over the course of weeks, not minutes or hours, and it wasn't fading. In this, he was keeping up, learning his place, discovering reality instead of exploring a temporary high.

He closed his eyes. Mental restraint was as much a survival skill as learning to perceive beyond himself. Expressing elevated awareness risked attention, examination. People were used to the type of contact born of ignorance, a language of protective responses and basic civility. Intelligent awareness made people uncomfortable, made people notice. Javier had jammed that into his head so hard he probably had bruises. *Do not give them your imprint. Do not give* anyone *reason to remember you. You are a boring fuck. Only boring fucks stay alive.* Even passively, there was more to learn about people around him than they would willingly reveal. Already he'd confirmed that preoccupation with sex was a driving theme and not just with men. At its best, it was tasteful and provocative; at its worst, evil and debasing. By far the most common vibe was that of depression. It weaved itself through most minds, even if only intermittently, pervading the group mind like an unshakeable background melody. Part of him wanted to help, to emit a soothing, reassuring vibe to help lift everyone on the plane. Though strongly tempted, he knew it would be an advertisement to the Comannda and might even backfire. Experiments had to wait. Instead, he spent the first couple of hours sifting through his meta-store of memories, reliving them in a lucid state of recall. It definitely beat the in-flight movie about a senator's wife falling in love with the president.

Halfway through the flight he finished memorizing Allen Crichlow's dossier. Dozens of questions stood out, things he'd need to properly cover his ass. So much left for imagination. If this was to be a primary identity there better be a whole lot more coming.

An attendant appeared and offered a pillow. Her long hair made him think of Kaiya.

"Please, thanks."

Every night since their time in old London, he'd taken pills before sleeping as insurance against dreams. More mystery. They would only say it was crucial he take them, that his life could depend on them. The warning had seemed more than a bit overdone. He touched a pill in his jeans pocket. The thought of catching Kaiya in a lucid dream was a powerful draw.

In a plane traveling over the dark Atlantic, he could say he nodded off without realizing it...

He re-stuffed the envelope and sat on it, reclined his chair, and relaxed. Someone nearby had freshened their perfume. The scent somehow brought to mind Paris or the Mediterranean. He recalled the last evening at Kaiya's trying to break the cipher code. In slow motion he saw the expression in her eyes, the curve of her lips, her hair as it fell forward like silk. Memories flowed, comforting and familiar. Eventually the drone of the engines and the hiss from the overhead air vents lulled him toward the shoreline of sleep.

He dreamt, but not lucidly.

In the din of a darkened manufacturing plant, lights slid past. He lay on a moving conveyor belt and watched behemoth machines pulse red, orange, and green. Robotics worked busily all around, hissing and beeping in a random symphony. He sat up. The high ceiling, dominated by a domed skylight, lit up from the flash of spot welding.

Beyond the skylight the Milky Way galaxy made a brilliant spectacle and dwarfed whatever facility he was in. He looked down the conveyor and saw a split point ahead where a connector belt veered left and his continued straight.

The split point approached, as did a vague uneasiness. The random tones and static started to fire differently, slowly arranging into a semblance of order. He glanced up at the skylight just as two long shooting stars crisscrossed the night sky to form a symmetrical X, as if the planet were being marked from outer space.

The conveyor carried him along. Thirty feet remained to the split point. Twenty five. *Stay or roll left?*

Something was wrong. The machines' cacophony was a signal. Straining to find meaning in the halting patterns, he looked up once more and saw a bright greenish-white comet streak down past the skylight on a trajectory that could only lead to the factory's grounds. Then, as if in frustration, the machines formed an unmistakable pattern, delivered with a sudden increase in volume.

"SYS-TEM!" And again, "SYS-TEM!" He passed the split point, the divider now alongside him.

"LEFT! LEFT! LEFT!" The machines vocalized perfectly.

He lashed out and grabbed hold of the divider, the belt like sandpaper tearing at his clothes. He rotated to get his feet against the divider then pulled and bounced with all his strength until he fell onto the other conveyor path. It trundled along while he examined the raw and bleeding skin beneath his torn clothing.

The machines were looping now, a soft rolling pattern that sounded like 'woo... woo', over and over. It was a sound of relief or contentment that made him wonder what danger he had avoided. Slowly it broke up until the tones returned to random patterns.

An overhead paging system crackled to life, the voice drably male. "You are approaching Ring One's boundaries. Please review your programming guide and select only the appropriate programs for the core. Thank you."

Ahead in the dim light of the plant, the conveyor belt ended in a huge rotating Petri dish. Dozens of skeletons lined its edges. He tried scrambling back but the conveyor tore at his hands. The belt folded underneath and he dropped down into the glass enclosure. The walls stood over twice his height, too slippery and high to scale. A glance at the skylight revealed low clouds, possibly smoke, obscuring the view of the galaxy.

He shouldn't have trusted the machines.

The dream paused then, as if time was a component and not a constant. It slowly dissolved and left him awake and uncomfortable in his seat.

The hour before dawn in the County of London proved delightful. Cool air and openness helped counteract the long flight. He'd slept until landing but memory of the dream had left a funk. Threaded with symbolism, it felt threatening and worse, relevant. The treadmill fit, a perfect representation of life since the file arrived. He'd trusted the machines only to find out they were part of a trap. An allegory for the Runa Korda? The comet, a symbol for what? Alien contact? And why didn't it impact? Or had it? The petri dish was the most revealing because it mirrored the feeling he'd had since the hospital – that he was an experiment. Or perhaps it was mankind that was the experiment.

Following instructions, he arrived by cab at the Hilton at Canary Wharf. The hotel stood sleek and modern, surrounded by the Thames River on three sides. Checking in was a slightly nervous affair. The clerk's awareness was palatable, reading his vibe without revealing much of her own. Javier's training kicked in and he babbled about how excited he was to be in London for the first time. The business visitor slash tourist. *The boring fuck.* Nothing shifted in the woman. He accepted his room card and thanked her without having gleaned a drop of information from her. Naturally contained or something more?

He headed for the elevators. Spots of energy drew his eye; every time it was either a person or a hotel security camera. *Could meta energy be seen? Transmitted via electronics?* The questions he'd forgot to ask piled up.

He entered his room on the thirteenth floor where full length windows revealed a sunrise breaking over central London. In the mirrored wall of the entry he saw the face he'd chosen. Handsome but not striking. Average but not boring.

He unpacked and took a shower. All his little scars were absent, replaced with new ones. As amazing as their body crafting expertise was, it all paled compared to the timeframe in which it had occurred, including the healing. No incision lines, no suture marks of any kind. The doctor had declined explaining how, saying only, "You are in fortunate company, Austin, in fortuitous times. However, I recommend not getting hit in the face in the next couple of weeks."

The meeting at a pub in the Epping Forest on the outskirts of London wasn't until dinner time. They presumed he'd sleep but for the moment the thought wasn't desirable nor were the instructions to stay put in his room. Instead, hunger and visions of a big English breakfast led him to the door for a walk. The hotel restaurant couldn't be too much a travel violation.

The phone rang on the night stand. He went to answer it.

A stranger's voice said sternly, "Tsk, tsk. Use room service. Check your pillow, now." The line clicked off. They were with him, then. He had to tear open a pillow to retrieve a cell phone from its center. It booted up and within seconds rang.

"Greetings, program." The same stranger's voice, now clipped from encryption. "I know I suggested Germany or Thailand but I suppose London will have to do."

"Ramaet?"

"Not a name you should repeat, but yes. I couldn't resist being the one to call. Heard you've been through hell. Again, I'm sorry for that. Can't say I didn't try to warn you, though."

"Why did you send it to me?"

"Got to save something for tonight. Order up breakfast, take a nap, watch the tube, but don't leave the room until quarter of five and keep the phone with you. See you at dinner."

The sheer enchantment of the forest rolling past the cab's windows mesmerized. The woods suspended energy, lingering with memories that spanned centuries. Austin almost expected a band of knights on horseback or a king's hansom under escort to appear up the road.

Despite the mansions, cottages, and small stores dotting the countryside, the woods dominated with their aged splendor and stories. They quietly tolerated the artificial growth around them. A shady glade surrounded by a dense thicket of trees came into view, its opening like an arch formed by Arthur's magician. The desire to enter the glade and process the energy nearly made him halt the cab. Things had happened in that clearing. A great many things in time. It was sad to see the driver oblivious to it all. His mood was that of civilized irritation at having to drive so far from the busywork of the city. All the lost tips.

The cab slowed in front of an old four-story hotel with the words 'Kings Oak' lettered across the second story. The pub was on the first floor with a crowd packed in, visible through windows. A parking lot brimmed with people coming and going. A wedding reception was underway somewhere on the grounds, evidenced by a decorated limo in the lot. Half a dozen touring motorcyclists pulled away as Austin paid the driver. He enjoyed the driver's surprise and relief at the remarkable tip.

"Hey chap! Yes, Allen, isn't it?"

A pudgy Brit stepped forward, hand out – the kind of Brit that looked out of place without a butler's uniform. "Don't think me daft but I'm up from the residence down the road, sent to fetch you. Martin Williams." They shook hands. "The pub's full and while the restaurant's a muster at Mexican food, the steak is sometimes a tad naff. If you'll come with me, there's a proper English dinner scheduled for you and friends."

"I think you're mistaken, I'm to meet someone here for dinner. Perhaps you're thinking of another Allen?"

His red cheeks rounded in a smile. "*Back in* the day... I'd have thought maybe. But no, I am well acquainted with your face. Please, dallying won't do. Maybe this will help."

The cell phone in his pocket vibrated with a text.

"Might want to check that."

Go with him. -Edward

He could only nod. "Lead the way, Martin."

"Please, call me Williams."

They set out in a sleek brown Jaguar XF. Williams pointed to a sweeping open space the size of a football field as he drove.

"High Beech, birthplace of the British Speedway."

"Car racing?"

Williams shook his head. "Motorcycles. Dirt track racing, 1928. Imagine thirty thousand people crushed in and around that expanse. Yes, thirty thousand. 'Twas all the rage. They'd only expected about four thousand. Oh the crashes! Bloody marvelous times those were."

Dense forest lined the road on their left, manor houses to their right. A formidable estate loomed, surrounded by wrought iron fencing. A spiral tower rose from the third story. A mansion sprawled in an L-shape to cup the grounds in a cozy manner. Williams steered towards the already swinging gate. A stone driveway led to a roundabout with a water fountain in the center. To the left, the driveway split off towards a shaded garage area. Williams pulled up in front of stairs that led to a pair of oversized doors inlaid with stained glass.

"And welcome to Shamrock," he said, climbing from the car.

"Shamrock?" He paused, aware of a gathering sense of enigma. Almost physical, the flow took its place amidst other impressions.

"Aye." Williams opened the stained glass doors to a foyer with another, much smaller fountain at its center. "They're gathered in the gazebo down back, enjoying the snacks Edward insists upon. He'll spoil his dinner, filling up. Often does."

Four wide steps led down to a great room with a fireplace fit for a beach bonfire. A wall of windows revealed an expanse of lawn so green it seemed to make its own light, even in the shade.

Williams opened a pair of French doors to a brick patio. The mansion sat atop a hill with the back lawn rolling down and then out to a fence of trees and bush surrounding the property. At the edge of the patio Williams indicated the gazebo below. "What'd you like? An ale? American beer? Dinner's about half an hour out."

"Ah, whatever you'd drink, thanks."

"Trustin' lad, aren't ya? Me personal? I'd be drinkin' what they 'ave down there."

One thing was clear: fairytales weren't based solely on imagination. Shamrock could give rise to a hundred such tales, as beautiful and mysterious as it was. The air itself held the enigma, so different from the rest of the woods. Driving in, he'd sensed the history in the forest, the stories bound in the spaces. Here it was different. It actually drew out more from imagination than it gave. He'd never visited a place so neutral yet so full of possibility.

He started down the steps with a rising pulse. Eyes were upon him, featherlike brushes of scrutiny. Staying passive, he soaked up enough information to know a mix of trained and untrained minds lie ahead.

The gazebo had a table surrounded by a dozen chairs, nearly half of them occupied. Two faces stood out. Edward's was a welcome sight – the other belonged to a blond woman, sensually magnetic but far more noticeable for one reason: he could no more read or manipulate her than he could a rock. Holding her hand was a mellow guy without a ripple of ego. Sitting next to Edward was a wiry, reserved fellow with cropped hair and mirrored oval shades. Beside him sat a rough looking hombre of Spanish descent, clearly untrained.

Edward stood to greet Austin as he topped the stairs.

"Good to see you again, Mr. Crichlow." His grin was genuine, as was the warm handshake. "Compared to our last visit, you look like a new man."

"Coincidentally I feel like one, too."

Edward gestured to the wiry fellow with the shades. "Austin, this is Sean, our chief technologist."

He could have guessed; Sean exuded a measured and precise vibe like he thought in code. Sean said his welcome with a slight nod.

Edward went on to introduce Soldado. "He is a professional associate of this gentleman," he indicated the man sitting with the blond, "whom you've had contact with but I believe this to be your first meeting. Austin, meet Johan."

It was him. Older, not what he'd imagined at all yet inexplicably familiar. The hacker came around the table to greet him.

"They say the stiffest tree is most easily cracked, while the bamboo or willow survives by bending with the wind."

Austin shook his hand. "Bend to not break, yes." A teaching of the Tao, it embodied all the lessons and sacrifices so far. "I'll admit that at one time I imagined quite a different meeting."

"I don't blame you. I only knew it could be important and should live beyond what I did with it. You appreciate that now, no?" He returned to sit by the woman. "This is Anki, my very good friend."

They exchanged nods. She said, "I know so much has happened. I hope things will turn out okay."

She meant his dad. "That makes two of us. Nice to meet you."

Edward offered Austin a glass of wine and raised his own, calling for a toast.

"To new family and friends. To change."

• • •

Anki followed Edward towards his study, more winded than she should have been thanks to her pounding heart. They'd just finished dinner and he'd asked for a private talk before they rejoined the others.

Her hopes soared.

He knew something about her, had to. Her hyper-empathy was a mystery, as much a curse as a blessing. No one got away with feeling anything without her feeling it too, or at least sensing its charge. Long ago she'd learned to segment from it, to preserve her sense of self. Little by little, she'd learned to use it but only sparingly as it could be a most uncomfortable gift. She hoped they would help her with training as they had Johan.

"Please, sit down. Relax," he gestured.

She settled into a leather chair before his desk.

He sat down and regarded her. "How are you feeling?"

He referred to the modifications and surgery. "More sensitive, as if that's possible. I wasn't expecting it. Some advanced notice would have been nice."

"I'm sorry for that. It does take some getting used to."

A spell of silence grew awkward.

He said, "So, tell me, what am I feeling?"

It wasn't hard to realize Edward gave off no feeling. Rare was the person who wasn't emoting *something*. Since he wasn't, she tried to probe him. At first there was a sensation of calm and contentment but then she caught something more, a sense of anticipation. Hidden, suppressed, but having glimpsed it, she had confidence it was there.

"You're feeding me."

"What exactly?"

"That you're expecting something. Something great. You've waited a long time for it."

Edward looked down at his desk and smiled before looking up again. "Very good. Not many people can read at that level."

"Okay..."

He turned his computer monitor around to face her. "Watch this video. Which of the people in the crowd is unreadable?"

Before she could reply, a scene at an airport appeared, the footage from a handheld camera pointed at a boarding line. About two dozen people were in the frame. "It's not reliable—"

"Try. You've got less than a minute before they start to board."

Once she managed to forget the screen and focus, the passengers were fairly easy to read. There was one, a male, that couldn't be read — flat as the screen itself. "Third from the last, in the tan suit."

"Now probe him."

"It's a recording!"

"You're already reading the recording. Try probing him."

She did, despite the awkwardness. It lacked the give and take, the live response, but surprisingly there was something — the same kind of block that Edward had shown. Now, though, it felt hollow, as if through a tunnel or tube. Still the reading came through the recording, which meant through time, an even more surprising experience. She managed to sidestep past the block and press forward to find a murderous rage.

"Oh hell. He's going to kill someone. He's about to go ballistic."

He nodded, releasing satisfaction for her to feel. "Let me rewind it a bit. Now, who in the line is serving up a fake emotion?"

Emoting on purpose. "Ah. Okay, wow. The woman? Fifth from the front. She's bored on the outside but really very agitated, I think. I don't know how I missed that."

"You didn't have a reason to look, is all."

"Who are these people? And how did you know I could probe them on a recording?"

"Some were our people. Not the angry man. And I wasn't certain you could. I had a hunch."

"A hunch?"

"When one spends time with those gifted in the meta arts, they tend to absorb the gifts."

"But I haven't."

He turned the screen back facing him. "A few questions for you. First, do you like lemonade?"

She laughed. "What does that have to do with anything? Sure I like lemonade."

Edward nodded. "Is your absolute favorite color orange?"

"Yes."

"Do you love museums, late eighteenth century especially?"

She paused, then forced a laugh, uneasy at the intrusion. "You can stop the demonstration. I know you read minds."

"I assure you I am not," he replied quietly. "When you hear flute music do you think of your mother?"

"Edward." She stared. "Please? What does this mean?"

"When you were a little girl did the rumble of trains frighten you beyond all reason? Do they still?"

"Enough!" she blurted. In the abrupt silence, she probed him hard. What she found was deep love mixed with relief – and a raging current of conflict beneath it all.

"Fascinating." He sat back in his chair and sighed. "*Flùr air a' raon.*"

"What?"

"*Flùr air a' raon.* The flower growing in the field."

She didn't hide her irritation. "Please share the joke because I don't get it."

"Who is Sarah Debeere?"

"A friend of my mother's."

"What do you know about her?"

"She found me online a few years back. Why do you ask?"

"She's helped you quite a bit, hasn't she?"

"Yes, she has."

"A wealthy woman. She gave you the money to buy the internet café."

"Loaned, but yes. What's the point, Edward?"

"Sarah is of the Runa Korda. You've been protected since you were twenty years old."

She shook her head. "Protected? Me? Why on earth?"

"A short story will explain, if you don't mind hearing it. A long time ago someone had a vision of a woman of great power who would fall at the hands of our enemy but might come again when our needs were the greatest. That woman was named Clare and she came to us in the summer of 1880 from within the Korda. She was killed in the San Francisco quake of 1906."

"You loved her. My God, how old are you?"

He returned her look. "Many people loved her. She returned as predicted, almost forty years later."

"Returned? As in reincarnated?"

"Essentially yes. Few know the story and you are one that must. You cannot, however, share it with anyone. Not even Johan. Will you abide such secrecy?"

"I'm wondering if I want to know."

"You have to, but I need your word. Johan will know in time. For now it is for you alone."

"Okay." She nodded. "You have my word."

Convinced, he continued. "Clare returned with her metabody and memories intact. In her twenties she was being trained in the latest meta arts by a man named Steffan. He and Clare soon created a child. However, as the most unfortunate of circumstances would have it, Steffan was being tracked by Comannda. They tried to subjugate Clare."

"Subjugate?"

He hesitated. "Subjugation of the body. Where they remove core meta essence and assume the physical shell. The meta essence becomes lost."

She recoiled. "Like a ghost? They can do that?"

"Yes. Their attempt half-failed in that Clare was bumped from her body but her essence was not lost. Sadly, she lost both her body and you, her baby daughter."

"Me?" The spacious study constricted as her world suddenly shifted. Her mother's name was Margaret, not Clare. "Then who raised me?"

"I'm sorry, Anki. The mother you know was a stand-in, though no less loving and genuine a person. Margaret was happy to inherit the life she did and she did love you."

"Are you saying she was Comannda?"

"More like ex-Comannda but that's a story for another time. Relax. Please. Yes, there are some things that I cannot share with you yet. I know this is difficult but it is absolutely necessary. You must trust me."

"Um, I have a problem. There's *a lot* more you're not telling me. I can feel it." She rose to her feet and paced, overwhelmed by what he'd said and afraid of what he hadn't. She felt twelve again and she didn't like it. Sitting in the school counselor's office listening to a police chaplain explain how a burglar had killed her mother. Only it wasn't her mother – or was it? It was so long ago but keen empathy made for vivid memories. Margaret *had* loved her as a mother. Absolutely had.

She focused again on Edward. "You're holding something back, a really big something and that scares me."

Edward nodded, as much to himself as to her. "At conception, Clare and Steffan shared in the creation of your meta. Just as the body is a result of two bodies combining, so is the meta a result of two metas combining at the same moment, however briefly. Clare and Steffan are your parents and you are inextricably linked to them."

She nodded, absorbing. "But what happened to Clare? Her essence? And where did Steffan go? My father?"

He shored up noticeably before answering. "Stefan was killed trying to protect you and Clare. When Clare was knocked free of her body, Steffan's last act was to help hide her essence somewhere safe."

She froze, feeling an immense truth bubbling up within him.

"And where was that?"

He leaned forward and held her gaze.

"Within you."

Chapter 12

Nearly all men can stand adversity, but if you want to
test a man's character, give him power.
- Abraham Lincoln

After dinner the group gathered at a conference table in the library. Johan was subdued, wondering what Edward and Anki were meeting about. Sean sat listening to Soldado and Austin go around and around about Johan's break-in at InterGen.

"Well, look at it this way: he was about to plunder your facility and that could've cost you your job anyway. I see it all the time." Soldado's beguiling smile offset his frankness. "That Rocom hack was high level NSA shit, man. Never seen a backdoor like it. Crafted so sweet. Permission to walk on water, worldwide. Jesus fucking Christ. Then ol' Johan here had to fuck it up. That's legend. Pure legend."

Johan shook his head, only half minding the talk. "Blame Austin."

"Um, there was a packet storm on the inside port," Austin said. "You couldn't have knocked on the door any louder."

Soldado slapped the table and pointed at Johan. "Ah *ha!* You *did* fuck up. And I know just what you did. You used the first binary for the flash, didn't you? Someone didn't read the fucking readme!"

Johan shook his head again, quietly embarrassed. "I know for a fact I'm not the only one who doesn't read instructions."

"Ha!" Soldado barked. "Shit, don't sweat it. I'm just knockin' yer balls. We all make mistakes." He gulped more wine before adding, "Of course, some are bigger than others. God this is good juice."

Edward and Anki entered the study and joined them at the table. Williams filed in behind and opened cabinet doors in the wall to reveal a projector and a laptop. A screen descended from the ceiling. Anki sat next to Johan and slid her hand into his with a short nod to say everything was okay.

"What is left in the bottle is the last for the time being so don't fight over it." Edward said. "I will need your undivided attention, please, thank you. Your time in training has purposefully lacked significant details about the Comannda. Let's make it all simple and clear, shall we? This rock has landlords of the worst kind. By controlling the attention of the human animal and by selectively focusing its development they have stunted natural evolutionary processes for ages, all to maintain the keys to the kingdom. They are the very definition of tyrants, the corrupt elite behind all corrupted systems. What was meant to be ours by ancient design is not. Instead, we have inferior development and inferior understanding of ourselves and that of the world around us. Most people cannot yet imagine what they are being deprived of. Human awareness is like a lens that has never been properly focused. That... *that* is the legacy of the Comannda.

"There are the exceptions, as you are aware. You might consider the Runa Korda to be a kind of accomplice – aware of so many of the secrets, yet holding on to them. The fact is, humanity is hostage. There are so many trip wires in place that if I began to name them, you'd likely despair and walk out on us. Yes, it is bad. Yes, we are gravely challenged not to trigger those safeguards by releasing truths. But there is no excuse for giving up or giving in. We must evolve our tactics so that one day we can disable those safeguards and overcome them. Note that I said 'must evolve'. At no point in the foreseeable future is dumping the High Truths on the public a viable plan. Already aspects of the truths have been de-vitalized, made out to be the realm of kooks and bad science fiction. Further exposure now would only serve their agenda which is why we work to avoid it. That said, certain segments of humanity are closer to being ready than ever before. Though fractured and disorganized, some have begun to tap the source of their consciousness and experiment. They see through the cultural smokescreens and recognize the possibilities. They are intermingling in the grid with increased intimacy, though still ignorant of its complexity. One's fantasy seeds the reality of others, a mechanism that is predictable and which can lead to eventual catalytic evolution in consciousness.

"The Commanda are aware of all this. Conventional control bases are fragmenting as the previous programs lose their effectiveness. Intelligence has blossomed in the masses. Free thinking is on the rise. Rogue culture is breaking the bindings. Efforts to restore pre-Information Age levels of control are failing. Religion is diluting as fast as spring waters run and the supplemental institutions are not taking hold. Their 'science of the mind' concept has so far failed to capture the imagination of the *monje*, or free thinkers, so acceptance is low. The more creative monje are tapping media such as movies and books to promote wide-scale elevation of meta-physical thinking. Mankind is beginning to bloom like a weed under concrete, finding the cracks and pressing upward to the light. This growth is being offset once more with guerrilla tactics: global economic downturn, extreme class division, political upheaval, terrorism, viral disease, drug addictions, food supply tampering, and unprecedented cultural poisoning and redirection using technology and media."

"But that's not enough, is it?" Austin asked. "Those things have solutions, especially if people figure out they are all avoidable."

"Or intentionally created," Anki added.

Edward nodded. "Quite so. The global mind is beginning to grasp what is wrong and what is possible."

"The global mind?" Soldado asked.

"It is what governs the eventual actions of the species. Up until now it has been consumed largely by chaos. It has begun to understand that a very few with great power are behind what's wrong with the world. The Comannda cannot allow action on that understanding. Chaos and their fictions must prevail for them to remain in control."

"So what are they planning? More chaos?" Anki asked. "World War Three?"

"That is an option. The underlying framework is certainly primed. However, seeding justification for war on that scale is much harder today than it was fifty years ago. People are more aware. Transparency in the information age makes too many details visible. Communication allows for verification. Stories are harder to sell."

"Then what's their plan?"

"That is what we are trying to learn."

"Obviously they want to keep people from learning the truths and uniting," Johan said. "Unification at the level of the mind would open gates they could never close. I'm curious about the Runa Korda, though. What are its plans?"

Edward regarded him. "The secrets are like fire, the unaware like children. At first you protect them from fire, using it to insure their survival. When they are ready, you teach them to handle it themselves. Thus far, we have been insuring mankind's survival. Slowly, we are teaching. If the secrets go out now, humanity will burn under its own flame."

"Teaching?" Johan pressed. "A few stragglers like us at a time? What about the other nine billion?"

Edward pursed his lips before answering. "Like the monje, we move awareness towards truth. Unlike the monje, we know the end lesson and the dangers in reaching for it too soon. We work at the lower levels with knowledge the Comannda do not have and try to undo the damage they inflict upon the people. We stir and spice the waters of culture. We protect and build the foundation for meta awareness and someday, meta intelligence. The monje can be incendiary, reckless, distracting. Their methods are like grenades. Oftentimes their message is destroyed by the medium, only serving the Comannda."

Again Johan responded. "Why don't you work with these monje then? Influence them if nothing else—"

"Do you suppose we don't?" Edward interrupted, his demeanor finally less than cordial. "That we haven't?"

"I'm sorry, it's just not easy to see your work. The world's a mess."

Edward looked down at the table and allowed impulse to pass. When he looked up it was with a measure of patience. "I have spent the last hundred and sixty-four years of my life on this effort, Johan. At some point you will be given the chance to review what we have done. Until then, I can only hope you will become more trusting of my lead and learn something along the way."

The room fell silent. Austin and Johan shared a glance. Soldado let out a whistle and mouthed *'a hundred and sixty-four'*.

"How long have the Commanda been in control?" Anki asked.

"They began over four thousand years ago. Think Sumeria. The first cities, first writings, and first with the wheel. Mathematics, irrigation, laws, and astronomy. A sudden and prolithic advancement that included the discovery of meta and Saoghal. They knew to keep it to themselves and as a result the world would never be the same." Edward offered a critical eye to his guests. "Yes, we work with the monje as best we can. It is very dangerous, for them as well as us. We work in key areas where culture is defined and mass propagated. The news media is the front we are losing on the most. Journalism is being hedged more severely than almost any time in history and it's being done without the obvious trappings of oppressive government."

Sean joined in. "They control the governments, the industries, the political landscape, the monetary systems, the media, and the most important technologies. Through all that, they bind culture and thus the highest level of group minds. The Runa Korda is laying a foundation I can assure you, but in ways you might not recognize. We have grown the Confrere, a network that includes key members of state, industry, and military that help in many ways. We are making real progress."

"They're holding back medical technology as well?" Anki asked. "Cures, medicines?"

Sean nodded. "To a degree that is tragic. Same with energy. Everything is orchestrated to leave mankind wanting. They both create and satisfy the needs. They are in control."

Johan asked, "What are the safeguards? The tripwires you mentioned."

"That is not for you to know yet. When the need arises, you will know them."

"Their numbers then? How many Comannda are there?"

Edward considered the question. "Speaking in terms of organization, their Group Three appear at the top of every government, military, and industry. They are the scene manipulators, the fabricators, and the rule changers – the elite corruptors. They control with money and fear, just as they themselves are controlled. They are typical human animals, keyed to the needs of their handlers and are not very meta aware, if at all. Their Group Two are far fewer and are trained in meta specialties and the arts of coercion. G2 are involved in every major campaign, every significant development that shapes history. They assure execution of the plans and make it all 'fit' in the accepted public narrative. Group One is the inner ring, comprising the central planning and core operations body. We have no idea their number but it must be relatively small, likely in the low hundreds, maybe less. Above them, we know of the High Comannda, a body of twelve that oversee everything."

"Where do they operate from? They have to have bases."

"All over the world. Command and control is designed redundantly and insures survivability. There is a central base, however, that they call the Core. We know only that it is underground and one of the most secure and defensible places on the planet. The ultimate goal is to learn its location but right now our focus is on their network and their plans." He looked at the group. "I know you are curious but we need to continue. Time is short."

Despite a growing list of questions, Johan raised his glass. "To longevity." Hesitant smiles spread around the table. He sipped his wine. A group with such power could exist indefinitely, theoretically. That the Runa Korda had managed to hold on in defiance of the Comannda seemed suspect unless they'd made a pact. In that case, either the pact protected them somehow or they were subservient to the Comannda in some way. The latter would make Edward a liar and them pawns. He smoothed his thoughts. There wasn't sufficient knowledge to judge.

Soldado muttered something about wanting a bus ticket to the Fountain of Youth.

Edward continued. "The trends we see support the idea they are planning something unprecedented. Something to reposition man's attention on survival, on the basics."

"Enter the digital world." Soldado emptied the last of his wine.

Sean nodded. "Their plans require movement in the material world. Political changes, financial transactions, contracts, equipment deals, and so on. Analysis of such movement provides pieces to the puzzle but the foundations for their plans are stored in their systems. They rely heavily on technology and keep it ahead of the mainstream. However, we're catching up in key areas and are close to climbing up their tailpipe and looking around the engine. Soldado has agreed to work with our teams to finally break into their network. The goal is to intercept and interpret Comannda communications directly from their own wire. A presence there could change everything."

"And it could lead us to the core of Totem," Edward added. "Which takes us to the present. Soldado, Mr. Lathrop is waiting in the room at the top of the stairs. He has a special briefing for you and some new concepts that need your review."

Soldado made a face. "Eh, work. Let's all hook up around another bottle of the good stuff later on." He pushed back from the table and headed for the door.

Edward said to Anki, "I need to speak privately with Johan and Austin. You'll find the great room offers diversions, as does the game room and library."

Johan looked at Edward, asking if it were necessary she leave. Edward nodded.

She stood and squeezed Johan's shoulder on her way out. "Later you won't choose Condrieu over me, I hope?"

"A bottle of Condrieu *and* you. I shouldn't be too long," he said.

Edward waited until she left. "Williams, the door please. Alright then. First with you, Johan. During my time, no one, Korda-born or not, has ever shut out a squad of korjé without extensive training."

Korjé were the hunters, the thought police. Groups one and two.

Johan spread his hands. "Well, I guess that makes me special."

"It makes you valuable." Edward tossed a small wooden block onto the table. "You know what that is, Gerrit Bartel."

Stunned, Johan faltered, trapped in a moment. He tried to recover. "And you're a carnival ride, Edward. What can I say?"

184

"There's more to your story, Johan. Vincent and Juliana Bartel were gifted members of our family. They were Instructors."

Johan went still.

"You witnessed their murder. Eight years old, two years shy of Initiation. Your grandfather, not one for the Family, chose to keep you from us and raised you without our involvement. We honor those decisions. When you disappeared, you did so quite effectively. That was fifteen years ago. We thought you'd been killed and so imagine our surprise when your DNA threw a match. Not quite a prodigal son but nonetheless we are glad you are with us. It explains your gift."

He closed his eyes. The dreams, the old hunted feeling, the paths he'd been led down. The circle was complete, the healing a rising chorus in his soul. There were no accidents, just as he'd always believed.

"What about my gift?"

"Just as you learned to speak by listening to their speech, you also learned how to think by their unique way of thinking. Between two Korda flows a language unto itself. You were raised with and impressed by that flow. It explains why you were so distant from everyone else growing up, why you drew judgment on people that others couldn't understand and why some people felt uncomfortable around you. You looked right through them. It is why you are so good at shifting identity, adapting to people's needs. It is how you isolate wrong doers and sustain a nomadic life, or I should say 'lives'. You know the multitude of ways people can think and be and you can emulate them like a skilled stage actor. You are tuned to the meta field, to the true nature of people. A typical Korda child. You had wonderful parents."

"You knew them?"

"I knew of them. I met your father briefly in Washington in sixty-seven but we never worked together. I know you have questions but it's late." Edward shifted attention to Austin. "How are you feeling? Any more headaches?"

"None like the ones after the first treatment. The other pills help."

"That's good, very good. Well, the anomaly, you are. A natural traveler. From where does your ability stem? Any ideas?"

There was no knowing, could be none. He shook his head. "Seems a lot to do with imagination."

"Why do you say that?"

"Because imagination creates," Austin replied without thinking.

"Precisely so, Austin. Imagination is normally seen as important because it encourages visions of what is possible. At the near end, imagination fetches concepts and plays with them, birthing new relationships and ideas. Indeed, without imagination," he shook his head, "you are content to work with what you know. An abundance of contentment is what prevents people from learning more about meta and their connection with the world. Thank you, culture. With sufficient imagination you begin to grasp the connections. Imagination drives curiosity, which in turn drives discovery. Again, at the near end."

"And at the far end?" Johan asked.

Edward reached for the wine bottle. "Do either of you mind?" He quarter-filled his glass. "At the far end, far from where we are... I suppose you join company with the Creator." He took a sip. "Between here and there lies the pitfalls of madness, no doubt for a reason. God's locked screen door."

Austin asked, "Aren't you suggesting that it's not just the Comannda keeping man's awareness in check, but maybe God, too?"

The elder shook his head. "No. The madness I speak of protects things greater than just Saoghal and man's journeys with his meta. The latter are within his reach, as the two of you can attest, albeit with their own obstacles."

"The biggest being the Comannda."

"True."

"What about these protein additions? If they work, I'm told I'll be disturbing the quantum foam with my thoughts. You know that's kind of scary, no matter how cool it sounds."

"You are a solid subject in that regard. We know you have the control and moral code needed to work it safely. Of course you will also be monitored and trained. Do not worry yourself unnecessarily. So, you answered my question – you don't know how you came about your ability. Nor do we. It is an anomaly we wish to understand and help you grow."

Austin hesitated before asking, "Is it possible that my dad– I mean, he seemed to know something. About how they did things."

"Could he have worked for the Comannda? It is possible of course, though we've found no indications. I encourage you to keep an open and positive mind in regards to him. However, if you begin to feel contact from him, any impressions at all, let us know right away. We have no way of knowing his fate or allegiances at this point."

Austin could only nod.

Edward stood with his glass and walked to the window. "It's important to know that the two of you are joining us during what most of the Runa Korda consider to be defining times, times that were once predicted by those who have such vision. We're approaching an apex that involves the kind of conflict that will define mankind's future." He turned to look at them. "You have been made to wait on the topic of aliens. I can tell you now that humans are not unique in their intelligence nor in their technology. I suspect we are garden variety. What makes us somewhat different is the degree that the Comannda have been able to limit our evolution. By now, most species like us would have crossed the language line into meta-enabled communication, would have smoothed the differences that still plague our societies, and would have used technology to erase physical suffering entirely. It is this hostage-like existence that has drawn the attention of our more evolved neighbors."

"They want to help?" Austin asked.

"Some would like to, yes. In fact, they have been trying to the extent that they are able."

"Why not just fly in and take out the Comannda?"

Edward smiled. "If only it were that easy, they would. No, it is up to our majority to create the future. We have to climb the mountain as one or not at all. To do that, we need to free ourselves of our own bindings."

"We'll never make it then," Austin said. "Like you said, the world's a hostage."

"The world is asleep," Sean said. "Lulled by a story that keeps them dreaming the fucked up dreams of the Comannda. Our job is to awaken them without hurting them. But first we have to keep the Comannda from destroying all our work and the world with it."

Austin shook his head. "Why can't the aliens help? Seriously, if they are more advanced, they should. Or don't they subscribe to moral imperatives?"

"They are more advanced in ways that you will find hard to comprehend, Austin. They seek balance for us, but cannot tip the scales unnaturally. It is just so. What they *are* doing is keeping outsiders from coming in and taking advantage. The universe is a very big place. For that alone we are in their debt."

"So we're left to take out the Comannda on our own."

"Fundamentally, yes."

"Sink or swim."

"As it has been and must be."

"What are they called? And how alien are they?"

"They are called Mu, from their ancient language meaning 'people'. They are everything we are but in different measures and in a more evolved state."

"Mu? Really? Any relation to references in the Tao?"

Johan said, "Mu is the term for the original non-being from which being is produced. It is pure awareness, prior to experience or knowledge."

Edward shook his head. "I can't speak to that. What influence they have exerted in our history is not shared nor catalogued. I can only confirm they are masters of awareness."

Austin straightened in his chair. Once again the familiar pendulum of inevitability swung into view – only now it was gigantic, involving an alien race, a shadow government, and the possible devolution of the modern world. Only a month ago such a reality would have been bizarre and nightmarish. He idly tapped the smooth oak of the conference table. Thoughts of his dad and Kaiya and her mom and all his friends and neighbors surfaced. So much sacrifice just to be at that table, only to learn the most powerful people on earth were considering knocking everyone back to the Stone Age and that advanced life forms were standing by to watch. Awe of the enemy churned, driven by the facts. Awe quickly gave way to a stronger emotion, that of anger. *They had no right.* They just *didn't*. No self-made committee of man-gods had the right to manipulate an entire planet, to determine who evolved and who didn't, who ate and who starved, who lived and who died.

"Austin," Edward said. "Are you with us? Is something wrong?"

Nodding curtly he replied, "Well yeah, I think there is, yes. We need to stop the Comannda. Flat out *stop* them. This can't continue. We can't let it happen. The Mu can't. It's insane and completely wrong that they don't help."

"We agree, in principle," Edward started with an annoyingly patronizing tone, "but there is a bigger picture to consider, an approach we must–"

Something snapped and floodgates gave way. Words spilled forth of their own volition. "An *approach?*" he asked. "This *approach* has lasted how many hundreds of years? Your *awareness* of their powers and manipulations has been used *how* to stop them? All I see is an army of savants dedicated to a cause I don't quite get. What *is* your purpose? What have you been *doing* all these years? Tell me your secret empire doesn't include newspapers and media outlets around the world! Tell me your Confrere couldn't break out the truth!" Momentum carried him. "Hell, with the technology used to reshape us, I bet you could come up with an AIDS vaccine or a cure for cancer pretty damned quickly, Edward. Or have a ship land in Times Square and let them reveal the truth about our overlords once and for all. Why in the fuck do you dance and prance around and not *do* something?" Unbridled now: "Or maybe you really are just like them, working for your own goals? Too much stock in the drug companies perhaps? Who pays for your mountain getaways and country estates? Too damn comfortable, are you? You're just like them!"

A shroud of silence slipped over the room. Johan's gaze flicked to Edward, then back to Austin. Something had gone suddenly and oddly wrong.

Edward disregarded the outburst entirely. "Back to the matter at hand. Evidence has accrued over the past year indicating something big. As Sean will tell you, our technology–"

"Fuck this." Austin knocked his chair over backwards. "You're all fucked up." If he didn't get out of the room now, he might burst. He headed for the door, knowing vaguely that it was him that was fucked up but not why.

Sean stood and Austin's head jerked violently to the side, as if struck. Anger spread like fire in dry grass. Control slipped further.

Sean said, "You don't just walk out on a meeting this important."

The words splashed like fuel, sending him scrambling for a way to strike back. He descended straight to his core and out into the grid, out into the space between them. He focused on the space just in front of Sean and with all his might punched *movement* there.

A slight wind puffed Sean's face. He laughed.

"Keep that up and you're going to chap my lips."

"Fuck you!" he shouted in a torrent of anger. "Fucking cowards! You pretend nobility and– and *sophistication!* Sipping fine wines and lounging like the rich. You chase Big Brother's tailpipe when you could be helping the world. You could have made incredible changes!"

"Fuck me?" Sean pointed at him. "Fuck *you*, the hypocrite who's spending thousands of dollars turning your house into a shrine to artificial intelligence and imagined wealth. How many times did you stop by a shelter and teach basic computer theory with your laptop? Or share some food or give out blankets in winter? Hmm? What was within *your* ability to help? Why didn't *you* do something? How about doing *anything* that didn't directly benefit yourself? And now let me ask you: what have we done? You don't really know yet, do you? So shut the fuck up and sit down, asshole. You've got *a lot* to learn."

Briefly, the sheer insanity of the moment struck him but pride and fury forced him towards the door, unable to form a response. Three strides out, his legs folded and he landed painfully on the floor. Rage flashed, both at Sean and himself for his outburst. He pushed to his feet. A red orb, cartoon-like and swirling, formed in his mind's eye. It absorbed all anger, amplifying it, understanding it, forming purpose. Beyond the orb lay the room, the grid of marbles in perfect clarity. Sean was right *there*. Right fucking *there*.

Edward sensed the change too late. "*Austin*—!"

Riding the high of intuition and rage, he smashed the imaginary red orb into the grid, aimed directly at Sean. He hadn't expected the loud *crack*, nor the bending of light as the orb punched into the grid, force modeling the marbles into like states, causing a high-speed domino run with explosive effect. Sean barely angled his head clear. The hazed ball shot by and burned the side of his face before searing into the wall behind him. Johan leapt to his feet and moved to tackle Austin.

"Enough!" Edward bellowed.

Austin's rage expired the next moment and left him dangling in disbelief and horror. The orb dissolved but not before it went through the wall and destroyed an adjoining ceiling. Sean responded by sitting down, squaring his cuffs and losing all the emotive charge from a moment before. If he was in pain he ignored it masterfully.

It was Edward. Austin felt him emerge from the patterns of his thoughts, a ghost rider, a chameleon that had played him like a video game. Then three more emerged, others who had helped.

"We bound your control. The rage needed to surface to push your limits. Now we know." One by one, they blinked out of Austin's stream. "Now we know."

Johan stared, stunned. "What the fuck was that? And what do you know?"

"Prophecy tells us of the Change, a person with gifts that will help end the Comannda's reign."

"Gifts?" Austin asked. "Bullshit. You increased the proteins. You're turning me into a god damned weapon." He righted his chair and leaned against it, fishing for calm. He indicated Sean's raw face. "You knew I could do that?"

"No. Once again you exceeded expectations."

"This is nuts. Telekinetic killers? Javier did it in L.A. Are you trained to kill with your mind, too?"

Sean shook his head. "It's not what you think."

"It's not?" He looked to Edward. "Well? What is it then?"

"The proteins mean nothing if you can't use them. Sean is one of our strongest TKs. The same levels in him change nothing."

"I'm maxed out," Sean confirmed.

"And Javier killed by disconnecting meta, not with telekinesis," Edward explained. "I know of nobody, besides yourself, that has ever been able to do anything like that," he looked at the hole in the wall, "in Raon."

Chapter 13

It is a magnificent feeling to recognize the unity of complex phenomena
which appear to be things quite apart from the direct visible truth.
- Albert Einstein 1879-1955, German-born American Physicist

In his bedroom on the third floor, Austin finished reading Kaiya's last message in disbelief.

She wasn't going through with it.

Her face was her own, she couldn't let them change it or make any of the other changes. Despite the warrants for murder, despite her face plastered on every post office bulletin board across the country alongside Mac's, she couldn't bring herself to let them cut her up and be reshaped into someone else. It felt like an admission of guilt. She wanted to wait it out and see if circumstances changed.

It wasn't a complete surprise. A traditionalist in some ways, the thought of such a drastic and permanent reformation would screw with her badly. The pictures they'd sent of him didn't help, seeing a stranger instead of his familiar face. Still, she had to know there were no good alternatives. Hiding in secret in a foreign country was perhaps the only option and even that posed risks of eventual discovery. It was no way to live. She was smart enough to realize that, which bothered him. Until she allowed the changes, she wouldn't be able to join him in his new life or have any kind of real life herself.

Careful to phrase his reply, he avoided pressure or criticism. She had to arrive there on her own. But it sucked. *Man it sucked.* To hold her again was all he could think of. Drawing her into a dream was a compelling temptation.

He stood and paced the room before opening the French doors onto a small balcony. From the high perch, he took in the beauty of the evening. The grounds' lighting complimented the celestial canopy above. The gazebo floated as an island of illumination, inviting in the velvet night. The forest's spirit tinged the darkness beyond. Stories amid stories waited to be told to a patient and listening soul. His wasn't the one, tonight.

Motion below caught his eye. Johan and Anki walked hand in hand headed for the gazebo. Their bond was like psychic glue, visible from a distance. The sudden roar of envy was as embarrassing as it was painful. It should have been Kaiya and him adding to the forest's memory.

He retreated and gently closed the glass doors.

• • •

Sean sat with Edward in the study reviewing the latest updates. "Still haven't found her."

Edward grimaced. If recovered, she'd likely not be the same. "I am surprised they have not tried anything yet. Such leverage."

Sean nodded. "As distasteful as it may be, we must continue corresponding in her place. If he goes to the dream state to look, it may be the only way we find her."

"And they will find him. We need to get him to the next stage quickly."

"Why not tonight?"

Edward shook his head. "No, he is running on reserves. Tomorrow we will begin."

"And if he tries on his own tonight?"

"He was lucky on the flight in and I let him know it. Bràthair will monitor. What of Anki?"

"She's stable. Not looking within, a bit scared at what she may find. Anchoring herself with Johan. Clare's keeping silent, as you requested."

"Good. I don't want to risk losing either of them."

• • •

Forty yards past the gazebo in the darkness they rested, regaining their breath. They'd coupled like wild boars. Cool air descended from the stars. The night surrounded them, filled with a chorus of crickets and mockingbirds. If ever there were to be a perfect moment it had to be upon them.

Anki ran her hand along his stomach, gently scraping with her nails. "I think I'm getting used to it."

"I imagine you are." Using a method provided in training, they were able to climax together without hitting the radar. In their private bubble the contained orgasm was twice as powerful and far more intimate. "We could get rich just teaching that."

She ran her palm over his chest and kissed his shoulder. "What is Edward having you do?"

"Don't know yet. We were sidetracked."

"What did I miss?"

"Austin. Turns out he has some latent gifts they're drawing out of him. Semi-unpleasantly but pretty amazing. Not sure why Edward had you step out. I'll talk to him." Not sharing the energy blast with her was difficult.

A shooting star made a brief dash across the heavens.

"Don't bother. I'm sure he has good reasons."

• • •

Across the street, a child held his mother's hand, bewildered by the crowds and the noise. No more than seven years old, he had to have heard the explosion and was frightened. When the crowd pulled the man from the shallow river, they'd beat him mercilessly before the Serbian police took him into custody. The man had vomited continuously from the old and weak cyanide pill he'd taken. How much the little boy had seen was impossible to tell, but the lollipop idle at his side suggested perhaps too much.

Austin knew the man was the attempted assassin of the Archduke. Just twenty years old, a dropout with a father who beat his family, he'd been recruited by the fellow who would assassinate the Archduke. He knew these details, but didn't think how. A glance at his watch showed the hands on ten-thirty. Further down the street, the last of the wounded were taken away for treatment, victims of the thrown bomb. Somewhere in the crowd, the other would-be assassins still lurked.

He turned and walked eastward up Appel Quay along the motorcade route. There at the corner was Schiller's Store. The store was important. Again he didn't know why or how he knew it. The Archduke was due back this way but with the attempted assassination no one knew for sure if he would return. Unsure of himself, he loitered for ten minutes, keeping an eye on the store's single door and on the boulevard. People were angry, looking at any stranger two and three times, suspicious.

From the crowd emerged a thin young man, hands in pockets. Unlike those around him, he gave off a vibe, a second layer that revealed ill intention. How the crowd couldn't read him... As he approached, he glanced at Austin and quickly away, uneasy with what he saw. He walked right into Schiller's. As the door closed, Austin caught a glimpse of Kaiya inside.

His heart leapt and he started towards the store, then checked himself. A confrontation could hurt Kaiya. If he waited for the assassin to come out there may not be enough time to save the Archduke, something he knew he had to do. The decision came down to wanting to protect Kaiya first, to be there between her and danger. He walked towards the store.

At the entrance he saw the small boy from down the street. When he reached for the door handle, the boy stepped in to block his way.

Pointing with his lollipop, he said, "You can't go in there, mister."

"Where's your mum? You need to run along now, and quickly. Something bad's about to happen."

The boy's face was stern. "No way. You have to stay outside, or you'll find out."

He squatted down to eye level with the boy. "And what will I find out?"

The lollipop lowered and the boy shook his head.

"Well then, I need to go in, I have something important to do." He stood. "Step aside now."

"No, mister."

He looked around. The mother was nowhere in sight and people were busy watching the street. He took the boy by his shoulders and forced him away from the door.

"No!" The boy screamed. He punched Austin hard in the nuts and shouted, "Now wake the fuck up!"

The smell of toast and bacon filled the stairwell as he descended into the great room. A ghost pain lingered in his groin courtesy of the vivid dream. He hadn't intended to fall asleep. One minute he was thinking of Kaiya and the next he was dreaming.

A sign labeled 'breakfast' stood prominently next to the open French doors. From out on the patio he saw the table filled with food in the gazebo below. No one was there yet. He called out for Williams. The butler appeared from the kitchen.

"Good morning! You must be starved."

"I'm a bit hungry, I suppose. Where is everyone?"

"Just not roused yet, apparently. Food is ready in the gazebo. If you need anything I'll be down there shortly."

"Will Edward be joining us?"

"I don't know but I expect if he is, it'll be soon."

He walked down the steps with the morning sun warm at his back. In the shade of the gazebo he built his plate and poured orange juice from a carafe. His mood was a bit off despite the bright new morning. An underlying tension pulled him down. Probably worry about Edward finding out he'd not taken the pills. He'd just been counseled about it, too. He took a seat and started in on some waffles.

Out at the tree line, a lone figure stepped onto the green and began walking towards him. Something wasn't right though he couldn't say what. Williams hadn't returned. No one else around. Perhaps it was a test. It started to feel like one.

He stood and went to the edge of the gazebo, drawn to the figure.

It was a woman, her intentions a stark contrast to the brilliantly lit morning. Her aura roiled dark and–

He recoiled.

This was who he wasn't supposed to find while crossing the ocean in his dream. No tiger's head to warn him off now. Fear slipped in, tainting control. Her dark brown energy narrowed to focus on him. Intentions became clear: she was there to end it, to end them – to end all interference.

He immediately formed the red ball, its cartoon energy no less powerful than in the study. He mapped its trajectory in the grid. Now though, the grid was different. The granular, tactile connectivity was missing. Instead there was just uninterrupted space.

He faltered with the thought that the ball might not work here.

Here. A thought followed – *where is 'here'?*

The woman's angry face came into view, recognizable as the check-in clerk at the Canary Wharf Hilton. The next moment found him standing at the check-in desk, the gray of dawn again creeping through the hotel lobby windows. The space-time shift hit him like a punch in the head.

"Can I help you?" Gone was the threatening glare though she remained as unreadable as the first time they'd met.

"Yes, I uh, I have a reservation." Another dream, then. Too powerful to break. *Who was driving?* Panic rose.

"Your name, please?"

The question was different this time, asked too eagerly. His name *meant* something to her – she needed to know it. He looked beyond at a glass display. In the faint reflection he saw himself but without a face.

"You know, I'll be damned, I think I have the wrong hotel. I'd better call my agent to check." He retreated across the lobby. In every reflection there was a white blot where his face should be.

Outside the hotel he veered onto the sidewalk. A lorry lumbered by, trailed by three cars impatient to pass. He slowed and checked back towards the hotel and saw no one following. Crews arrived to start their day at a construction yard across the road. The building's steel framework loomed overhead. Someone was driving the dream and it wasn't him. *Or was it?*

He kept moving and watched the sparse traffic for threats, searching for a clue, an out, something. Between two buildings he saw light spilling out onto the street from a store front. The front door stood ajar with a sign overhead that read, 'North Pole'. An upscale pub and restaurant, open before dawn. The tables and bar inside were all empty. This was an anomaly, something to check out.

He climbed a pair of steps and was immediately taken by the quiet within. Not a soul in the joint but still lit up for business. The chairs were all down around the tables, ready for customers. The neon around the bar burned brightly. The wooden floor creaked with every step, audible to anyone down the hall in the kitchen. No one came. A piece of paper lay on a table near the windows. In black ink it read, "Santa's helper is in danger. Head to the South Pole."

Across the room, just past the bar, a white neon sign over a hallway read in cursive, "South Pole".

He followed the hallway to a bank of descending stairs lit with more neon signs advertising beers. Rounding the second set, he stepped down into a bar with blue and purple lighting. It reminded him of the cantina scene from Star Wars but without all the patrons.

He followed the layout around the bar and stopped.

Kaiya sat on a couch, dressed up for a night out.

She looked up from her cell phone and smiled, as sexy as the first time he'd met her.

"About time, nushi. I was worried you wouldn't find me."

She stood and walked to meet him.

• • •

Johan sat by the French doors in Austin's room, watching Anki tend to a sleeping Austin. Edward lay in the bed next to him. Both men wore black sunglasses.

Sean sat in front of four small monitors on a push cart laden with computers. Each monitor showed different imagery. One of them was of Kaiya in a bar.

"How is that possible?" Anki asked. "How can you see into his dream?"

He pointed to the glasses. "They're *shùils*. Real-time visual intercept at the optic chiasm, the point where the two optic nerves meet to combine visual data. Everything they experience flows through the brain. We're just tapping the stream."

His expression soured.

"What is it?" Anki asked.

"Edward's blocked out. They have Austin and he's not fighting it. They're fishing for clues about his identity and location." Sean stared at the video feeds. "This may not end well."

The Comannda had drawn Austin to the Sarajevo dream. Edward's attempt at intervention only made him think he'd woke – the Comannda pressed again and locked onto Austin, drawing him fully into their dream.

"What next?" Johan asked.

"They're trying to bridge to his body and push a tracking signal from there. *Bràthair* are doing their best to block them but will fail soon."

"Bràthair?"

"Our brothers, working beyond their bodies. We need to get him out of here."

Williams heard from the doorway and left to prepare.

"And where to? They'll triangulate," Johan said. "You know they will."

"I said we can try."

"Stay." Edward's voice broke like ice in the room. "Something is coming."

Johan joined Anki and Sean at the screens.

• • •

Austin held Kaiya's hands, soft and warm in his own. This was what he wanted. Like the dream in old London, he wanted nothing more than to sink into her. Fears had painted the earlier dreams, creating near nightmares. Finding her in this way was well worth the trouble.

"This is all my fault," she said. "If I would've let them do the surgery we'd be together by now. I guess tonight is all we'll have for a while." She went to embrace him. "Let's make it last."

Looking into her eyes, he hesitated. "Um..."

Her eyes weren't the glassy caramel brown he knew. Instead they were blue and had begun to shift. He held her at arm's length.

"Austin, what?"

Her eyes grew and changed shape until the unmistakable eyes of his mother looked back at him.

"Mom?"

Kaiya's face contorted. "Leave him alone! He's not going to—"

Pale colored skin spread outward from her eyes, replacing Kaiya's light olive tone. Her head wobbled and then began to change shape and size, as did her cheekbones, nose and chin. In a bubbling of morphing energy, Kaiya's head was replaced by his mother's. Her familiar pursing of lips gave him the chills. It had been years since he'd seen that expression.

She fixed him with an intense glare. "Austin listen to me and listen good. This isn't Kaiya and you have to get the hell away from this dream. Get out, now. Your father—"

Kaiya's terrified face snapped back into place. "Austin, they're using your memories to steal my soul! If you leave me now, I'll never wake up! Please!" She gripped his forearms desperately. "Help me, I'm scared!"

"Biiiiitch!" Her mouth gaped and her voice changed again midway through, her face once again his mother's. "I should have fought harder for you when I was alive. If I'd only known. Your father—" She struggled against unseen powers. "Go now, run, Austin! Wake up, keep running until you do! *Goooo!*"

The last ended in a howl as her mouth grew and opened wide to reveal rows of razor-sharp teeth. Her face morphed larger and blood-red eyes bulged with a look of murder. Her body swelled and veins appeared. Claws extended from her fingers and pierced his arm.

He screamed. With a vicious effort he launched the creature across the room and ran for the stairs.

• • •

Anki flew across the room and hit the wall, shattering a glass picture frame before falling to the floor. Johan and Sean rushed to help her. Blood stained her blonde hair.

"I'm okay, I'm alright," she said. "He's trying to break free. We need to help him."

Johan told Edward, "Do something."

"We are," Sean replied. "Just didn't see that coming. He's tapping his power."

"That's wonderful as long as he doesn't tap us to bloody pieces."

• • •

The creature hit the wall and bounced back in the shape of a four legged beast. Its metamorphosis complete, it growled and followed Austin's path to the stairs.

Just a dream – just a fucking bad dream!

He rounded the corner at the landing and took three steps at a time. Instead of reaching the first floor, he arrived at another landing. He turned and climbed another flight before arriving at yet another landing. "Fuck!"

"*Austin!*" The words were half growl, half Kaiya's voice. "Come here, Austin! Right *now!*" The rapid click-tap of claws echoed. There was no end to the stairwell, and worse, the bar was still just one flight down.

Lucidity grew, teasing with possibility. It was his dream, too – had to be or else they'd already have him. He thumped the wall and found the hollow space between studs. He climbed up the next few stairs, turned back, and ran with all his might. He busted through the wall and stumbled headlong into a thick bush. Blinking away dirt, his eyes adjusted to sudden daylight. Smoke passed through tall trees and stained a blue sky. The bar had vanished.

"Here! I have him in sight! Here!"

A soldier in Roman armor called out before starting down the grade of the hillside with sword at the ready. Austin scrambled to his feet and ran, grateful to be wearing his own clothing. He could easily outrun the soldier.

Flit-thunk! An arrow struck a nearby tree. He turned in time to see two archers letting fly their missiles. More soldiers appeared over the rise.

"Shit!" He broke left to follow the descent of the hillside, zigzagging as he went. *Where the hell was Edward or Marcel or any of them?*

• • •

Edward removed the glasses. "I cannot help him but Cathbad will try."

"Cathbad?" Anki asked.

Edward told Sean, "He and Mug are going in. Use their relays for viewing." To Anki and Johan he said, "Cathbad leads the Runa Korda. Mug is his Second. If anyone can break Austin free, it is them. The Comannda have suspended his rathad in the dream state. There is no waking him here," he gestured to Austin's body, "as long as they have him there. If not for his mother, their trace would've gone much easier. He's fighting them now. It buys us time, at least."

"Was that really his mother?" Anki asked.

"The dead can appear. Or he may be working this out for himself. The good news is he's trying. He has powers he hasn't yet realized." Edward donned the shùil again. "Do you have them?"

"Yes," Sean answered. "They're waiting outside Hunnenring."

Edward met with the two elders at a brook below a hillside fort accompanied by a squad of bràthair. Morning mists swelled from a forest aglow with the rising sun. An apprehensive Mug squatted to splash water on his face while keeping an eye out. Cathbad joined Edward in counsel.

"Be ready with the Concord of Ascension. You must keep it formal and strong. The Family must not falter."

Edward nodded. There was no questioning him, regardless the danger. "Aye and well."

Cathbad gazed up at the fort and the hills beyond. "If the Words of Kornilian are correct, Austin is the Change." He looked back at Edward. "I won't let it end like this."

History indicated druids kept no written records, using oral tradition instead. While true, the Words weren't just words – often they were actual memories passed on since the earliest families. Most important were those of the *welets*, druids known to glimpse the future. The Words of Kornilian surfaced between them as they waited.

...by the firelight the band huddled against winter's brace at the foot of the mountain. Forced into nomadic life by the hunters, the nine were destined for the Strait of Gibraltar, less than a month away with God's hand upon them. Brother Pierce had weakened, unable to keep food down as a result of the poisoning by the innkeeper at Horta de Sant Joan. Before first rest Brother Kornilian bore the message to the group again, speaking the words only, as the message had passed thinly into his keeping, without original vision. "He that would move the wind, that would Travel the world as a boy, and that would appease the animals, will be the Change. He that would master Saoghal and move without peer in the World of Dreams, will be the Change."

Predictive visions of the welets had proven valuable for hundreds of years, accurately forecasting up to the second World War. Since then, events had gone strange, incompatible with the Words. Worse, there hadn't been a welet born nor found in two centuries, bearing credence to fears the Comannda were gaining control over the mysteries. Kornilian's salvage of a vision involving the Change continually fired the family's will to survive. Austin's appearance and abilities marked him as the Change, save for his lack of dream control. The rise of the Runa Korda against the Comannda was nearly at hand and he had to be made ready.

Mug stood, still apprehensive. "Sir, we are to begin." He turned to the squad. "Prepare!"

In ones and twos, the bràthair disappeared, off to form protective barriers around the meta cores of the two elder druids. Should either be caught in a dream, the bràthair would be the last defense against invaders seeking to track back to Raon to reveal their location.

Cathbad nodded and closed his eyes in prayer.

Edward said his own, especially for Cathbad. The man was nearly four hundred years old and his passing was as inevitable as ever. To have him face the Comannda now and fail could bring division to the Family, a strife that would dishonor the Concords agreed to so long ago. He prayed for success.

A distant horn sounded from beyond the fort.

"Entry's made, the path is in place. God's strength to you both."

• • •

More archers appeared, more arrows cut the air. Trees and their roots made for treacherous footing. Every step seemed his last, a fated arrow surely in flight. Austin knew that if one were to stick they would have him. He zigzagged towards the wall-high thickets some twenty yards away. He cringed as he neared the vegetation. To scout for an opening would leave him exposed so he built momentum and aimed for the bushes, bracing himself.

He barreled into the thicket and abruptly halted in a flurry of green – only now, the branches and vines were replaced by two sets of hands holding him in place.

He stood in a clearing, instantly familiar as the one seen during the cab ride through Epping Forest. Looking beyond the entrance, he saw no roads or buildings – just trees and sunlight dancing with shadows on wild grass. The two men holding him wore battle robes made of leather armor inlaid with metal studs and rings. One of the men was infinitely old, not so much by appearance but by aura. They looked like old world druids.

"Calm, Austin, be calm. We're here to guide you from the dream." Jumping ahead of the suspicion forming, he said, "Keywords to authenticate: trainer Marcel, protector Meng, knightly Edward, Kaiya love, missing father, wise Javier, dead Jacob. Now, can you align with us?"

Still catching his breath, it took a moment to process what he'd heard. "Yes, yes, I see, I get it. Now how do I wake up?"

The druids relaxed their grip but still held his arms. "We're doing what must be done. We hide in the spaces between their own creation, pacing them. It should end soon."

"Who are you?"

"Korda. Nothing more until you awaken. Do nothing but relax."

He tried to empty his mind and just stood with the two men, waiting. Breathing slowed. His eyes wandered. Such a beautiful land; an unavoidable thought. The grass was untrodden, the trees clustered to form a private court with one entrance. A calm saturated the clearing and held all the magic and history he'd glimpsed before. He could imagine a night here, stars and moon overhead, where the spirits might appear to converse with the living. The earth's voice seemed to rise from the silence, a rumbling force that spoke directly to his soul. The next moment, the druids tightened their grip as the rumbling voice became the thundering approach of horses.

Both druids looked alarmed and pained. The younger druid shook his head.

"I can't...."

"Nor can I. Be brave, Mug. Come!"

The older druid led them towards the trees just as mounted soldiers appeared through the grove's entrance. One stood in his stirrups, balanced a long pole, and hefted it with all his might. Mug turned and deftly palmed the pole midflight to direct its force into the ground. Shouts erupted from all directions. Soldiers appeared from between the trees and filled the gaps. The clanging of swords on shields created an unnerving cacophony. The elder druid halted. They were surrounded.

A gray-bearded rider in elaborate armor stayed his horse and shouted over the din, "Aha! Yes! Yes! *Quiet!*"

The sword beating and shouts fell away.

"Cathbad, leader of the Runa Korda! I am honored at your presence. Simply delighted. You've made this foot chase much more interesting. And why *are* you here?" He appraised Austin visibly. "I cannot wait to learn of the youngster's abilities. Do you care to share them with me here, in a pleasant space? Or would you rather wait for the hell I've designed especially for you?"

• • •

Sean gave the warning.

"I know, I know." Edward rose and removed the glasses. "Better to submit him to Gwynvyd where he might one day come again."

"What? You're going to kill him?" Anki asked.

"Look for yourself. He doesn't realize his power, he isn't mastering the dream. If Cathbad can't help him escape they are worse than dead. Would you have him become a puppet? A weapon against the world?" He looked back to the screen. "They have them, it is unmistakable. Now leave, go. Bràthair are losing ground."

Johan stood. "I don't believe it. There is a way, I feel it. Put me in. Sean, give me one of those dream pills. I can get him out."

Sean brushed him off. "You've not the skill for this. Leave now or witness the death."

Johan crossed to stand in front of Edward.

"*Listen*, old man. *Something's* telling me I can save them. I just *know* I can. Put me in now, while there's a chance. If you need to, if I fail, then kill me, too. If Austin is the Change, if he's the only chance to beat these devils, then I have to try. *You* have to try. Give me the damn pill and take me there, now."

Edward scanned then, searching for Johan's motivation. Indeed there was certainty there, and a coiled, familiar energy. Above all else there was altruism, pure selflessness, beyond what he could imagine even from himself.

"Send word to Cathbad's carriers and raise more for this one." He silently blessed Johan. "Deliver him to the dream, quickly."

. . .

Blood flowed in a steady trickle above Austin's swollen right eye. His hands tingled numb from the wrist bindings. Rib fractures made breathing difficult. No longer a dream or a nightmare, reality had been recast. Edward's warning traveled across time. *This is not a job. This is a life choice.* This *was* happening. Troops encircled the clearing. Their long shadows darkened its grass. The Runa Korda leader, Cathbad, knelt nearby, tied and held by soldiers. The younger man was strung up to a makeshift gallows. The Roman general's droning litany completed the elaborately staged scene.

He looked away. The agony of his body couldn't compare to the suffering at knowing he'd failed everyone that mattered, including the world itself. Somewhere across the kaleidoscope of reality, Kaiya waited for his next email, ignorant of his impending death. Somewhere his father existed, aware or unaware of the events unfolding. He grieved for life and for what it could have been, for everyone.

"Young man!" The general called to him. "I sense you could use a shot in the arm. The guest! Make way for our guest!"

A black horse emerged from the other steeds at the opening of the clearing. Sitting atop, wearing armor similar to the general's, was a vision of Kaiya, her hair drawn back in a regal manner to emphasize the graceful lines of her face. Her beauty complimented the original nature of the glade and accentuated the evil soiling it. She guided her horse next to the general's and looked at the dark-souled bastard in a familiar way.

He gloated. "I'm sure they didn't tell you, boy. Shortly after you spoke with her on the phone we saved her from the death her body met. She has since learned what real living is about. In fact, she helped us reach you. Don't be too critical of her. She wants the best for you, just as we all do."

Captured? Body dead? Fear and rage filled his core.

Nearby, Cathbad muttered, "Just a dream." A guard kicked him in the face.

"I'm sorry, Austin," she called out. "I know this is a shock, but it's amazing, just amazing what's coming. Just don't resist and everything will be okay. Trust me, babe, it's amazing, just amazing what's in store. Say you'll give me a chance to show you."

He glanced at Cathbad. His face was half-buried in the ground under the weight of a soldier's knee. Mug, rope tied about his neck, stood perched on a shield held up by a pair of soldiers, awaiting his

fate. *All the world's a stage and we are merely players.* The druids were likely
the only chance of rescue yet were helpless. Bargaining felt pointless
but seemed the only way of controlling the outcome.

"Only if he allows these two to live and go free."

"No! *No!*" Again the soldiers beat Cathbad silent.

The general appeared to weigh the offer. Too soon, he nodded.
"Agreed. Let the laundry down." The soldiers complied and lowered
Mug to the ground.

Kaiya turned to ask the general something. Receiving a nod, she
bowed her head in thanks and dismounted to join Austin. She
approached and knelt before him. As in the basement of the bar, she
filled his senses. Her eyes searched his. In a low, quick voice she said,
"Break free now, babe, *now.*"

In response, she was flung backward the distance to her horse.
Before she struck the steed, she vanished, leaving her clothes to flop to
the ground.

The sky exploded in billowing clouds that stole the sun and turned
the air cold. The general's voice echoed to the heavens.

"Find her! Find the ignorant whore who might have been queen!"

Thunder pounded the air so it seemed about to shatter. "Prepare
to die Cathbad, leader of druids. But first, behold." He gestured to the
guards surrounding Mug. In a uniform movement, they pulled back on
the rope and propelled Mug into the air by his neck. His body recoiled
wildly as they jerked the rope. "There hangs the second most powerful
of the secret family. His attendants have done the deed for us." The
general turned to Cathbad. "Bring him to me!"

"No," Austin shouted, "*Don't do this.*"

The guards lifted the old druid and dragged him across the ground.
Hope left at last. The forest clearing would be his last memory of life.
He cringed as they dragged Cathbad by.

The druid turned his head and said, "It's coming."

A scream pierced the gloom, the wind suddenly rising. The scream
sounded again, a banshee seeking souls. Soldiers turned outward as
one to form a shield around the clearing. The general swung about on
his horse to seek the source. The guards bearing Cathbad dropped him
and drew their swords.

"Come one, come all!" The general yelled. "Yes! Come find your
leader! He's awaiting your rescue!"

The wind. He closed his eyes and focused only on the wind. It
played across his face, rising and falling, as if probing. *I need your help.
Please, hear me, understand me. Dream or not, you are the force I seek. Help us.*

Rising in response to every word, the wind rushed through the trees and flowed in ever stronger gusts until it became a howling force, tearing leaves from trees and pageants from poles. The soldiers looked to their general. His own bluster receded, the biting concern clear in his eyes. The scream sounded again, unnatural above the roaring wind. The general panicked.

"Kill them, kill them both now! Now! *Now!*"

The nearest soldiers prepared to hack.

The scream exploded once more. Bodies flew away from a shimmering outline, the shape unclear until it ran headlong into the line of horses just behind the general. Suddenly visible, a large white horse rammed them. Its squatting rider launched into the air on impact. Adorned in black leather armor, the rider soared over the general and landed in a tumbling roll in front of Cathbad.

Johan shouted, gripping the sword hand of the nearest soldier. He plunged the blade into the Imperial's groin and issued a hell kick to drop a pair of soldiers. He grabbed Cathbad's collar and heaved him towards Austin ahead of the attackers. Troops rushed to close the circle while others notched arrows and drew to fire.

Lightning crackled and forked in the air above Johan, lancing out to strike the nearest soldiers dead. With another soul-piercing scream, he reached for Austin as a volley of arrows let fly from the rim.

His palm braced his head and the madness ceased.

Silence carried echoes of the violence in a dizzying stillness. Light from attic windows revealed an old man at the head of a stairwell, staring on in approval.

Cathbad slowly stood, taking in the scene. "Vincent?"

"Cathbad. A battle, then?"

He nodded. "A friend has fallen."

"Fallen from their grip, I pray the Wild Wood. It was close for you, no?"

"Aye, it was. None closer. Your son saved us."

Johan strode forward. "Father, you were right. It is a noble fight."

"And you are learning. I'm proud. So very proud, Gerrit." He turned to Cathbad. "It has begun?"

Cathbad confirmed. "The Words are once more correct but in an imprecise way."

"How is that?"

"Your son, and this one," he indicated a still-shaken Austin on the floor with his back against a trunk. "*They* are the Change."

PART II - Conflict

Chapter 14

Against stupidity the gods themselves contend in vain.
- Friedrich von Schiller

Austin surfaced to the murmur of conversation. Memories trailed from the dimness of sleep. A stab of loss and panic shot through him upon recalling news of Kaiya's death. He shifted his head to find Anki sitting next to him. Johan and Edward stood with Sean by the French doors. Conversation halted.

"Is she alive or dead?" he asked them. "The truth this time."

Edward neared. "Forgot to take your pills, did we?"

"God damn it, tell me."

Edward leaned in close, eyes sharp as daggers. "Before you dare raise your voice, you will consider what your desires have cost us *this time*. One of the greatest druids ever to advance the Family is gone, having tried to save your life. What I choose to tell you is this: I sorely wonder now if it was worth it."

The bite of Edward's words paled compared to what followed. Edward jammed the true meaning of Mug's life hard into his mind, obliterating ego and birthing a guilt that threatened to consume him. Mug had helped pioneer technology, avert wars, cured diseases, created new defenses in the dream world, and most lately discovered the quantum-physical mechanisms behind telekinesis. A legend in time had been forced to sacrifice everything simply because he'd wanted to see Kaiya again. Mug's death was his fault.

He recoiled when released, battered by the knowing.

"We don't know her fate," Edward answered. "They may have her or they may not. But yes, her body was lost at the safe house. The same with Mac and our brothers."

He pushed up onto an elbow. "You knew? All this time? Is that what the future holds with the Korda? Lies? Games within games?"

"She may still be alive, Austin," Anki said quietly, "just not with a body."

"The 'game' is to prepare you, to preserve your continuity," Edward said, his vibe narrow and sharp. "Your progress is vital, the timing everything. As for Kaiya, we don't know. There is a chance she escaped their hold when Johan broke into the dream."

"You never mentioned they could do that. Stealing souls from their bodies? That's a hell of thing to leave out, don't you think?" He shook his head, struggling to keep up. "Look, you have no idea how sorry I am about Mug, but why lose both? We have to find her."

Sean stepped forward. "He said there's a *chance* she escaped. It's more likely they have her still. If so, there is little we can do. Then again, she may have gone on to Gwynvyd. There are fates much worse, Austin, though we hope she is within reach. There's no telling at this point."

"And if you do find her?" he asked. "What then?"

"Hopefully we'll cross that bridge. You need to focus on the here and now." He went to unplug the monitor cart.

"Will she have a body again?"

Edward crossed his arms. "You wanted the truth and that is we will do our best."

He looked to Johan. "You've got the power. Edward just said it. You can help find her and bring her back."

"He already offered," Edward replied. "His success tonight was due in part to the element of surprise. Until we better understand his abilities, he won't be out on anyone's behalf."

"If she's free then she's just wandering. I have to go back to find her. I have to."

"You require much work before you'll be allowed back."

"Really? And what if she's running out of options?" He imagined her swimming under a sheet of ice, just visible but unable to break through the surface. "I need to find her. She needs me, I can feel it."

Sean shook his head. "Meta contact is only half the battle. There is the matter of binding her to a body again. Not an uncomplicated matter."

Edward pressed his displeasure into the moment. "Understand, too, your girlfriend is not the only life we are trying to save."

He stifled a stream of replies born of desperation and frustration. Yes, there was much more at stake than just Kaiya's life, but it was maddening to know Johan could help find her and wouldn't.

"We're not giving up, Austin," Sean said. "We're already working on a plan."

Edward headed for the door. "We will resume briefing an hour after sunrise. Also," he looked to Austin, "until further notice, we will meet every night to take the pills."

Anki stood and squeezed Austin's shoulder. "I'm glad you're okay."

Everyone but Johan left the room. He crossed his arms and said, "Looks like we're on the hook for saving the world."

"*Right.* I couldn't save Kaiya. Hell, I couldn't even save myself."

"Bullshit. You did what you were supposed to. If you hadn't, I wouldn't have learned what I did. And listen, I may be some kind of dream weaver but you, man, you're going to turn their world upside down. We'll do this together. You heard him. It's prophecy. Have a little faith."

He couldn't help but recall Meng's instructions on forming an island in his mind to call home: *If you don't, you will drown in the pain of loss and of memory.*

He drew a sharp breath and let it out slowly. "I'm trying."

"You are right, Austin," Edward said when they gathered again in the library. "No one told you about soul stealing. It is not easy to do and does not happen that often."

"So what does it mean?" he asked.

"Subjugation. The bond of meta is severed from the body and the essence captured. The latter step is difficult and requires specific knowledge to perform. There are only a handful of us that can do it and for good reason."

"You'll be able to recapture Kaiya then? What about a body?"

"It is possible to join meta essence to a body. The process and ethics involved are topics for another time. We will address Kaiya's fate when it becomes necessary to. Right now, a briefing before we split up. Our time here is almost done."

On the table sat a silver attaché case. He rested a hand on it. "I spoke briefly of the Change but there is more to know. Prophesied over five hundred years ago, the Change was to be a person with powers allowing the Runa Korda a chance at altering the course of history. By that I mean at least stemming the worst of what the Comannda does, though most believe the Change will allow us to topple the Comannda altogether. How that would play out is debated as the Words are not clear. Some believe it can be done without exposing the secrets all at once. Others believe it will trigger Armageddon. Certainly the Conflict is shown as being a tumultuous and grave period. I think it is safe to say it has begun. We now know the Change consists of you two and that you are both with us. Our goal is to keep you safe and help you master your abilities. Alignments are occurring that offer confidence we are on the right track. We will do our best to prepare you for whatever lies ahead."

Anki nodded. "Prepared is good."

"To start, you need to know more about your modifications." He popped the latches on the attaché case and turned it to face them. Inside, several gray metal tubes of various diameters and lengths lay ensconced in fitted rubber molding. He withdrew a small penlight from the case and shined its light at them. Unscrewing the lid revealed the battery compartment. He slid out the three tiny disc shaped batteries, flipped each, and re-inserted them. "Reverse polarity. The light won't work. But the more important functions of the pen now will."

He stood and held the pen light against his belly, which earned him looks.

"Press and hold the clip for three seconds. The signals emitted will start a reaction according to the setting you select. There are four settings, the first always being 'neutral' or your natural state. The second is olive, as found in Asians. Third, brown as found in Hispanics and the fourth is mulatto. Each setting has a shade parameter determined by screwing the pen's clip right to left, lightest to darkest. You will have up to two minutes of conversion time while the melanocyte alteration occurs and pigmentation becomes uniform to the programming." He held up the penlight. "First function then, is to alter your skin color."

Austin shook his head in amazement.

Edward stowed the penlight in his shirt pocket and retrieved a pencil-thin aluminum tube from the case.

"Anki, you asked about the holes at the top of your gum lines. Our answer was contrived; they aren't for sinus drainage in case of infection." He lifted the briefcase's rubber molding to expose a screen and keypad. It powered up at a touch, revealing a computer generated image of his profile. He tapped a few keys and placed the tube near the screen.

"Low power signal for program download." He unscrewed the cap from the tube and slipped the open end between his teeth and lips. At the top of his gum line his face bulged and began to throb as things moved, sliding rapidly from the tube into his face. He emptied another tube in the same fashion at the other hole.

"What the...?" Anki stared. Johan watched, mesmerized as the druid's face pulsated with the movement of whatever crawled around inside it.

"While grotesque, these are my personal bio-cats. Like caterpillars but created specifically for this service. They will traverse catacombs woven under my face to a pre-set location and then expand and stretch themselves according to the program, thus shaping my face. They will even act as temporary tie-offs, cinching muscles and tensioning cartilage to help reshape areas such as my nose, eyes and lips."

"Biological?"

"Yes, our own basic lifeforms."

Edward's skin had become noticeably darker and areas of his face had smoothed into a different shape. His brow appeared fuller, his lips and cheeks ample, and his eyes more oval. "Once in place, they will lock and retain their shape and position. Their cellular cohesion and function is maintained by absorbing nutrients from the walls of the catacombs, which are membranic. Their energy source for motor systems and locking is achieved through bioelectromagnetic effect and is boosted when you are in urban areas where heavier fields exist."

Anki put her hands to her cheeks. "I'm supposed to put bugs in my face?"

Edward nodded. "You will get used to it. It helps that the biocats are coated in a mild local anesthesia in the tubes. But even dry they are not intolerable in motion. There are also creams that induce localized swelling to achieve a desired facial topology, though the effects are time-limited. Now, this pen also drives four more functions."

Edward's demonstrations revealed the other bio-tweaks made to the three at the table.

"Dynamic retensioning of muscle within the vocal folds allow for pitch alterations. After voice training, you will be able to vary your voiceprint by assignment."

Fingerprints were also dynamic although the cellular perforation process was unbearable for some without a local anesthetic. Pain and itching could persist for an hour or longer depending on the individual.

He twisted the cap to enter another mode. "The pigmentary layers of the eye's iris contain cells with pigment granules. Each of you have irises with modified cells that respond to nano-transmitters which in turn receive orders by this signal. Chromatophoric alterations recolor the eye within seconds."

He replaced the pen in its slot. "You'll have your own cats, pens, and the unit to program them, called a deck. There is also a two-in-one smart phone if you can't use the pens."

The three stared at the stranger before them. The now-black man with a baritone voice and a slight French accent continued.

"The ability to change these physical properties extends your field usefulness by many factors. You will be trained how to gracefully make the changes in different situations without revealing yourself. Take careful notes. You are in a most valued group. You are now Atharrachdainn. May your secret serve you well."

• • •

Director Tomov stood on a dais at the front of the conference room running the debrief. Orb cameras rose from the table on thin stalks to allow the Executive Board telepresence. Behind them stood two G1 agents replete in black, their faces hidden behind formless masks. They scanned continuously, reading him to his core.

The conference rooms' black glass walls and tabletop displayed imagery and video from the operation in question. Stills of the various subjects lined the walls. Videos looped scenes and one large video at the front of the room was paused, showing the outstretched form of Peter Brusse mid-air, moments before his dream rescue of the druid leader and his charge, Austin.

"Extensive analysis has failed to explain how A2, Peter Brusse, initiated this level of control. There was suggestion that it was made to appear as Brusse but in fact managed by some other method, possibly combining."

An Executive with a Saudi accent spoke into the room. "What does this mean?"

"It means the priests have actuated yet another extraordinary response to protect their charge, Austin Bakken. Volgograd is nearly there with combining so it's possible the druids have succeeded ahead of us. In which case Brusse is just a figure, not a single entity with extraordinary power. Of course, Austin may be even more valuable, given their willingness to use Brusse in such a revealing manner."

Another voice, synthesized to disguise, asked, "What is Austin's value?"

"Still unknown."

"What of their prophecies?"

"I cannot speak to that directly, sir, without sufficient information. You are aware what the legends state. We see one subject exhibiting unprecedented influence in the mesh."

"This must be resolved."

Director Tomov nodded. "Highest priority has been given to locating both targets. Patterns have been issued to all Signus teams and

G3 are fully involved in the coordination. Overseer is engaged. There have been no incidents suggesting further release activity at this point."

"Locate him." The synthesized voice said. "Locate them both and contain them. Lead this effort, director. All resources. Utilize Decimation Protocol if necessary. Whatever it takes. Do you understand, Director Tomov? Whatever it takes."

• • •

A white Citroen van sped along a lane draped in the shade of English oaks. Thirty kilometers outside Epping Forest the farmlands and old growth forests shared land with country manors and small townships in sleepy elegance.

City life seemed a sickly perversion by comparison. Here the accomplishments were in the order of the fields and the crops they yielded, in the standing homes and structures from centuries past – not in the model of Mercedes or BMW you drove or in your zip code. There was a harmony and quiet dignity in the way the people worked and lived here.

Sean drove while Austin stared out the window.

"What's that?" he asked Austin. "You've got a willow's look on your face."

"I just like it out here. America hasn't got the grace England does."

"Grace? I think you haven't traveled much. Grace is Milan or Venice or Athens or Bucharest. But I think I know what you mean. Okay, here we are."

Sean pulled off the road and stopped under a stand of trees lined with tall bushes. He took up a camera bag. "If anyone asks, we're just out taking pics. If pressed, we're taking stock photos to sell on the internet. I've got the business card."

"Farmland pics, got it. Big demand for that." He grabbed his own bag.

"Just another assignment."

They climbed out and pushed through the bushes. Beyond, an expanse of recently-tilled field stretched outward a quarter mile, half that across. Splotches of partially dried dirt made for good contrast. Sean produced the camera and began shooting. "Get started."

Austin took out a spongy yellow ball and tossed it on the ground. Dropping into the grid was easier now. The sense of 'touch' came from a direct experience of meta – rathad, the seventh sense. The ability to feel the underlying structure of the physical world allowed him to target it, to become entangled with it. Beyond that, it came down to the still-mysterious conversion of intention to actuation. Once connected to the yellow ball, he wanted it to roll and it did. Like in a lucid dream, the dreamer in him arranged for the change to occur.

"Float it."

The ball rose into the air without effort.

"Good. Now the empty can."

He tossed an aluminum can to the ground. With only slightly more effort, it rose into the air and spun slowly.

"What's Atharrachdainn mean?" he asked Sean.

"It's Celtic. To change. To become something else. Now try the full can."

One at a time, he floated the objects from his bag, each one heavier than the last. The red brick was the heaviest and was much easier this time. Handling two at once wasn't something he could do yet. As expected, Sean instructed him to try. The yellow ball floated upward and hovered. Splitting attention to reach for the empty can caused the ball to fall. It seemed a case of either or, no matter what he tried.

Sean saw him struggle. "Alright, let's try something else."

At the edge of the field was the tilling machine used to turn the field. It was a smaller unit, no more than six feet wide, designed to be pulled behind a tractor. Sean nodded towards it.

"You kidding? That's gotta weigh half a ton."

"Last night's increased dosage may help. Can't hurt to try."

"Don't be so sure about that."

Wrapping his attention around the tiller was awkward, probably because the thing was just so damn large and heavy. The obstacle was even considering that he could move it. Over the next several minutes he managed to focus and really feel the machine. With some mental adjustment, an understanding came. Heavy yes, but when he thought of moving it, a feeling grew. The same intention that let him lift bricks blossomed by degrees until he thought he might actually be able to lift the tiller.

Sean sensed the change and looked over. "There you go. Be careful with it."

In his mind's eye, the machine became a three-dimensional cutout, its form something he wrapped his entire rathad around. Potential surged.

"Here goes."

The flash of effort immediately narrowed his senses. The field and sky and his own body disappeared – leaving only the machine and its relationship with Raon. The grid was just X, Y, and Z and he was going to move that thing in Z, straight up.

The tiller creaked under an imprecise pressure. A fender guard bent inward.

"Easy does it," Sean said, amazement in his voice.

"Ain't nothin' easy about this," he said with clenched teeth. The tiller raised several inches from the dirt before a headache burned outward like lightning forks. He panicked and set the machine down with a thud.

"Good fucking job, mate. Most impressive."

He circled back into the shade of the trees rubbing his head, staring at the grid before him. He'd spent a lifetime taking it for granted – knowing now that it could be altered so severely with just human thought was both intoxicating and frightening as hell.

"You're telling the truth, I hope," he told Sean.

"About what?"

"About me being the only one who can do this kind of TK. That neural protein research is exclusive to the Runa Korda."

"As far as I know we're the first."

"So they could have this tech. They could have found someone like me."

"It's possible, sure, but we've had no indication. None. You worried about duking it out with another TK?"

There was that but what he didn't say or even think about was the fear of being turned into a weapon without the freedom to say no.

"Something like that, yeah."

• • •

The windows of the cottage looked out over an unkempt yard facing the English Channel. Johan wiped a pane clean to watch the waves march in, an endless army on a suicide mission to dash against the stone-lined shore. The old man lived there alone and like a biological chimney he smoked his pipe nearly constantly. The cottage held two small bedrooms, a bathroom, kitchen, and a living room made into an office. Covering the walls were paper sketches pinned three and four deep or more. Some were detailed and drawn with care, others were hastily done and only roughly suggestive. Faces, places, scenes, and storyboards of all kinds filled the living room and spilled onto the kitchen's walls.

Two easy chairs faced the windows, a small table and lamp between them. The lamp's shade was a sickly mustard color. The curtains, too, were nicotine-stained. The house sat still in time, evidenced by magazines dated three decades ago and furniture much older than that. The phone, buried beneath sheets of sketches and newspaper clippings on an antique desk, was the only visible hint of the modern world. A small woodstove might have been nineteenth century.

He waited and listened while the old man finished work on a sketch.

His name was Pons, a Frenchman, another long-toothed druid probably older than Edward. He spoke four languages and had forgotten three others though he cussed fluently in all seven. He demonstrated that while he worked his sketch. Pons was thin, of average height with tousled gray hair cut short, probably with scissors from the desk. His gray beard was similarly short but kept more neatly. He wore farmer's overalls, old brown boots, and a plain white t-shirt. Beneath the beard, a pale and wrinkled face focused on the paper. Still trying not to gag on the smoke, Johan considered going outside again.

"Alright, then. That will have to do." Pons folded the sketch in fourths and tucked it into a pigeon hole in his desk. He turned to face him. A pipe hung from the corner of his mouth.

"An honor to meet you, Johan. I did not mean to be rude. I forget how important time is to people."

"You sketch your dreams."

"I do. I'm no welet but I've got sketches that depict a lot of what has come to pass. That's what I do – study dreams."

"I'm here to learn more about them."

"That you are, yes, and more. I expect to eventually learn from you but we have to get you rolling first. What you did for Cathbad was bold and reckless, which just so happened to be the exact thing needed at the time. I hope that was instinct because it will make my job much easier if you already have it." He emptied his pipe into an ashtray and stamped out the embers. "Go and crack the windows, open the door. You aren't used to the smoke and I shouldn't be."

They sat in the easy chairs and enjoyed the breeze off the channel. Long weeds swayed outside the windows, a lazy dance accompanied by the surf's lapping against the concrete beachhead beyond the yard.

Pons produced a toothpick and used it in place of the pipe. "You understand, no one wants you going into Saoghal making dreams that attract every damned korjé there is. It is like real life: to control the experience you need to temper your intention at all times. To control your intention, you need to know you are dreaming."

"Lucid dreaming."

"Yes. You will become *aware*. Night will become another kind of day. You will find it is a high buy-in until you are used to it. Don't say I didn't warn you."

He studied the yellow-orange nicotine-stained windowpanes. Sunlight passed through them and emerged a sickly semblance. A little like his former self passing through the gauntlet of change.

"Relax, you will get used to it," Pons said, reading him. "Just takes time. You've had your basic training."

Seagulls squawked overhead, soaring on channel winds. The same winds rang the chimes on the porch. In the distance a ferry churned the sea white in its wake.

The flow of meta reached and left his brain. Sensory imagery and memory-born associations mixed to create the always-new pinnacle of emotion, the subtle paint on the canvas that formed reality. Each moment, captured in turn, fed back into the meta in an endless loop of creation, yielding awareness, experience, and memory.

He breathed deep from a rising breeze, sensing all the awareness flying around unseen corridors of reality. The world was alive with consciousness.

"What about dreams then?" he asked Pons. "What can you teach me?"

"Well, you already know that sleep is the act of unplugging from the grid. We withdraw all but the life cord of the droichid, withdrawing almost completely into our meta-self. For recreation, as problem solving exercises, or whatever the reason, we dream. A dream is a stage set by a meta in Saoghal, a bubble of reality unto itself. Everyone spawns these bubbles because everyone dreams. The Comannda's korjé are rangers in this realm. They take control of a dreamer, of the reality, unless the dreamer is also lucid. In that case it becomes a question of power and cunning. Not lucid or overpowered, a dreamer becomes imprisoned for as long as the korjé can manage. The imprisoned cannot wake up, cannot plug back into the grid. The body is suspended. This you saw with Austin. The good news, Johan, is that you have no match. Or shouldn't, if the Words are right."

"So I kicked korjé ass, eh?"

Pons smiled. "Yes, you did. But who knows what would have happened had you stayed longer to fight? Hmm? That is what we are going to try to find out today. Right now, in fact."

"Right now?" He reached into his pocket for the pillbox Edward gave him.

"No," Pons put up a hand, "you won't use those. You are going to learn to dream on the go."

"On the go."

"Yes," Pons twisted the toothpick in his mouth. "You daydream, right? Everyone does. Far more than we realize. Even while driving."

"Pons, those are thoughts. Hardly the same as dreaming."

"You think not? Many of the same components are in play. People interact with their meta store and throw things on the stage, in a bubble. They are lucid dreaming without realizing it. I am going to teach you to hijack the stage."

He stumbled over the implications until they culminated in one unavoidable realization: he was talking mind control.

"You're going to teach me? Now?" he asked.

"I am going to try. You must make the proper leaps." Pons blinked several times before continuing. "Now, there is a benefit to being right next to someone you want to drag into a dream. It takes most of the work out of it, provided you know what you are doing. Distance is a factor for most. For me it is." A butterfly flew in the window, fluttered in a circle, and left through the doorway. "You extend right into their meta flow, but quietly. Do a little number with the local loop, at the brain stem. Some call it 'planting the tree' or 'setting base camp'. Then you enter the droichid and follow their flow into Saoghal."

The window panes seemed more orange than yellow. Probably the angle of the sun.

"Once there, you spawn a dream via their meta, one that perfectly matches the grid around them. You do this by using fresh physical data from the meta stream in the local loop. Their eyes, their ears – every sense flows in meta, giving you the ingredients to create the stage. You can imagine the dexterity this involves, yes? It takes practice, lots of practice. You must be careful, so they don't detect it, so they are not distracted by the act of constructing it."

The drapes began to sag, lengthening on the rods.

"And then once built, once synchronized, you will have slipped your dream over the top of their reality. A joining. A merging." He paused, eyeing him. "You are doing quite well in the realization that you're now dreaming lucidly. At this point, most people become emotional. They feel disconnected from their body and are scared to death of me or thinking they've lost their mind. But not you. I am impressed. I should probably thank you for your restraint, because I imagine you are holding back."

"I am." Glued to the druid's every word, he resisted trying to take control and focused instead on what he'd just sensed. Just like *that*, they were dreaming the druid's dream. "How is this possible?"

"We daydream." *Together*. Pons' voice resonated in the center of his mind. He resisted blocking it out.

"You're not holding me in this, are you?"

I was, but you feel it now, of course. You could break it if you wanted but please don't, not yet. I've wonderful teaching tools here. Get comfortable now, and relax. Trust me.

Pons proceeded to describe the technique to initiate dream control, coupling his words with concepts born from thought. Learning this way made the knowledge familiar and easier to transfer.

It is like a mini-dream unto itself, Johan. A dream inside a dream. You form it and trust its validity, trust your sense and the intended outcome. With practice, it will drive any dream. You understand?

He nodded.

Satisfied, Pons continued aloud. "Now you have the concept of the local loop and how to manipulate it. What I'm curious about right now is if you can break from this dream. I'm going to harden it, clamp down as much as I can, and then see if you can shake it off. Are you ready?"

He tried to nod but couldn't. The same paralysis from the cave dream had suddenly set in.

"Try to stand."

Nothing responded from head to toe, save for his eyes. His heart began to pound madly. Seconds passed. Pons watched him.

In the cave, he'd found an edge which led him to an entirely different scene. Such a move might be dangerous here, considering the Comannda's interest in him – plus, it was too much like running away. *This* was the dream he had to control. Instead of looking for an edge to tear at, he searched for what was driving the dream: the spout, the source.

Under intense scrutiny, a difference between waking and dreaming became apparent. Aside from the melting curtains, the color changing windows, and now the thousands of ants burrowing up from the flattened carpet, the dream version of the old man's house held an underlying evanescence, as if the room might shift under the right circumstances, might *give*.

But how to push?

Edward's insistence on imagination's importance led to the solution. Pons had explained exactly how to drag someone into a dream: extend across the grid into their meta stream and up to their meta body to spawn a dream. That meant *he* was the inadvertent dreamer in his own meta body. That fact revealed a transcending lucidity that he snapped to instantly. A veil lifted and he woke from the dream. The windows were a proper nicotine yellow, curtains at normal length, the carpet free of insects.

The old druid smiled. "Bien. Très bon! The best kind of student. Now, I will do it again but then I will go a step further and bridge to another dream hosted by an associate. A transfer, you see? You will then be a guest in *her* reality and when she hardens it, you will become twice the prisoner. Try to wrest control from her."

Johan nodded and studied the carpet. A chance to beat him at the game. If he could detect the druid's initial incursion into his awareness, there'd be a chance at figuring out his entire method.

It came as a delay, a ripple in time. Tiny, subtle, and nothing after – it had to be the druid. Locked onto the knowledge of an intrusion, just the fact of it, he became supremely lucid in the moment, waiting to act.

Pons' expression grew serious. He rolled his toothpick idly between his teeth but otherwise sat still, pensive. The surf crashed beyond the yard, a punctuation in time. A breeze stirred the chimes and swirled dust motes through sunbeams. The moment drew long with all the elements of a standoff.

Pons nodded in a gesture of acquiescence. "I think I need my pipe." He stood and walked to his desk.

The druid remained there in his flow. Without knowing what to feel or what to look out for, instinct led the watch.

Pons loaded his pipe and tamped the tobacco. He appraised him with a critical eye. "You know, if everyone had the uncommon awareness you do, we would either be well on our way to a brighter future or digging our own graves. Of course, it is the former we aim for."

"How many can do this?"

"At this level? Only a handful. Until now, perhaps."

"Why? And why can I?"

Pons shrugged. "It is what makes us different."

"Did they think you were the Change?"

"At one time I was considered a candidate, yes. Same with the others."

Johan looked around the room. "You don't leave this place, do you?"

"Rarely. I am all too familiar with our beloved space rock. Dreams, now, they are worthy of exploring. New and meaningful. Tied to the underpinnings of mankind and thus to the future."

Johan nodded, unwilling to relinquish his post. Something began to reveal itself. A sense of *otherness*. Too nebulous to isolate, it sought to bury itself in his common, everyday sense of self – he would soon lose track of it. Pons was on the move.

A memory surfaced of gold panning in Switzerland with his parents. Sifting out ordinary rock in the hopes the heavier gold would remain. Still bearing strict attention, he did just that and let the ordinary fall away, as he had when fleeing Amsterdam.

Like a tiny hidden nugget, Pons' awareness was revealed within his own, the druid's meta stream waiting to be followed. He wasted no time and shot straight into it, a nearly instantaneous trip into Pons' local loop. There he found a busy junction of energy, thought, and emotion – a truly well oiled, if chaotic, machine.

Three things happened almost at once: Pons raised a block, Johan effectively denied the block, and then Johan stalled, an oversized sumo sitting atop his opponent without knowledge of the rules of the game.

"Are you sure you haven't done this before? Please be careful." Pons sat down at his desk and slowly lit his pipe.

"How can this be?" he asked. "We aren't daydreaming now, and we're not asleep."

"There are levels of consciousness that most people keep, or acknowledge. A convention, if you will. You and I are breaking from that convention. 'Heavily blurring it' is a better description because reality is anamorphic. We're raised to experience it in linear, unimaginative ways because that's the most effective and comfortable means to build and tightly control societies. As you can see, there is so much more to life and perception." Smoke streamed from the pipe. "Now, since you're here, see if you can trace to my core. The meta flow might seem thicker the nearer you get, if that helps."

That he'd managed his awareness so long and even held the druid at bay felt like an accomplishment, as if he'd beaten a wizard at a game of spells. Still so much to learn, though. The druid's meta stream flowed more dense in one direction, awaiting only his intention to join it. He hesitated at the thought of crossing into Saoghal.

Nothing ventured, nothing gained...

Arrival happened as a gunshot – in an instant, hundreds of years of memories and emotions assaulted him, a vast catalog of human knowledge and wisdom bound by an overwhelming love of existence and thirst for survival. One could easily drown trying to absorb even a portion of it. However, a sense of duty stood out powerfully; a duty to the Family first, then to all of humanity, to the entire planet, and to –

"Okay – deep stab, that. Quite piercing. That's all you need right now," Pons said quickly, jolting him back in a one-two punch of unexpected imagery and bland, blocking emotion.

He went to catch a glimpse of what else Pons was duty-bound to but the druid was in the way, protective and defensive of those memories, of something bigger. He yielded in respect.

Pons redirected the moment into something positive. "Unless you care to try to spawn a dream from my meta."

The challenge eased the moment and engaged curiosity. Several concepts of how to do it came and went, all of which proved useless. Again, he remembered Edward's discourse about imagination. At once an idea came, simple and powerful: *start imagining*. Fully centered in Pons' meta, he imagined a street in Berlin. A world flickered into being, was gone, and then reappeared with a steady push. They stood on a snow-lined street outside a bar, the night air biting-cold. Two women under a covered patio smoked and talked. Music thumped from a nearby club. Pons looked around and nodded.

"You have it. You are a natural, Johan. There's more to learn, but at this rate, you won't have much homework."

Chapter 15

To map out a course of action and follow it to an end requires some of the same courage
that a soldier needs.
- Ralph Waldo Emerson, 1803 - 1882, American Poet, Essayist

An autumn-tinged evening descended on the London burb of
South Lambeth. Brick row houses lined Killyon Street. Streetlamps
reflected from shiny hoods and windshields of cars parked along the
curb. A half a dozen youngsters perched on a low wall. Their voices
rose and fell, lost in the sounds of traffic and trains running the nearby
line. The 8:45 from Brixton rumbled into Wandsworth Road station.

Sean sat on the porch steps of the flat chewing jerky with a beer in
hand. A couple walked a pair of French poodles past. The woman
gabbed of adulterous intrigue in the neighborhood while the man
looked as leashed as the dogs and far less enthused. A cab drove by,
too fast for the narrow lane.

A few minutes later Sean stood, timing it. A swig of beer. A bite of
jerky. Again a swig. He glanced left and saw a second couple turn the
corner. Austin and Anki arrived right on time.

"Evenin', mates," he said as they approached. "Party's on the
inside."

Johan banked the cue ball and struck the nine into a corner pocket.

"Well played." The old man shook his hand. "I suspected you
were a shark."

"Thanks for not cheating."

Anki entered the sunroom-turned-billiards hall and went directly to
Johan. They embraced, kissing.

Soldado looked up from his notes. "Looks like we're all here."

Austin stood in the doorway. "Bloody fine evening for a shindig,
but why the rat's hole?"

The old man brushed past him. "Blending, is all." He wore an
untucked dress shirt over jeans and the face of an old Italian. It had to
be Edward. "Congratulations, by the way. I knew you'd push the
boundaries."

"I had a good coach," Austin said, indicating Sean.

"Just pointed you, is all," he replied.

After dinner, Sean drew crimson drapes closed in the sitting room and turned up the radio. Anki helped pass around glasses of wine.

The flat brimmed with secondhand store furniture. A worn couch and mismatched Morris chairs filled the narrow room. Poorly hung track lighting lit the room along with a pair of buffet lamps on battered end tables. The stale odors of past fraternity parties mixed with the berry-scented candles Anki had found in a hallway drawer.

A laptop rested on a coffee table with a fist-sized cube plugged into it. Anki took a seat between Johan and Austin on the couch.

"Thank you, Anki." Edward raised his glass. "Now, a toast to each of you, for the progress you have made is historic."

They all drank.

"Johan, your power in the dream state has never been seen before. Austin, your affinity with the grid will change things in ways we cannot yet imagine. We are grateful for your alignment and have already learned much from you. Soldado, your insights into frequency channeling and distributed associative encryption resequencing may well be the breakthrough needed to gain a beachhead on their communications. Mr. Lathrop has only the highest praise for the way your mind works. And Anki, your finely tuned empathic sense will continue to guide us, your very presence a reassurance that we are on the right path. Believe it."

"Okay, Edward, why the buttering up?" Soldado said, smiling. "What's the meeting about?"

"Time is pressing on an issue of great importance. Our immediate action is necessary. You may consider this your first commission."

Sean clicked the lights off. The cube shot an image to the wall. The face of a Japanese man in his sixties stared into the room.

"Yukitake Sakuma, oyabun of the largest yakuza crime family in the world, the Ookami-shita. As godfather, his expansionist policies brought him power and wealth far in excess of any of his predecessors. They bring in billions of dollars a year from extortion, gambling, guns, drugs, real estate and more. Stock market manipulation, internet porn, construction kickback schemes, they do it all. A significant amount of that wealth is due to work done in the digital territories. Soldado, I'm sure you're familiar with the yakuza's 'digital warriors'."

He nodded. "The Dejitaru. Pure digital. We've contracted with individuals and small cells. Mostly bag jobs on tight databases or proof of concept threats. Some thrash attacks and data drills. They're expensive but we've used them on Asian targets because they know associations and routes in that part of the world. They move like light through glass, even in Chinese space. That's why they're expensive to get."

Edward glanced at the oyabun's image. "Sakuma's Dejitaru bring him great wealth, a wealth he wisely shares with them. Out of the estimated forty thousand members in the Ookami-shita, as many as four thousand are Dejitaru. Compare that to your five hundred in the Underground and you get an idea of what they are capable of. Our interest in their operations recently uncovered this man," the screen split to display the photo of a white male in his forties, slim with an intelligent face but otherwise unremarkable, "a Comannda Group 2 agent. He greases the wheels of the unwashed masses, influences thought processes, and uses money and other incentives to secure cooperation. To make agreements with the yakuza in this manner is expected, as they tend to honor them when made face to face. Getting Sakuma's commitment saves them the task of manually driving lesser bosses from behind the scenes. He is one of a few we have ferreted out and are trying to keep track of."

"What's he up to?" Johan asked.

"He's been working on Sakuma to bring him into a deal he's resistant to. Encounters are shielded, any and all observation blocked. When he's alone, we sense Sakuma is disturbed at the proposal, but we can't get in to learn the details and he speaks to no one of it."

"He's been muddled." Sean added. "Active shielding in the grid and in Saoghal. We could only skim stray emotions and watch, ready if they slip up."

"During a recent meeting they did. We pressed in. What little was harvested suggests involvement in a local operation with worldwide implications."

Sean picked it up. "Interpreted, we see the Dejitaru running concerted net attacks against the US and EU. Likely infrastructure with extra emphasis on financials. Why this bothered the godfather so much isn't clear. It implies he didn't trust the proposal or he doesn't like what the attacks would bring about. This yakuza connection may yield the best intelligence of what they're planning."

The slide changed to an image of a nearly destroyed black luxury sedan.

"The Comannda's need for the Dejitaru must be timely and great. This morning the oyabun was involved in a car wreck. Before they could finish him off, bràthair interceded and stole him into a dream.

The bond to his body is thin but he may still make it provided the body is maintained. If the godfather dies now, the syndicate falls to his son, Ukita, whom we know is willing to do whatever the Comannda wants. This must be delayed, at least until we know more."

Austin asked, "If you have him in the dream why haven't you figured what it is?"

Edward shook his head. "Attempts at forcing lucidity have failed. Which is why we need you, Johan, to assume the dream. You may be able to do what others have not, as well as ward off attempts to recapture him. As for his body, his wife managed to install an army of Ookami-shita warriors in and around the hospital to protect her husband. It won't be enough. The Comannda will be enraged at our involvement and will act soon." He turned to Austin. "You leave for Tokyo tonight. We want you in place to help protect Sakuma."

"You're serious?" Austin asked. "What can I do that his warriors can't, besides maybe get myself killed?"

"Sounds dangerous," Johan agreed. "Why the risk?"

"Because what we do requires risk and he has to start somewhere. From a field position, he'll be surrounded by positively aligned forces. The Confrere have assigned anti-terrorist units to the hospital so risk is low. Training means nothing if you don't apply it." Edward stood and paused, taking in the three on the couch. "Anki, you'll go with him, as a traveling companion. You'll gain field experience and help further with his self-discovery."

The idea didn't set well with Johan but he kept silent.

"Anki is uniquely qualified to help Austin. A cab will arrive in a few minutes." It rang with finality. "Soldado, Mr. Lathrop wants to use this time as a sampling of their communications net using your hypothesis. I think you'll appreciate what he's setting up."

The flat's door stood open, a cab visible at the curb. Anki sat in the back, having said her goodbye with Johan. A chorus of crickets subsided in the nearby shrubbery as Edward and Austin stepped out onto the porch.

He turned to regard Edward, who nodded.

"Go on, Austin. Out with it."

"Yes, I'll say it. You'll use Johan for this but not for Kaiya? At what point do you think it becomes anything less than cruel? If you're holding back, do me a favor and tell me now. Is she really gone?"

"I've withheld nothing since you dreamt. I simply do not know. I give you my word, Austin, we will use him to find her. This assignment will be a test. If he can operate safely on Sakuma's behalf, we'll know Kaiya will be safer when he goes to look for her. It is the right order for the circumstances. That's all I can offer."

He looked away. A cricket dared a chirp. The sweet scent of honeysuckle on the night air took him back home to evenings with Kaiya, to dinners on the patio, lying out looking at the stars under the pines, and watching television with the windows open. He ached to hold her again. It was torturous to think she might be gone forever.

"Austin. There is no randomness, nor is there chance. Trust things are evolving as they should, with our understanding or without. Go now with Kaiya in your heart and a love of the mystery and the power you are joining with. You will find what you need. You will be complete."

There was nothing to say to that. It was in the old druid's eyes, the truth of his words. To protest would create weakness at a time when strength was needed. He could only continue to trust – in Edward, in the Runa Korda, in the universe.

The druid offered his hand and he shook it before leaving to join Anki.

From the porch, Edward watched the cab pull away and disappear down the lane. Long moments passed before the crickets resumed their song – hesitant at first, then with growing confidence.

• • •

Johan stood on a raised dais in a room that stretched a hundred yards in all directions. Slate-gray walls and floors offered no texture for the eye, nothing to distract. On the dais were two chairs. Tom sat in one, Sakuma in the other, looking upward as if at the stars.

"You're in, thank Christopher," Tom said. "Feel 'em? They're trying to distract me and draw him away. It may not look like it but I'm doing the equivalent of a wind sprint here–" An apparition of a mother figure appeared before Tom. "Uh, see, it's hard to talk and control at the same time when you're the center of so much attention." Tom's exertion was plain, even in the dream. "I'm the second handler. We almost lost him in transfer from the first. They want him bad and are teaming up. We'll be outnumbered soon. Look, here's the deal. He... he thinks he's on the shores of the Pacific, stargazing with his buddy from the army." Sakuma muttered something. "He hasn't been lucid yet, which is bad because he's not making much sense – hold on."

Tom turned to the muttering old man. "Eh, Sakuma? I can't hear you."

"I said the night will tell if we get off the island or not," he looked over his shoulder, right through Johan. "I swear they are closer now."

"No, no, they are still in the cages. Relax Sakuma, the tigers can't hurt you. Think of other things. I still want to hear about the job the American wanted you to do. Relax and tell me about that."

The crime lord shook his head and sighed as if he'd not heard.

"Same thing I get, every time. Tough nut. It's time to transfer him to you. I heard you did well in practice so this should be cake." A gurgling roar echoed from the distant walls. "Uh, okay, I'll set the path, you just need to follow it. The moment you reach the door and open it, it's all you. They are bound to be all over him, so you'd better be good about slappin' 'em down. It's both our butts, you know? You can use this as a template or do whatever you want. I'm going to scram. They've got enough vibe from me to nail me to the cross, I think. And the door is a push, not a pull. Questions?" He was eager to dump out. "No? Okay." He nodded to the left where a stone path appeared and ran all the way to a door in the far wall, a football field away.

Johan took a few strides and stopped, looking back. "Um, any way you could...?"

Tom nodded. "Sorry." The door slid towards them, the walls stretching pyramid-style to keep up. "Better?"

"Much, yes. Thanks."

The wooden door appeared heavy with metal bands of reinforcement and symbols etched into its frame. A worn brass thumb-lever handle dully reflected the room.

He stared at it. Premonitions poured from the handle, possibility and intention from dozens of minds striving for a chance at control. This was nothing like they'd practiced. He glanced back at Tom.

Tom grimaced. "Don't make this all for nothing, man. You can do it." The wall behind him had slid forward as well, half again nearer than before. Frantic shadows formed against its pale gray surface. The druid was losing it.

He reached for the handle and stopped. "How will I know I've got control? What if they grab it first and let me think I have it?"

Tom shook his head slowly. "You're gonna have to do better than that, man. You have to *know* what's going on. One thing: don't doubt yourself. That'll jack you up, invite them in for the keys to the castle.

Just do it, man. You're the master." Despite the encouragement, fear etched Tom's eyes. A failed transfer could mean their capture or worse.

He faced the door. It breathed *others*. Anki's question rose like a prognostication. *What if they team up on you? Is that possible?*

He faltered. Tom's distress passed through the dream in a wave.

A voice from deep within sounded, an almost sacred import. *See the outcome beforehand, son, then live it that way. Take that which is yours to take, that which is right.* Emboldened, he grasped the brass handle, its bitter cold unexpected.

He shook his head. "The last surprise." He thumbed the handle down and threw all his weight into the door.

A bright light split from the widening gap, consuming everything.

When the white light flared, taking him, time and every damn thing else with it, a single thought appeared as a guide: *you get what you give.*

What he put out, came back to him. What the others put out, was coming back to them. With a universe that returned what it was given, there was little room for doubt. *He with the least doubt wins out.*

In the burst of insight, he snatched the crime lord from the vanilla void of possibility and snapped to a non-space, a barren zone in the extreme of Saoghal. In the distant, unused space, he wrapped a million mile-thick shell around them; no gaps, no cracks, no weaknesses. Perfect density for perfect isolation.

In a hollow dot at the center of the impossibly large construct, in a glowing spherical chamber, utterly and completely alone, they sat on a platform. Long sought tranquility descended.

"How the hell did you do that?" Sakuma asked, suddenly alert.

"Awake now, yeah? Good, because I have a few questions."

"Don't hold your breath, mercenary. I've given my word."

He raised an eyebrow in response. "You've been lucid the entire time, haven't you? Clever. And your word, huh? A little bird is telling me it's not about your word. No, something else has your tongue."

"Your kind wouldn't understand the value of a man's word. Now tell me how you did this!"

"Control, tomodachi. That's how. Something they don't let you have. I understand they have a job for your Dejitaru but you refused. Why?"

Sakuma said nothing.

"They're going to do something awful, right? And you're out now, almost. Thing is, you don't care about your life, but you do care about someone else's. That's it, isn't it? Yes, I can feel it. Even now, on the edge of death, you care more about one person than what, a few hundred thousand Americans? A few million Europeans? Hm? Who is it? Your wife? Your son? No, not him, he's an ungrateful shit."

Conflict moved across his face, the flickering of resolve.

"Show me. Go on, show me who it is! What one person alive today is more important than the deaths of *all those people?*"

In the silence that followed, the chamber grew pink then red, darkening to crimson. Johan shook his head. "Sad. I suspect your soul is nearly decayed, Sakuma. I say nearly because you realized what they ask of your Dejitaru is wrong. You stood up to them and now you're in over your head, life in the balance. But you're thinking of your duty to *one person*. If you meet that duty, you reap your personal reward, which is what? Preserving your honor? That's called selfishness, not honor. In the end, you are a disgrace to the principle of Japanese honor. Since you stumble so heavily with the concept of honor, I won't try to explain why you also fail as a man or as a father–"

"Silence!" Sakuma shouted. "You know *nothing* of honor! Nothing of the kind of man I am! You disrespectful *child*." He spat. "That you have such power in this dream world is surely a mistake. I will not listen to you insult me for things you are ignorant of!"

The wedge took, emotions shifted free. He pressed to expose more. "Ah, *honorable* Mr. Sakuma! You are right, I am mistaken. You peddle drugs, sex, and weapons. You blackmail people, you poison governments with bribery, you steal and sell people, destroy lives, and so much more. Oh yes, you are so *honorable*. Look, friend, you may be Musashi incarnate but in *this* life you have lost your mind. Your honor is twisted, your–"

"They have my grandson!" he blurted.

Sakuma buried his head in his hands. Frustration and guilt exploded in waves. Images spilled onto the curved walls. Johan recoiled in surprise. A young boy no more than five years old, smiling in plush gardens, laughing atop a Ferris wheel, sleeping peacefully under blankets. A little voice filled the chamber, its sound torture for the crime lord, "*Sofu! Sofu!*"

Grandfather.

He looked up, face streaked with tears. "I cannot explain my *life* or the culture into which I rose to power. I cannot *sit* here, talking uselessly to you, while Ryota is captive and scared! Do you see? My arrogance brought this upon me! In arrogance I believed I could bargain with them, that my *power* would protect me. Then the dark men took Ryota and what did I do? My *pride!*"

His face scrunched in grief, rolling tears saying what his voice could not. He struggled to continue. "I refused. Refused to be outdone, to be... overpowered by weakness. My own grandson! He has done *nothing!*"

He buried his face again, the images fading. "Now I am in this hell, or dream or wherever, twice a prisoner with no power at all. And Ryota... Ryota will surely meet death unless I keep my word."

Johan sighed. The man was a walking contradiction, opposing values all siloed and valid despite their operation in one mind. Capable of every crime, yet with the marrow of a loving grandfather.

"Sakuma. I cannot help Ryota, not at this moment, but I am willing to try, if you help us. Your son will soon ascend to your position and proceed without you, dishonoring you further, no? Your Dejitaru are poised to conduct operations that will bring harm to many. Ask yourself, why would the dark men bother to keep their promise to a man they chose to kill? If Ryota is still alive, they will use him against your son. Do you trust your son to protect Ryota?"

Sakuma looked up. Cognitive functions returned though draped in emotion. "No. Ukita has no heart. Another of my failings. Ryota would suffer. It is unthinkable. But... what the dark men promised is far worse. Madness. Should I reveal their plan, Ryota will die in the–" Fierce lines creased his face as he winced, holding it in. "He will die, too."

In the hesitation, Johan saw fire.

The oyabun straightened. "I am selfish, yes. I want Ryota to live. And so Ryota will live. I will die. Others will, too, but it is necessary for his life. It is the last gift I can offer him."

"You really are dreaming, aren't you? As intelligent as you appear, you'll turn away the chance to save millions of lives? If there is honor in having put Ryota's life at risk, or even sacrificing it – which is what you've likely already done – it is in the act of stopping those plans, of stopping Ryota's father. Tell me, sensei, tell me that you don't know the truth of this?"

Indecision wrought Sakuma's soul, palpable in the space between them. His face dropped into his hands again and he groaned softly.

"Ryota..."

• • •

The Lear jet banked tightly as the pilot prepared for final approach. Tokyo's evening splendor filled the windows. Anki held her breath, both for the lurch and the wondrous display of light. It was as if the Japanese love for technology had worked its way into the city's design, visible from above. Still, old anxiety spiked at the thought of being lowered into the mass of humanity.

Stop. One person required her attention. Only one. She glanced at Austin. Edward insisted she could help him develop the mastery he needed. That faith rested on her empathic talent but also on the fact that Clare lurked beneath, perhaps influencing. How much of it was Clare and how much of it her own gift was unclear, but the 'flower' that would return to help the Change wasn't going to be her.

She shuddered slightly. Clare's emergence still loomed as a frightening, life threatening event despite Edward's reassurances. The only real indication of her truly belonging to the events unfolding seemed to be Pons' sketches. She wanted to believe they suggested her survival. Singing to the world at the end. Though her mother being the seed from a star didn't make sense, unless her 'reincarnation' was just a story to cover something else. A child of the stars? Or was all of humanity star-spawn?

The plane hung low over the city and passed by an electric blue Ferris wheel. Answers would come, eventually, in whatever the future held.

Austin stirred and looked at his watch. "Eight hours. Wonder what they got under the hood. Hey, you okay?"

"I don't fly well," she lied, turning to the window. "I'll be good back on the ground."

The jet lowered towards the runway. The reflection of Tokyo's lights on the bay was replaced by the view of industrial buildings. Landing on solid ground felt like a welcome embrace. She touched her face again, grateful the bio-cats responded like flesh and not like skittering bugs. Alive, but only in the most technical of terms, they were more like synthetic robots. That bit of logic helped with the process of letting them crawl in through her mouth. Still, the urge to gouge her face had been intense.

The cabin door slid open and the co-pilot emerged. "We'll be pulling up at the VIP terminal. A courtesy shuttle is waiting for you." He offered a friendly wave before retreating again. "Konbanwa."

Their shuttle van turned onto a narrow two-lane street just outside the airport. The air conditioner blew cool against the scented air of a tightly-packed neighborhood. Incense, cooking, the muddy river, and the smell of ocean permeated the cabin. Their driver, an older Japanese woman named Yonezu, drove confidently past stacks of apartments. First floor shops sold everything from grocery to cosmetic to electronic goods. Bicyclists appeared from side alleys and veered sharply to avoid the van. Only minutes from the airport, Austin was lost. The horizon was all power lines and two and three story buildings.

Yonezu turned into an alley and pulled up alongside a two-story residence lit by a streetlamp. A red door waited.

"Knock one time, then three time quick. You answer, 'yoyaku' to the question. *Ha ji may ma shitay.* Nice to meet you."

Austin pulled the door closed and the van rolled off into the humid summer evening. They stood holding their briefcases, listening to muted chatter from families in surrounding buildings.

"Hope she got the directions right." He went to the door and knocked as instructed.

A metal mail slot next to the door opened slightly. A female voice asked, "*Onamae wa?*"

"Yoyaku."

The door swung open and a striking Asian woman stood in a pale jade dress, motioning. "Come in, please."

They stepped up and inside into cool air and a room with brick walls. He realized the outside of the building had been built as a shell around an older industrial building to create the appearance of a modern residence. Surely cheaper than razing the old building and starting over. Each interior window had a matching window on the façade outside. In the living room, European furniture contrasted with Japanese art and electronics. A tight spiral staircase led upward and a downstairs hallway extended to what looked like a dining room.

"I am Constance. You are both hungry and tired. There is food prepared and your room is upstairs. But first," she opened a folder taken from the coffee table, "a moment, please. You are?"

"Daniel Harutaka, my father's only son, vacationing in Hong Kong. I'd planned to visit him before we left. He suffered a heart attack and we are on our way to hospital."

"Please study your father's dossier carefully. Your updated papers are included." She handed him the folder and turned to Anki. "And you are?"

"Vickie Harutaka, his wife of three years, no children. Never met father."

"Very good," she nodded once. "There is additional background for you to read, as well. Please, if you would both spend a minimum of one hour with those documents. Daniel, you have a protein drink waiting in the kitchen. Edward offers best wishes for a successful outcome. Your room is the first door on the left upstairs. A bathroom is across the hall. Please, I will need your decks to update them." She smiled. "Do you have questions?"

He shared a look with Anki. "Uh, what's for dinner?"

Chapter 16

A moment's insight is sometimes worth a life's experience.
- Oliver Wendell Holmes, 1809-1894, American Author

The taxi slipped through Tokyo's morning traffic. The driver timed his lane changes perfectly and took side streets, honing in on their destination. Austin watched and admired his efficiency to keep his mind off his nerves.

"This isn't so bad." She smoothed her hair and ran a hand down her arm.

His eye twitched. The underlying tissue and muscles were cinched unnaturally to form his Asian appearance. Constance had applied gel to his face that caused localized swelling. The bio-cats' work combined with his swollen pale olive skin made him a body double for Daniel Harutaka. When he spoke, his voice box tickled from the unfamiliar resonance.

"It could be worse." *If only the stomach gymnastics would stop.* He countered them by reviewing the dossier from memory, focusing on the details he'd most likely need to use.

"Relax, Daniel. It'll be alright."

Twenty minutes later the taxi pulled up in front of St. Luke's Hospital. They emerged into the shadows of the twin towers of St. Luke's Garden across the street. The taller of the two skyscrapers rose fifty-one stories over the city with a connector walkway at the thirty-second floor. The hospital's eleven stories were dwarfed by comparison.

"They don't mess around, do they," he said.

"No," she replied, immediately aware of eyes upon them. "I suppose they don't. Let's hurry, I'm concerned for your father. Time could be short."

Inside, a volunteer at the desk found Mr. Harutaka's room for them. "High Care Unit on the fourth floor. Elevators are there."

Sleek and modern, the hospital lacked the typical chemical sterility and boasted more of a Four Seasons feel. Two hospital workers and an older Japanese man dressed in blue waited for an elevator with them. Off to the side, two suits stood by the stairwell like guards.

Anki rubbed his hand to comfort him. "Maybe he's come to by now."

He shrugged. "I don't know. We'll see."

"You know you care about him. Why be so difficult? This is the perfect time to let the past go. He needs to hear you say it. Give him some peace."

The elevator car arrived and the doors slid open. He removed his hand from hers. "I'll be fine. He's *my* father."

Put off slightly, she remained quiet as they rode the elevator. He went passive and extended to the three strangers. Something about the man suggested aggression. He probed further and found it to be only strong American disdain. The two workers got off on the third floor.

The doors opened on the fourth floor and they stepped out. The man in blue brushed past them.

"There." Anki pointed to the HCU sign.

Another sign pointed the opposite direction, to the ICU where the crime lord was situated. A yakuza suit stood against the wall, surveying them as they passed.

At the HCU nurse's station they showed identification and were taken to Mogami Harutaka's room. Light from the window softened the old man's slack face and bald head. The room stood bare of any personal effects, as if he were just a prop. In a sense he was. A callous thought, one he immediately regretted.

A woman approached and greeted them.

"I am Niwa Uchime, physician's assistant to Dr. Tomoe. I am sorry that Dr. Tomoe is not available right now. However, I can provide you information. Your father remains in coma," she looked at her watch, "thirty-two hours after the cardiac event. We have conducted EEG scans on the brain as recently as this morning. The findings are considered grade three, which unfortunately offer no definite positive prognosis."

"Grade three?"

"Yes. We see dominant theta activity in the brain with no detectable normal alpha activity. To have grade-three EEGs at around thirty hours is concerning but not indicative of a final prognosis. The chance for brain damage increases dramatically the closer to seventy-two hours coma gets. Further testing is scheduled for later this evening."

He asked, "So he could already have brain damage?"

Niwa nodded. "It is possible, yes." The silence grew awkward and long. "That's all the information I have for now. Do you have questions?"

He shook his head.

"There is a restaurant and ATM on the first floor and a convenience store at the basement level. St. Luke's Garden is across the street and has many restaurants. A connecting walkway is on the second floor. We have special rates available for you at the hotel, as well. If there is anything you need, please see the nurses' desk and they will be glad to help you."

"Thank you, Niwa," Anki said.

"Of course." She withdrew graciously.

Austin took a chair across the room from the old man. *Halfway to brain damage.* Anki sat down near the door, the same concern for the man on her face.

He rested his head in his hands and proceeded to seek calm. Two men's lives hung in the balance, neither regarded as important save for extracting knowledge from one of them. Once extracted? Edward's instructions were clear but limited: keep Sakuma alive until called and told otherwise. Memories of Marcel's grilling DFA scenarios bore a whole new dimension as he listened to the soft wheezing of Mr. Harutaka. Would they even try to revive the old man? Could they?

Anki cleared her throat, a sign he needed to get started. He sat back in the chair, crossed his arms, and extended his legs. Anki produced rosary beads and began to pray silently.

"I should have taken those sleeping pills," he muttered. "Didn't sleep at all last night."

Further relaxed, he waited several minutes before letting his head tilt to one side, as if asleep. He extended passively, a small dome of awareness at first. *Good thing.* Someone nearby was heavily scanning for meta sentience in the grid. Riding the feedback from that scanning, he extended further, bit by bit, until a direction came clear: the ICU. They had someone near Mr. Sakuma – near the *target* – actively scanning people for threat. One radar to fool? How many more hands on deck? To find out required the next step which, as practiced as he'd become at it, still felt like a drop off the rim of the Grand Canyon.

Just a little walk.

The step-by-step approach to traveling still worked best. From a top corner of the HCU room, he saw the fuzzy image of Anki sitting near the glass door, working the beads. His own form, stretched out in the chair, lacked a face. The next instant he stood by the bed.

Mr. Harutaka's face was blanked, a reminder of his hostage status. Briefly, images of his father locked up in a cell came to mind. *Also hostage?* He buried the thought and moved into the hallway. Anki looked up and nearly at him, as if sensing him, before resuming her prayers.

He drew himself inward to hide before venturing out. Past the nursing station and down the hall towards the elevators, he eyed every person in sight for recognition of his movement. The guard remained posted by the signs with no indication of energy blob or other awareness. However, something... *big* lay ahead in the ICU wing.

The elevators chimed. Doors slid open to reveal a group of men with bulky sport coats. An uncomfortable hospital administrator emerged first and led them towards ICU.

Austin relaxed. They were the SAT units, the counter-terrorist defenses Constance said would be in place. He followed them past the reception counter, still trying to resolve the feeling of *bigness* looming. A SAT peeled off and entered the waiting room. One of the men appeared to be a commander because he issued instructions as they went.

The hallway hooked right. The intensive care unit lay on the left side, the critical care unit on the right. The special teams spread out and took up positions.

At a central nursing station, a SAT joined sentry near an Ookami-shita suit. They looked awkward – anti-terror police and the syndicate working together. Austin followed the commander into the ICU to Mr. Sakuma's room. Two SATs took up sentry outside.

Austin passed into the room and found the crime lord's face blotted out. Various tubes ran into his arms. Life support systems blinked and bleeped softly. An Asian woman sat on the edge of the bed with her hands wrapped around her husband's. Mrs. Sakuma nodded to the SAT commander. She spoke in Japanese but it was clear she was thanking him.

The commander bowed slightly, an unexpected gesture. Mrs. Sakuma seemed to swell. He turned to leave and Austin followed him into the corridor.

That they could possibly need his help seemed remote. Only the feeling of something big still bothered him. Something *big...*

He moved around, looking in various rooms. The closer he got to the east-facing windows, the heavier the feeling became. It didn't make sense. What was so big? The feeling of death? He stepped through plate glass windows to inspect the area outside. Nothing. Sliding up into the fifth floor he found administration offices. Only two women worked there, a receptionist busy with paperwork and the other in a large office studying a computer. He sank down into the third floor, apparently a dayroom of a psych ward. A woman in pajamas rocked with arms around a pillow.

"Yureeeeeiiii!!" The woman screamed, threw her tissue box at him, and ran for the nurses' station to pummel on the glass.

He recoiled through the ceiling and into the fourth floor again. She'd seen him or some aspect of him. He'd have to run that by Sean. Way too much commotion, in any case. Still the feeling of something big loomed. He retreated from the windows and the feeling lessened. Anki might know what to make of it.

With the thought, he opened his eyes.

Anki was gone. Her rosary beads lay on the floor.

• • •

The comm sounded. CoreOps again. Director Tomov answered and listened, slowly nodding his head.

"Yes. Understood. Of course. I agree. Confirmed." He closed the connection and marveled at what he'd just heard. An agent had taken up position at the hospital and found that whoever had Sakuma locked down wasn't aware of the underlying meta resonance technique. That suggested the Korda's new and powerful controller was not fully trained. The agent would start the resonance via Sakuma's body. Whoever had him locked would become a beacon, broadcasting that signal. They had only to detect it.

"Ops, establish an open relay channel across all units, authority code U42, mandatory. Schedule execution for ten minutes from now with a sliding go-slot no wider than three minutes. And send a runner with some blues and a Coke."

He itched his nose. They had no idea where the controller was so the resonance would be sent globally. A massive and risky undertaking. Interrupting so many units, so many operations. An unprecedented and aggressive strategy. Outside the box.

Something Overseer might come up with.

• • •

"Damn. Still can't reach him. He's completely cut off." Edward cursed softly. He rose and removed the shùil. "He isn't monitoring Sakuma's core meta feed. They're going to use it."

Sean stared at Johan's sleeping form. "He's too strong. We need better control."

"I'm quite aware of that. They're going to set up a pulse at St. Luke's. Get Austin involved. Clear access through the SAT commander. Get at least five of Rodelli's best to try and reach Johan. If you can't get them try the Tedesco family. If a pulse goes out we're in trouble."

Sean indicated Johan's prone figure. "Shall we try to move him?"

"Not yet. However, have the van readied then send staff home."

"Williams?"

"Him, too. Cullstone's stables will be his to clean if he balks."

• • •

At 2:17am Greenwich time every available unit in G2 went passive, sensing. Given a ten second sample of what to feel for, hundreds of sensitives around the globe expanded their reach to their effective limits and beyond.

Within fifty seconds, the command to cease and resume was broadcast: a unit had located the resonance.

• • •

"Signus status?"

"Signus 8 is formed with the reporting agent who will be airborne in five minutes. We've already got north of London in a vector and will begin narrowing it down when translocation begins."

Director Tomov shared a glance with his Ops officer. "What do you think?"

She shrugged. "Could be big."

"Get every aero team we have in line with that heli's twenty. I want them half a mile back and ready for AMS. Have Oscar prepare a scenario for local authority but I want to see it first."

"Confirming aero support with All Methods Strike readiness. Engaging Overseer analysis."

• • •

Austin fiddled with a pen at the counter and waited for one of the nurses to get off the phone.

"Please, ah, yes. My wife, did she say where she was going? Maybe the restroom?"

The nurse said she'd headed in the direction of the bathroom and the elevators.

"Thank you." Panic fell back a few notches. He headed that way. One of Sakuma's men stood near the stairwell across from the restrooms. On impulse he asked, "Excuse me. Did you see an American woman with blonde hair go in there?"

He nodded towards the stairwell. "She left. With a man."

"No, she wouldn't have. Blonde, about this tall?"

He nodded. "Left in a big hurry."

Panic flushed. "What did he look like, the man? Did they go up or down?"

"Tall man. Blue suit."

"Up or down?"

"Up."

He raced up the stairwell, rejecting terrible thoughts. Kidnapped? Gunpoint? Mind control? Pent up tension and fear collided with frustration. To *strike out* at the enemy would feel so good. The air in the stairwell suddenly flooded with potential, responding to his urges.

He stopped at the fifth floor landing, trying to arrive calmly. Up, or in? The question hammered the moment. *Energy...* her energy had passed by, leaving a trail. He extended out into the stairwell and listened, feeling for Anki.

Full in the doorway, empty up the stairs.

Basic, imprecise, but it was all he had. He pulled open the door. Another of Sakuma's men looked over, surprised at the sudden movement.

"A blonde woman with a man in a blue suit, which way did they go?"

The guard shook his head. He appeared offended at having been surprised. "Don't know."

Frustrated, Austin extended, feeling for her energy. It was there but spread out. The guard looked on, ready with his suit unbuttoned. Cover or no, Anki's life was on the line and perhaps Sakuma's as well.

"It is my wife and I fear for her safety. Please tell me where she went."

The guard spoke dismissively. "No clue." *What are you gonna do about it?*

What the guard saw was a rice cracker staring helplessly at him, pulse throbbing in his temple. What he didn't see was him sizing up his

9mm SIG-Sauer and the unlatched holster it rested in. Meta brushed against the weapon. A round in the chamber, safety on.

He looked around then said in a low voice, "Mrs. Sakuma wouldn't approve of you being so rude to a friend."

The guard's suit flapped open as the pistol broke free and slipped into his waiting palm. He thumbed the safety off. "Now which way did she go, baka?"

Shock and fear replaced cockiness. "That way."

Austin let the clip drop to the floor, ejected the round, and handed the gun back. "Stay quiet. I'm on your side, asshole."

He strode into the administrative wing with the guard's confusion and disbelief at his back. Exhilaration mixed with anxiety and fear. The hall forked. Right or left? To the right was east, where the big feeling had been. He strode in that direction. A woman emerged from an office but sank back at the sight of him. *So much for arriving calmly.*

Two doors braced the end of the hallway. He tried one and found it locked. The other was also locked but was all about Anki – her energy seeped from the door. Down the hall, the woman peeked from her office and retreated once more.

Things were about to fall apart. The mission was to keep Sakuma alive but something else was in play now. Something big.

• • •

"Sir, anomaly reported. Sakuma's guard on the radio talking about a wizard on the fifth floor."

Wizard... "Keep the panels at a distance but ready to move in. No early warnings. What's Lilly's status?"

"Last poll indicated no changes. Quiet and pulsing the target."

"Give her a call, make sure she's ready for anything."

The control room display showed video from a heli night flying over forested countryside. The occasional light of a home passed by. A sudden banking accompanied radio traffic.

"Signus 8, Black Jack Five at apex. Map mark is Epping Forest. Be advised, signaler now being dampened or blocked. The reader estimates we're less than a click from target. Maybe three dozen buildings in the zone. Recommend deploying all available to cordon and have the pulse pattern varied to throw off their blocking. We need another thirty to sixty seconds of strong signal."

"Damn!" Director Tomov glanced at the incident map still focused over Tokyo. "Tell Lilly to vary the pulse using deceptive cadence ending in V. Signus 8, join with 6 and 11, they'll be there any second. Track it fast! I want the druid location now."

"Sir, Lilly isn't answering her phone," the Comms officer said. He turned in his chair. "The guard is saying his gun flew out of its holster and landed in the wizard's hand, like magic. They've got a bender in there."

• • •

The metal strike plate sheered away from the doorjamb with a wrenching report. Austin bumped the door open to a secretary's anteroom. He checked his breathing. Perception grew sharper. Anki's energy wafted like heat waves. The door ahead shimmered with immense potential. It felt like he could bust the building wide open with enough intention.

Another doorjamb crumbled and he slammed the door open.

Time compressed to the smallest units imaginable, so granular it seemed to stand still. In that space, information flowed. A man stood near the door with a long-barreled pistol trained on two women standing behind a desk. One was Anki, a gun held to her head by the other, an Asian woman. The woman had begun to pull the trigger at his entry. In the small gap of the moment, intention flickered and the grid responded: her pistol broke her index finger as it snapped from her grip. The weapon discharged silently at an angle, the round missing Anki's skull before it slammed through the ceiling tile and lodged in the ductwork. In the next moment, he wrenched the gun free from the man's grip and received it midair. It was the man from the elevator, dressed all in blue.

Anki struck the woman with her elbow and broke free from her grip. "Shoot her, now! Shoot! She's helping track Johan!"

"*What?*" A cell phone rang on the floor in the far corner of the room.

The woman stared blankly at him.

"Now!" Anki moved towards him, ready to take the gun. "Shoot her now, damn it!"

Despite the woman's impassive expression, fear coursed from her like thick syrup.

The man spoke. "Do it or I will. Save the mission."

The woman stared back. He couldn't do it, couldn't put a bullet into a woman. *Where?* In the head? What if it hit her eye? She'd scream in agony. He'd have to shoot her over and over again, a bloody mess.

249

He imagined her crying as he pumped bullets into her. It had to happen, she had to die, for whatever reason. Suddenly doubt arose; he wanted to know *why*. The first time to kill someone – he needed to know *why!*

"Damn it, she's fucking with your head! Kill her!" Anki took a step towards him. "She's signaling back through the dream! They're *tracking him* right now! Do it!"

He trusted Anki, felt the truth in her words. He would kill the woman but not with the gun. Instead, he gathered a wad of potential at the base of her throat and punched it against her spine, severing it. Her head snapped forward and her torso fell to the desk. He cringed at the spine protruding from a gash in the nape of her neck. *Too hard.*

"She's still doing it!" Anki took a step towards her. "Okay, okay, she's leaving. Leaving, leaving... gone. Otani, what now?"

The stranger replied, "We go back to our loved ones on the fourth floor and pray Johan gets what he needs soon. My weapon, please?"

"Who the hell are you?" He pointed at the corpse. "And how'd you know where to find her?" He turned to Anki. "Why didn't you warn me?"

Otani answered, "Later. The mission is still primed." He took his gun back and headed for the door. "I'll smooth the guards. Resume your roles. Go to the elevator. If asked, you got off on the wrong floor. Move quickly!"

• • •

The newly formed Signus 16, comprised of four panels, approached the fifth floor at the director's command. They halted as a flock of druids fled the scene.

"Priests, a dozen or more."

Their patterns dissolved, escaping the grid. The lead entered the office to find the body.

"Agent down."

Control responded. "Confirmed. We just lost the pulse. There's a bender operating in the building. Spread out, locate, and track. Mind the exits. We have units going in now."

"Control, we have no visual reference."

The director cut in. "Get in there and look around. He's probably near Sakuma. Use your damn instinct! I want to keep him on or near the fourth floor."

• • •

Toda and Honda finished the last of pre-flight checks as their Japan Airlines 747 cargo freighter turned on to runway 34R. It was Honda's first flight with a fully digitized flight deck, which meant no flight engineer. There was more information to look after despite the automation and myriad of displays. Training had been very thorough yet he still felt a bit edgy.

Honda keyed the radio. "Tower, JAL923 requesting clearance for takeoff, runway 34R."

"JAL923, cleared for takeoff. Contact Departure on frequency 120.8. Enjoy your flight."

"Copy that Tower. JAL923, rolling for takeoff."

Honda tried to enjoy the surge and thunder as the craft accelerated down the runway. A clear blue sky awaited them, a good sign. He squeezed the rubber Totoro figurine in his pocket. A gift from his daughter for luck.

Transitioning to flight, all systems were green, as expected. Three kilometers out Toda banked to a northerly bearing and climbed to six thousand meters. The city stretched out beneath. Honda imagined his wife taking lunch in the break room at her work, sitting by the window, watching the planes take off.

"JAL923, change course to zero four five degrees, maintain ascent to altitude."

"Copy change course to zero four five, maintaining ascent to altitude." Honda relaxed a bit.

"Not so bad, eh?" Toda said, banking gently to meet the new bearing. "Everything's right there where you can see it. The system will tell you when something's wrong. No need to worry."

"Yes, I see. Still takes getting used to. I feel like I'm missing something."

As the pilot began to level the plane out, he suddenly grimaced and grunted, holding his chest.

"Toda! What's wrong?"

"Take... take controls." He struggled to release his harness. Honda took hold of the flight yoke and set about leveling the plane on bearing. With a pained expression, Toda climbed out of his seat.

Honda keyed the radio. "JAL923 declaring flight emergency. Pilot is having a heart attack. Requesting clearance to land. Please advise!"

The pilot leaned against the bulkhead and held his chest, muttering with tears forming in his eyes.

"Toda! What is happening! Please, tell me!" The tower squawked with new bearings. He radioed confirmation then glanced back, only to receive a vicious blow to the face, the first of many as Toda went berserk.

Sixty-five seconds later, flight JAL923 banked hard and fell into a dive.

• • •

Johan shook his head. "You would sacrifice thousands in the hopes he is spared. What kind of people do you think you're dealing with? Do you imagine them honorable? They took Ryota as a way to make you cooperate. You refused them, Sakuma. Nothing you do now will change their mind about Ryota. They tried to kill you and they won't rest until you are dead, especially after this time with me. Ryota may be alive, but it won't matter if you don't tell me what they asked you to do." He paused, letting it settle in. "You know now what we can do. You don't help me, I can't help you. If he's alive, we are his best hope to stay alive. And you know this is your very last chance to make a fair deal, to invest in something greater than yourself. In something greater than even Ryota."

Sakuma cringed, looking away. Nothing was greater than the boy. Still...

He shrank in resignation. "I am to die. My threads are weak. So much I should have done differently. Much I did not regard properly." He sighed. "Ryota must have a chance to live. For him, I will listen to you. I will believe you are right but only if you give me your word that you will seek out Ryota and free him."

"Sakuma, you have my word. I will fight to find Ryota and bring him to safety. And not just for you."

The crime lord straightened, a last effort at dignity.

"I will share with you their request – no, their command, and what it means to my country. To many countries."

• • •

The nurse at the HCU desk smiled as Anki and Austin approached hand in hand. "You found her."

Austin nodded back. "Yes, yes, thank you."

They entered Mr. Harutaka's room and took their seats. He quietly explained the big feeling and asked if she could sense anything.

"Besides how it makes you feel, no."

The cell phone at his side rang. He answered. A rushed Constance said, "Airplane about to hit hospital, ICU side. There's a stairwell down the hall. Get down and out."

He pulled her into the hallway. "Go down now, as fast as you can. Get down and out of the hospital, now. Now!"

She tried to protest so he propelled her towards the door with invisible force. She hit the door hard enough to open it. "Go, god damn it! Go!" With a frightened look, she disappeared down the stairs.

The feeling of *big* pummeled him as he jogged past the Oshitama guard at the elevators. The impression suddenly made sense – it was something big *about to happen*. He rounded the corner to the ICU ward. Two SAT units pulled their weapons on him and commanded him to stop. Already nervous nurses ducked into patient rooms to hide.

He pointed at the windows and shouted, "Plane! Kamikaze!"

Visible beyond the nearby buildings, the Boeing 747 leveled out from a dive with its tail pitched at an angle. Dark exhaust contrails plumbed from straining engines. It was lined up and headed for the hospital.

He saturated the group mind with the knowledge of impending impact. Shouting erupted and people ran. The SAT units held position until fear won out and they fled as well.

He walked to the window where the big feeling rooted him to the spot. Flashes of peripheral movement threatened to steal focus; what looked like faces, ghoulish forms. The plane. Impact – ten seconds? As in the office, time slowed, the grid sprawling out before him. Memory of the general's attack in the forest clearing came. Mug's daring handling of the thrown pole became an inspiration. Outside, seen between buildings, a murky river flowed.

Scale. It's just fucking scale. He extended into the grid, felt the *big* feeling there, the sheer potential like a mountain landslide waiting release. He reached the plane and knew it was too huge, moving with too much momentum to affect... directly. There was only one option and he took it, forming intention and tapping the immense potential like a spike into a glass wall.

The grid responded in a flash of change. A roar erupted as the air sucked away from the hospital, accelerating and cooling in a turbulent stream towards the jet. The sudden flow grew stronger, spinning off mini-tornadoes as it mixed with the humid summer air. He fed it until it seemed it might take on a force of its own, as if nature had been awakened and joined in. The massive movement created a howling whine with undertones of rumbling thunder. Patients cried out. The floor swayed. For a staggering moment it seemed the flow was too strong, like it might damage the building itself.

The 747's nose cone crumpled when it encountered the wall of wind. Its sheet metal body crinkled and folded as rapid deceleration stressed holding bolts. Cargo shifted violently to impact the weakened framework and split open the fuselage. Torrential winds sheared compressor blades to create explosive catastrophic engine failures. The wings deformed and rent open, spilling fuel into the air that ignited with the engine fires. The resulting fireball slewed into a stream taken away in the wind.

Like a fire extinguisher emptying its charge, he felt the extreme drain and dimming of consciousness. A headache bloomed, threatening focus. He pressed both hands against the window and channeled the pain as best he could, leaning into the effort. As he'd seen Mug do to the incoming pole, he used the wind to direct the ravaged remains of the aircraft towards the river below. The twisted fuselage clipped the corner of a building on its downward arc. Impact in the river threw a tremendous wave into the air while debris rained down. A trunk-sized piece of cargo crashed onto a nearby bridge. Cars swerved and collided.

The howling abruptly subsided and he crumpled to the floor, barely able to breathe. Consciousness dipped and returned, accompanied by the pain in his skull. He laid on his back, unsure if he'd taken it too far. Flat-line tones sounded from multiple monitors in the ICU. His heart slowed, as if confused. It seemed fitting that he might also die. Sunlight streamed against his face, warming his skin and somehow anchoring him in the moment. The big feeling had gone but death had taken its place nearby.

"How—?"

He looked up at the voice. Mrs. Sakuma stood with a single guard at her side.

• • •

A portable generator rumbled from a municipal utility van parked next to the high school a block from St. Luke's. Inside, four technicians dressed as workers sat at laptops wired to an improvised and complex piece of electronics. Thick bare wires ran up the walls of the van and snaked across the ceiling, held in place by spot cement and twisty ties. They'd been in the area five hours, already exceeding the safe limits for presence, but were unwilling to give up. They were too close.

"Another fragment! Solid hit with that sequence. Open the parameters for it and shut down the others. Apply resequencing mime on all inherited nodes."

A technician worked the console furiously. "Done."

Thousands of tiny bars in red began turning green, one by one. *Sequencing matches!*

"Oh God…"

The matching turned into a cascade as the new algorithms began exponential returns. In seconds, the sequence was complete, the screen filled with green.

"We've got a stream!"

The assembled audio playback kicked in.

"–threat. Probably worse. It's your call. If you're going ahead with it, I want time to clear out of the city."

"Acknowledged. Begin moving your units to regress points. Assume the protocol will be used."

Soaring high on their success, the four resisted cheering aloud and instead scrambled to save the settings. They'd tapped the Comannda's communications layer using techniques proposed by the Bootstrap project team. The possibility became greater that similar techniques might work on the net, as well. The breakthrough overshadowed anything else in the moment. One technician patted the device, proudly saying, "Enigma has nothing on you, Booty."

The team leader climbed into the driver's seat to get them moving back to the lab. The intercept content sounded ominous and needed immediate relay.

"Keep scanning in the test range. There's bound to be more."

• • •

Three cars and an hour later, Austin stepped into the living room of a residence in the Meguroku ward, southwest of central Tokyo for a surprise meeting with Constance. He wore a new face and clothing.

She bowed and offered congratulations, her new regard of him apparent. "I am glad you are okay. You are something special, no?"

He bowed in greeting. "How did it go with Sakuma?"

255

"A success." Her answer was subdued. Something suppressed.

"And my traveling companion?"

"She is returning home already."

"Ah, I see. Maybe you can catch me up?" At her look, he added, "I mean tell me about Sakuma's interview."

She didn't respond immediately. Instead, she led him to a sofa facing windows with a view of the urban park alongside the house. Women walked while children pushed scooters on the paths.

"There's a problem," he said.

She nodded. "The mission succeeded but the information gained is not available. I am unable to brief you. You must leave Tokyo immediately."

Not allowed to brief. "I nearly died today and now I'm supposed to wait half a day to learn what threatens the world?"

Her appeasing look did nothing to soothe disappointment, nor did her offered flow of sensual meta, a combination of formal apology and intense desire. Beneath it all she tried but failed to hide urgency and fear.

He stood. "If it's that bad, maybe I don't want to know."

Chapter 17

Neither the sun nor death can be looked at with a steady eye.
- Francois De La Rochefoucauld, 1613-1680, French classical writer

The surface of the loch caught the last rays of a setting sun and danced them against hills blushed green in the height of spring. In the center of the loch a circular stage floated, detailed with twelve majestic chairs. Each chair sat with its rear legs up against the edge and was separated from its neighbors by twelve feet. In each chair sat an Executive.

Fitted in a gray Italian suit, Bastion stood and walked to the center of the circle. He spoke with a magnified voice found only in dreams.

"As you have just heard, Gaulic interference is at levels without precedence. They would have us believe the Bohemian legends have some kind of truth to them."

Ganzai, fifth Son of Pablo in the southern realms of the Americas, cleared his throat.

"Is it possible they've learned to combine their benders?"

Bastion shook his head. "There was only one. Cameras confirmed that. He had to be carried out, suggesting a tremendous effort."

Maria de Oro, Sequence Three of Grecian Royalty, suggested the priests may have achieved the feat in stealth. "Volgograd is close to achieving combining. If the priests have already succeeded, we need to know. I recommend we go back to investigate further. The hospital staff will have received stray impressions. We can learn more from them."

Bastion turned to Maria. "And thereby prevent J86 execution for Tokyo? Your veiled philanthropy is duly noted."

In the distance, a large serpentine figure launched from the water. Its shadow blocked the sun's rays before it fell back with a great splash. Bastion paced the platform. He pulled a cigarette case from his jacket and prepared to smoke.

"Oh please," Maria said. "Either they have the most powerful telekinetic in history or they've learned to combine their benders. We need to know which is the case. And no, I don't think J86 for the world's most populated city is at all appropriate for the situation." She looked around the circle. "Do any of you?"

Bastion stopped pacing and faced Maria. "They need to know how stupid they are for playing the prophecy game. The Conflict they dream of will cost them dearly. We establish that now."

"I've an idea," Ganzai said. "If it is just one gifted man, and frankly I suspect it is this Austin fellow, then lure him in. Use the girl's core as bait. If he eludes us, then use J86. One lost city should get them in line again. Tokyo's the largest but I'd hate to see all that lost. Pick another – Toronto or Hanoi or Johannesburg. Follow with threats of more. They will have to cave. They simply must."

Some nodded their approval.

Maria said, "If they believe they have their Change, they won't cave. They will press forward to their destiny."

"Then they press into death." Bastion flashed memory of Nagasaki and Hiroshima. "*We* are in control, Maria. Destiny is *ours* to make, not theirs."

Nora Brennan, the quiet patroness of Eastern lands, rose a thin voice. "What about A2?" she asked. "Peter Brusse. He stole Cathbad and Austin from Shang's own dream *and* held us at bay from the yakuza boss."

"Surprise accounts for the former, poor coordination for the latter. I have no doubt that we'll take him down. Oscar, what work has been done to identify Peter Brusse?"

Overseer, following the proceedings via Bastion's neural linkage, checked the logs.

"G3 PROCESSED DNA RECOVERED FROM DEN HELDER MULTILATERALLY AGAINST INTERNATIONAL POLICE, PRISON, MILITARY, AND MEDICAL DATABASES. NO MATCHES WERE FOUND AND NO FURTHER PROCESSING WAS REQUESTED."

"Why no record for him?" Nora asked. "Or has Oscar been breached?"

Overseer responded. "THE DNA SAMPLE HAS NOT BEEN FULLY PROCESSED AGAINST G1'S GAUL ROSTER."

"What?" Bastion demanded. "What do you mean 'not fully processed'? That's the first database to check!"

"THE DEFAULT QUERY FOR THAT DATABASE CONTAINS AN EXCLUSION FILTER FOR DECEASED MEMBERS HAVING DIED MORE THAN TWENTY YEARS AGO."

Bastion caught his rising anger. Instead he forced a sigh and stared directly into the orange sun resting on the hills. Large black sun spots bloomed on its surface, dimming its rays.

"Determine the origin of the filter, then run the query without it." He turned to Maria. "Another example, no? If this continues, I'll have Oscar expand and run it all."

"Who's to say it wasn't Oscar's fault?" she asked.

As if waiting for the remark, Overseer responded.

"THE EXCLUSION FILTER WAS CREATED SIX YEARS AGO AND HAS BEEN UTILIZED PERIODICALLY BY VARIOUS DIRECTORS. THE MOST RECENT APPLICATION WAS ORDERED ON APRIL 22ND, 2015, BY DIRECTOR HENLEY. THIS DIRECTOR WAS TERMINATED MAY 3RD, 2015, AFTER THE COALITION INCIDENT."

"Henley, yes. And no one removed the filter since? Delete it and allow no restrictions on that database without my approval."

"ACKNOWLEDGED. THE QUERY RETURNED ONE MATCH. PETER BRUSSE IS GERRIT BARTEL, SON OF VINCENT AND JULIANA BARTEL. HIS PARENTS WERE TRAINERS FOR THE GAULICS AND SPECIALIZED IN MIND-BODY ATTUNEMENT AND DREAM CONTROL. THEIR MORTIFICATION WAS SCHEDULED FOR AND EXECUTED ON SEPTEMBER 12, 1978. THE BOY WAS PRE-INITIATE AND ALLOWED TO LIVE. HE WAS RAISED BY HIS GRANDPARENTS OUTSIDE THE RUNA KORDA AND DISAPPEARED TEN YEARS LATER. RECORDS OF GERRIT'S BIRTH ARE ABSENT FROM ALL PUBLIC DATABASES FOR UNKNOWN REASONS. HE HAS AVOIDED DOCUMENTATION SINCE."

"That explains some of it," Bastion said. "I want him captured or dead. Focus on drawing Austin in, as well. I want him alive. If anyone comes up with ideas better than Ganzai's, let me know immediately. In the meantime, pay close attention and keep your guards in place. Anything more?"

Cormac raised a question. "Overseer bypassed CoreOps in suggesting the system-wide detection of the controller. Should we be concerned? Or have new protocols been adopted?"

Bastion nodded. "Neuristics is looking into it. No need for concern. The safeguards allow for rollback of the AI at any juncture. Now, anything else? No? Then we adjourn. Thank you."

One by one the Executives winked out of existence. As always, Maria de Oro was the last to share the dream with him.

"So quick to use violence, Bastion. You must know others see that as a weakness. A sign of unmanaged fear."

A ring of lights in the platform began to glow in the gathering dusk. Orchestral music rose from the waters around them.

He walked over to her. "You're mistaken, Maria. It is simply impatience, not fear. Their impetuousness must be addressed. I see benefit in destruction where you do not."

"Oh I understand the benefits, but I also understand moderation. Too often, you don't."

He stared into her eyes. "Moderation. How far from that to reconciliation? To sharing control?"

Maria shook her head. The implication that she would advocate sharing control with the druids was a dangerous one. Though brilliant, he was not without delusions – delusions that seemed to be growing in size and frequency.

"Asset management, Bastion, has absolutely nothing to do with treason." She held his gaze firmly. "Killing Tokyo is wasteful and dilutes control. It is balance we seek, remember? Focus on the targets and use force wisely. That is the proper response."

He slowly nodded before walking the circular platform. "We'll use the AGTs. Austin's capture and our study of him will resolve the issue."

"And this dream maestro?"

He waved dismissively. "We saw this in the girl, remember? He is as inexperienced as she and just as distracted. More so, perhaps. I detect quite an ego. I've already received the after action on the Shang incident. Foster's group says they've broken it down and are on top of his technique. We wait for his next move and then lynch him. With a horde if need be."

"Something tells me *start* with the horde." She looked away, across the now murky water to the hills. Shadows stole their color, a precursor of the darkness to come.

• • •

Existence would end the way she thought it might. Inevitably and simply. Under the motionless sun, lying on the heat-baked sand and dead palm leaves, the blackness would eventually converge on the shores of the little turd of an island. Once her refuge from the searchers, it would become her dying place. Sadness for the little boy surpassed that for herself.

Introduced shortly before the trap at the forest clearing, she and the boy had connected immediately. His fear and longing for home mirrored her own. She'd already lost so much of herself to General Shang and didn't want him to suffer the same. When the chance came, she'd taken it, shearing from the dream. He'd hung to her side at every subsequent jump, through every scene, adapting as fast as she had. Despite not having spoken a single word, he remained with her, trusting in her every move.

What small sense of reality she retained seemed artifact now as she stared at the black clouds looming. Ten miles out? It had begun as a blurring of the horizon, slowly growing into a storm approaching from all sides. With it came a sense of endlessness, a palpable sensation pervading the dream. Ryota had stared and stared, his little eyes seeming to read more from the clouds than she could. The one glance he gave her before retreating to the palms conveyed only sadness. Changing again was pointless and he knew it, too. The black wall of clouds was meant to make them run. She felt the trap, felt their certainty. Running would only give them pleasure, some kind of benefit.

Lying on her back, she squinted into the blue, ignoring the tempest bearing down. The sun shimmered with a familiarity born of years under its gaze. It wasn't hard to forgive its punishing rays because of the reminder of home it offered. The island itself, though, had become a symbol of her desolation, of the end. For the millionth time, doubts about breaking away from Austin resounded. Too rash? Hurt or helped him? Had it paid off? Was he safe? Knowing she'd saved him would mean everything.

Instead, there was too much room for doubt. Time was nearly gone. In its place the endlessness grew, an indistinct and troubling perception. The next shift would be a leap into the blackness, into whatever ending neared. She closed her eyes.

Time.

Tears formed, hot with regret. She hadn't had *time*.

Chapter 18

If one has to jump a stream and knows how wide it is, he will not jump.
If he doesn't know how wide it is, he'll jump and six times out of ten, he'll make it.
- Persian Proverb

Hard wood floors reflected the flames dancing in the massive stone fireplace. A dozen candles flickered to light the corners of the great study. Dawn's gray filtered through window slits cut into the stone wall. Cathbad stood by the fire lost in thought.

Many times the Comannda had managed ingress into their ranks, swatting with deathly effect. Such encounters bore lessons, one of the most important being division. Later interrogations would have meant the collapse of the Family if not for the learned segmentation of the units and the ability to scatter and reform. Still, any hierarchy had its binding roots, even if only visible from on high. Bringing the Change to Cullstone might be frowned upon by others, just as sending Austin to Tokyo had been. As leader of the Korda he was used to criticism yet at this point he'd begun to have his own doubts. There was no guidance, no definitive Words to use going forward. It was his own interpretation of the trackways guiding his choices and the trackways were weak and numerous. No matter how they prepared, the Conflict was going to be a chaotic affair whose duration or outcome wasn't even hinted at.

In one thing the Words were clear: the Change would do things their way. Edward's contingent had fled Shamrock only to encounter a barricade staffed by four black ops G3. Johan's masterful application of Pons' techniques on all four guards simultaneously allowed them to drive around the blockade without the guards ever acknowledging their presence.

Legends were born from feats such as that, just as they were from Austin's incredible work in Tokyo. They signaled first dawn in the Conflict; perhaps the last clear signs that the old Words were in alignment. The news had already spread hope and unification throughout the Family. The enemy's wireless communication network had been compromised and their network would likely soon follow. These were the times he'd dreamt of and worked towards. Surely the Lord of the Wood was watching over them closely and influencing events. To lose faith now was to jeopardize hope itself.

He turned from the fire and cast about the room. For the hundredth time he missed Mug's presence. Still sallow with grief, he strayed to a window. The surrounding emerald hills glistened in the muted light of morning. The single ribbon of road crested and disappeared in a shroud of mist that held the valley.

He sighed, hoping to expel the growing weakness from his bones and from his spirit. Creative DNA sequencing extended the major systems but did little for a soul too long in the world. A familiar division resounded, threatening resolve. Half of him yearned for the songs of the Faerie, for release from his mortal shell. The other half wanted to grind the face of every High Comannda to dust, to hear the hammer of Truth ringing across the heavens, releasing humanity from its bindings. The danger inherent in both desires permeated every thought. To flee was to abandon the planet to peril and chance. To fight was to risk conveying the wrath of the Comannda to the nations of Earth. If only the Mu could take a stand...

With a jerk of his head he dismissed thoughts of abandoning the fight or being rescued. *Weakness of spirit, indeed.* The Change was at hand. There was hope.

The sudden rising drone of an engine preceded a biplane dropping into view from over the top of the castle. The yellow-bodied relic soared down and over the field, banked lazily and settled onto the green with practiced ease. Bradley O'Connell turned the craft around and stopped it near the driveway. In the second seat, Johan rubbed his chilled face before climbing down. Williams came out to welcome him and to greet the old pilot again. The warmth of their exchange touched Cathbad.

A moment later, Anki dashed into view and exploded into Johan's arms. He smiled despite himself.

• • •

Beyond the village of Killearn, the two-lane road stretched from Glasgow's outer edge towards the misty hills and lochs of the north. Acceleration welded Austin to his seat as Sean engaged the Vauxhall's 6.2 liter V8. The druid wore his mirrored shades despite the gray morning.

"Don't worry. The road knows me," Sean said.

He chuckled then grew quiet. "No word on Kaiya then."

"No."

They passed ivy-draped mills and clapboard houses surrounded in mist. Green fields rolled by, occasionally split by creeks and wooden bridges. Sheep and goats grazed on grass laden with dew. If England felt graceful, Scotland was timeless.

"Edward said she might have broken free but wouldn't know how to return. If she's not being held, that would make her sort of a ghost, wouldn't it?" he asked. "Wandering?"

"Brave conclusion, that. If Edward is right, she's in danger of being led to Gwynvyd. What you would call heaven. Wandering in Saoghal, dream to dream, she'll eventually go beyond, yes. They'll come for her."

"They?"

Sean shook his head, downshifted into a curve, and pulled g-forces coming out of it. The druid wouldn't elaborate. Couldn't? Goose bumps pricked his arms at the thought of Kaiya wandering lost in a nether world of dreams.

"They who, Sean? Angels?"

"Something like that. She'd go the way of Mug."

No. Johan *had* to seek her out now. It would be a condition going forward. A requisite.

The road grew more winding and hugged the shores of a loch. Steep hills and patchwork forests surrounded the deep lake. An occasional country home rested nearby in the majesty of the land. They rode in silence, the pitched growl of the Vauxhall the only sound.

He thought of Kaiya, tried to reach out to her. Imagination or not, it seemed he could feel her. If it really were her, she felt sad, deeply sad. He squelched the flow of guilt that followed, knowing it was a wasted expression. If he had failed her, guilt would have its day.

A crest in the road revealed a quarter-mile expanse of green bowled in on three sides by tall, forested hills. A sprawling brown stone castle sat nestled at the far end. Out front, a yellow biplane dotted the lawn.

Sean looked over. "Welcome to Cullstone."

The morning mists surrendered to a sun that shone around clouds. Lunch was taken in the nearby hills reached by horseback. Cathbad insisted they enjoy the afternoon with no concerns for other matters. The directive sat well with the group with only a couple of indirect violations. When Anki's horse became agitated, Austin spooked it further when he tried to calm it from within.

"Practice later," was Cathbad's response.

They returned to Cullstone's stables as long shadows fell over the meadow but before the mists returned. They took dinner in the study and Cathbad used the time to tell stories of the successes and setbacks in the last few centuries.

The breadth of influence allowed by the meta arts was further detailed. Used on people at the highest levels of conventional government, G2's techniques swayed opinion by subversion and coercion and made control of world events almost academic. Crafting public opinion had always been their strength and priority, as was keeping themselves untouchable and unknowable. The rise of humanity's knowledge and innovative thinking became the challenge. Curious minds always sought to discover more. Technology allowed the injection of both violent and non-violent controls and revealed that humankind was as easily programmed as any computer. On the whole they were as predictable, too. The Korda's efforts to alter the paradigm posed severe risks – those who enjoyed control would not easily have it taken away. Achieving balance between survival and progressive change was a constant battle for the Family. Cathbad shared three particular stories of daring counter-Comannda operations that left Austin feeling more obligated to help them than ever, despite resentment for the delay in helping Kaiya. The past could not be allowed to become the future, especially when there was so much potential otherwise.

Williams traded Austin's empty plate for a full stein. Johan, Anki, and Sean sat on the next couch while Cathbad sat at his desk. Conversation halted when a young man entered with a violin and bow in hand. He took up position amidst the candles and with a nod from Cathbad began a soulful, entreating solo. Williams returned with a mug of his own to sit next to Austin.

Cathbad came around the desk to stand in front of the fireplace. In each hand he held exquisitely detailed pewter beer steins. Stone gray eyes regarded each in the room, as if gathering their presence. His deep voice wove into the violin's story, a natural joining.

"The day I met Mug Ruith I remember well. Hours old he was, a pudgy face latched onto Murdina's breast. Peering left and right, so curious. Quiet lad, but hard as hell to get to sleep. Always wanted to know what was going on. He surely kept track, growing up. That involved nature led him back to me and eventually to the daring advances made in the sciences. His vision forced history to bend closer to a day we all believe can come. That he was taken at the start of the

266

Conflict, at a time when vision is so desperately needed," he shook his head. "I won't say I understand it, but I trust things are as they need to be, as they've always been."

He gazed beyond the room. "Mug, I feel you at the edge of the world, looking back. You want to know the ending but it's not yet at hand. Rest easy friend, for the Creator has provided. Go lad, explore like you know you want to. You've earned it. But keep an eye out and when you see me, have fond Words ready on my behalf."

The violinist finished and silence fell upon the room. Cathbad raised both steins. "To Mug Ruith and his journey through Gwynvyd!" They all stood and loudly echoed the toast.

Cathbad drank deeply of both steins then whirled and threw one into the fire. It clanged and came to rest against others lining the floor of the hearth. He dismissed the violinist and took up a chair near the fire. He toasted again.

"To the Change. May the bastards fall easy and harm not the children of the Land."

The druid leader's expression sobered as he took them all in once more.

"The Comannda behave like God because they control the system that allows them to. They've set up humanity so the truth would only tear them apart. The combined truths of meta, the Comannda's system of control, and the history of repression would destroy civilization as we know it. We must be mindful of that fact. The Conflict is our responsibility. As long as there is a High Comannda Council, as long as there are ranks vying for the control they wield, as long as the Comannda rule Saoghal and Raon as they do, there is no real hope without our intervention. Already we've crossed boundaries and they are preparing a response." He nodded in thanks as Williams refilled his stein. "They have much to lose and will utilize extremes to protect all."

The great fire crackled and warmed the room. Destiny seeped from the rock of the castle walls in the silence following Cathbad's words.

Johan spoke. "They have indeed prepared an extreme response."

"What is it?" Austin asked. "What did Sakuma tell you?"

"He confirmed something we had suspected," Sean said. "He spoke of a device installed in the city of Tokyo. A device nuclear in nature."

Austin nearly choked on his ale. Anki looked from Johan to Sean.

Sean continued. "There is reason to assume other cities are similarly laden, however, we have no confirmation nor signs of immediate threat. This just means they have the mechanism for great control over governments and over us, though they don't know we are aware of it yet. The devices have been kept from us, probably to keep us from looking for them."

Cathbad nodded. "Knowing this makes our job that much more important. Soldado's work with the Bootstrap project yielded the first real success in penetrating their systems. We've resolved at least one of their wireless encryption methods and have achieved our first intercept."

"Excellent," Johan said. "That means the network isn't far off?"

"We're encouraged. Deployment of more wireless intercept devices in Tokyo has begun. The Booty teams located a central carrier in the city. It's the logical place to hard-tap the network. Because it's a military installation, the network will be more dangerous to access and test from. With Soldado's help we think we can do it. If we can break the network, we'd be into voice and data intelligence."

"Which is why we must all be ready to act," Sean added.

Ready to act. Austin met Cathbad's gaze. A flicker of recognition in the druid's eyes preceded the rise of tension.

"You've something to say, Austin."

Thoughts of Kaiya steeled his resolve. "I've waited."

"That you have."

"I agreed to help as long as I could help my family. Both my dad and Yuni are still missing. Kaiya is at the edge of life and you're asking me to ditch all and join in the fight. I'm ready to act, yes, but first on her behalf. The Korda has ignored its promise. You *get* this, I know you do."

Sean leaned forward. "Of course we get it. I wonder, though, if *you* get it, the rest of it."

Austin's defenses deployed, a presence in the room.

Cathbad explained. "Imagine Johan goes into the dream world, seeking Kaiya. Powerful draw, he'd be. Good chance, if she's still in Saoghal, she'd be drawn to him, to his dream. But so would *they*. Think, Austin. Announcing his presence in the least understood aspect of our reality is not a good plan, son."

"You know he's more powerful than any of them."

"We know he's *been* more powerful than them. What if they learn to mimic him? Reproduce his methods? That's what we seek to do. Maybe they've done it, or will. Then what? Then he's exposed unnecessarily, forced to fight his way clear, just to survive. Which is why I must ask you: would risking the loss of Johan now for the sake of one beloved person be your best advice to the Family?"

A chasm yawned wide, separating the two men. In the depths between lay the unwelcome truth that Austin couldn't face. Wouldn't. He left the couch and strode to the candles.

"That wasn't part of the deal, Cathbad. Edward knows it. You know it."

Sean stood. "There isn't time to—"

Cathbad raised a hand for silence. "Austin. It is true. That promise was made. And now I ask you, will you be patient while we position ourselves to take advantage of the element of surprise? What little we have must be capitalized here and now, at the start. You know this, you get it. You risk much by asking Johan to expose himself to search for Kaiya. Will you consider waiting?"

The leader of the Runa Korda knew how to lead, how to make a man follow. There seemed but one option in the moment –

–*No*. If not now, when? How long could Kaiya survive before going beyond? And what then? The reality of losing Kaiya struck. *Gone forever*. Forever was for their love, not for their separation. Guilt would mar the rest of his days if he didn't do what he could right now.

He faced Cathbad. "I regret Mug's loss, I truly do. I'll carry his death to my grave. But on this, I must say no. Johan is the master of dreams, he is what the prophecies said. He can do it, and he can bring her back. That is *not* asking too much."

Johan stood at the fire, staring at the glowing embers but following every word.

Cathbad went to Austin. "Yes, Johan is that, but the prophecies do not say what will be. *How* he uses his power now could end this before it begins. Is that what you really want? If Mug's death is heavy upon you, what will the Korda's fall feel like? I'll not even mention the rest of the world. Are you prepared to lose Kaiya and your father as a result of your desire to rescue them? You and Johan are the Change. You are *both* needed. Think, son, *think*."

It wasn't fair. Damn near everything was stacked against Kaiya. Could she hold on? Was she even still in Saoghal?

"Fucking *hell*." He spun and strode to the windows.

Kaiya would say it herself: it was about the world, not her. It was about a civilization's fate on a rock spinning in space, about billions of lives, both present and future. Fate pinned him to the moment, to a hellish choice. Reason settled in, an acid cloud eating away hope for Kaiya. He couldn't ask Johan to expose himself now. The best he could do was bury anxiety and fear and entrust her fate to the hands of a higher power.

He closed his eyes, holding her dearly in his heart and mind. *I give her to thee, so that she may be safe and free*. Somehow it felt right, despite the uncertainty and pain.

"What are the Dejitaru supposed to do?" he asked.

Johan answered, "They'd be given a free pass. All networks spanning the planet would be open to them. Financial centers, banking networks, civil, government and military systems, on public and private networks. Information would be filtered, replaced, and massaged to set the stage. Totem would do most of the actual work, of course, far beyond what the Dejitaru could do alone, but the work would appear done by men."

"Global chaos is required to bring about the kind of change they seek." Sean said from the desk. "The fallout from the Dejitaru's work would include depositions, scandal, coups, and assassinations. Political upheaval would quickly reshape governments and corporations to the highest levels, led by Comannda surrogates in positions of power. Advanced terrorism would be leveraged to prepare the justification needed for widespread martial law. It's all poised right now and would occur over the span of months only. Beyond that, wars both civil and foreign would be selectively waged to plunge regions into isolation. Communications – satellites, internet, phone service – all would be segmented and access strictly controlled at the military level. The borders of the lands would be imposed upon the internet. Purely an exercise in domino effect on their part. All of it would act as the perfect silencer of truth, no matter how loudly we shout at that point. This is the level of division they've long sought. Their System Seven."

"System Seven?" Austin asked, remembering the dream of the factory machines. They'd called out 'SYS-TEM' over and over. "Why seven?"

"Because six systems have been implemented prior," Cathbad answered.

"And just how long have they had these systems?"

"Second century before Christ. Think Sumeria. Think introduction of law, of military, and most importantly, of government."

"Fuckers." He saw his own reflection in the narrow window. Unseen beyond the hills, Glasgow and the surrounding villages formed a group mind where contentment pervaded the bulk of the harmonies. He withdrew quickly and considered what was to come. Man would fall further from the chance at awareness and into the throes of war and circumstance. All to maintain control.

"What are we supposed to do? The three of us."

"You are the knives, Austin. We are the surgeons." Cathbad gestured. "The cancer is widespread but we've monitored the growth so we know where to act."

Sean signaled agreement. "You don't live under a tree for two thousand years without learning a thing or two about its branches."

He turned to Cathbad. "Where do we start?"

A smile of gratitude formed on Cathbad's lips. "You are a good soul, Austin. We start by stopping the Dejitaru and cracking the Comannda network. Now," he motioned to Williams, "it's time to welcome you into the Family as three of our own. Traditions bind us and serve us well, this one especially so."

Williams retreated to the desk and received three thick pieces of paper from Sean. He came around and gave one to each. Old and yellowed to near brown, the scripts were faded and cracked in places.

Cathbad returned to the fire and bade Austin to sit with his friends.

"You've sworn and demonstrated allegiance. You know the enemy. You've come face to face with them and made it away, on Raon's land and in the waters of Saoghal. You've shown mastery of the secrets and have proven trustworthy. You understand the world's fate hangs in a balance more dire than ever before, and yet you stand ready despite the danger. You have true souls, worthy of our respect and love." He grew grim and focused on Austin and Johan. "They know you two exist and they will act. First to take you, and failing that, to destroy you. Anki, you remain a secret but one they will uncover. They will see you as an empath first but will figure things out. You will become a target as well, count on it."

"Is this predicted?" Anki asked.

"Yes, as far as the welets go. The rise of the Change, the return of the helper, the start of Conflict."

"And what then? What is seen of the outcome?"

"Only great chaos, the potential of which is too much to read. The outcome relies upon our actions. Now those," he indicated the parchments they held, "are the commandments of the Celtics, one of the last truly spirited civilizations. The words may seem fanciful to you now but in time and with the grace of the Creator, you'll come to understand their meaning. Please, read them with me now."

As one, they read.

"Give thou thine heart to the wild magic, to the Lord and the Lady of Nature, beyond any consideration of this world.

"Do not covet large or small, do not despise weakling or poor, semblance of evil allow not near thee, never give nor earn thou shame.

"The Ancient Harmonies are given thee, understand them early and prove, be one with the power of the elements, put behind thee dishonor and lies.

"Be loyal to the Lord of the Wild Wood, be true to the Lady of the Stars, be true to thine own self besides, true to the magic of Nature above all else.

"Do not thou curse anyone, lest thou threefold cursed shouldst be, and shouldst thou travel ocean and earth, follow the very step of the ancient trackways."

Crackle from the fire punctured the silence that followed.

Cathbad was again far away, treading memories, only this time he shared them with the others in a vision. Mug stood in front of the lodge at Cutler Fell, beside the great fire, for the first time declaring the same commandments as his own. Mug's loss, the latest, brought to life all the others gone before him, a gathering of the fallen. Of all the death caused by the Comannda, that of the Family hurt the most. Only the knowledge they'd lived lives a hundred times fuller than most brought any respite.

"You are welcome to the Runa Korda, to the Family. Your arrival was seen long before your dream of life began and I'm honored and grateful for your presence. What you bring to our future remains unknown. We can only guide you towards the goal, which is to safely ease the Comannda's grasp on humanity. They ought not be the hoarders of knowledge and of good life. Forced ignorance and shame must be removed so that the great design can flourish. Man's rightful evolution must be untethered and allowed to be. Truth and eventual peace must reign."

• • •

Austin stood in the dark chill of early morning, hands in pockets, forty paces into the green clover. Ground fog spilled down from the hills and flowed around Cullstone's sides into the meadow where he stood. A quarter moon glowed through the milky haze above. The odd, repetitive call of a bird carried from the wooded hillside.

He felt the hacker's meta ahead of the footfalls. Johan appeared, several paces off.

"Damn beautiful, isn't it?" Johan asked.

Kaiya's eyes stared back from the moon. "Yes. Beautiful."

"They kept me from my own promise, you know."

He looked over. "What's that?"

Johan told the story of Sakuma's grandson and of his promise to save the boy in exchange for the Comannda's plans. "Edward forbade I look for him. Too much exposure."

"Jesus, that sucks." He stared at the moon. "I'm not sure I can just sit here knowing Kaiya needs me."

"You won't have to. I'm going to look for her. Tonight."

"What? Are you nuts?" He looked back at the castle. "Or did they approve? I mean—"

"We aren't talking about this, we're dreaming. They have no idea."

Austin struggled with the sudden juxtaposition to dream and with Johan's display of control. He'd forced him into a dream state while standing outside.

"And the bràthair? They monitor us."

"They see a version of this in mine, randomness in yours."

"Um, okay. This is nuts. What if Cathbad is right? What if the Comannda track you down?"

"Anything's possible, but I've been studying this realm, especially where it overlaps with the waking world. I feel how it works. I've given them the leg up they need, I've been doing what they want. I'm all for taking apart the Comannda, but I'll be damned if I'm going to be the Korda's puppet at all times. I'm going after her and the boy. Ryota is innocent and I gave my word. I'm going to teach Cathbad *my* word means something."

Fear rose. "So does their warning, Johan. You could take down everything doing this. The Comannda have *nukes*, man. Millions of people could die. Think about it. Really think."

The meadow darkened and rain began to fall in heavy drops. Austin held out his hand and looked up, shocked to see the moon a crimson red. A blood-red drop spattered against his wrist.

"Forget the nukes," Johan said. "They won't use them. Not over this. They don't really know what they're up against yet. *We're* the Change, Austin. I do my part, you do yours. Cathbad was right, timing is everything and I'm not waiting around. If we don't press them, they'll never look for Ryota and they'll let Kaiya die. This way, they'll look for Ryota. They'll find his body but may need your help to recover it. Do this for me and I'll bring Kaiya back if she's not already gone. I won't let them decide her fate any more than I'd let the

Comannda. It starts now. I'll find you when I have Ryota. Be open to me. Be ready to work with me."

Without warning, Johan faded away.

The rain subsided, the blood gone. The moon glowed brightly again, textured by the rolling mists. The bird had fallen quiet. The peace of the place married itself to his soul, a sudden joining. The universe settled in, an intelligence spanning all before and all to come. What mattered was the preservation of good, of that natural rightness due all righteous beings. Threats against good had no right to exist, were to be eliminated by the strongest in nature. That it was his job now struck a chord of awe and fear reverberating at levels he'd never felt.

As if waking from another dream, vivid realization sank in. A wrong move, a wrong *thought*, and failure could descend, taking so much with him. The same was true for Johan... Johan, who was going to seek out Ryota, right now. On his own. With no backup. No help.

The nukes....

He believed in Johan's abilities, but the risk was still far too high. He turned and ran for the castle.

"Anki, wake up!"

Anki started. "What? What's wrong?"

He pointed at the sleeping form at her side. "He's going after Ryota and Kaiya."

"*No!* Why? How do you know?"

After hearing the story, she turned to Johan and punched him in the face and then again, splitting his lip. "Wake up, you bastard!" She pummeled his chest with both fists. "Damn you!" she shouted. "We must wake him. He'll get us all killed."

Sean arrived at a run with pistol in hand. "What is it?"

"He's gone after Ryota," Anki said. "I should've known. Damn, I should have *known*."

• • •

Dawn's song played to the quiet of night, signaling her eventual arrival. Cathbad sat in the study in his bed clothes, gazing at the fire. The familiar pressure of substantial fate ground against the silence, threatening. Things were in motion beyond his reach, altering everything.

Footsteps sounded in the hall and Sean appeared in the doorway.

"Selfish and short-sighted. The son of a bitch! It's like a stab in the back. I would kill him given any other circumstance."

Cathbad spoke low, to the fire. " 'Once found, the Change will divert the stream, coursing through harsh lands unseen by man, until choice and chance become one in the first Acts of Conflict. Be them sturdy of character and true of soul, and be thou also, for survival of Good relies on such.' The last of the *welets'* Words. I fear they come true tonight."

"Should we try to stop him?"

"No. He'll find Ryota where Kaiya dreams and then the korjé will strike. That is the natural way of things – he will succeed or he will fail. This is his choice.... and our chance." He closed his eyes. "Move him to Belfast. And raise our bràthair. Raise them all."

Chapter 19

Would you learn the secret of the sea? Only those who brave its dangers, comprehend its mystery.
- Henry Wadsworth Longfellow, American Poet (1819 - 1892)

Of course the old druids had good reason for caution. They'd played the game for centuries, learning hard lessons of survival along the way. They'd operated within the limits of their situation, preserving the secrets, their family, and worked towards a more certain future.

That was respectable but didn't mean his way would be the same or that it should be.

No druid had ever moved through Saoghal with such power as he, nor had any Comannda. The ultimate reason was not lost – opportunity to enact balance was greater now than ever before. A reason to wait wasn't forthcoming and in fact appeared unwise. Time was short, the enemy still in control. The people behind the manipulation deserved nothing less than justice for their treasons against humanity. To impart such justice and save mankind required a better understanding of the playing field. What better way to learn than by settling a debt to Sakuma and making good on Edward's promise to Austin?

At the doorway of his dream, the shimmering blackness of Saoghal stretched out without end, a universe of consciousness where souls lived, dreamt, evolved, and departed. It was here that he would impact destiny, starting with his promise.

To seek Ryota required a sense of the boy's soul, his meta imprint. Johan drew upon the oyabun's memories from their shared dream. Visions formed – a happy child, filled with wonder and joy, safe with his loving grandfather. The soft voice, calling '*Sofu! Sofu!*' Ryota... little Ryota.

He cast off into Saoghal's night to find him.

Darkness soon gave way to green fronds rustling in the wind, shading the boy from the sun. His mother sat on a bench nearby talking on a cell phone. Ryota rolled a truck over the warm brick patio and made his motoring sounds soft so he wouldn't disturb her. This was home, a memory of Sakuma's. He pulled away from it.

He tried again and focused on Ryota's essence.

Darkness again gave way, this time to swirling textures of black. He'd arrived somewhere with a great many minds nearby. Rather, he was *among* them, as yet unseen. Concepts mingled, distant and strange. Involvement. Disruption. Mutiny.

A yellow face emerged from the ebony. Simple black eyes, a slit for a nose, and thin lips, all framed in a narrow, pale, sun-colored face.

"You endanger more than yourself, dreamer." An eerie voice, neutral of gender. Images of fiery holocaust flickered, unwelcomed. "Impulsive and dangerous. Very dangerous."

The face faded despite efforts to hold it there. Darkness swirled, the place stranger still. Faint bells rang, water splashed, and distant voices intoned, layers of them. He found himself free and withdrew to the safe house in Oostendorp, to the living room.

The encounter spawned questions – questions that shook foundations, stealing focus from his mission. The Mu? Had he found them or had they sought him? He forced them all aside. Kaiya and Ryota had to be found first.

A sense of Cathbad permeated the room – necessity and synchronicity drove the dream. He softened, allowing it.

The doorbell rang.

He descended the stairs and checked the glass. Sean stood on the porch with a woman. He opened the door, ready to act.

"You've made up your mind about this ill-planned treasure hunt, so I'll spare you what I'd like to say. Instead, you're going to need to know where to put Kaiya's core. Get a sense of this woman, right now. She's your lighthouse. Hand Kaiya off to her, she will be the container."

Johan ignored the druid's terseness. "Container? You don't have a body for her?"

"No, I haven't had time to get out and shop for one. Maybe I'll look online tonight, find something with one hour delivery."

"Fuck you, Sean." He looked to the stranger. "What's your name?"

"Amanda."

He explored the woman's presence, a finger dip into her pond to sample energy and map her patterns. A Spaniard. "You know Marco and Rachel?"

"I know of them."

Johan looked to Sean. "And Ryota?"

"You jumped the gun. You wanted shit to fly, you have it. But we're looking for him, as fast as we can." He turned to go then stopped. "We'll talk about this breach of trust if we all live through its effects."

The two vanished.

• • •

Williams stood amidst the candles, waiting. Cathbad sat by the fire, alone in thought.

Sean came through the door. "Soldado is done. The prototype is being field readied. They'll make the attempt at Ichigaya in three hours' time. And we've located the boy. A clinic in west Tokyo, all knit up with threes and twos. There's no time for anything near graceful or safe enough by our local teams and I doubt Johan will take very long finding Ryota's core."

It was a nine hour flight. Cathbad acknowledged the dilemma. "But you have something in mind."

"Actually, it's something Austin has in mind though he doesn't know I know."

"What's that?"

"Since before Tokyo he's been levitating himself in private. From what I see it's become almost effortless compared to lifting objects."

Cathbad looked up in alarm.

"No, I didn't see him do it, but it's legit, solid. He's been doing it. There's a link between his thoughts and his body that we need to explore. Whatever it is, he can manipulate his body far more easily than anything else."

"Why hasn't he told us?"

"The same fear. Of doing things he doesn't want to. Of becoming a weapon for anybody."

"Yet you're about to propose he fling himself across the globe and confront them at the clinic? I don't like it and I'm sure he won't either. It's madness."

"It's only madness if you compare it to the past. What he can do now is what matters. He's already thought about long distances and speed. He wants to try." Sean shrugged. "You said it, the Change will direct things. If he doesn't get there, how else will we retrieve Ryota's body? They aren't going to just give him up."

"Yes, but good Lord, it's a trap. So much coverage for the boy? They know his value. Things are unraveling too fast."

"It's either that or you pull Johan back."

Cathbad stared in the fire. "Risking both at the same time. It's madness..."

"Yet the trackways lead there."

The old druid slowly nodded. "Indeed, they seem to." He looked up. "Confirm it. Measure his effort while levitating. Increase the dose if need be. Prove to me that he can sustain it, Sean, through the rescue. And show me a bulletproof exit plan. Meanwhile I'll see what the Confrere can do to help."

• • •

"I didn't fucking tell you because I didn't want you to know, get it?" Austin paced the kitchen at Cullstone. Sean leaned against the counter. Anki sat at the breakfast bar. "There's got to be a part of me that is private, that exists away from the Runa Korda. Just because I'm not as advanced as you doesn't mean I shouldn't be able to keep certain things private. You have your privacy, right Sean?"

"Relax," Anki advised. "You're going to pop a heart valve."

"No, I'm not gonna relax. This is serious shit."

"Yes and no, Austin. I'm able to fully protect myself. You're still new and so you need monitoring. Skimming keeps us in the loop and helps keep you safe. That's the reality for now."

"Okay, but you know it's something I wanted private. That doesn't count for anything?"

"It's a god damned breakthrough, Austin. It's phenomenal. You can't keep that shit in your pocket. It's the path we need to be on to understand not only telekinesis but maybe our own placement in the universe. You are literally thinking yourself into a new relationship with Raon. The implications are tremendous. You can't be afraid to learn more about it."

"I can't? What do you know about my fear? Is it natural to do this?" He rose into the air and hovered, causing Anki to gasp. "Let me tell you, this doesn't feel natural, man. It feels like I'm breaking the law, nature's law, and somehow, some way, I'm gonna get busted for it. And now you want to increase proteins so I can fly myself around the world? That is nuts. You're nuts. Really, really nuts."

Anki gave Sean a warning glance.

"Alright, I'm hearing you. All I know is that Johan's out there and will most likely find Ryota's core. If he's successful, he'll grab it and will need a place to land it and quick. The best, safest place is the boy's own body. I've told you the situation at the clinic. Now you tell me a better way to get his body than you going in and getting it. No one can do it as simply and as directly as you. No one."

Austin lowered to the ground, shaking his head. "Propelling myself thousands of miles over oceans and desolate wilderness using only my mind is not simple, it's *insane*. And supposing I make it, I'd have to bust in and fly the boy out to safety, eliminating any threats along the way. For all I know they have a TK waiting there to swat me like a fly." He gave Sean a hard look. "What I really want to know is, why even suggest something like this? If I'm so rare and important, why risk my life?"

"It seems like a risk, but there's more to it. More than we understand. Situations arise. Options appear. We're led to the answers if only we listen. Cathbad knows how to listen. And as crazy as it all may sound, Johan's actions are the signals. Your abilities are the exact fit for the situation and the only thing standing in the way is growth on your part. Growth that is meant to happen."

The two shared a long glance.

"The trackways," Austin said. "Ancient trackways. What does that even mean?"

"It means destiny leaves footprints. Each footprint is timeless and is connected in some way to the ultimate outcome. Listening to the path leads to knowing."

"It's not exact."

Sean shook his head. "Nothing ever is. But it's possible to sense a direction."

"And you're saying this is the right direction?"

"Yes," he said. "It is."

Austin paused, reflecting on the very same feeling Sean spoke of. He had to admit the direction was there, like a flow. Things were taking shape, the form already familiar. Johan must've known what he could do. *Be ready to work with me.* He could fly and there was a reason. Had to be. Helping Johan was part of it. He felt it, almost knew it.

That didn't mean he had to like it.

Early dawn broke outside the garage behind Cullstone where he stood with Sean and Anki. Wearing doubled up thermals, jeans, three shirts, a Kevlar vest, electric socks and glove inserts, and adorned in black riding leathers and boots, he was as bundled as an astronaut and about as protected. On his back he wore a low-profile parachute, on his wrist an altimeter from Sean's jump equipment, and on the other wrist a GPS device with his route programmed. He wore a holstered Glock on his right hip.

His body was ready. His mind understood what to do. His fear still felt like a fever, though. Thousands of miles, at speeds better suited for metal-plated jets. What would a bird strike feel like? "Stay above six thousand feet and that won't be a problem," Sean said. "Stay below eight thousand and your breathing will be fine." And aircraft? "We'll plot your flight on the GPS away from known routes."

Despite the fear, successful testing made the journey seem possible. He'd shot north across the Scottish highlands at seven thousand feet without a problem. The GPS calculated a speed of nearly a thousand miles an hour and truth told it was easy. Too easy. He'd formed a piercing dome to split the air and reduce drag. Almost no effort. He could go faster. Hard-iron butterflies flittered in his chest still, but he was confident enough. He would go for it – to earn a chance to save Kaiya and to help the boy win his body back.

Sean was displeased with Johan though he kept it to himself. He spoke over the hiss of spray paint as he primered a motor cycle helmet black to match the outfit. "I need to fill you in with a few details that you probably won't like. The Comannda have a type of aircraft they use a lot. Not your usual craft." He stopped spraying and glanced at Austin. "They are fast. Broken laws of physics fast and they're tough. They can split through an airliner like a pile of kindling." He resumed spraying. "There's a few of them in their fleet—"

"Wait, wait. *UFOs?*"

"—and if they catch wind of you out there playing superman, they'll target you if they can. It's unlikely, of course, because they won't know you're up there. And no, not UFOs. They made them."

Williams entered the garage carrying a dark duffle bag and a plate of food. "This ought to do. I've lined it with Kevlar, thermal padding and fur—"

"Wait a second!" Austin stood, dazed. "Sean, why the fuck didn't you tell me this before?"

"Relax, Austin," Anki said and took the plate of food from Williams.

Sean set the helmet down. "Because we don't see them being a significant threat. They're antigravity transports, best we know. Yes, they can be used for intercept and ramming. But in your case they won't even know you're up there. Still, just watch for them. They're normally jet black when you can see them—"

"When I can see them? What the—"

"Typical saucer shape, like two frisbees put together. Watch for sudden holes in clouds, that sort of thing. Yes, they have metamaterials bending light around them. Not perfectly, but it's impressive. Again, it's highly unlikely they'll be involved. Here," he took the duffle bag from Williams, "this is Ryota's seat for the ride to safety. There's a med kit in case you get hurt. It's got the joiner strap so you can wear it in front, under the jacket. I updated the GPS with two more safe drop points, so there's five to choose from. Now, grab a bite to eat and then I want you to try it again. Use route number three on the GPS. Try ten thousand feet and go faster. I want you confident before you set out," he glanced at his watch, "in twelve minutes. Williams, see if the clinic floor plan is ready, please."

Austin accepted the food from Anki and stood there, still in shock. Anki led him to a bench outside the garage.

"Relax, eat. You need your strength. I'll get you some water."

Despite Anki's advice to relax, a thin line ran right down his middle, once more challenging belief in what was happening. Terrestrial UFOs. Questions popped like fuses, each one more urgent than the last. Did they have weapons, too? Lasers? What about killer satellites? Would he be targeted? What else hadn't they told him? Out of the jumble one thing stood certain – things would well and truly never be like they were.

He heaved a big breath and let it out. "*Shit.*"

Anki came from the garage with a cup of water. "Okay now, seriously, I could feel you from in there. You've got to stay grounded." She sat next to him. "What's got you most worried?"

"Are you kidding? You name it." He took a bite of fried chicken. In the silence between them, a mesmerizing feeling grew that calmed and centered. Time slowed. Details stood out. Light from the east had woke the morning birds and brought the horses out to the pasture for a walk. Their energy fused with the beauty of the morning. The castle's brown stone seemed to glow as it shed night's hue. An overriding peace colored his every thought.

"Thanks for that, Anki." He took the offered cup and drank. "Damn. This is really happening?"

"Yes, Austin. It is."

"Why me? Of all the billions of people... *why me?* I've got zero qualifications for this. I'm more apt to fail, you know, than, than a whole lot of people. I just don't understand why *me*."

"You said it yourself, you've always wondered at the mystery of life. It's in your nature. And somehow, some part of nature is more open to you. There is one thing you need to recognize and fully accept: you have the right soul for the job. That has to be your best qualification. I don't believe you would have been given the gift otherwise. I'm sure of it."

Sean stepped out, patting the helmet. "It's dry enough. Whenever you're ready." At Anki's glance, he added, "Sorry, but time is short."

• • •

Director Tomov woke to the sound of the comm. He noted the time.

"Yes?"

"Sir, Gerrit is out and headed for the girl."

Four minutes later he emerged in the control room. "Initiate priority live-log to the Executives. Are we synched to the cloud? Good. Java, please?" He took the vacant command chair. The touch screen before him updated noticeably with four gold indicators along the bottom – four Executives already linked in.

"Ops, status?"

"A watch-listed revenant led to proxy contact with Gerrit. Signus 5 was tracking the target but was unable to make the leap after contact. Fortunately they achieved a strong reading. He's going for the girl and her little friend."

"Excellent." *By the book. No mistakes.* "And the boy's body?"

"G3 has it secured. Riders are standing by at the clinic with the recognition pattern for Austin. Reinforcements have been ordered."

"Fit the clinic for detonation, fast. I want to level it with a word. Confirm scenario J86 as an option for the region. No mistakes, people. Not one. We make history tonight and it better be the right version."

"Sir, scenario J86 is enabled as an option. Executive authorization required for execution."

Scenario J86 was least preferred but if things went that way, so be it. Not his job to be concerned with the outcome; the target's actions would determine the results, not him. He called up the feed from Signus Alpha. The little island filled the screen. Kaiya sat with the boy, talking to him, soothing him. Under G1 observation since the last hop, she realized they were trapped. As soon as Gerrit merged in, all three could be contained.

"Signus Alpha, confirm your panels are ready."

"Confirmed, director. Currently twelve linked with two more in briefing, due shortly."

"Good, because he's on his way."

"Bring him in, sir, we'll bag him."

• • •

Hurried plans made Noboru queasy. Nothing done hastily ever seemed to go well. Normally there was time for meticulous planning, for crafting an operation like a well written application. All tight code and efficient functions. In this case there was almost no time.

The call came just as he prepared dinner for Kou, the Shitzu he'd adopted from the family two floors down. They were moving to Honshū and could not keep the little rascal. Noboru had made the mistake of holding him on the elevator ride up. Amazing what six floors and a pair of moist, imploring eyes could do. He put the beef mixture in the bowl and left it at Kou's feet before hurrying to the roof.

Rows of bee hives glowed a milky white beneath the pole lamp. He walked the narrow aisle between them and made sure he was alone before he knelt before one. He slid open the storage door beneath and retrieved the hidden comm link. From a brief transmission, he received instructions. The queasy feeling began upon hearing 'highest priority' and deepened at hearing the announced job and timeline. Two hours to deliver a team of two into the defense ministry's communications building! Third basement!

Asinine! It couldn't be done! Yet even as he thought it, pieces of the solution began to form. By the time a response was required, he knew two things: he'd received his riskiest assignment yet, and Kou would need a new master if things didn't go just right.

• • •

Austin stuffed the map in his jacket and closed it up. The last try was better and had done much for confidence. The grid's potential was at peak response, flowing in line with every intention; pliable, focused and stable. That he was about to propel himself six thousand miles to arrive in Japan's evening sky wasn't something to think about – it just had to be done.

Anki and Sean stood aside when Cathbad arrived to see him off.

He clasped his shoulders. Gray eyes spoke concern. "What Johan isn't considering is how far they'll go to destroy you both. Pay attention. Be open to me, Sean, and Anki." He narrowed his eyes. "I wish this weren't the path but damn it, it is. Be aware, be in tune, and you may just save everybody's skin. Godspeed, lad." He stepped back.

Sean clapped his hands once as he came forward. "Remember, take as many breaks as you need but keep them short. You really need to push for speed. Follow checkpoints and wait at the last one. Use the flashing light to guide you in. Once you're on the roof, an old man will give you instructions. We'll be monitoring you every step of the way and will guide you as needed. Be open to us. Any questions?"

"Dozens if I stopped to think."

"Then Godspeed, Austin." Sean shook his hand. "And watch out for the AG units."

Thoughts of anti-gravity ships made his stomach spin.

Anki stepped in and hugged him tightly. "Be strong. You're the Change. Make them wish they'd never messed with Mother Nature." She was right – they *had* done just that. Anki touched his cheek before stepping back.

He slid on a thermal mask followed by the helmet. After fastening the straps he paused to face the three. In that moment, the two druids and the empath felt as close as family.

"Am I clear?" The bràthair would scan to be sure the hills and skies held no observers.

After a moment Sean nodded. "Clear."

He imagined a grand exit and knew it would work. Intention turned to reality: the grid folded in closely, braced him, and like a slingshot flung him upward. In a flash he became a dot in the morning sky then vanished from sight altogether.

"Holy living hell," Cathbad muttered, craning to see.

Sean nodded. "He's got it now. The Change, indeed."

• • •

Ryota finished covering his legs with warm sand and patted it down. Buried up to his waist, he appeared content and resumed staring at the storms pressing in from all sides. For the first time wind blew in the tropical dreamscape, introducing cooler air. The sun hung overhead in its usual place to light the tiny island despite the approaching gloom.

Kaiya walked along the water's edge looking for something unique in the clouds, anything to take advantage of. After three slow laps, she found nothing. Control had wilted long ago. What little she had left she clung to in the hopes it might matter in a crucial moment, like when the storm fronts collided at their island. They would, she felt it.

She returned to Ryota and put on a smile. "You look comfy. A sand blanket." He looked up. She tapped her temple. "Smart, very smart!" He seemed to understand.

The wind gusted stronger, a reminder time was short. They'd worn her down all too easily. Her initial burst of creativity had freed them but it hadn't taken long for them to retake her. *Weak*. Before this, the idea of lucid dreaming belonged to Psych majors and coffee house beatniks. She couldn't have imagined the reality of it before. The people who tried to save Mac had to know about this dream world. She'd expected them to try a rescue, yet saw no evidence of one.

She looked directly up, shielding her eyes from the sun and the too-perfect blue sky. What was beyond sky in a dream? What space did a dream occupy? Dread suddenly became more than just a feeling. The winds whipped harder, growing persistent. The towering black clouds loomed closer, converging in the counterclockwise flow of the wind.

Everything was closing in. Everything was going to end.

She knelt next to the boy and patted him on the back, receiving more comfort than she gave. He wasn't suffering from the same panic – only a sadness beyond his years. Helpless to do anything, she thought of digging in next to him.

Inspiration struck, though admittedly weakly.

"Ryota, you are *very* smart. We need to dig a hole." It was all she could think of – to do nothing was madness squared. She dropped to her knees and began furiously swiping the sand aside. She squinted hard at the wind-whipped grit.

"Close your eyes, Ryota!"

He watched her through slitted eyes before climbing out to help. Already the sand in the shallow hole was more moist, better to form a burrow to escape the coming storm.

"Thank you, Ryota, you understand me! Yes, here, dig. Dig a big hole. Wider – there, good. It will be our safety cave. Safe is good, yes!"

Somehow believing made it more likely so.

• • •

Eight thousand feet was the sweet zone as breathing came easy and the distance to the earth proved breathtaking. The Norwegian coastline slid by on the right, backlit by early dawn. *I'm flying, through the sky.*

He stayed focused and tuned, scanning for anything in his path. Confidence grew with every passing moment. The GPS fluctuated but read just over a thousand miles per hour. The symbiotic nature of the connection with the grid grew. The sense of expenditure and recovery evened out, as if he were both giving and receiving energy in the quantum process. Gratitude for the gift was unavoidable just as was the pure, uncut amazement at flight.

When the cold grew bitter, he imagined a warm bubble of air and one formed. He pushed harder until the speed indicator rose to two thousand miles per hour. He crouched to look behind. The warm bubble leaked like exhaust into the cold air, forming a contrail – just like in the first dream at Kaiya's apartment except it wasn't purple or made of curiosity. Here, it was an arrow pointing to his passage. Moments later, the contrail dissolved, the dome hardened to contain the warmth. He couldn't help but recall Edward's words about joining with the creator at the far end.

The thought proved more breathtaking than the flight.

Faster. The dome grew longer. The GPS digits showed almost three thousand miles an hour. The shoreline fell away and open sea claimed every horizon, enveloping him in a solitary portrait of watery nature. Clouds slipped into view only to be pierced and passed through, flickering by in strobe fashion. The GPS vibrated and changed to the next checkpoint, an estimated ten minutes out. A slight turn southeast towards Russia....

He pressed a button to read final ETA. Less than two hours at this rate.

Mom, I really hope you can see me now.

• • •

By the eighth hour behind the console, sleep always became a problem. No matter how much rest the night before, the eighth hour dragged like a walk in thick snow. Right between lunch and the end of the shift, the black hole of sleepiness beckoned, numbing every sense.

Following routine, Sergeant Kislyako stood and stretched. Whoever invented the twelve hour shift needed to be shot. He wasn't old enough to remember the days of six hour shifts and vodka and women at lunch, but he'd heard stories. Someday he'd retire and have all day to himself. He'd never look at a screen again. Ever. The radar station at Severny Island could rot further into hell and he'd not care.

One of the most useless duties imaginable. Like America would ever really launch missiles?

He eyed the new black boxes recently installed in the racks by the young shchenoks.

"You're lucky to have a job, Daniil. Fucking computers taking over everything."

He sat back down and ignored his sore legs. He adjusted the scan range and bit his tongue doing a double-take at the screen: a single faint return, moving at missile speed. He increased the radar's intensity, narrowing it by three measures. The altitude was too low. Either a stealth craft or a new missile of some kind.

He cursed and picked up the red phone, more awake than he'd been all year.

• • •

"There! Good, get closer. Focus. God damn… Oscar, how fast is he moving?"

Overseer calculated and responded. "ESTIMATED SPEED IS THREE-THOUSAND MILES PER HOUR AT EIGHT THOUSAND FEET."

"Heat signature?"

The view switched to thermal to reveal a vague, localized heat with none trailing. "How is he pulling *that* off?"

The commandeered American spy satellite followed the bender's flight as he approached land. Director Tomov sat back in his chair, juggling implications.

"Send in the riders, I want a track on him *now*. Get AGTs on his tail, maybe they can lock on and provide guidance for the riders or vice versa." *Or they can ram the fucker.* "Issue stand down orders through the Russian defense ministry, flag it as equipment malfunction and get Oscar in there to make it real. Make sure the U.S. gets word, too. Black out all satellites in his path, current or future. He's headed for Tokyo. Open a channel to the demo team." He looked on in private wonder at the man in flight. "Zoom in." The image revealed no propellant signature, no structure or engines of any kind. Only a parachute.

Orders issued, the control room fell silent. All eyes stared at the screen.

• • •

The doors to the NRO satellite operations room burst open. Heads whipped around.

An Air Force major shouted, "Everybody out, now, now, move! You!" He pointed to a wide-eyed satellite operator. "Stay put. Move people, *move!*"

The facility commander, General Fagan, and a civilian entered the room accompanied by two Security Police officers with hands on their side arms. The lieutenant in charge approached, questions forming on her lips. The major put up a hand and thumbed her to the exit. The guards followed her out and closed the doors behind them.

"Stay seated." The major instructed the lone operator. "What's your first name, soldier?"

"Patrick, sir."

The major handed him a piece of paper. "Can you find this, Patrick?"

The twenty-four year old from Los Osos, California, scanned the paper. Coordinates, heading, speed, altitude, size – less than two meters? Time stamped three minutes prior. He cleared his throat. "I can try, sir. I'll need to access–"

"Do it!" General Fagan barked. "Whatever it takes."

"Yes, sir!" He worked furiously at the console, entering override codes spit out by the major, displacing scheduled controls until he locked onto MISTY-4, an NRO satellite passing over far east Asia nearest those coordinates. A control directive failed – the screen came up black.

"Shit," he muttered, intensely aware of eyes on him. He decoupled, relocked, and reissued the control directive but still got black.

He turned. "Sir, either that's equipment malfunction or we're being blocked."

The general exploded. "Blocked? Who the hell can block us? That's our fucking satellite!"

The civilian asked, "You're patched over SDS?"

"Yes, sir, SDS."

"Switch to Milstar, SDS-2 class. Pick the nearest one. Good, now use the K band downlink to reach the Misty on the diagnostic port."

Patrick hesitated. "That would require line of sight calculation–"

"No, it doesn't. Arrow down to the last menu item. Press ALT and SHIFT together and press the number six key on the keypad."

Several new menu options became available.

"There, option S2S. Sat to sat."

"Wow." A list of satellites appeared. "We want 186."

A minute later, the link completed. A diagnostics menu filled the large screen. "I'm in."

"Now use the Config menu. Access.... Multilink Protocol.... fourth item down, Override Options. There, disable the Force Override option. Now, go back to Access. Security... Diagnostic Password. Change it to something, just double damned don't forget it. Good, save it. Now, back out, switch to SDS and attempt control of the Misty."

Whoever he was, the guy knew his shit, Patrick thought. But who had locked them out? He recoupled, locked, and issued the control directive. The room lit up brightly from an out of focus image of mountains on the screen.

"Someone's been looking at this target, coordinates are in line. Give me a second to catch up."

Twenty seconds later, he found the projectile and established a track lock. He zoomed in on the target, onto the–

"Patrick, what you see is beyond top secret. Which means you *don't* see it and this never happened. Do you understand?"

"Yes, yes, sir. I understand." He dared look again, his heart pounding.

The major reached for the nearest STU phone. The civilian asked, "Where will that trajectory take him?"

Patrick tore his eyes from the screen to run the calculation. "Over a desolate section of Russia. He'll pop out in the Sea of Okhotsk in... ten minutes at that speed. On to New Zealand if he keeps going."

Further zoom allowed for a detailed view of the flyer. Two small tubes, no jet pack or other means of propulsion visible.

"Borden here. Confirming stand down. Repeat, no threat." The major hung up and looked over at the operator. "Patrick, you have family?"

"Yes, sir, I do."

"I see. That's good. Again, this never happened."

Patrick replied carefully, "No, sir, it most certainly did not."

• • •

With the backdrop of the Milky Way galaxy framing it, MISTY-4 hung in apogee, the longest stretch of its high elliptical orbit, conveying imagery back to NRO receiving stations via relay satellites. For previous spy satellites apogee meant downtime; MISTY-4 utilized gen-after-next optic systems that allowed for continuous high resolution focus from an apogee twenty-five thousand miles distant.

In a split-second event, a black blur struck the twelve-hundred million dollar satellite and sent it hurtling like a pinball into outer space, its solar arrays and antennae flailing from a smashed core.

• • •

Austin slowed over the western edge of a shoehorn peninsula jutting from Russia's mainland into the Sea of Okhotsk. He descended vertically through the gloom of dusk, steering between trees until his feet touched spongy earth. He released the grip of flight – vertigo from the sudden stillness nearly toppled him along with the wind. A thousand feet above the sea, atop a steep quarter mile slope to the beach, he stood surrounded by wilderness.

The GPS marker read 'rest b4 last CP'. The two hour flight hadn't taken much out of him – though imagining the rescue had. If the element of surprise remained his, things would go much better. If not, the hell-in-a-hand basket effect would surely apply. Johan had started this but wasn't the one in line to do the real dirty work. Thoughts of having to kill people only turned his stomach tighter. For Kaiya, though, he would do it.

He pulled off the helmet. The zigzag route over land had been exhilarating, especially the mountain peak flybys. He took a seat at the base of a moss-covered tree and looked out over the sea. To the far right, distant lights of a city lined the horizon, a twinkling coast. Everywhere else water met the horizon in a beautiful but desolate union.

Watching the sky deepen in the west, he could pretend the world wasn't topsy-turvy. For a moment it was a beautiful planet, devoid of confused people, empty of power struggles and unchecked greed. The sphere was just a home, a firm and stable place in the universe, created for life with such varying beauty that even a lifetime wasn't enough to appreciate it all or very well. In that pretend place, the questions were gone, the truth self-evident. Humans were meant to *be* here, together in peace.

Reality crashed the vision. Instead of just *being*, they had the Comannda. Led astray, corrupted, set up for failure, taken advantage of. Thousands of years' worth of growth, stolen from humanity early on.

The magnitude of his place in history struck again – *I am part of what can change it.* Half of the Change, up against a system so powerful, so prolific and advanced it had kept itself hidden for centuries. Instead of surging with confidence, he shrank in retreat to the small, comfortable world he'd left behind. Kaiya stood in the shop the night Johan broke into InterGen, an angel in the flesh surrounded by technology. He imagined her sitting alongside him at a campfire, content after dinner, talking of anything and everything. A walk to the lakeside and a bit of stargazing–

He shook it off. *Stop dreaming. Man up. Make it happen.*

He pulled out the printed notes and his penlight. The boy's room was on the top floor, the fifth, with a north facing window. He looked at the photos. Rip out the window, neutralize guards, sweep up the boy. IVs? What else would he be hooked up to? Breathing tube? It could be complicated. Speed would matter. He checked the GPS and looked through the five programmed locations where he could safely drop the boy off. Having options was good.

He noticed the wind had died down and a calm pervaded the woods. Nature drew his attention, basic life flowing from the insects, animals, and the trees themselves. For long moments he dwelt in the space, feeling it, being felt by it. The world was alive, down to the smallest elements, reactive and in some manner intelligent. How else could his thoughts result in the grid changing like it was? The observer impacted the observed – in a way more sophisticated than most scientists could imagine. Whatever secrets lay at the core of Raon seemed to have roots in Saoghal. It was all very designed, entwined and dependent, like the inner workings of a Swiss watch.

Time. There wasn't much of it. He stowed his notes and stood to stomp off the cold. Intention flowed and was met by the warming of his feet. Again it felt like standing on the border of a dream.

"Okay." He put the helmet back on and checked the GPS. Over sixteen-hundred miles left. Potential rose and with it, excitement.

"Time for me to fly."

He couldn't help but think, *I should have brought music.*

With a few quick, deep breaths, he leaned forward into the grid and lifted from the ground, back into weightless flight. He descended over tree-tops to the shoreline then shot outward to skim just above the sea. For a time flying low and hidden felt good but he needed speed at altitude. He shot upward in an arc. Thrill coursed and his heart pounded against his lungs. For a moment he dared envision a future beyond the danger – a glimpse of what he could become.

The next thought was of Icarus and the sun.

• • •

"Problems, sir. Still no reacquisition of Austin and Signus reports Eden approaching. Pattern is stable."

Director Tomov looked up. "Where is Gerrit?"

"No data, sir. However, Signus impressions indicate between one and two hours until contact with Eden in their current state."

Hell. The garbage truck of the universe, coming to clean up at the wrong damn time. Nothing could touch it, nothing could stop it, and nothing could communicate with it. If you were cast-off, you were scooped up. Just a cosmic energy collector, automatic and inconsequential. He'd long ago lost interest in the ethereal presence others deemed as God's Gatekeeper. To see God in it was just leftover cultural programming. The universe simply liked to keep a clean house. Nothing mystical in that.

He sipped from his cup. The Korda were working a bold plan, using both targets at once. The AGT teams were in synch now, aware of the bender's bizarre flight and ready to track his approach to the clinic.

Kaiya remained firmly cornered but still free within her own meta, the best way to attract Gerrit. Of course, leaving her free also left her open to collection by Eden. To steal her back now would complicate everything – extend the conflict and allow room for failure. The bender and Gerrit had to be contained or eliminated.

"Prepare to retrieve her and the boy but only at the last possible mark, is that clear? I want that *clear.*"

• • •

The vast bed of Tokyo's lights spilled to the horizon once more, a nuclear-powered array of LED, florescent, mercury, and neon. Arrival over the city came as a sensory rush compared to the nature he'd traveled through to get there. Below, avenues crawled with activity, full of cars, busses, and people. The city itself pulsed, a breathing ocean of consciousness – not a lucid dream, but in reality.

The GPS indicated arrival at the checkpoint, a quarter mile below. He searched for and found a white and red light blinking erratically atop a building. He lined up and descended rapidly, a tiny shadow slipping from the sky. He set down near a table and turned off the flashing strobe light. After his eyes adjusted, he peered around. Air conditioners and solar panels mixed with organic landscaping to create an odd ensemble. In one corner a shallow koi pond complimented a rock garden. Plenty of shadows to hide in. He felt alone, no hint of meta nearby. If the old man was there he was damn good at hiding himself.

He took off the helmet and ran a hand through his hair. Six thousand miles in just over two hours. Amazement dimmed under the weight of what might come next. The GPS showed ten miles to the clinic. Butterflies swarmed at the thought of facing armed guards – a sickening flurry of wings scratching his insides. He squeezed the grip of the Glock at his side. The sooner it was over, the sooner he'd know if there was a chance to be with Kaiya again.

He took cover under an awning near the koi pond and waited, helmet in hand. Hopefully no one came out for a smoke or a stroll before the old man arrived. At the moment, he couldn't recall a word of Japanese except for one: *kamikaze*.

• • •

Evening settled on the compact mid-rises of the Kanda Tacho district. Cool air swirled into the tiny balcony six stories up, carrying with it music from the apartment below.

Noboru pulled on a Peace cigarette. Japan Tobacco, trendy and typically comforting. Tonight the irony made him want to choke – he felt nothing of peace. In the narrow street below, a woman walked back from market with plastic bags like weighted balloons. She stepped around them as they swung with her gait, her torso weaving expertly in a practiced system of motion. Again he checked his watch. Less than two minutes before the mail server would crash. He'd get the text alert, wait another five, and then call Central Security. He fought rising nausea. He'd never had to put anyone into the building before, much less two.

The muted ocean sounds of city traffic reminded him of travel, of escape. He longed to be on the subway to Shuji's house instead of working for the Sensei. But he had no choice – debt required repayment.

Thirty minutes later, Noboru stood at the entrance to Building E and stared up at the massive bulk of Tower A, trying not to panic. Clammy palms, bowels loose with fear. Severe queasiness. Hasty planning. Daring moves. *Still a good plan...* a new mantra.

Helping some was the expertise the operatives displayed so far. In the properly branded van, wearing what he'd ordered, they'd said exactly what he'd instructed them to. Not really surprising but still impressive. The two carried bulky laptop and equipment cases, part of the gear they required. More impressive was how they moved and talked: just like repairmen. Unworried, a bit boastful with their techese chatter. Trained to mimic the very air of a computer serviceman? To talk the talk? The Sensei didn't screw around. They did things right, made things easy for him. Only they usually gave him more time; never before had action so fast and risky been required. *Calm. Be the calm.* He could almost imagine that he hadn't triggered the server failure and that this was a real service call.

Almost.

Central Security sent over Mori, an officer cadet Noboru had never seen before. The young cadet opened the main doors and halted them in the lobby while he powered up the x-ray machine and wrote on a clipboard. He wasn't talkative – maybe a sign he wouldn't be nosy and push to accompany them. Sometimes they did. Noboru hoped and re-hoped he wouldn't insist on coming along. The plan got far more sketchy if he did.

"Company?"

One of the operatives answered easily. "J.I. Technical".

"Names?"

He rattled off their names.

"Reason for call? Server?"

"Mail server down. ID 8011. Two hour response guaranteed."

The cadet looked at them before nodding, unimpressed. He turned the clipboard around.

"Sign there. Place bags on the conveyor, your metal objects in trays. Belt buckles, USB sticks, gum wrappers, anything metallic."

Noboru breathed shallow as the bags slid into the machine's chamber. One by one, the cadet inspected the equipment. He peered intently. "Are those power supplies?"

"Yes, they are." The Sensei feigned respect at his technical knowledge.

Bags cleared, cell phones and belts back on, the moment came. The cadet walked around the x-ray machine and looked to Noboru.

"Call when you are done. They need to be checked out, as well."

"Yes, of course. I'll call."

Still a good plan...

Chapter 20

Thought has been constantly evolving and we can't say when that system began.
- David Bohm, American quantum physicist

A bird's-eye view showed the van racing along the A8 headed west towards the ferry, thirty minutes away. Anki sat in front of the screens watching, sick with worry though still angry for the danger Johan had created. There were probably a hundred more appropriate ways to get what he'd wanted but he'd chosen this. She wanted to say it was out of character but in truth, what did she really know? In this, Johan was like most others she'd known and had been disappointed by through the years. Unpredictable, driven by inner needs. Still, he was so much more than anyone before. There was no denying it or her soul-bound devotion to him. She would go the distance for him, no matter how far or short it might be.

She'd last seen him prone in the hidden compartment of the van's floor, looking too much like a corpse in a coffin. She wished she'd taken the time to dab the mess of blood from his split lip before they set off. Now the bràthair were out, working on his safe transport and also protecting Austin, seen atop a roof in Tokyo on another screen. From the basement entertainment room of Cullstone, they watched the flows captured by shùil. Sean focused on the team in the defense ministry building. Cathbad sat with templed fingers, involved and distant, eyes fixed on the screen relaying Johan's shùil. It showed gray except for an occasional glimpse of chaotic patterns and every so often a tiny island at the eye of a storm.

"Is he stuck or in trouble?" Anki asked. "I don't like this."

"Still waiting as far as I can tell. For what I don't know. He knows Austin is ready. The storm is narrowing quickly."

"This is all so bizarre." Tense as piano wire, she remembered to breathe. "More than I imagined it would be."

The barrier between waking life and nightmare had thinned, so much so it seemed the very air were ready to shimmer. Both Johan and Austin were flying on instinct. Everything hinged on their ability to be and do exactly what was needed. Their inexperience was a dangerous factor.

She turned away to look for something to ground or at least distract her. Recessed lights softened the oak-featured room. A billiards table took up one end of the room. The bar's backlit drink shelves looked inviting. *To drown all this away.*

She picked up a cue chalk and examined it, diving into its familiarity. Margaret – *mom* – had loved to play. Sunday mornings at the pool hall were some of her best childhood memories. She twisted her thumb in the worn depression of the cube, transferring the colored dust, then admired the blue shade of her digit. Transferring... *digitally.*

She looked up at the images on the screens. The videos were fed live, digitally, but from where? Besides three guards posted outside, they were alone here. Without bràthair, the imagery had to be flowing over networks to reach Cullstone.

She went to Sean with her question. "Isn't it risky? So many encrypted streams could draw attention. Aren't you worried about Totem tracing them here?"

Cathbad and Sean looked at her. She caught something dark from them both.

Cathbad stood. "There are no transmission lines. It's a closed system. Here in Cullstone."

"Oh? Then where are the bràthair?" Something wasn't right, he was hiding something. Shielding out of concern for her. Sean turned back to the screens, already refocused.

"We haven't had time to properly introduce you to everyone on our team here, Anki. I wouldn't say this moment is ideal for it, but I can't see holding off, especially now that you've sensed what you have. We'll be a few minutes, Sean."

He walked to the bar and behind it, to the narrow door of the wine cellar.

"Follow me, please."

They descended into a cool room with a low ceiling and more recessed lights. Six rows of wooden racks stood filled with vino. Cathbad walked to the far right row and followed it back. He knelt and removed a single bottle. Unscrewing a thin false bottom revealed a membrane keypad. He entered several digits before putting it back together and in its place.

He stood and turned to the opposite side of the row, along the wall. "As you recall, the brain is the only organ directly involved in the marriage of the meta to this world." He gingerly pulled on a rack which slid towards him on hidden casters. He pushed it off to one side to expose the wall. He pressed against it and the entire section swung inward. A steady hum escaped into the cellar. He turned to her, blocking the view beyond.

"You're aware our sciences have allowed us to stem the pace of aging. Unfortunately, we all eventually yield. One of the triumphs in our mimicry of Comannda technology is that of the preservation and sustainment of the brain well after the body's other systems have failed. You are about to meet seventeen souls who volunteered to 'stay on', as it were, in the service of the Runa Korda."

He stepped aside and gestured to a narrow room that reminded her of the aquariums of Den Helder's pet shop.

Along a wall the glow from two rows of tanks filled the space. Each tank contained a human brain, complete with stem, suspended in a black frame. Wires ran in and out at various points.

Anki gasped. Over a dozen sets of eyes peered in her direction, each orb in its own stand braced in a collar of sorts, with movement facilitated by micro motors tensioning lines attached to the collar. Optic nerves trailed back into gray mass. LCD monitors lined the opposite wall.

"My God..."

"Cullstone's own bràthair. Take a moment, probe them. You will see they are here of their own volition."

It was true. Each was content, in control, though most were distant, involved, as if dreaming or working. One in particular, the last one on the bottom row, was definitely present in the room with her. Drawn to it, she stepped closer and gasped. Gray-green eyes followed her approach. The draw intensified. Obviously the yearning to connect was not just her own.

She squatted. Eyes stared as if drilling to find comprehension she had yet to achieve. She could only bat at threads of intuition, some stronger than others.

"This one knows about my mother."

"Yes he does, and about a great many things," he said, measuring her reaction. "He wants to share with you. Sit, rest. Allow him in. You are in good company." He started to leave then stopped. "What you learn is for you alone, for now. Austin and Johan don't need the added burden right now. One crisis level at a time."

Anki nodded. Cathbad left then, closing the door behind him.

Tank lamps reflected off the submerged organs to cast a ghoulish light. Circulating pumps and equipment fans hummed. The eyes watched, waiting. Slowly, she felt a change in vibration, a signal of someone extending. She closed her eyes and relaxed, feeling the presence and allowing it to pass her outer firewalls. It was male and had a familiar quality that made trusting easier.

His arrival brought the merging, something only she and Johan had shared at that level. Her heart beat soundly, a physical reminder of what was happening. Here, the male presented much differently, more paternal and wise. His intention to paint a world dream preceded the gentle movement away from the narrow room. She allowed herself to be led.

From the comforting cradle of his mind, he spoke to her in a voice as spacious and warm as a summer sky.

Anki, no matter what you learn from me, promise that you will never forget how much good is still possible in this world. And remember how much I love you, your mother, and all of humanity.

It fit, then.

"Father?"

Yes, Anki. You have questions but let me guide you now. There are things you need to know. You are strong, but some of this will challenge you.

• • •

Cathbad returned from the cellar and went to the screens.

Sean pointed. "The Shiru team is at third basement. They're attempting the physical connection."

"What's it look like?" Cathbad asked.

"All the Ethernet ports to the backbone are full, either in use or linked through a loopback to detect access. No open fiber switch ports, either. To add Bootstrap they'll need to tap either the copper or fiber."

"Audio up, please." Cathbad sat near the screens.

A monotone narrative by the bràthair provided a running translation over the faint and chaotic audio interpretations of the shùil technology. "—requires physically splitting the cable open to touch the copper wires. Time consuming and messy. Yoshito is saying the fiber tap is less noticeable, faster, and everyone agrees. However, light loss is detectable if they are monitoring it—"

"Use the fiber tap," Sean urged.

A close-up showed his message made it through. A clamping device went over the exposed fiber length and an intercept fiber was introduced to tap the light signals.

The bràthair intoned, "Coupling is successful. The device is receiving encrypted data. Bootstrap will attempt to read it now."

Several moments later the Shiru team pumped the air with their fists.

"That's it," Sean said, "Soldado did it. The game's on. It's finally on."

Cathbad leaned back and took in the other screen. "Johan hasn't moved yet." The weight of responsibility pulled at his bones, at his soul. The fate of Tokyo, the most populated city in the world, hung in the balance. They *had* to locate the nuke.

He prayed to the Lord of the Wildwood, a most sincere and heartfelt prayer for success.

• • •

Marik arrived back from a long day spent at Toshiba replacing five server motherboards all fried from a power line fault. The extra hour to isolate a damaged CPU dragged right over his plans with Nomaai. If he hurried, the night might be salvageable. Gates to the building's garage rolled open and he immediately noticed two blank parking spots – one too many.

Inside the office, the missing van's keys hung in the lockbox. The dispatch log showed nothing and a call to Bebe confirmed what he had feared: one of J.I. Technical's vans had been stolen.

• • •

Colorful and complex, the user interface for Soldado's Bootstrap program filled both laptop screens. The technicians mumbled quietly to each other, tapping madly one moment, frozen the next, deep into the screens.

"They are stacked, modular. Look at the code groupings! Start with the H group, there. Route them to the filter."

"Keywords ready. We can only sample so much, though."

"Preview, open the preview window – good. *There.*"

Both technicians gazed, a look of nearly religious awe on their faces.

"Good God, look at the amount of data. He was right. It's already building the parsing nodes."

Soldado's retro-AI worm, Q, did exactly what it was designed to, recognizing and querying the constructs formed in the network stream, a passive mapping of content type and relationships. It was learning the form and method of Totem's transport protocols in order to extract meaningful representation of the data. The results were served up to the Shiru team's interface.

"Try another group, this looks like diplomatic intelligence. Route B group."

Noboru grew increasingly nervous. He asked whether they were going to search the whole alphabet.

"Relax, Noboru. We are within parameters."

"Of course, of course. But please, all possible haste!"

They continued to pore over the screens. "These appear operational in nature. The series refer to notations on the J group, I'm almost certain. Switch to J."

Noboru walked to the wall and sat down. The team was good but now they seemed about to take a long, long time. If security came, he would fall over, as if knocked unconscious, an unwilling victim. If by some miracle they got out undetected, this would be the last job, the last risk. A familiar oath, but this time...

• • •

Director Tomov gazed at the storm closing in on Kaiya. Eden was in a stable approach, its intensity felt and gauged by rangers familiar with the force.

"Prepare to grab them," he ordered.

"Signus Alpha is ready to grab. Safe estimate shows free zone ends in three minutes fifty."

No sign of their rescuer. Disappointment didn't begin to describe it. Fourteen panels linked, ready to shut down the target, and Gerrit hadn't made it. Not a ripple or a whiff of him.

"Grab in three, then. Slide the time as necessary. Update and recap the bender's status."

"No change, sir. He hasn't been seen."

Comms312 interrupted. "Sir, Oscar has alerted to a probable breach to the VisCom network at the defense ministry in Ichigaya."

"Probable breach? What does it mean, a probable breach?"

"Details on screen, sir."

A stolen IT services company van and a service call at the ministry communications building by the same company.

"Send a panel out to investigate."

"Sir, we're overextended with Signus Alpha. Shall I–"

"Yes! Break out a panel from Alpha." He remembered the gold dots glowing on his personal LCD. In a more controlled voice, he added, "It could be related."

No mistakes.

"Panel dispatched. Grab updated to two minutes five seconds, sir."

He again eyed the three remaining gold dots, the minimum required to execute J86 in one city.

"Confirm J86 is still enabled."

A moment later, confirmation came.

· · ·

Only yards from shore, black storm clouds raced counter-clockwise. Their bulk rose thousands of feet into the sky, lit with flashes of lightning. Thunder cracked the air. The eye of the hurricane had tightened to become a twister with a narrowing center.

Kaiya stole a look up from their sand burrow. A single shaft of sunlight pierced the gloom, robbed of its warmth but not of its hope. Again she tried to force change, imagining a steel plate to shield them. Again nothing happened. Stuck in a nightmare with no way to wake up, she was finally helpless. *What did I do to deserve this?*

She hunkered over the boy's tiny frame and hugged him tighter. The thought of him being ripped from her arms was too much to bear.

"Kaiya?"

Her head whipped up in time to catch a flurry of wind-blown sand in the face. Who'd called her name?

"Kaiya?"

The voice cut through the roar of the storm, like a voice-over on an entirely different soundtrack. She ducked back down and listened intently. Long seconds passed with nothing more. It was a trick, a way of getting them out of the safety of their hole, the symbol of her defiance. If she held any power left at all, it had to be in maintaining their place.

"Ryota!"

The boy shifted in response. It wasn't just her imagination.

"Kaiya!"

The voice seemed from beyond the dream, from the waking world – but she couldn't wake up! Were they finally trying to save them? Intuition said yes. She couldn't stand the thought of missing their help. She yelled into the squall, "Here! We're here!"

Thunder pealed and the wind tore at her hair. The storm wall toppled high overhead and converged to blot the sun. In the sudden darkness, lightning flickered. The island shifted, a small lurch at first, then as if starting to rise. Two of the palm trees rose like twigs to disappear into the streaming torrent of the twister. The boy screamed and tried to stand.

"No Ryota! No–" She felt a groping hand against her knee and screamed also. It found her calf, then slid to her ankle and pulled her leg violently down into the sand. She kicked but the heavy, wet sand held her leg. Lightning flashed as Ryota slipped down to his hips. "Nooo!" She prayed then, as hard as she'd ever prayed. *God, please take us now, take our souls and lead us to peace. God, please take us now, take our souls right now and lead us to–*

"Kaiya! No! Stop praying for that! Live, girl, live! Stop resisting and come with me! Austin needs you!"

A brilliant light split the darkness from above. The roar of the wind died off and the twisting storm slowed. Gone was the sun and blue sky, replaced by a heavenly downpour of white light that saturated the clouds and turned them gray-blue. Peace soaked in, numbing fear until it faded completely. Nothing would ever hurt her again, nothing could ever bring her pain again. She was going *home* – a home from a long, long time ago.

Another tug almost tore Ryota from her grip. With an effort, she looked down into the boy's terrified eyes. "No!" She screamed, splitting the silence. "Leave him to me!"

The voice and grip would not relent. "Come–" another violent tug and the boy slipped completely under the sand, "–*on!*"

The luring light forgotten, she began to scream but stopped when another voice, sharp and quick, filled the dream.

"Copy that. Signus Alpha to grab now."

The clouds peeled back to reveal more of the brilliance above. From the retreating billows emerged black birds, thousands of them, all diving towards her little hole in the island. They grew larger as they neared, revealing shiny black claws amid a flurry of wings. Their wild cries pierced her soul.

The hand on her leg released and instead surfaced from the sand.

"Come with me, Kaiya, or you'll never serve Austin sweet and sour pork again!"

There was no time to analyze that. Riding instinct, she took hold of the outstretched hand and allowed it to tug her into the gritty darkness below, back towards Austin.

God, she hoped back towards Austin.

• • •

"Signus Alpha in pursuit."

"Damn it!" Director Tomov pounded his armrest. "How did he *do* that?"

He stood and pointed at the display. "Somebody tell me how he slipped past fourteen fucking panels! Forty of our best trained minds and no one saw him? Someone tell me!"

No one dared speak. The panels sliced through the mesh, tracking residual energies of the three targets, maneuvering split-second switchbacks, morphing imagery – countering an endless stream of tricks as Gerrit barreled through bubble after bubble of unsuspecting dreamers. There was just no getting ahead of him. Two panels dropped off, casualties of the sudden alterations.

"Keep the linkage together – communicate! Stay cohesive, damn it. Get into his stream!"

The visuals grew more chaotic. Rapid shifts presented realties at mind-boggling speed. Three more panels fell off, unable to stay on the chase. Another gone, then another.

"Nine panels. Eight. He's wild. Hard to track."

"Get those panels reconnected. Shut him down!"

Tomov tried not to panic. No one had ever been so dynamic and agile, so dimensional. No one had ever moved with such confidence so fast in the mesh. The control room began to swim. He planted a hand on a console to steady himself and looked away from the screens. "Patch me to AGT Ops. And get me double blues with Coke."

The AGT director came online. "Tomov, what's happening?"

He exhaled heavily and turned back to the screens. "He's got the boy. I don't know if we'll stop him. Standby for the bender. I'm certain he'll be there for the pick-up of the body. And J86 is still on the table."

"Understood. We'll take care of him. Keep this line open."

"Right." The panel count dropped by another two. Gerrit was wearing them out, plain and simple. The panels had trouble reconnecting – the speed made synchronization nearly impossible.

The AGT director announced, "Heads up. There's a mix of birds in the air out of Yokota. Seven Hueys and a C-130. Scrub of the base comms shows reference to a training sortie but no word on what the 130 is doing. The Hueys are spreading out all over Tokyo and the 130's on its own circuit, outside our zone. No precedence for a night sortie of this design. I've got someone working on the roots. In the meantime, you might want to get in there and see if we have anything to worry about."

He directed his ops officer to coordinate rider teams to join the AGTs for intercept and inspection. He sat down, waiting for his blues.

History was about to be made alright, and not the preferred version. In a way, the scenario was inevitable, had been for years. If not here, then Zurich or London or Malaysia or wherever the breakout occurred. The number of incidents unraveling in the past year alone... too many indications of subversion growing right under G2's nose. He looked up at the incident map and couldn't help wondering if Stan and Laura still lived in Tokyo.

Overseer's voice broke into his thoughts. "ANSWER READY."

"Answer to what?"

"THE ANSWER TO YOUR LAST INQUIRY REGARDING TARGET A2 AND HOW HE SLIPPED PAST FOURTEEN PANELS. THE ANSWER IS APPARENT: TARGET A2 HAS SUPERIOR GOVERNANCE IN THE MESH."

"No shit, Oscar." He looked at the gold dots and decided he didn't care. "No *shit*."

Chapter 21

Deep into that darkness peering, long I stood there, wondering, fearing,
doubting, dreaming dreams no mortal ever dared to dream before.
- Edgar Allan Poe

Once Johan had Kaiya and Ryota securely in his keep, split-second leap-frogging proved to be almost fun. While the pair sat alone in a train car rolling through the Swiss Alps, he extended his reach farther than ever, pummeling through Saoghal like a god.

There were mouse holes to crawl through and skies to disappear into, crowds to absorb him, and children to hopscotch over his chalk line form. Under the pews of a church in Luxembourg and out a stained glass window to become a bird that flew to a tree down the avenue before shrinking into a drop of rain blown by the wind. He struck a branch and split into two, curled around the curve of the drop and exited the dream only to join a nightmare in a house fully engulfed in flames.

An old man, face streaked with tears, sat in a rusted wheelchair and listened to screams from family trapped upstairs. Caught off guard, Johan shrank and flew into the glowing embers of a door frame, emerged briefly in the openness of Saoghal, then slid down and away towards the billions of dreams that awaited.

He kept the stints brief, morphing at every chance, shifting emotion to blend into the scenery. He was a young woman entering a doctor's office one moment – the weathered door of a lighthouse facing a rising sun the next. Confidence grew by measures until it appeared inevitable he would completely lose them. He shook free of *that* feeling before it could be used against him, too. *Leave nothing of your self behind.*

Vaguely, the notion of fatigue presented itself, a shocking first suggestion of limitation in the dream world. He didn't slow and felt no different except for a gnawing realization that every snap of change that he affected became one more trick expended by his core – so that he would become that much more familiar to them if only they thought to pay attention. *Someone would.* He tried to set that aside but found it far more sticky a thought than anything he'd encountered so far. He was tiring and they had to feel it. Time once again became the enemy.

Amanda. He would deliver Kaiya to safety first. To accomplish that he couldn't have a posse trailing him. Creativity remained fluid, the playground of Saoghal still an ocean of possibility. An idea formed from that ocean, one that held promise of something truly ingenious if the realm operated like he imagined it did.

In the smallest, most private molecules of his existence, he began to build a false world, a pseudo-dream of the most typical kind. He installed a simulation of his shifting meta engaged in some of the same tricks he'd already used. He added several "leaps", ghostly paths of sim-meta to form a deceptive trail for them to follow. The process was slow and incredibly tedious, attended to between real dream jumps and morphs with great care and timing. They could not be allowed to see what he was creating. For it to work, where it led could not appear familiar.

If the idea of fatigue had surprised him before, its actual effects, felt now in the complex efforts of dream weaving, shot thin bolts of fear into his core.

• • •

"Sir, he's slowing–"

"I see that." Director Tomov stood. The blues amplified the good news by factors. "Panels are up by four, now five. He's wearing down. There's no way he could keep up that pace, I knew it." He hadn't, but that wasn't for them to know. "Signus Alpha, stay alert, your target's weakening."

"Confirmed. He's also leaking fear. Starting to unravel."

On screen, the target raced into another dream, a field of yellow wheat blowing in the wind under blue skies, lit like the afterlife. Signus Alpha shrank to the size of an ant and raced among the tall columns of wheat to follow A2. In a blink he shot into a light beam. They managed to follow, bouncing to the upper atmosphere before reflecting back against the eye of a man walking across the field towards his wife in a reunion dream. A2 shot into the darkness of the man's iris and made exit from the dream. They tracked him into another, a school boy's fantasy where a beautiful teacher unbuttoned her blouse.

"He's reaching his limits, sir. Back up to thirteen."

The director nodded. It was only a matter of time.

• • •

Johan clamped down on a feeling that threatened to get away from him – the feeling of pure joy and relief. Controlling his happiness proved almost as hard as managing the dream weaving. He was finally *free*, alone with his two charges in the placid blackness of Saoghal. He distanced himself from the cunning construct he'd made for his pursuers – proud of it but unsure how soon they would escape.

He had slowed some, allowing them into his dream, and then masterfully transferred them into *that*, a cornucopian bubble of worlds inside worlds, like a Pandora's box. With luck, he had time enough to secure Kaiya and the boy.

• • •

Snow laden mountains gave way to countryside similarly buried; an occasional stream, jutting trees, or farmhouse broke the blanket of white. Ryota sat at the window and gazed farther than his eyes could see, likely dreaming of things familiar.

Kaiya rested. The stress of arrival on the train had passed, replaced by hope that she might actually make it back to the reality she'd once called home. That there were dimensions beyond that reality made perfect sense now. Dreams could not be experienced if they didn't have some basis in the fabric of the universe. Before, she'd only glimpsed them as a passerby, remembered them infrequently, and considered them a chemically induced abstraction. She'd never imagined the underlying, coherent space that allowed for the experience in the first place. New understanding grounded her and offered a view to reality that before would have swept her away in a hysteria of denial and avoidance.

In the beginning, she *had* fallen into the depths of insanity, a lucid sensorium whose memory would forever haunt. General Shang's introduction to bodiless existence had redefined evil and mortified the shallow bowl that once contained her world. Yet, in that shameful lunacy – from it – a rearrangement of identity had occurred, forming a cogency of self that never would have manifested otherwise, even after the progression of an 'ordinary' lifetime.

She was more than she'd ever imagined.

Character strengths she'd recognized before were dimly lit tips of self that hadn't yet been fully exposed. Weaknesses and faults were in

311

fact shards of greater traits not completely realized or managed. Emotions were not blindsiding forces scratching to be let in: they were the very components of her being and as such were utterly valid and beautiful in their complexity. The whole of identity held depths that had yet to be illuminated, leaving her infinitely curious and powerfully endowed with a sense of soul and of the present moment.

In the now, sitting next to Ryota, she existed in the exquisite knowledge of self, pondering the efforts of someone she'd never met who held her fate in the balance. Hope burned deep. Hope to return to the world to live more fully than she ever thought possible.

Ryota sat up and strained to see down the tracks.

She stood and leaned over to see. A town lay ahead and the train was slowing. She entered the aisle and beckoned Ryota to join her at the door. Together they watched the edge of a modest township slip by. The train rumbled slower and slower until the station came into view and the brakes were applied in a squealing symphony. The arrival felt good.

Two men stood on the platform. One held a lantern in the shape of a lighthouse. The door opened and Kaiya urged Ryota to step down. One of the men stepped forward and said with the same voice from beneath the sand, "No Kaiya. Home is further on for him. Your return is now. Come, say your goodbyes, please."

"But—" She stared into eyes deep as oceans that impelled her to understand.

"Please, Kaiya. Timing is everything."

With that, she hugged Ryota, giving him every bit of love in her heart. She ran a hand over his hair. "You are wonderful. I hope to meet you when we're awake someday."

He nodded and said in a little voice, "Me, too." He stepped back as the doors closed and the train blew its whistle. Steam swelled into the cold air. He waved from the window.

"He *can* talk!"

The man took her arm and guided her towards the doors of the station. "It's time to return, quickly now. Brace yourself. I'm told this next step may be unsettling. Please relax and do not fight it, regardless of your fears. Safety lies just ahead."

• • •

Austin circled around to the far side of the koi pond and leaned against the low wall, listening to the street noise below.

312

I'm in Japan. I flew here from Scotland. I flew myself here...

Once again the surge came, an avalanche of awe and disbelief that any of it were real. *Fucking surreal*, like a bullet train in a crazy dream that just wouldn't stop. To wield the power left him feeling like God, an altogether frightening sensation. It took an exercise of focus and calming before the feeling subsided.

He scanned the sky. Only a helicopter passing high overhead with a baritone thump. Adrenaline waned, its slow withdrawal a drain on his senses. Concern for Johan added a layer of mental fatigue. If the hacker lost to the Comannda, if he were to be captured, things would go bad so fast... again he tried to clear his thoughts and be calm.

"Warning."

He spun at the voice and almost sent the frail figure sprawling. Wrapped in a black kimono robe, an old man with round eyes and a gaunt face stood staring at him with a look of perpetual anticipation.

For a moment it felt as if he'd fallen into a dream.

"Target is booby trapped." The voice was as frail as the man's body. "Get up there, overhead. Wait for the big flash before snatching the package."

Done with the message, the old man walked away. His body dissolved in the shadows while his pale head floated until it, too, disappeared. The encounter felt like a visit from the dead.

He donned the helmet and worked the straps. A flash? What kind of flash? And why should he wait up in the sky, exposed to the AG craft? It didn't make sense.

He floated a handful of tiny rocks from the roof into the air and dropped them – the grid was tight, responsive to intention. He leapt over the edge and rocketed skyward. The surge felt good, the propulsion intense. Properly miniaturized in the sky, he followed the GPS north-west and scanned constantly. Distant aircraft dotted the night. Nothing black and no holes in the clouds. He stirred the grid, hardening it against any surprises.

The GPS signaled arrival at the final checkpoint. Directly below was the clinic, lost somewhere in the field of lights – lights that included emergency vehicles. It was a medical facility but why so many? He spotted more flashing lights from units heading towards the area. It might be a ruse to help cover the grab. He'd have to wait for the big flash, whatever that was.

Seconds drew into minutes that felt like hours. Sitting in the sky with his feet dangling over the city below made him feel exactly like a yellow duck in a shooting gallery. The conclusion came of its own accord: he couldn't wait, couldn't just *sit* there. He thought of making a quick dip to find somewhere safe to watch. The yellow duck feeling suddenly turned to one of someone staring at him, as if drawing a bead. Panic struck. He spun full circle trying to spot the threat. Just the high altitude breeze and him – and perhaps an invisible observer. He forced his attention downward, afraid of missing the signal for him to act.

"Fuck this," he muttered inside the helmet. "Next time, I do the planning."

• • •

AGT-3 slipped into position in the stratus and drifted just beneath the clouds. Its pilot keyed his radio. "Target located, five angels over the clinic. Please advise."

An infrared signature combined with the organic filter made the subject easy to spot. The pilot centered the targeting daemon's lines on the glowing red dash two kilometers distant: a man, floating unaided two miles up in the air. The briefing didn't do justice to actually seeing the phenomenon.

The response came. "Lock it up and prepare to follow. Two and Five will join you shortly. Standby."

"Lock established. Hard targets approaching from the northwest, eight clicks out. Looks like Hueys hustling."

"We see them. Keep yourself faded and await orders."

"Copy that." He fiddled with the view of the clinic below, not wanting to miss the pyrotechnics should they let them off. Based on the report and what he saw right now, the guy could probably counteract the explosive effects. It would come down to agility, speed, and tactics.

He massaged the rubbery skin of the control stick, both excited and nervous at the prospect of the chase.

• • •

The forty-eight story Metropolitan Government building towered over the streets of Shinjuku Ward. Two blocks away, operators ran a Booty machine from a utility truck. Experimentation had yielded two additional active channels and a third clarified just as a transmission crossed mentioning a target's acquisition in the sky.

Certain it was an important intercept, they passed it to the bràthair scouring the city for the nuke. They in turn relayed it to Cathbad and Sean in the basement of Cullstone.

• • •

Johan stood in the aisle and stared out the train's windows across the top of an alpine forest. The snow covered trees stretched away into the haze of a covering storm. Ryota sat, alternately looking at Johan and out the window.

"Why are we hiding?" Ryota asked finally. "I want to go home, too."

The boy was bright and imbued with a Zen calmness not typical of his age. He was curious, absorbing everything. Until now he'd remained mostly unruffled; with Kaiya's absence, he'd apparently reached his limit. Brown eyes looked back with a profound need Johan readily connected with... he wanted his mama and his *sofu*. He wanted to be safe again.

"I'm trying to help you wake up again. Until then, I protect you."

How much Ryota understood wasn't clear until he replied, "Are the bad men still at my house? If they are I don't want to wake up."

"That's right, we don't want that. I'm trying to find out now. I want you to be safe." *I promised that you would be.* Ryota turned back to the window at the same moment a strong presence arrived carrying the familiar shade of the Runa Korda. Johan saw Cathbad's face in the small window of the door to the adjoining train car. The door was designed as the only approach to the dream.

Cathbad wasn't alone. Two men stood behind him, draped in dark trench coats. Cathbad's glance conveyed their purpose as bodyguards. Johan unlocked the door and slid it open. Cold air and carriage noise filled the car.

"They'll wait beyond," Cathbad said over the din. He stepped in and closed the door. The druid met Ryota's curious look but withheld comment. "Austin needs you. He's over the city and in grave danger. They have anti-gravity craft poised to strike but he's too wound up for us to warn him. You have to reach him."

"Anti-gravity craft? Fantastic. What more have you withheld?"

"Remember, you rushed things. Your education is far from complete. Right now it is time to warn Austin."

"What about the nuke?" Johan asked.

"We're working to find the location. Go and warn Austin."

315

They both looked at the boy.

"Shall I remain here?" Cathbad asked. A sincere offer but also a measuring of how much Johan trusted him.

"That's fine. What do I tell Austin?"

"To get out of the sky. The grab for the boy cannot happen now, anyway. There are complications."

"What kind of complications?"

"We're also working on that. Now go. Go now, please."

With a glance at the two men in the next car, Johan shifted free of the dream.

He focused on and followed the threads that bound him to Austin. Closer in, he encountered the shield of bràthair protecting Austin. He passed through them and bore the brunt of their surprise before his identity eased their fears. Austin's meta vibrated with an over-strung resonance, discordant and panicked. No wonder they couldn't reach him.

He sank in to synchronize.

They've locked onto you with antigravity ships.

Austin's heart leapt at the intrusion. A shimmering field of potential rose around him. Another memory surfaced, more powerful than the others: *They'll target you if they can.*

It was too much. Austin bolted straight up into the clouds and then shot off blindly through the darkness.

Stop, Austin!

He ignored Johan's command – no half-baked plan was going to cost him his life.

You're not going to leave.

The hell I'm not.

You're breaking the deal.

No, the deal wasn't about dying – and Kaiya isn't back.

She's returned. She's safe—

Bullshit! I'm not stupid.

The hell you aren't—

He tried to block out the hacker but failed. Kaiya's voice chimed in. *Owned by a hacker, babe...* anger trailed the memory.

Stop fighting me, it will only get you killed. Think, then act!

Austin had long ago learned to recognize the sharp contrast of good advice, even in a polarized fit of emotion – a hard-received gift from his dad. He slowed. Johan injected again, this time with knowledge of the handoff of Kaiya to Amanda. He saw a woman sit up, disoriented, struggling to focus in her new world. *I delivered her safely. She's joined with a new host for now. You can't reach her because she's shielded but she's okay, you have my word. Now I need you to keep yours. Remove Ryota from the clinic.*

Austin pounced on the imagery and dissected it to feel Kaiya's essence in the memory. It was her. She was intact, safe within another's care. Intense relief drowned out his fear and he stopped. There was no question now – he needed to help Johan and Ryota.

He imagined life support systems dangling from an empty bed, a small boy's lifeless body in his arms. *No! You will do it quickly, so I can bring him back.*

But there was danger at the clinic. The understanding of explosives ringing the facility came. The druids had called in a bomb threat to multiple agencies and the media and made sure a guard found one of the devices. Evacuations were underway. *They think we're using local authorities to save the boy. They won't be expecting you. If we do this together and you strike fast, we'll make it. Go now and pull him free.*

"People will see me," Austin said aloud. "How do you explain me flying in and tearing a hole in a building? You can't explain that away. They'll be forced to use the nuke."

No they won't. It was dark out. The hole would become the result of a faulty oxygen delivery system that exploded. Fabrications would explain away whatever stories did surface. The system would self-heal itself. Johan laid in more imagery to convey the Comannda's momentary weakness in Saoghal – he'd trapped dozens of korjé in an elaborate dream. It was the most opportune time to act. *Austin, do this for me, now. Keep your word.*

The prophecy implied they had to work together to succeed, to act to make change happen. Johan had already come through by extending himself beyond limits to lose the Comannda and return Kaiya to safety.

He had to try.

I can do this... his own thought, from a very deep place.

• • •

Thirty-nine Delta rangers faked out. The target untraceable.

Director Tomov glanced at the screen. Nine gold dots now. Which meant three were in the Core, watching locally as the fabric of the mission came apart.

How the dream construct existed without A2's presence was both amazing and deeply troubling. The gold dots stared back from the screen, unblinking. He knew the Executives contemplated his fate and the fate of millions. The seconds passed, an eternity of suppressing thoughts of how things could possibly get worse... because it seemed they might.

The riders sent to investigate the defense ministry found an operation underway, complete with priests shielding their operatives. The druids managed to isolate the building from the automation system and engage emergency locks on elevators and doors. Military units were due to reach them any moment.

The AGT director announced the bender had been reacquired. "Fourteen clicks due north, at nine-thousand feet. Bring your riders in on AGT-3's beacon. What's your ETA?"

Ops429 threw up hands to signal four-five.

Director Tomov replied, "Forty five seconds." He tried to sound calm and only half succeeded. "I need more riders, all priority. I don't care what it takes, I need more power in the mesh."

• • •

Poor Noboru. It should have been me.

He could imagine his sister Akiko's voice lamenting his demise. She didn't know it but her survival was the rope that bound him to the Sensei. They'd cured her cancer as promised, the only cost being his continued cooperation. He looked at the two Sensei huddled around their laptops and tried not to be resentful. This mission would save "many, many innocent lives". He chose to believe them.

They'd hacked the facility's security module, shutting them in. Any hope of getting out without incident was dashed with a few keystrokes – forces topside would waste no time finding a way down. Death was on the table and he decided he really didn't want any part of it. He sat against the wall, now prohibited from getting any closer to them. They were near their goal and could not afford risk of intervention by anyone.

As if cued, a rattle sounded from the hallway. The elevator shaft.

"They're coming," Noboru hissed. He laid on the floor in the far corner like a casualty. One of the Sensei broke away and stood with a view to the elevator doors. Unarmed, he would surely be the first to fall.

The other Sensei blurted, "Hai! Look, it's here, it's right here. Built into the communications tower. See there? They just powered up the ignition computer!"

Tower A, looming 220 meters over the city, was a beacon at night seen for miles. Noboru resisted sitting up and asking what in the tower required starting.

"Isolate the control stream and jam it."

"We need more time!"

A dark object tossed from the hallway clanged when it hit the floor and rolled. The last Noboru saw was a flash before putrid green smoke exploded into the room. He held his breath but panic made short work of his air supply. His skin grew hot and painful. When he could stand it no more, he let out his air.

The first intake of acrid smoke was his last – he gagged at the burning in his throat and nose. He opened his eyes and immediately they stung as if on fire. He thrashed in pain for what seemed an eternity. When the darkness came, he embraced it with all his being.

• • •

In the misty clouds over Tokyo, Austin laid out his intentions to his unseen companion. Johan lurked just above his subconscious, riding the stream, reviewing.

That's good. Johan approved of his plan. *Now, if you're ready? Before they move him?*

Impatience, the driving force behind everything that Johan did.

Things are changing fast, I feel it. Austin received Johan's push and then understood – the boy could be murdered during the confusion of the evacuation.

"I get it, I'm gone."

He blew through the clouds and emerged just below their cover before leveling out at speed. He scanned continuously while eyeing coordinates. A few moments later he didn't need the GPS anymore – dozens of emergency lights flashed far below. He arrived overhead and saw evacuations of the clinic were underway.

"Let's do this..."

INCOMING!

He instantly turtled inside a hardened field, hoping it would–

Thwak! The bright grid of the city spun madly.

The quantum field protected him against the strike, negating the g-forces just as in flight. He looked for the ship but couldn't spot it.

Thwak! Again, the world spun, only this time he'd felt the strike in his bones. Energy dipped and focus wavered.

"Fuck!" he shouted. "Where is it? Help me out here!"

At your three o'clock and low. Crap, there's two of them. Abruptly, images of commandos boarding a train flashed. *Abort! Get out!* Johan fled in response to a threat elsewhere, his fierce apology fading as fast as his presence.

"Shit!" Left alone, he shot downward with the thought of hiding in the city. He braced for what might be a far worse strike.

It came but not as expected – he rammed into a disc-shaped craft that suddenly appeared in his path, the impact stealing focus completely. An electrical current lashed through his body and numbed every muscle. Worse, it scrambled all sense of meta and the grid. He lay sprawled on top of the craft, limp and stunned. A glance outward revealed they were moving. Behind and above, two more black craft flew into formation. With no tug of centrifugal force, he realized he was in a field with its own gravity. The lights of the shoreline appeared. They were headed out to sea.

He willed his legs to move and with great effort, they did. In slow motion, he began to crawl towards the edge of the ship. In response, the current increased. His eyes spasmed in their sockets. Muscles shuddered and failed. Breathing became a struggle. Realization struck: he'd been captured. Panic roared.

Help. Someone help, please. The plea echoed in his head, as weak as his body. To keep his lungs pumping air was all he could do. A pulsing pressure in his ears grew into a baritone thump that grew louder. He recognized it finally, the chop of a Bell Huey. As fast as it came, it faded.

Help.

The city swung into view as the craft angled and lashed around to a new bearing. Abruptly the current stopped flowing and he slid off the craft into free fall. He glimpsed the AG ship, no longer black but a grayish-silver, also dropping from the sky. Not far off, a fiery ball that had been a helicopter lit the night. Memory of the stunning current ran through his bones. Wind whipped his weakened arms and legs. Darkness and water loomed below.

Come on... rathad was fuzzy and indistinct. He struggled to focus. A sense of bràthair returned in fragments of thought. He recognized urgency and intention.

Come on! He forced meta outward until it flowed once more into the grid. Warm and fluid, it filled every sense, returning control. He pressed intention and slowed to a stop. The bràthair wanted him to flee, which was perfectly fine but he didn't know which way to go. In the darkness, miles from the coast with only starlight to guide him, the only place that seemed safe was down, to the water, away from the flying ships.

No. Johan resonated clearly in his mind.

"Where did you go?" he shouted. "What happened?"

An intrusion. You need to get to the downed craft.

"No way. It's headed for the bottom of the ocean."

No. Move quickly. A strong notion of direction rose. *This way, move!*

"God damn it." Again, following not leading. He took off in that direction. "What happened to it?"

Gunner in the Huey fired a beam weapon to scramble the magnetics of the drive. It will reset itself in just a minute. You need to get to it before they do.

"I'm not going underwater. And there's at least two more ships."

People died to save you and get a chance at this. You won't need to go underwater. Slow down. Head to the right. With nudges and words, Johan guided him to the ocean's surface. Just visible under the water was the grayish-silver disc.

You need to raise it up and pop the door.

Before he could ask how, Johan interrupted. *Raise it up, now!*

Hovering just over the water, he reached out and felt the grid, felt the ship's weight. It wasn't nearly as heavy as he'd imagined–

Its drive restarted. Hurry!

–it was the water that was heavy, not the ship. Intense focus further drained him but the craft rose, water streaming away from the hull. The drive had restarted and the ship was hovering in neutral. He landed on it.

"Where's the door?"

Feel for it.

"Nobody has ever been in one?"

Not Korda. It has a pilot, they know that much. Hurry!

He crawled over the ship and found a seam near the edges. Tugging hard did nothing except give him time to wonder if the pilot might still be alive. He imagined cracking open a hatch and being shot in the face. He stopped pulling and scanned for life instead.

Nothing at first, then a tiny bump of something. The faintest sense of meta, subtle to the point of feeling alien. Passive, he waited, hoping to feel something he could latch onto and explore.

What are you doing?

"Seeing if the pilot is alive."

He isn't.

"Well something in there is."

No time! Force it open. If he's still alive, deal with him.

"Quiet."

Carefully, he extended to the soft meta. It remained elusive, ghost-like. The further he extended, the less he felt of it – and the more he felt he was being scanned in return.

Hurry, Austin!

He placed his face close to the hull. Something knew he was there. He formed and released a resonance message that suggested he was peaceful and wanted to come in.

Nothing came back. He sent it again.

No return.

The pilot has to be dead. Come on, damn you!

A moment later, a hiss sounded and a portion of the ship slid away. A dim light and an awful stench escaped. He peered in.

A man strapped to one of two command chairs sat with his head to one side. Laying around the cramped interior were food containers, bags, and other belongings flung about when the gravity field failed. The stench was that of death, something he had never smelled before.

In, go in. Get the body out. Move!

He climbed in and set about freeing the body from its harness. A small remote was clipped to the man's belt, which he pocketed. With an effort, he lifted the body free and sent it flying out the hatch into the ocean.

"Gah!" He searched a bag and found a shirt to wipe the chair where the man had died. It, too, went out the hatch.

For fuck's sake, Austin, check the controls or get out.

"Will you relax? It smells like shit in here."

Four choppers down and two craft heading this way. It's your ass.

He slid into the command chair. The dim meta remained. Resonance had worked before so he tried again.

In response, the hatch slid shut.

Did you do that?

"Sort of."

Who are you in contact with?

"I have no idea."

Look around, is there room for someone?

"Not unless they're flat under the floor or stuffed in some side panel. There's a bunk bed, otherwise it's tight."

Three displays above the chair lay flat up against the ceiling. The tip of a control grip was recessed in the chair in between his legs. The best he could do was resonate a request to go into 'active flight mode'.

It was enough. The screens swung down and the control stick rose up. A dial also rose from the chair's arm. With the response came a brush of meta, an unintentional bulbous protrusion related to identity. Not a name but an essence, one that flowed like liquid green glass.

He didn't think about it – he simply reached for the essence and attempted to merge with it. The next instant found him in regret.

Flattened and thinned to an intolerably minute thread, he held onto the last of his own identity like a breathing straw. Information appeared, shifted, merged, and slipped away, its ebb and flow in synch with the world outside. Whatever it was, it had only a small amount of meta flowing through its core but it carried an immense volume of data. Its rathad was highly defined and focused on what felt like a million things at once. Everything was state and properties, down to the molecular level. He barely remembered to breathe.

A complex weave of variables appeared; felt, sensed, but not all understood. Its connections were made of energy, akin to thoughts, the variables themselves suggesting values too alien to comprehend. It was scanning him so deep it felt it might scrub him into nothing.

In the next moment, the screens filled with graphics depicting status and sensors. Two craft had just arrived. A resonance message struck him with a force so powerful he jolted in the chair.

What happened?!

Memories that couldn't have been suddenly were. He rose and went to a panel and removed its thumbscrews. Inside, rows of plastic-covered modules filled a chassis. He scanned the labels until he found one in particular and pulled it free. On another module he pushed and held a small button.

What the hell Austin?

"Remote access disabled." He returned to the command chair. One of the screens showed a menu indicating new user set up. He initiated the voice recognition option and spoke a sentence aloud.

A male voice replied, "PATTERN IDENTIFICATION RECORDED. VOICE RECOGNITION ACTIVE FOR NEW USER."

He thumbed a switch on the control grip. The background of the displays became the front window of the ship, shown in infrared and augmented with an artificial horizon and grid lines.

What did you just do?

"Made a friend, I think."

He turned the dial until the two craft were out of his path, then slid it forward and racked the stick to the side. The horizon spun and the two craft fell far behind.

It felt as if he'd been flying the ship for years.

• • •

AGT-3 rose from the ocean and shot south, spinning on its axis like a corkscrew before leveling out. Radio calls were ignored.

Director Tomov ordered the other two AGTs to pursue. Both remote control and self-destruct commands failed to reach the rogue ship. Flight telemetry still flowed, allowing CoreOps to track its movement. A new user was at the controls, a fact that made him sick to his stomach. The skill with which the craft was being flown suggested an inside job. It also meant the ship's offensive elements could be used against them.

The craft shot past the island of Okinawa headed for Taiwan.

"Sir, AGTs six and seven are set for intercept. They are requesting permission to take out three."

"Only on my mark. We won't have a damned Roswell in Hong Kong."

On screen, two additional units scrambled from northeastern China and India. The ships' speeds and maneuvering ruled out use of satellite beam weapons. It would have to be a dogfight.

The director blinked at the screen. The designator for AGT-3 had disappeared.

"What just happened? Did we get him?"

"No sir. Telemetry just failed. Last track was 100 klicks south of Taiwan. No visuals from two or five. It's gone."

The gold dots on his panel felt like tiny nukes about to blast him to oblivion.

PART III - Control

Chapter 22

We are bemused and crazed creatures, strangers to our true selves, to one another,
and to the spiritual and material world -- mad, even, from an ideal standpoint
we can glimpse but not adopt.
- R.D. Laing, 1927-1989, British Psychiatrist

In the half-light of the woods, gnarled trunks rose alongside young trees from a bed of greenery. Cries of wild birds carried on the winds through the woods. Johan walked with the boy along a dirt path smoothed by time. A sky wrapped in the gray of winter peeked between gaps in the canopy overhead.

Johan answered Ryota's unasked question. "Almost there now. Really close."

The korjé had found the approach to the train and had pressed it. A burst of collaboration with Cathbad's thugs had allowed him to escape with the boy. Saoghal was starting to feel far smaller than he ever thought possible.

The path turned to skirt a tremendous redwood and ascended into heavier shade. The wind lessened but the air grew colder and damp. He took Ryota's hand and led him from the path to the base of a knotty and ancient-looking tree. Pressing the center of a knot split the trunk open to reveal a rough doorway. It swung open to expose a set of stairs that wound down and away. Candles tied with a looped string hung just inside.

"Take one, Ryota."

The boy stepped through the doorway and lifted a candle free. Its wick glowed orange before raising a soft flame.

He squatted in front of the opening and held the boy's hand. "Follow the stairs. Light the other candles you find and be careful. You must not come back up the stairs, no matter what. I will come for you when it's safe, okay?"

"Do you work with my grandpa?"

"Sort of, yes."

"Is he okay?"

"He's okay, yes, but he left on a journey, a lot like ours. He misses you and loves you very much."

Ryota looked down the stairwell and then back. "Do I have to hide for a long time?"

He squeezed his hand gently. "I'm not sure but probably not long. Don't worry, you will be okay. Hurry, now. I've much to do in a short time."

Fear passed from the boy just before he began down the stairs. He was a brave little soul being pushed near his limits.

Johan closed the hidden door and turned to listen. A gust of unexpected cold air blew in as a chilling reminder of the effects outside forces were having on his protected world. Given reason to research, experiment, and push their limits, the korjé hunted now with greater intelligence, combining their experience. Their raid on the train had nearly succeeded, a sign of their progress. Triggers set up all around this dream space should keep him apprised of threats as long as they weren't detected first.

The forest faded and was replaced by the inky wash of Saoghal. He went to Cathbad and found the druid desperate for his attention. Cathbad drew him into a simple living room at night, lamp-lit with shades drawn in privacy. Subtle emotional detail woven into the fabric of the dream induced feelings of familiarity and of trust. A neat trick.

Only the druid leader wasn't pleased.

"This *won't* do. Either be more open to me or—"

Johan threw up his hands. "They're getting close, playing smarter. I'm trying to keep you from danger. You know about the ship?"

"Yes, but do you know what you're doing? Really know?"

"I'm learning as I go and you know it. But yes, I know what I learned."

"And if they learned it, too?"

Johan sighed. "I didn't have much of a choice. Whether or not you planned for this, I still have to survive. Raising the stakes, exploring what's possible... I'd say that's just part of the damn game at this point."

"This *isn't* a game. What you're doing is dangerous."

"Saoghal was already dangerous, just like Raon. I'm not going to play by anyone's rules, especially if it means limiting my defenses. You, them, and God are going to just have to deal with it. Now, about the ship? And whatever Austin's in contact with? It has to be the Mu, right?"

Cathbad nodded. "The ship, yes. It's possible the Mu have acted on our behalf but I find it hard to believe. In any case, we need time to study it and Austin's contact. Tell him we'll soon have a place for him to bring the ship. It may be a game changer but right now there are other challenges."

"Like what?"

"We leaked more to the Americans, enough to give them reason to want to investigate the tower at Ichigaya. Unfortunately the Comannda are not taking chances." Burning remnants of another downed military helicopter stole the moment, a recent memory.

The vision challenged Johan. "The nuke is *built into* the tower? That's simply fantastic. How can they *not* set it off now? If it's found it would reveal conspiracy."

Understanding came, delivered by Cathbad in a rising flow.

The blast would destroy a large portion of central Tokyo. To the world it would appear a terrorist act. The few who knew better would support the lie out of necessity, helping the cover up to protect against future retaliation. Those that didn't would be silenced by their own ranks. Such was the Comannda's effect, as it had been for centuries. Contingencies within contingencies for every possible situation – and always potent leverage to force outcomes.

Johan suppressed a shudder and stared into the darkness beyond the living room. Millions of lives at risk. Every possible action he could imagine threatened either himself or the Runa Korda. He looked back at Cathbad, into eyes that understood helplessness despite possessing unusual power.

"What *can* I do?"

"Nothing yet. We need time to locate other bombs. The Confrere are helping with that. Soldado is using Booty to study Commanda network protocols and learning how to move around. He may be our best hope."

"And what about Anki? Prophecy says she'll help us."

Cathbad took up a chair, fatigued even in the dream. "Yes. Yes there is that." He weighed the moment and came to a decision. "To understand the prophecy, you must know more."

He related Clare's story, of her gifts, and of her passing in the San Francisco quake.

"When Clare died in 1906, we had begun to better understand the droichid. In one of the first ever successful attempts, Clare was embedded within a volunteer, Macy. A rough experience for both at first. They learned to cope, though, and spent the next forty years joined."

"Forty years? Why so long?" Johan asked.

"Research was slow. The Comannda hunted us. Scatterings interrupted progress."

"Scatterings?"

329

"Druid hunts. It requires changing one's psychic imprint to break the family's links in case someone is captured. Homes abandoned, identities changed. Regathering occurs over time, though some never rejoin. In the early 1900's, we experienced no less than five family scatterings. By the time Macy grew old, we'd made progress with droichid. A suicidal woman was found, about to kill her newborn and herself. We intervened."

"The seed in Pons' dream, 1942. You bumped the child for its body?"

"I know, playing God. In this case it was for prophecy. Without Clare, it cannot be fulfilled. She was raised in an orphanage outside the Runa Korda for her safety. A perfect child, as you may imagine. Loved her new body and family and made everyone around her happy."

"Of course. A second chance at life, knowing what she knew before."

"All the while monitored closely. In her twenties, Clare grew close to one of her monitors, Steffan, the one who had transplanted her into her new body."

"So Steffan fathered Anki?"

"Yes. No one knew he'd been targeted for investigation by the Comannda. A high ranked G1 agent had enough to bring Steffan offline for interrogation. Instead she kept the findings to herself."

Johan sat on the arm of a couch. "She? Why?"

"In favor of developing a relationship with him. She'd become emotionally and physically obsessed, both bad marks for one of her standing. Steffan was aware of her obsession but not of her affiliation; he thought her a harmless Natural and a sensual one at that."

"He failed to scan her then. He didn't go deep enough."

"A mistake he keenly regrets. In his defense, it was his first encounter with a G1 level agent. He'd kept a proper psychic distance due any Natural, but she was more than that. Once the G1 learned of Clare and their new baby, her response was to try to knock Clare to Gwynvyd and take over her body. A devious and not uncommon act for lesser Comannda. Steffan caught the attempt and a struggle ensued.

"The G1 knocked Clare free and took over her body. Steffan managed to tether Clare's core while he fought off the intruder's attack. He tried not to harm the body and sent a call for help. Unfortunately, his wounds were severe. When he thought he might not make it, he force-bonded Clare's core to Anki, a move the G1 didn't recognize.

"Good lord. So Anki's mother is still within her?"

"Yes."

"Does she know this?"

"Until recently she did not."

"Hell. What a head trip. You asked her not to tell me?"

"I did. She is our most important link to a future we need."

"So where did the agent go? And what happened to Steffan?"

"The G1 escaped in Clare's body and took Anki with her. Steffan was near death. He'd been ravaged and bled out from knife wounds. We were able to preserve him, you might say." He described the technology used in the tanks at Cullstone. "The G1 was in dire straits. She had already broken enough rules to earn death if discovered so her next step was puzzling. She discarded Clare's body and struck a deal with a prisoner, a woman. She gave her a new life with the baby."

"Why not just destroy both? I mean, they were the evidence."

"I don't believe she had intended to kill Steffan. We shielded him upon finding him, so perhaps she thought he'd died. Protecting his daughter was the only gesture left. Or maybe she realized he'd been saved and wanted to use her as leverage. Knowing her motivations for hiding Anki is important."

"Because she might have a soft spot."

Cathbad nodded. "And not a small one."

Johan paced the room. "What happened later to Margaret, the surrogate mother? Why was she killed?"

"I don't know. It's possible she had second thoughts about their deal. Or maybe it was the agent's way of setting Anki completely free. After Margaret's death, Steffan managed to re-establish linkage with Clare and Anki. She had been left to the system as an orphan, all ties to the Comannda severed."

"If you love something, set it free?"

"Perhaps. We've been guarding them over the years, right up to the morning you knocked on her door. We agreed early on for Clare to remain hidden from Anki until the Words proved true. That time is now. Soon Steffan will help her emerge."

"What will that mean for Anki?"

"She'll work alongside her mother, at least for a time. We'll work on separation when it becomes appropriate."

"And her kidnapper? Where is she now?"

"Names used then mean nothing now. She was a G1 agent, of the inner sanctum, and still exists corporeally. All indications are that she was promoted into the Council. I'm betting she was, anyway."

• • •

A kilometer under the sands of the Saudi Arabian desert, a bullet train arrived at Ring One via the Jeddah line. It emerged from one of four tunnels and slowed to a crawl as robotics scanned and sprayed the exterior of the train. Troops boarded at the head and tail of the train and swept towards the center.

Bastion sat, hands folded in his lap, and waited with his guards as the gate troops processed them with their scanners. The twenty minute ride from the western port city of Jeddah had allowed him time to rebalance his energies and feed on a dish of local Kabsa. The loss of the ATG was more unsettling than anything he'd experienced. The effort to achieve equipoise proved considerable but infinitely necessary. The Council was due to meet to decide on the events unfolding. For that he needed to be as in control as possible.

The troops finished their sweep and disembarked. The iris doors for the next segment opened and the train accelerated towards the Core.

He keyed his comm. "Update."

"AGT craft have been unable to locate unit three. A fifth American helicopter with scanning gear had to be removed as it neared Ichigaya's tower. Command chain analysis is underway. We expect control and recall of all aerial scanners shortly."

He took the news of Ichigaya carefully, resisting the instinct to rage. Someone on the inside was aiding the Korda – it was time to find out who.

The druids' uprising would be quelled with Ichigaya's detonation. Certainly no more than two strikes would be needed as long as Cathbad still had to answer to all the families.

Eleven heads swiveled towards the sliding doors.

A severe Bastion strode in wearing a traditional Saudi robe, brown and flowing. He briefly surveyed the seated group before stopping at the curved window wall that overlooked the control rooms. Screens below showed imagery of the various targets being sought.

"Is it possible that someone is helping the Korda?" he asked.

The question landed in the room like a bomb, its implications like shrapnel. No one wanted to field an answer for fear of receiving attention or suspicion.

"Come now, really. It's a fair question, isn't it?" He turned to face the Executives. "How else would Austin have gained entry to the ship? Or bypassed biometrics to activate flight mode? How else would he have known how to fly our ship? Or to disable flight telemetry?"

He scanned them all, a rough and disturbing rifling meant to uncover any treasonous elements. The group endured it without comment. Such scans had become more common.

Maria spoke after he had finished, in a voice that conveyed reason. "Our pilots and engineers are well kept, Bastion, but that is not to say they are impervious to shadowing. They are allowed leave topside."

He sighed. "Shadowing? Then perhaps our rangers aren't doing their job."

Maria turned to Nora. The Eastern Executive reported all flight operations teams had been subjected to a level one scan.

"The results are in. They are all clear."

"Trainees? Retirees?"

"Also scanned and cleared."

"Conduct an audit then. Cormac, see to it."

"Of course."

Full audits disrupted downtime, rattled nerves, and usually uncovered unpleasantries, but it was the only way to touch everyone.

"Now Tokyo. Ichigaya is close to exposure. What happened and what are we doing about it?"

"The sortie was authorized by a captain new to the unit," Ganzai said. "PostOps determined he'd been managed by the Korda and knew nothing of the plan. The beam operators conspired with two of the helicopter pilots. All four are dead and gone. We're working to insure ministry officials prevent investigation of the tower."

"Conspirators are dead and gone, eh?" Bastion turned to Maria. "It appears the Runa Korda are experiencing many convenient leverages during the start of their Conflict."

She gave no sign of entertaining his jab.

"The question now becomes, what to do?" He began to pace. "They know of the nuclear threat. Prolonged effort at keeping it hidden is ridiculous and risky at this point. Either we topple the tower and retrieve the device or we use it to shut down the Korda. It seems to me that now is the perfect time for the latter. Does anyone disagree?"

An awkward silence followed. Unspoken was the disregard some had for the elimination of so many people using J86. Others approved but remained passive, knowing the minority would need to be dealt with. Behind the silence, the expectation that Maria would speak grew.

And so she did.

"An extraordinarily wasteful choice. Arrange for the tower to fall and recover the device. An errant aircraft crashing into it would suffice to—"

"It is *past time* to shut them down, Maria." His tone carried finality. He addressed the others. "You recall the simulations. J86 was designed for this. Yes, we opted for less destructive methods, but the situation warrants it. The plans are valid. We can make them return the ship. System Seven can be advanced."

In the silence that followed, Maria gathered herself.

"Bastion," she started, trying a reconciliatory tone. "Executing J86 in Tokyo exceeds the parameters for System Seven and complicates everything tremendously. The vision is not post-apocalyptic, or wasn't supposed to be." She turned to the group. "Do not forget that citizens are well-trained. They are as docile as they are going to be given the environment. Controls are in place. Any attempt at information breakout will be dealt with by Overseer and G3. The AGT will be dealt with. We'll turn our technology to the task and it will be located. This bender and Gerrit are the biggest concerns, but we have recourse there, still. The Volgograd teams are close to combining. They will insure capture. Think of what we could learn." She looked to Bastion. "You always say, 'know your enemy'. Losing Tokyo will only make them more desperate. Let the threat to Tokyo and other cities stand. Activate the first elements of System Seven. Move up the schedule. Give the priests something real to think about. Let us use the control we've worked so hard to achieve."

Bastion appeared to digest Maria's logic. He turned to the screens. "Oscar, show us the J86 map."

A spread of the earth appeared on a screen, spotted with red indicators. Maria sighed.

"I propose a test. Cathbad and the families are too invested in what they have built to allow it destroyed. The bulk of the families will not allow for nuclear holocaust in a city," he gestured to the map, "much less all of these. I propose we utilize J86 incrementally. Destroy one city and then issue an ultimatum. The families will be required to turn over their bender and the ship and abandon their prophecy."

Ganzai agreed. "The Korda need to be checked hard."

It appeared the only compromise Bastion would likely make. In a silent vote, most of the group agreed to the test.

"Oscar, issue activation of all sites to the ready state."

"Bastion–!"

"Maria?" His glance froze her mid-sentence. "We *will* be prepared. Once we confirm the existence of the nuclear grid, they will go looking. If found, we lose those options and gain irreparable visibility. We must be ready to exercise J86 to its full capacity or our position weakens irrecoverably."

Overseer responded. "AUTHORIZATION FOR GLOBAL ACTIVATION OF J86 SITES REQUIRES EIGHT EXECUTIVES IN CONCORDANCE. ELEVEN ARE PRESENT. VOCALIZE APPROVAL NOW."

"I approve." Bastion said immediately, as did Ganzai and Cormac. He eyed the others. "Well?"

The leap from one site to the activation of all sites unsettled some in the group. Still, one by one Executives offered verbal approval.

Moments later, Overseer confirmed activation of all twenty-three sites to a ready state.

• • •

The smoke from Soldado's cigarette filled the darkened sixth-floor room of the Luxze Hitotsuba Hotel. The glass balcony door, cracked open for Noriko's benefit, let in the evening breeze from the coast. A game show played on the TV. High energy host, attractive players, lively audience, lame contest, low budget. The show was a hit. To her credit, Noriko didn't appear interested in it.

The hacker ashed in the styrofoam cup and tried not to look too engrossed in what was on his laptop screen. The teams had located another access juncture based on his recommended analysis of dark-fiber ownership and sub-leases in the metropolitan area. They had just installed a remote proxy in the offices of a major video production firm. From the coast of Kyushu, five hundred miles from Tokyo, he ran a hack deep into enemy territory looking for information on the nukes. What was turning up had his heart skipping beats.

"You aren't going anywhere you shouldn't, right?" she asked from her chair. The prostitute façade annoyed him with its cheapening effect though it served well for cover. His bodyguard was exceedingly attractive and intelligent otherwise. Intuitive as hell, too, though supposedly not gifted in the meta arts.

"Right."

She crossed the room and took up position next to him on the edge of the bed. Musky perfume, pheromone enhanced. He felt it coming, tried not to tense...

"That's Booty!" She back-slapped his shoulder. "Damn Sam, why lie to me like that? You're supposed to be hiding, not dangling your dick in the wind."

"Easy now, missy. I'm not anywhere I shouldn't be."

"Bullshit! " She kicked off her heels. "Shut it off."

Fuck. The idea of getting his ass kicked by a chick for doing the most important work on the planet was so ludicrous it blew his mind. "Look Noriko, I'm only skimming, not touching. *Read-only* shit, okay? And I'm five-deep remote, get it? Five fucking hops, safeguarded, crisscrossing three continents. Plenty of protection." She looked ready to stuff the laptop up his ass. "*Noriko.* Someone's got to do this."

"Not you. Turn it off." She balled both fists and shifted to a Kenpo stance.

"Christ, girl, see here?" he turned the laptop. "These are conversations between a central core and systems across the planet. See this purple set of rectangles? Those are copies of command sets that just went out. I'm about to find out what they mean. I'm finally in where I need to be!"

"Not my job, Sam. You're on the net playing hero. Constance gave me orders. Kill it or I will. *Now!*" She was fit to kick his ass.

"Okay, okay, Christ. Fucking relax, I'll back out," he said, daring to stall, "but I have to do it carefully, get it?" He turned the screen back. "The worst fucking thing I could do right now is cut this off wide open like it is. There, I'm closing up the far end synch pattern. Another second... okay, good, it's closed."

Lying, biding for time, he saw the first command sequence come up as translated. "Okay, closing the farthest corridor. Good." He clicked for the results.

Ready-state activation.

"Shit..."

"What? Turn it off!"

"No, no." He held up his hands. "It's fine now, it almost didn't close, that's all. Fourth corridor's synch pattern is ending now. Relax, relax, it's closing out safely." He pulled up another sequence, hoping she wouldn't try to study the screen. "Uh huh, okay. Clear of the fourth. Starting on the third... give it a damn second."

The next sequence matched the first, another activation, though neither contained anything resembling coordinate information. His gut said things were about to go to shit – *completely* to shit – all around the world.

He looked up at Noriko. "Get Constance on the phone, quickly. I need to talk to her right away."

"What, Sam? You fucked up, didn't you?"

He stood and dropped the laptop on the bed, advancing on her. "Dozens of nuclear bombs are being armed around the world *right this second*," he hissed through clenched teeth. "Get Constance on the phone now right fucking *now*."

She paled but went for her purse, intuition winning over orders.

• • •

For the second time in three hours, Austin watched the sun dip towards the western edge of the world. Hovering off the coast of Somalia, he'd just finished a brief but intense resonance session with the entity he'd named Geo. If his new friend was to be trusted, the Mu weren't the benign, hands-off semi-benefactors Cathbad thought they were. Though he wasn't given specifics, the impression was unmistakable: mankind was an easy target, universally speaking.

Johan hovered just out of sense, waiting for the okay to commune. Surprisingly, he seemed to have honored the request to stay clear and let Austin make his own discoveries with whatever he was connecting with.

A twist of the dial brought the lights of Somalia's coastline into view, shimmering in the distance. He stared at the monitors in between bites of a protein bar from the pilot's bag. So much had happened in the last four hours. So much to think about. Tired didn't describe the feeling.

Johan nudged.

"Yeah, alright."

He was instantly present. *So let's have it.*

"Did you really not eavesdrop?"

A hesitation, then, *I can't sense it directly.*

"You what? What do you mean you can't sense it?"

When you are connected to it, you go gray. It takes you away.

It was clear he didn't like it.

"That's pretty weird, isn't it? What does it mean?"

Johan didn't respond. A moment later, Austin realized it was because he'd left and come back, this time with a harsh vibe.

Very big problem to deal with.

"What?"

Johan shared news of the bomb in the defense ministry communications tower at Ichigaya, as well as the knowledge that other cities were similarly laden and now activated. Twenty-three, if Soldado's intercept was correct.

"Twenty-three? Ah fuck no. Where? How many in the U.S.?"

Not sure. They're working on finding them. By the way, they want a look at this ship. Real bad.

"Yeah I'm sure they do."

Mistrust leaked like ruddy water. There was no escaping the resentment towards Sean for grossly understating the threat of the antigravity ships. He'd almost died as a result. He wondered what else they were holding back or what other danger they would put him in.

Johan picked up on it. *Maybe you need more time to get used to this ship, eh? Before you turn it over to them. Come pick me up. I'll be at the Milltown cemetery in Belfast in about two hours. See what more you can learn from your Geo and don't get yourself caught. And don't be late.*

"But the bombs—"

Exactly. I've got an idea.

"Shit..."

Relax. You'll like it.

• • •

Two floors up from Desmond's Bar and one up from the restaurant, a small bedroom served as storage and occasional crash pad for those regulars too drunk or too unhappy with their mates to go home. Cardboard boxes stood ceiling-high, partially blocking a window. In a wooden chair at the window sat a big brute of man, dozing chin to chest. A narrow gap between the boxes and the window led maze-like to a hidden space against the far wall. Just three feet wide, an army cot filled most of it.

Lying on the cot, Johan stirred and opened his eyes to find himself wedged between a wall and a mountain of boxes – plastic cups and napkins, by the printing. The urge to piss was overwhelming. Hunger made waves, too – and someone was cooking. He went to sit up but stopped with a throbbing head. "Fuck." Being back felt marvelous, to just *be* without having to worry about form, function, or vibe... a solid, unchanging body. He just felt badly hung over.

A head popped around the box wall, with a beard and a wool cap.

"Ah, grand. I was gettin' worried for ya." The fellow finished side-stepping the gap into the hideaway. "I'm Brogan. Been yer lookout."

A scan revealed he was contracted help, not Korda. It seemed they'd put some distance between them.

"Thanks. Eh, I *really* need a go at the loo. Could ya point me proper?" With Brogan's help he clambered to his feet.

"Yer name's Killian Casey of Chapelstown, by the way." Brogan shuffled the gap and led the way to the door. "Yer a photographer. School pictures and such, travelin' on holiday. Low budget, Killian." He produced a wallet and handed it to Johan.

"Right. Look, I need you to call your handler and have them bring me two Kevlar vests. Within the hour." A hall with low ceilings led to a small bathroom. The smell of food was stronger at the narrow stairs leading down. "And I need some food."

"Kitchen's still open. Beef, bird, an' a bottle of Bud for ten quid." Brogan said. "I'll make the call."

"Thanks." Just before his bladder burst he squeezed into the cramped privy and managed the best piss of his life. Eyes closed, he shifted briefly up to the edge of Saoghal and peered out...

All too near, the korjé probed patterns he'd used previously. Anki's thread was strong as she was in route to meet him. The thin line to Kaiya felt worried; poor girl, she'd just have to wait. A quick check with Ryota's covering team confirmed the Comannda had allowed the boy to be recovered, though only to his father's care. Guards remained. Retrieval would no doubt be risky.

He pulled all the way back, finished up, and made for the stairs. He suppressed a mental image of da Vinci's Last Supper, a sign of worry about being tracked. *Don't doubt yourself... that'll jack you up, invite them in.* He thought of Tom and wondered if he'd made it away from Sakuma's dream that day. If he had, he owed him a drink.

Desmond's chicken was delicious, marinated and spicy. The beef was on the dry side and the beer icy, the way Johan liked it. He could've done without the karaoke blaring up from the first floor bar, but happy drunks and good food beat all the gloomy alternatives. Brogan's role as guard kept conversation safely mundane. The TV over the cash register streamed images of the helicopter crashes in Tokyo. Terrorists with handheld surface to air missiles were blamed, supported by grainy CCTV video showing a launch. The Comannda knew how to heal the system alright. He savored the simple act of looking away as much as he did eating the food. At least here he had a choice.

A waitress brought the check. Atop it was a note.

"Hmm," the Irishman grunted after looking it over. "Room's doubled up to a hundred eighty euro. Takin' 'vantage, they are."

A woman came up the stairs. The dark hair and face were unfamiliar, but the taut lines of her jeans and her energy made him smile from ear to ear. He stood so she spotted him.

"Mind if I join ya?" The lilt of her voice could raise stones.

"Jenny! By all means, do. I was just thinkin' a gal would make the evenin' finer still." He caught her by the waist and they embraced fully. "Will you ever forgive me?" he whispered in her ear.

"Take me upstairs and we'll see."

Johan lay on the cot with Anki, spent and drifting with her in the twilight of shared thought and feelings.

With Steffan's help, she'd begun the slow and cautious reunion with a mother she didn't know. The greatest shock was learning that instead of having lived thirty years in some kind of psychic cocoon, her mother had discovered how to observe with clarity Anki's experiences. For the last eight years, she'd been a passenger to most of her thoughts, emotions, and even dreams. All the intimacies, petty moments – all the highs and lows. Not all the time, but most.

At first Anki felt both violated and guilty but then she grew angry. The intense empathy she'd suffered was likely enhanced by her mother's presence. Steffan helped her understand that it wasn't Clare's intention or fault. Without that sharing of the outside world, madness would have taken hold for good, a state her mother already endured the long years prior. Learning to reach and observe Anki's reality had saved her. Together they revisited memories and Clare revealed where she had tried to help, gently guiding her thoughts at the most difficult and lonely of times. She had been there for her, trying to do all that a mother would have done for her.

Johan checked the time. Quarter to midnight. He signaled and they edged their way out of their nook and headed for the hallway. Brogan appeared at the top of the stairs carrying a box.

"Bring it with you," Johan said as he passed him.

She nudged Brogan. "Time for a walk. Across the street to the cemetery."

"Um, right." He turned to follow. "Anything special I should know?" Despite the guard's tough exterior, he hid a deep-rooted fear of cemeteries at night.

Anki shared a knowing glance with Johan. "Nah. Just keep an eye out."

They slipped out the bar's side door and made their way across the street to the cemetery. After scaling a wall, they hiked a quarter mile through a sea of graves, stone columns, and headstones seen by the half-light of the city's glow. Johan slowed in the midst of a poorer section where plots lay flat and edge to edge. The cemetery grounds ended at a nearby line of trees with marshlands beyond. The stillness focused Brogan's fear until he couldn't help but break it.

"What're we out here fer again?"

"I'll take that," Johan said, relieving him of the box with the Kevlar vests. He sliced it open and handed a vest to Anki.

"Fer reals, what kind o' meeting would ya have out here?"

Johan checked the time again. "Most secret, as you can imagine. I need your eyes, now. Scan that quarter and tell me if you see even a shadow. Should be two of 'em, no more than three. Jenny, you look thataway and I'll scan this way. I don't like surprises."

"You an' me both." Brogan hunkered down in his jacket and kept watch. A police chopper circled a mile or so off with its spotlight working the avenues.

"Brogan."

"Yeah?"

"Do you believe in vampires?"

He turned as predicted for a quick glance.

"Aren't you the gas?" He turned back, worried they might have sensed his fear of the graveyard. "Yeah, vampires and werewolves and fairies, too. I'm all 'bout them. In fact, my ex-wife was a vampire. Oy, damn straight she was." Suddenly, every hair on his body stood up. He knuckled down to make sense of it but the feeling passed after a bit. A bloody freaky place to be out on a bloody crazy night doing bloody weird things. He shrugged his coat tighter. "What time was ya supposed to meet again? Cause I'd say they were late."

When no answer came he turned, then spun around in terror. The bloke and his gal had up and vanished. "No farggin' way...." His pistol fairly leapt to his hand. He scanned the closest headstones a dozen meters off, trying to catch the gag. When he couldn't, it was enough.

He walked the first few steps, then broke into a full run muttering every bloomin' curse he knew.

Chapter 23

To win you have to risk loss.
- Jean-Claude Killy

The elevator settled at the basement. Doors slid open and Austin stepped into a familiar foyer. He loosened the 9mm in the hip holster at his side. Under his shirt he wore the Kevlar vest.

He jogged up the ramp to the security doors and peered through the glass. InterGen's server farms and central networking core lay just beyond. Rows upon rows of servers glowed in the darkened aisles.

It was no surprise InterGen would be tapped as a gateway. Their bandwidth was as fat as it got, with as much fiber feeding the campus as most small cities had. The perfect place to up and down convert the volume of traffic the Comannda needed.

Again he scraped two security cameras from the ceiling before flexing the grid to shear the bolts of the locks. He pushed through and proceeded left towards The Door.

Since his first days at InterGen, The Door had given rise to many jokes and not a few conspiracy stories. Murray wouldn't speak of what was behind the door at the back of the server room, saying only that it was subleased space. None of the master keys worked for it and only Murray had ever been seen entering the darkened space beyond. To think of what he could tell Matt and the guys now... the truth was more strange than all their stories combined.

He approached The Door and with a swipe took out the camera pointed at it. He sat, closed his eyes, breathed, then stepped from his body. He tried passing through the door and couldn't, confirming what Johan had already detected.

"Blocked. They're jamming meta in there. Gonna be messy. It's plan B." He stood and faced The Door.

Understood.

Potential surged and the door opened with a loud clack as the locks broke. Austin pushed left into a hallway and strode to a glowing biometric panel at a steel door. Another big shove slammed the door open.

A dark room lay beyond. He flipped on a flashlight. A ceiling-mount security camera peered from the corner. With a thought, the camera sheared from its mooring and bounced across the floor with its wiring dangling.

Night guard called it in. So far not moving.

"Okay."

Five thick fiber optic bundles rose from the floor and terminated in an array of switches. Two long rack rows held high-end Rocom equipment, all solid with activity. Every port taken, every fiber patch full, just as Sean predicted. No consoles, just networking gear and fiber.

"Four foot clearance."

Acknowledged.

The room's raised floors vibrated. Seconds later, the concrete block wall split open and broken chunks and dirt spilled onto the floor. The edge of the ship protruded into the room. The hatch opened and Johan emerged with a laptop bag while Anki stayed ready at the controls.

"No lights?"

"None that I could find."

Anki kicked on a beam from the ship.

Johan surveyed the gear. "Main fiber cores." He touched the insulated fiber. "Black box here. Would love to know what it's doing." He withdrew a fiber intrusion kit from the bag and started work. "Keep watch at the outer door. It may get ugly and quick. Keep them back, I'm going to need some quiet time."

"If you can, look for anything on my dad," Austin said.

• • •

Overseer registered the anomalies occurring at site NA16.

On watch status due to incident 901, the junction at InterGen Folsom had not been estimated as a high probability site for further activity. Analysis of available visual data suggested the estimates had been incorrect.

SUPOPS and CoreOps were notified of the intruder while OpAIs were engaged to review every security camera stream in the building.

• • •

"Fiber tap is in. Booty interface on screen. CAP is up and running. Recommended J block traffic filter enabled. I'm seeing the purple stuff. Yes, I already launched Booty2."

Linked via bràthair, Johan coordinated with Soldado on the infiltration. Booty2 was a variant of the original worm with a program stack designed to stealthily explore and learn more about the systems running on the network. If it could do so safely, it would eventually send reports back.

The contextual analysis program, or CAP, would help uncover location data for the nukes. Based on the assumption that a 'ready state' implied control streams that would carry status, the CAP would seek out, analyze, and follow key J block streams to try to learn where they went.

"Yes, I see them. They're tagged now. All J86."

At The Door, Austin heard only half of the conversation. The 9mm felt good in his hand though it would probably be the last thing he used. The mass of potential flowing in and around him was so great it seemed like it might activate itself. Once again something big loomed and it turned his stomach not knowing what. Johan's rushed plans seemed to have little in the way of predictability.

"You're right, four just popped up. Sending tracers out now. Damn you're good, Soldado. I take back everything I said about your mother and her mutated DNA."

To hear Johan laugh felt good though it did little to ease the feeling of dread growing in his gut.

• • •

The glass dividers between control rooms darkened to black. At the sight, Director Tomov stood up and faced forward so as to not lay eyes on the visitors. All hopes of keeping his cool were shot to hell. Footsteps sounded on the floor. He was sure it was–

"Mr. Tomov," Bastion called out as he made his way forward. "Status!"

"Sir–" He fumbled for words like they were muddy footballs. "Sir, Black ops are en route to InterGen, ETA two minutes. Panels are blind to the junction room which suggests Austin may be–"

"What does video show of the ship?"

"Sir, a ship isn't seen anywhere on video now or prior to the break-in. We don't know of–"

Bastion shouted, "What *do* you know, director?"

He almost fell forward. "Sir, we assume the ship is in use at the junction–"

"Shut up!"

The director's heart went still in his chest, long enough to feel the empty dread of impending death. It pumped once, then began beating wildly as linkage to his nervous system resumed. He stood, his face ashen with fear. To his left, someone came alongside his chair, neutral and silent. It had to be Maria de Oro. He wanted to bury his head in her calmness.

"Oscar," Bastion began, "prepare San Francisco for J86 execution."

Oscar answered according to protocol. "IMMEDIATE J86 EXECUTION AT SAN FRANCISCO WILL RESULT IN THE LOSS OF TWO-HUNDRED FIFTY-NINE GROUP THREE PERSONNEL, FOUR GROUP TWO PERSONNEL, AND NINETEEN FACILITIES RELATED TO PRIMARY CONTROL. CIVILIAN DEATHS WILL EXCEED ONE POINT SIX MILLION. ECONOMIC IMPACT FACTOR REGISTERS FOUR AT A MINIMUM." It paused. "VOICE APPROVAL BY THREE EXECUTIVES IS REQUIRED FOR SINGLE-SITE EXECUTION."

Maria cringed. The original plans called for evacuation of staff and incidental relocation of vital persons of political and commercial value. Then there was the city itself, a favorite.

"Bastion, InterGen is well outside the kill zone. This won't touch him."

"I am aware, Maria. We will not stand by while they hack our defenses. There must be immediate consequences. There *will* be."

She requested Overseer provide status on the systems at the InterGen junction.

"NO RECOGNIZED THREATS DETECTED AS YET. ANALYSIS CONTINUES."

"See? They have no idea what they are doing. Nothing has been heard in channels. Things are still secure. G3 will have them in moments. And if you must blow the city, then at least pull out the G2. There is time with the AGTs."

Bastion surveyed Maria with a stare that could strip paint. "Oscar, I approve J86 execution for San Francisco."

From behind Maria, Ganzai echoed his approval.

Bastion cocked an eyebrow at her delay. "Do we need to call on another to replace you?"

She felt the implied permanence of such replacement. The others in the control room masked their discomfort out of respect.

"Oscar," she began. "I... approve J86 execution for San Francisco."

"Single-site execution of J86 approved for target San Francisco, California. Commencing necessary sequences for final execution order."

"Give me a wide shot of the Bay! Move!" Bastion ordered, coming around to the raised dais. Director Tomov stepped forward out of the way. "I want to *see* the lesson the priests will never forget." He sat heavily. "These Words will never fade."

A satellite view revealed the luminous grids of city and suburbia. Streams of vehicles flowed along freeways and avenues. Homes and businesses glowed against the dark night. Almost a million people – working, playing, or resting after the long day. A long, ordinary day.

"Sequences achieved. Awaiting final order."

"Final order given. Execute J86 for San Francisco now, Oscar."

"J86 execution for San Francisco has commenced. Fail safe measures disengaged and placed to standby. Option to re-engage fail safe requires two voice approvals. Estimated detonation in one minute."

The already silent control room fell morbidly still.

• • •

"Execution order for Chevron Tower!"

"That's San Francisco!" Austin yelled back. He thought to run down the hall to join him when movement at the left end of the racks caught his eye. The flash and crack from an automatic rifle startled him so bad he struck without thinking. The end server cabinet slammed into a dark clad figure. Bullets sprayed around, striking the door jam and walls. In a panic, he crammed a fist-sized wad of force directly into the gunman's torso. Blood sprayed out against the wall and exploded from his skull.

From the right end of the row another figure appeared just as one popped up again on the left. Two grid punches to the head dropped them both. A grenade flew over the racks. He slapped it back and heard scrambling and shouts before the explosion tore into the cabinets.

From further back in the room someone said, *"Go go go!"*

Feeling the numbers approaching, he pulled deep and sent a wave outward that slapped the nearest row, toppling the burning cabinets and uprooting floor tiles. On the right, more gunmen appeared. He let loose a focused blast to knock them backwards into their team. The big feeling wavered, as if he'd stepped into it, defining its nature, its outcome.

"Get. The fuck. *Back!*" Another push toppled the next row of server racks. Electrical fires flashed and black smoke billowed. Vaguely he realized he was destroying the very servers he'd once installed. A sudden and distinct alarm went off.

The CO_2 fire suppression system.

In an adjacent room nicknamed the missile room, fifty canisters of carbon dioxide stood at the ready. Thirty seconds and the system would discharge. He yelled to Johan to see if he was done.

Not yet. I'm about to blow charges at the site. Keep them back.

At his confusion, Johan added, *self-destruct charges attached to the ignition computer. Chevron Tower. Firing it remotely.*

More black-clad troops appeared, firing freely as they cleared the racks. Shielding himself, he sent balls of kinetic killing across the server room. Blood and tissue splattered the walls. Six bodies fell in the aisle before they stopped coming.

A headache bloomed and the first fingers of exhaustion raked his core. Maybe fifteen seconds left before the suppression system fired. The smoke grew so thick he had to force air to clear a view. More energy gone. Seconds passed. The alarm kept blaring. The big feeling waned but did not disappear. He would shut the door and let the CO_2 system rob them of oxygen. Ten seconds? He backed up and held the edge of the door ready.

They came then – six grenades, thrown from different angles. He sent an arc up to meet them, batting them back. The punch of a bullet against his chest knocked him off balance and stole his wind. A gunner crouched low and to the left with a pistol in his hand.

Fuck! Anger fused with intention to create a tight and unforgiving response. The gunman exploded in blood and bared bones.

His head felt like it, too, exploded. He shouted in pain and closed the door. Spots dotted his vision. His breathing became short and labored.

He retreated down the hall to the inner steel door to take cover behind it. The grenades hadn't exploded so the pins hadn't been pulled. Just a distraction for the sniper.

"You okay?" Johan asked.

"Hit in the vest. Did you stop it?"

Johan didn't look up. "Yes. Working on the other sites. Keep them back. I'm almost done."

The alarm switched to a high pitch and was drowned out by the high pressure discharge of carbon dioxide. He raised the 9mm and readied his finger on the trigger.

Johan glanced up. "Away from the wall!"

Shots sounded. Puffs of white dust erupted as rounds passed through the wall. Austin darted across the room.

Johan dropped to his knees and shouted, "*Down!*"

A blast tore through the wall and knocked Austin down. A ringing in his ears stung and a wave of dizziness made the room spin. Blood flowed from his nose. He sat up to face the gaping hole. Smoke and dust billowed in the ship's beam, blocking his view. He fired three rounds blindly. A clank sounded and a grenade hit the ground, rolling to touch his right knee. He sent it back through the hole where it flashed. A concussion wave punched him in the face and sent more debris into the room. He coughed on blood streaming down his throat. The urge to breathe increased, courtesy of the carbon dioxide spilling in. Focus faltered, his eyes burned, and the ringing in his ears grew painful. There were more soldiers and they would throw more grenades.

He reached out. *Geo... Anki...*

He imagined the ship firing lasers at the troops, beating them back until he and Johan could climb back in.

The hatch closed.

"No! Don't leave!"

The craft spun in place then stopped. Sudden screams sounded from the other side of the wall.

Affirmation came, as if to say, *done*. The smoke from the server room wafted against an invisible wall. The ship's field had extended into the room to protect them from the smoke and CO_2.

Energy beam. Organs boiled in their own fluids. You can thank Anki.

He looked to Johan. The hacker worked the keyboard with one hand while holding a bloodied side of his head with the other. He said something but the ringing in his ears was too much.

"What?"

It's done. They can't set off the nukes. Not the twenty-three. He stood. *Grab the laptop. We have more to do.*

"Did you find anything on my dad?" Austin shouted.

Are you kidding? I had no time.

The ship burrowed back the way it had come, displacing earth in bucket brigade fashion using a wrinkled kinetic energy field. It re-emerged on the far side of the hill behind InterGen and shot to the upper reaches of the atmosphere.

Austin helped wrap a torn shirt around Johan's head.

"You need a doctor," Anki said.

He shook his head. "Not yet. Did you reach Geo?" he asked Austin.

"No. Nothing. Why? What's next?"

"There are four old nukes we need to reach before they're detonated manually."

The list of J86 sites made its debut electronically using the Underground's framework, reinforced where possible in the dreams of the Confrere. For those who endured the vivid imagery, sudden waking brought irresistible compulsion to seek out confirmation of the list and threats.

In zombies around the world, dead drop scripts activated to retrieve the message and recipient list. Emails went out. Files appeared in private folders. Hijacked VoIP systems called cell phones and after keyword authentication, played back recordings. All were delivered with impunity using Soldado's injected protocols, their existence forcibly omitted from Totem's OpAIs intercept processing.

The messages provided locations of the J86 sites and any notes available for each. Korda-aligned officials of the countries with devices in their cities were urged to intervene and facilitate control of the sites. Although the ignition computers had been blown, the threat of recovery was high. In the case of four older nukes, the threat of detonation was absolute as they were not part of the Comannda network.

"Identify Montevideo, Uruguay," Austin instructed the ship's navigation system.

The overlay marked the city with crosshairs.

Austin pointed the ship in that direction. "If we could just extract the AI from this ship, we could be rich. It's incredible."

"Yeah, until it phones home." Johan sat on the bunk behind them with eyes closed. "Second site is Florida. Miami, near the coast," he said.

"How about Montevideo? Where exactly is it?"

"Northeast of the bay. Don't worry, I'll guide you in."

Arrival at the coast of Uruguay revealed an unnatural cloud formation. As they neared, what Austin thought were city lights instead resolved to a field of fire beneath a massive plume.

He blinked furiously. "No..."

"What?" Johan asked, climbing from the bunk. "Oh God."

When Austin zoomed in, the damage was clear.

"No, no, nooo...." He stared, lost in the gaping hole of life burning on the surface. He imagined three more just like it, at the heart of cities. The sick feeling in his gut spread to encompass his whole being. He sat back and let himself begin to slide.

Anki grabbed his arm. "Austin, no—"

"What are you doing?" Johan asked.

He fell away from his body and pushed towards the fires, aware of the bràthair responding in alarm at his presence. The druids moved to shield him but he shunted them in the grid and fixated on the clamor below. He wanted to *feel* it, to feel what he'd caused. No filters.

Bending and folding to avoid detection, he arrived in the chaos of thousands of souls in the process of dying. Untrained and orphaned, the raw meta thrashed without comprehension, battling the slow withdrawal into Saoghal and the return to their core metabody. What should have been a familiar and safe retreat was instead much like their physical existence – a prolonged and confused journey without understanding, filled with doubt and fear. False premises proved poor footing as reality shifted to its basic, natural state. He felt for them, knew their suffering, but took refuge in Johan's description of the light that would soon gather them.

For the burned and stricken survivors there could be no consolation. He'd never known agony could have so many manifestations. It extended and joined with others, forming a wave of pain and misery that became its own character, a group-mind with a biting outflow of feeling. He followed it and found the reverberations joined with three others of its kind to impact the higher layers of Raon, coloring a hierarchy of group minds with pain, empathy, and fear. From a distance, he felt the weight of the world growing as news spread.

He retreated to the cover of the ship, dashed from the herculean experience of pain and suffering. Even anger felt useless in the moment. The glow of fires twinkled in silence. Tears welled. So many lives lost, so many still suffering. He'd been given the ultimate tools and still had failed to save them.

Javier's voice echoed in his mind. *Dying's part of what we're buying. Deal with it.*

He let go and began to sob.

Chapter 24

And nothing to look backwards to with pride, and nothing to look forward to with hope.
- Robert Frost, 1875-1963, American Poet

Four bombs, manually detonated. In each case, massive explosions obliterated ground zero and sent radioactive plumes into the sky. Each yielded no more than eight kilotons thanks to the aged plutonium isotopes – in two cases destruction was further limited due to placement.

In Montevideo, Uruguay, in a hidden sub-basement of an old Neo-Manueline-style residence, the hydraulic mechanism designed to lift the device through the second story malfunctioned, reducing the effective yield.

Similarly in Istanbul, G3 operatives failed to raise the device from its subterranean storage chamber beneath Gülhane Park. A gun battle with Turkish secret police in tunnels leading from the Archeological Museum forced an early discharge. Among the priceless casualties of the blast was the Kadesh tablet, the world's oldest peace treaty... and nearly a thousand lives.

In Johannesburg, a device detonated in the third floor attic of the main library flattened the surrounding banking district's high rises. The noon day sun dimmed under the dirty shroud and fires spewed smoke across the kill zone.

Florida's devastation was the worst. In the predawn darkness, a gardener's truck pulled into the driveway of a gated residence in south Miami. The driver disappeared into the backyard, a half-acre of lush grass with a pool facing north Biscayne Bay. Beyond the pool, a narrow, tiled water feature suddenly drained as a four foot section dropped and slid from view. From a hole beneath, a turbine howl rose and gathered loudness until lights came on in nearby homes. A deafening thump sounded and a black barrel-sized object shot out of the hole and arced out over the city. The blast succeeded in laying waste to fourteen square blocks of mostly residential homes and plastered radioactive residue over a four-mile radius. The resulting fire storm lit the night and swept through neighborhoods like a new virus.

By dawn's first light, mortalities had risen above ten thousand. Radiation poisoning would kill thousands more.

In the ensuing hours, some form of martial law went into effect in major cities across the globe. Militaries deployed, police forces patrolled, and news organizations delivered reports from all corners of the world.

The media settled onto theories by experts pointing to the radical Islamic elements already claiming responsibility for the attacks. Heralding their success as a sign from Allah, the radicals warned all world states supporting the Zionist infidels that more destruction would come unless drastic policy changes were implemented immediately.

The United Nations Security Council met in emergency session to assess the crisis and to insure every nuclear-equipped country was in communication. No misunderstandings or further attacks could be allowed to trigger an inadvertent war. Reports that more bombs had been located and seized in other cities could not be confirmed except in the case of the defense communications tower in Ichigaya, Tokyo. Allegations of American military involvement there prior to the attacks raised suspicions that the U.S. had withheld intelligence that might have saved lives elsewhere. The Iranian ambassador went so far as to suggest the U.S. might be behind the attacks.

Via secure satellite link, the U.S. ambassador to Japan, David Boles, joined the commander of PACCOM in denying the allegations and to confirm that a nighttime training sortie attacked by terrorists had triggered the rumors in Japan. According to Japan's UN representative, the bomb's discovery was solely the work of attentive computer technicians tracking hidden cabling found during an infrastructure survey. Speculation that the find may have triggered the other attacks could also not be substantiated but appeared a possibility. An investigation was already underway to determine how the bomb had been placed in the tower.

An exhausted Cathbad listened to the monitor relaying the UN session. No mention of secret governments or of the J86 list. The Confrere had done their job. The veil of secrecy held, at least in the moment. The korjé hunted the collaborators, trying to identify those behind interventions at the bomb sites. Protecting them was the main focus of the families.

He rubbed his temple. The Comannda had been desperate, incredibly so, to use the nuclear option. What they might attempt next was the greatest concern.

Sean sat with eyes closed, following the flow of events as they unfolded.

"Global markets have suspended trading until further notice. Russia and China both restricted international flights. A Lufthansa airliner just blew up over Africa. They are putting everything into play at once, seems like."

Cathbad nodded. "Closing their fist."

Sean opened his eyes. "Austin and Johan are safe. However, Austin is insisting on seeing Kaiya. Johan strongly backs the idea and won't leave him."

Cathbad weighed the risk. "Give him half an hour. And tell Johan I want a meeting with him."

"We should leave for Rome now. There's–" Sean stopped. The monitor of the UN had gone black. The familiar gravelly voice of Padrig of the Borcelli family broke in.

"Comannda's made contact. Their message is to abandon the prophecy and hand over the Change and the craft or the worst is yet to come. Cathbad, your new children are breaking up the world and all without a plan. This we cannot abide. Take the proper corrective action now or bear the split."

Cathbad responded sternly. "The Concords, Padrig. You know without unity every family will fall, either to their end or to the will of the Comannda. You *know* this. We all do. The ship and the Change are our greatest assets! Have you no grasp of what this means for–"

"No grasp? Lord of the Wood, I have grasp. What have you? By all appearances the ship is not *ours*, it is the Change's and they are doing what they will with it. Barreling around on their own. Cathbad, the time is nigh for you to step aside. You've allowed prophecy to drive us towards ruin. The families will not survive this path. Make good or let the Concords break upon your conscience." The screen flicked back to a view of the UN.

Sean cursed. "They've lost their minds. Padrig has it wrong – it is a *split* no family will survive."

"Agreed. We cannot stop nor break ranks. It is a measure of Padrig that he even considers it."

Sean frowned. "He is a fool."

"He is behaving like one." Cathbad slowly rose to his feet. "Though in one thing Padrig is right: it's time to focus the Change."

• • •

The path followed a gully through thick palm forest. Morning sun lanced warmth in thin rays. Wild birds went silent as Austin made his way downhill, their senses tuned to his passage. Thirty minutes tops and he'd already burned two just getting to the road. He touched his face, grateful to feel the biocats finally settle in their assigned positions. His old face, but not exactly. Kaiya would notice the difference. Kaiya, sharing a body with a stranger.

He reached the narrow rock and cement road as it bent and crossed a gully. Fifty yards along it ended at a gate, open as promised. Several multi-story condo buildings stood overlooking the azure waters of Banderas Bay at Puerto Vallarta's southernmost tip. From a set of stairs a woman bounded down and ran to Austin. She looked nothing like Kaiya, yet...

She called out, "Babe!"

They embraced and instantly Kaiya came through, dissolving a gulf that felt a hundred years old. With every touch, every breath, she was more there. All he could do was apologize, over and over. He'd never meant all the trouble he'd caused, or all the people to die. Pent up guilt overflowed like a swollen river and tears spilled.

"Babe, babe," she whispered. "It's alright, it's not your fault. You didn't mean for it to happen. I know that. Everyone knows that." She wiped the tears from his cheeks and eyes. "It's so good to see you. C'mon!"

She led him back up the stairs, eyes darting to windows, eager to get him inside out of view. They undressed to shower, something he hadn't done in days. The woman's body was beautiful, fuller in areas Kaiya's was not.

She tended him, cleaning him. Hot water splayed as they pressed into one another.

"Touch me, Austin. Baby, take me, please. Love me."

The world had gone strange, the notion of normal a fading memory, yet some things couldn't be changed. Wouldn't be.

"I love you, babe."

Together they opened the way, amplifying everything good and right in the moment. They climbed the heights of their love, abandoning completely the bittersweet knowledge that their stay at the top would soon be over.

Chapter 25

A little kingdom I possess, where thoughts and feelings dwell;
And very hard the task I find of governing it well.
- Louisa May Alcott, 1832-1888, American Author

At the northern edge of Velletri against the forests at the base of Mount Artemisio, the last of a worn road led to the house of Martin Moretti. At one time a modest Italian estate, years of neglect lent the property an almost disreputable air.

On the weed-lined lane leading up from the road, a gray canvas wrap covered a concession trailer used for making food at regional festivals. The two-story home's stucco and stone exterior needed paint and its tile roof was patched in several places. The porch was overrun by potted plants, many browned with neglect. Parked out front was an aging Fiat Spider with faded orange paint.

Past the house the lane became dirt and curved amidst dense stands of juniper and cypress trees. In a clearing beyond, a workshop stood with an oversized barn tucked away in the far corner, half hidden by branches. Most of the workshop's windows were boarded up and weeds grew knee-high all around the yard.

Austin and Johan emerged from a side door of the barn into the early evening dusk. Together they walked to the corner of the workshop.

"You don't trust them." Johan said.

He'd left the remote and the ship in the hands of the scientists and engineers. "It's not that, exactly. I just want to be sure I get to come back to it."

Johan clicked his tongue. "Of course you will."

"You said Cathbad's not happy with us."

"I said problems are making him unhappy."

A voice called out from behind them. They waited while an old man caught up. Martin Moretti's sons had helped cover Johan since his departure to look for Kaiya and Ryota. If his choice and all its consequences bothered him, he didn't let on.

He came alongside and joined them on the walk back to the house.

"You've been in touch with Cathbad? Then you know it has started. Three airliners down in the last five hours. Half a dozen bombings around the world, including the U.S."

Austin hadn't been told yet. "Nukes?"

"Conventional. Big ones."

"Where in the U.S.?"

Martin shared a look with Johan. "I'll tell you over dinner. Anki's making baccalà with Giani."

Austin didn't like being excluded from the flow of information. Mistrust and concern colored his vibe. That he spoke next about his father was no surprise.

"I want Soldado to use Booty to find out about my dad. And Kaiya's mom, too."

They had rounded the curve and were greeted by an old Labrador. Martin petted its head and again shared a look with Johan.

"I'm not sure that's a good idea," Johan said.

Defenses rose. "And why the hell not? What do you know?"

"Relax, Austin."

A sudden wind brushed the leaves overhead. "Don't tell me to relax. Tell me what you know."

Johan shook his head. "I only know about Kaiya's mother. Nothing at all about your father."

The porch screen door opened and Anki appeared.

"Nice of you to mention it," Austin said. "Where is she?"

Johan returned Anki's wave and looked at Austin. "Passed on, best we know."

Calming Austin proved difficult, even with Anki's and Giani's help.

The revelation of finding Yuni's body immediately led to suspicion that his father's fate was also being withheld. He even began to doubt his encounter with Kaiya. Worst was the feeling that Johan was not trustworthy either. So much erosion of trust at once left him angry and volatile.

It was Anki that finally pointed out that he hadn't slept since before arriving at Cullstone, some thirty hours prior.

"Think of all he's been through. He needs sleep badly."

He took dinner on the back patio alone. His assigned bràthair stayed distant to allow him room, though Johan knew others monitored him more closely. It was clear the Runa Korda intended to protect its interests and agenda.

From the dayroom, Johan watched Austin out on the back porch, drinking wine and fostering an angry mood, largely focused on himself.

Deeper in, fear curled around his core, birthing the anger and selfishness. Withdrawing offered a buffer against the realities beyond his control. It was an improper and imbalanced response, despite being natural. The concern was where it might lead him.

You need to calm down.

Austin shook his head at the message. *I killed Kaiya's mom.*

No, the Comannda killed her. Don't let her death give them what they want. Don't help them win. Step up. Move forward.

Thoughts of his father emerged in a stream of guilt. *So easy to say. It isn't your girlfriend's mom who's dead, or your dad's life on the line.*

My dad's life....? The assassin's long barrel pointed from the darkness.

Austin's unraveling was understandable but it was time for some harsh perspective. Without warning, Johan ripped his rathad free and slammed him into a dream construct.

Austin fell in a blue sky filled with debris and the nauseating smell of jet fuel. A seat twirled by. A small girl strapped to it screamed into the wind, blinded by blood from her torn cheek. The earth below grew, a slowly rising patchwork of color and texture. What should have been a woman cart-wheeled freely, her head and left shoulder missing. Tattered shreds of a blue polka-dotted dress clung to the torso.

"Don't pull this shit with me! I know! *I know* what you're doing!"

A spiraling chunk of burning fuselage arched towards him and grazed his fuel-drenched shirt. It ignited.

"You fucking—"

Shift.

Charred and flattened debris stretched out half a mile in all directions. What had been homes and people living in them were now only ash and scattered chunks of blackened bricks. Not a living thing remained, not even the memories. Farther out, part of the skyline burned unattended. Normally white high-rises stood sickly gray, their windows knocked out by the radioactive blast. Smoke edged the horizon in columns as if the ocean breeze refused to blow over a place of such death and sorrow.

Austin stared, his earlier anger awash in the reality of the place. In the next moment hills appeared, the sky darkened nearly to dusk, and he stood before a huge crater in the ground. Distant smoke rose from fires burning out of control. Another of the four killing zones. The sheer loss of life hung in the air, connected to a wailing sense of misery and sadness – families and loved ones grieving for their dead.

"Enough, already. Damn it!"

Between blinks, Austin stood at the bottom of an enormous silo, at the base of a snow white missile seven stories tall. The next shift took him to a situation room full of angry Israeli generals. Knowledge flowed like spoiled wine until Austin knew the world's problems were further wrapped in tensions known only to the politicos and ultimately controlled by Comannda. A possible nuclear apocalypse still lay in the future.

Austin closed his eyes, finally submitting. "Alright, alright." He exhaled heavily. "I get it."

Someone softly sobbed. He stood in a hallway looking in on a small boy crying over a woman shot and bleeding on the floor. Johan stood next to Austin.

"That's... that's you."

The boy Johan lifted a block and placed it over one of the bullet wounds. The imaginary block of medicine had no effect.

"Ah man." He turned away only to see a man lying on the floor nearby, also dead. "Jesus. *Okay*. I'm sorry. I'm no good at this, alright? Yeah, I'm scared and angry and you know it. My dad... and Yuni. She didn't deserve to die. No one did. And I don't care what you say, I know which of my choices led to this. I carry my portion of the blame and I'm going to have to live with it. I know people want to protect me, but if you know something about my dad, you need to let me know."

The scene faded. Johan stood with Austin on the porch.

"I don't know anything. We'll find out about him, I promise. Just not right now. For the record, I disagree with you. It's not your fault. It's bigger than you. It's bigger than both of us, has been for a long time. We didn't set this up, the Comannda did. They have to pay and they will. But to get to that point, the Korda needs us. It's our time to fight. We only get one chance at this."

Austin nodded. "I know. It's just that... it's a nightmare. It keeps getting more strange and I can't wake up."

"That's a big part of your problem. You need to sleep. Really sleep. You'll lose your mind if you don't. Ask Giani for help with that, I'm sure she'll come up with something. First, though, we need to have a little meeting."

"Cathbad's plans?"

Martin had shared details of the ultimatums from both the Comannda and Padrig of the Borcelli family. Cathbad ordered the search for Ryota's body and Austin's father to be left to lesser Korda. He insisted that without the right focus by the Change, the trackways would surely lead to a darker future. It wasn't hard to understand the truth of it now.

"Yes. After that you sleep. I'll ask Soldado to see what he can find out about your dad."

Austin stood. "Thanks, hacker. I guess I owe you again."

"Damn straight you do," he answered.

Johan spent the next two hours lurking, creating, covering, imitating, and disappearing in Saoghal. He absorbed and expanded throughout, gathering information and concepts, tying together the operational intelligence required for Cathbad's plan.

The High Comannda drove the machine, twelve elite meta bodies hidden somewhere in the endless sea of Saoghal, guarded by an army of korjé. Their invincibility had at its roots many factors but the most basic was the fact that they were simply unreachable. It didn't help that some bràthair believed they hid on a higher, as yet undiscovered and more complex level of Saoghal.

The search was worse than finding a needle in a haystack because this haystack shifted and convulsed constantly. Without some starting point, there could be no hope of tracking down even one of the twelve.

Luckily for Johan, they only needed one and Steffan had a scent to offer. The scent of a woman.

• • •

Austin brought his plate to the kitchen and rinsed it before joining Anki outside on the front porch with a glass of orange juice. She leaned against a column in the morning sun.

"Well, I bet someone feels better. A solid eight hours."

He leaned against the other column. The old Lab lay at the foot of the stairs. "Was that the team I heard drive in?"

"Yes. They're setting up now."

"Hm." He looked out over the suburbs of Velletri to a mountain range beyond. Clouds floated in caravans across the sky. "I'm guessing you're a bit nervous."

"More nervous for Clare, I think. Still, yes."

"Cathbad's sure about this?"

She met his glance. "He said it's been done but only with fellow Korda. In principle it should work with anyone."

"Principle doesn't protect rathad."

"No it doesn't." She shrugged. "Anyway, it's time."

They entered the barn through the side door and saw cables running from a van into the open hatch of the ship. Two armed guards stood to the side.

Martin and Johan sat in the command chairs of the craft, talking. At Austin and Anki's arrival, Johan pulled the remote from his pocket and tossed it to him. "About time you woke up."

"Good morning to you, too."

Johan looked to Anki. "Are you ready?"

She nodded. "We both are."

Austin leaned against the open door of the van and watched a technician make final adjustments.

"Vitals are all coming through," he said. "Shùils are synched up. I'm ready on this end."

Visible through the ship's hatch was Johan and Anki, laying on the bunk bed with sensors hooked to their forehead, chest, and arms. Martin sat next to them on a small stool. The pair's journey would be through Saoghal and on to the target.

Johan briefly connected with him. *Wish us luck.*

Are you sure about this?

Johan shrugged. *I've got a way in, as far as I can tell. If it goes bad, we back out and go for a ride. If it goes real bad, they pull the plug and we make for heaven's gate. Beats an eternity under someone else's control any day.*

Austin sensed a bit of false bravado but not much. *What if they've figured out your tricks? The infinite loop, for example? You could find yourself trapped.*

If I worry about what I don't know, I'll be no good using what I do know. I'm not going to worry until I'm out of options.

Let's pray your options are many, then.

Pray to the Lady of the Stars, yes. Or maybe to your Geo. Nothing more? Nothing.

From the cabin of the craft, Johan called out, "Let's do this."

Austin checked on the readings. Heart rhythm, body temperature, brain wave activity, rate of oxygen consumption, and skin resistance data filled the screens. Somewhere a lawnmower started. The dogs barked. The modified silence settled in the ears of everyone gathered. The technician kept to himself, as did the guards.

Several minutes passed. Martin glanced up from his chair. If things went bad, he would disconnect one or both of them from their bodies. Perhaps they'd be stored somewhere, like Clare had been. Perhaps it was too risky. Martin hadn't shared details of the plan.

Anki's heart rate increased while Johan's brain waves rose to high beta, indicating a very alert, possibly anxious state. On the shùil screen, a scene emerged.

The technician nodded. "Looks like he's found the target."

• • •

The two young women worked in the glow of hundreds of white candles, softly sponging their mistress while humming a song of the magician Vergilius. Steam rose from the sunken marble bath in the caldarium, its scented waters combining with the loving strokes to soothe Maria's worry and ease earthly concerns. Dealing with Bastion had stressed her like nothing in recent memory.

She reached up to stroke the slave's arm, earning a tentative smile. "More wine, please."

The woman stood to comply then froze when the first strains of a flute sounded.

Maria cocked her head, preparing a diatribe for the only one who could be so audacious to interrupt her privacy. She sat up and turned, expecting Bastion. The man she saw was not Bastion, nor a manifestation of his.

This man was beautiful, inside and out. A curly mop of hair adorned an alluring face further complimented by a graceful, muscular body wrapped in a pure white exomis and red cloak. He held her with a commanding gaze – instead of cruelty or coldness, his eyes bespoke temperament, love, and soul-piercing interest. A cup of wine and a bundle of grapes in one hand left no doubt who her visitor was meant to portray. She had never felt anyone so perfectly mimic the ancient Greek Dionysus, god of wine, ritual madness, and ecstasy. His mere presence made worship a compulsion.

The slaves pulled back, unsure of their place. Maria waved them to their marble seats. She stood, her wet skin reflecting the sea of candlelight.

"You are the powerful one, aren't you?" She watched him approach. "The Change of legend. A fitting avatar, as you must be mad to come to me in this fashion."

"Not so mad. And no, he will not know of this visit." He stood over her. "As long as you do not tell him."

"As if I haven't already."

She hadn't – perhaps couldn't – and he knew it. He plucked a grape and held it before her lips. The intimate offer birthed warmth that rippled across her breasts. Here was more danger than she'd ever faced and still she felt the thrill of lust. *Madness, yes.*

She turned away and stepped from the bath to retrieve her robe, feeling his eyes upon her. "Speak now before I change my mind."

"You're not so hasty, Maria. You respect your godly position too much for that. I wish the same were true of the others."

She cinched the robe and turned to regard him. "You don't know me."

"As well you know me."

"I know you are Gerrit Bartel, druid-born, and a pawn of priests." She poured a cup of wine. "I know you believe us to be evil beyond words, puppet masters of mankind. What else would the rebellious have you believe? Certainly not the whole truth. You would have been better off without them. Still can be." She walked to a warming bench and sat.

He circled the bath. "Maria, former G1 agent, risk taker, lover of men and apparently of Greek women. Now a member of the High Council, your rise to power was not without conflict, something that haunts you this very moment. Should they learn of your indiscretions, you'd be worse than done. Always at the precipice, you dare dream of an alternative path for the council, one that sees you dominant." He joined her on the bench. "And that, my lusty Maria, is why I am here."

He knew, had already passed barriers the others could not. Anxiety bubbled with fear as she pushed and pried at the seams to learn how solidly encased she was. For long moments she probed from a dozen different perspectives, searching for deception, any hint of a set up. After thoroughly raking the dream, she finally conceded to his control. Overseer was right – he governed the mesh like none other.

"I'm going to assume you are projecting some suitably erotic version of events for those that might monitor. Bastion is capable. I'm not sure about the others."

He nodded. "You're still being sponged. Without an audience as far as I can tell."

She gazed into vivid hazel eyes, briefly giving herself to the fantasy of a god courting her. He made it so, so easy. His power exceeded that of Bastion, that of several of the Executives, if not all, combined. Self-preservation felt attainable with collusion. Removing Bastion would simplify everything as long as he truly departed.

"Well then, let me start by saying you do not understand what the council is protecting against. Our methods may appear oppressive and inhumane but it is all meant to avoid the chaos that would otherwise manifest."

"You're standing in the way of a planet's evolution. How is that protecting anything but your control?"

"Evolution? Devolution more like. Are you not aware of the nature of man? Of the variety of subspecies? They didn't tell you, did they? Not all are created equal. There is violence in the DNA of some. Instability in others. Raising them from the murk of ignorance would not lead to utopia. Curing all disease would not improve the outlook. Without the systems, without our management, without our plans, mankind would unravel."

"You will not convince me, Maria, that your council is fit to preside as gods for an entire planet. Even you do not believe that."

"I can't say it for our predecessors, but we've made great strides in the last hundred years. The Runa Korda disagree, not surprisingly. Control of ultimate power always spawns differences and contests but the battle they've begun will not be tolerated. The Korda cannot replace our plans with theirs, no matter how fierce their desire. My problem is that Bastion's leadership may leave us with little or nothing to rule. There is a better way to manage our powers and our problems."

"Bastion then." He sipped from his cup. "How can I get to him?"

She nearly blushed at revealing his name. Unspoken goals suddenly came into focus. She hesitated. "I cannot be implicated. Even after you succeed, my complicity cannot be revealed. If it is, you'll think of Bastion as a feisty kitten."

"I intend to stop the obscene retribution under way. If you help me remove him and change the present course, I won't reveal your cooperation. You have my word. Beyond that, I have ideas that involve you and the Runa Korda."

Whatever his plans, she didn't doubt the promise or his altruism. It would have to do.

"Killing his body will be difficult but nothing compared to handling his core. You obviously managed to slip by my guards. Bastion's personal guard is many times that of mine and hand-picked. He travels with his own recovery crew to move him to a new host should his be damaged. I cannot turn you onto his core because he will recognize my sense as your source when you reach for him. If you manage to destroy his host and control his core you would need to keep him subdued until he is collected. You are aware of Eden? Then you know it can take its own sweet time. You'll be on your own, during and after. I cannot pull them off you in any case. If things fall apart and I'm discovered, you promise to deliver me to Eden, at all costs."

"That's reasonable. Where can I find him?"

His probe for information on the Core felt like a rough strip search. "Consider him beyond reach. I will arrange to get him out and about. There is a woman by the name of Samantha Sigler in a care home in Cambridge, the UK. She is autistic and posts a running blog every day. Look it up and stay on it. You'll get instructions from that."

"Will you be able to keep this from him?"

"Surely. I am experienced. There is something you should be aware of. Combining. I'm sure the Korda are working on it. Our teams are close to achieving it. Should they succeed, you would have one hell of a fight on your hands. You may want to check with your priests."

"Thanks, I'll do that." He set down the grapes and wine and stood, eyeing the two slaves. "Just so we understand each other, I don't expect a truce," he leveled his gaze at her, "but in exchange for your... *elevation*, I expect a resumption of peace in the world of man. A return of the status quo, at least. That is your preference as well, no?"

He needn't ask but she reassured him anyway. "My vision differs from Bastion's, so yes. However, if this new arrangement comes to pass, we will meet again to discuss the Runa Korda's future. There is so much you need to consider."

She motioned and the two slaves approached. The deal made, she loosened her robe and her demeanor. "I have half an hour."

"Perhaps another time, Maria. Enjoy."

The intense power left his gaze and was replaced by the energy of her own imagined god. She quickly breathed life into him, life modeled after Gerrit's Dionysus. It seemed quite possible he had outdone the original, something only a god could do. She lingered under his stare, unwilling to give up the fantasy.

"Come, Dionysus. You have been away from your earthly roots for too long." She reached out and drew him in by the hips. "Let us celebrate your return..."

• • •

Johan swung his feet to the deck, visibly shaken. "What a mind fuck."

"Almost, yes," Anki said.

"What happened?" Austin asked from the hatch. "Did she make it across?"

"Yes she did." Johan looked to Anki. "I wasn't sure she should go."

Anki nodded in agreement. Martin started a countdown timer.

Austin looked to ready to pop. "What *happened?* The audio was poor."

"Maria's her name and she's ready as can be. Either that or she's setting me up. We made a deal. She turns us onto the one in charge, we take him out, and she calls off the dogs. The guy's name is Bastion. I got a vague reading off her but nothing I could use to track. We'll have to hit him in the grid and then punch him home."

Martin grew concerned. "And you sent Clare over anyway?"

"She wanted to go," Anki said. "I don't think I could have stopped her."

"So now we wait?" Austin asked.

"First window is in three minutes. She'll try for details of the base first. If she wants to continue, we'll extend again." He laid back down, clearly exhausted. He explained the autistic blogger and the instructions to monitor the site.

Martin shook his head. "A website? I don't like it. Might as well point an arrow at yourself."

"We may not have a choice. I've an idea on how to watch it safely."

"Oh shit," Austin said. "I don't like it already."

"One minute thirty," Martin said. "Silence now and prepare."

• • •

367

Blackness.
Boundless.
Without time.
Without form.

Can you be trusted?
The question split the void as a shining blade, a defensive swipe at whoever was lurking.

Meaning bled into the darkness. Time faded once more.

• • •

"That was damn close. Too damn close."

Johan had again slipped by Maria's guard in order to wait for Clare's return. In the narrow nook of nothingness that had proved safe before, the executive's sudden focus struck like nails in his chest. While he struggled to maintain his sense of absence, Clare's gossamer thread beckoned. As if he'd split in two, one side paced Maria's attention while the other managed to bring Clare back. Had he blinked, she might have sensed him and known what he'd done.

A small part of him wondered if she had.

Anki sat in the living room with her head in her hands, consumed by the knowledge transfer with her mother. Martin sat with her, hand on her shoulder, calming as best he could.

"It's a bit much," he said softly.

"Yes," she started. "It's a lot." She looked up. The energy in her eyes and voice told Johan it wasn't Anki speaking but rather Clare.

"I'm going to need some help sorting through it. Maria is one hell of a character. Complex doesn't begin to describe it. And just so you all know, Anki's not trained for this. It's taking a toll. Don't think less of her."

Martin asked what she could share.

She looked to Johan. "Maria's impressed with you. In fact, she was still playing with your god like a three hundred year old cougar. And there is no doubt she wants Bastion removed from the picture. You've hooked her there. But listen you two... this woman is a threat. She is made of things stolen, borrowed bits and pieces of thousands of souls. For her, taking a life is no different than moving a chess piece. She also harbors love for all of creation, a love that encompasses the very souls she displaces. If that isn't a dangerous combination, I don't know what is."

Hers was the world view that had helped shape humanity for millennia. Knowing death did not mean the end, all matters of conscience were subject to interpretation. The call for balancing nearly lifted Johan to his feet.

Austin asked if there was anything about the Comannda's base.

"The Core, yes. I sought access but the lady has 'access' to so much that it was hard to filter without setting off alarms. I found something though. There's a building in the Persian Gulf, at the coast. It should be easy to find because it's round with scimitar-shaped arms coming off it. Maria held concern about it, a vague 'weak link' feeling. I'm almost sure it's a transport depot for the base."

"I see its form, yes. What about the base itself?"

"It's big. Radial in nature, with transport lines running out to distant ports. It's secure, remote, like another world. All underground. So much safety yet also a stifling that she dreads. She loves being topside."

"Where is it?"

"Distant from the depot and the coast. Totally landlocked. It felt surrounded by rock."

"Johan," Martin said, "I want you to work with Ginia and help Anki. I don't want her retreating. She needs to be with us."

"What about separation?" Johan asked.

"I do think it's time," Clare said.

Martin agreed. "I'll speak with Cathbad. Meanwhile she should spend time with Johan. Quality time, focused on normalizing her world as much as possible. How long before Maria updates via the blogger's site I don't know, but be there for Anki now."

Austin asked about the blog. "I know we're all on board with this Maria, but what if it's a trap? How are you going to monitor it without Overseer tracing?"

"I said I have an idea," Johan said.

"Yeah?" Austin said, only half smiling. "Why do I still not like it?"

Chapter 26

Confidence is the feeling you have before you understand the situation.
- Source unknown

Wind through the open side door of the barn carried the smell of rain. Austin sat on a chair facing the ship, forearms resting across his lap. An empty plate on the floor held the remnants of a spaghetti lunch. Six Korda engineers pored over the ship with equipment, poking, prodding, recording, and talking amongst themselves. The few stray words he'd heard referenced beam weaponry, radars, field generation, and metamaterials.

He'd patiently sought the small sense of meta that had blossomed in his mind and flooded him with knowledge of the ship. He entreated contact, paced by Johan and other bràthair. The danger was in attracting the Comannda or perhaps worse, the Mu. Geo had acted to give them the ship, so the tendency was to think it was in some way on their side. The reality could be different and Cathbad made sure they all considered it. Whether it was truly an alien entity or just made to appear so also concerned Cathbad. Further contact might provide clues. His own thought was that Geo was an outsider, more concerned with humanity's fate than with power or control. The impression was clear yet could still be a product of manipulation.

An engineer walked over. "Got your answer. It's a closed system complete with air scrubber. You can take it up and out anywhere you can steer it, as far as we can tell. Underwater, too, with or without the field."

"What about power?"

"It's got nuclear batteries but we have no idea how it's generating the fields it is. Best we can tell it's got some kind of over unity capability, probably in the sealed modules of the lower section. When you're ready I'll show you what we learned about the beam emitter and the different radars. You should be able to pull off your trick no problem."

"Great, thanks. I appreciate it."

"One more thing." The engineer offered him a black velvet bag with a string tie. "It's a stretch suit. Same metamaterial used on the hull, just different composition. The pilots must've used it for stealth operations outside the craft. Wonder where it's been, ya know?"

Reaching into the bag, he felt something like thin lycra. He pulled it out and immediately tried to make sense of what he saw. Touch contradicted what his eyes told him. The outside of the fabric blurred slightly what was beyond it. Only seeing the inside of the suit calmed his brain. He held it out at arm's length but saw nothing.

"Bizarre, isn't it?"

"One suit?"

"Only one. I'll be needing it back, of course."

Hell of a toy, Johan commented. *Bring it with us.*

"Do you mind if I take it for the ride? We'll be back in a short while."

"Fine. Just don't lose it."

Austin smiled. "I see what you mean."

· · ·

From twenty-two thousand miles away, Earth basked in light pouring from the star, Sol. Seen only through the craft's cameras, the view still held the eyes and hearts of all three in the cabin. Austin mentioned how funny it was that beyond the planet, the sun stopped being the ordinary bright thing in the sky and instead became the star that it was.

"Perspective is everything," Johan said and returned to the bunk to check his laptop. Anki sat in the co-pilot's chair alongside Austin.

Fine-tuning the radar and beam emitter to the frequencies used by satellite service providers would provide the connection needed to browse Samantha Sigler's blog. They just had to line up on the beam of a satellite without weakening it too much. To do so might attract attention.

"Alright, hold it. Tilt another two degrees. Okay, there. Now ease it forward just a nudge."

The Hughes HS601HP they'd researched and selected was an older Astra satellite servicing northern Europe. They'd found it after an hour's search in the wide field of geosynchronous satellites. With Johan's help Austin worked the controls to bring the craft closer in. Signal strength rose as they neared the beam.

"That's good right there. Hold it," Johan said. "Okay, I'm in. Need to forge another account if we're going do this regularly. Hang on."

Austin glanced at Anki. "How you doin'?"

She smiled. "I'm fine. We're fine."

"You sure?"

"I'm sure."

Johan cursed.

"And?" Anki asked.

"And nothing."

"No entry?"

"Not in three days. Last post is a photo of a leaf."

"We'll just have to try again later. I'm heading back."

"Wait," Johan said.

Austin and Anki both turned. "For what?"

"See, there's a little boy who deserves to have his body back and I know exactly where to get it. I want to do this now before they decide to destroy it."

"Johan..." Anki's tone carried a warning.

"I know what Cathbad wants but bràthair have monitored him since the clinic. Nothing's set up at the hotel where they have him. Sendai City, fifth story royal suite with a patio garden. Two guards. His dad's been there only once since he was recovered. He's on a portable ventilator and gets a nurse visit three times a day. Physically, he's available for a grab. It's eight o'clock and he just had his diapers changed."

"So that's why you wanted the suit," Austin said.

"What suit?" Anki asked. When he showed it to her, she shook her head. "I'm sorry but I don't get it. Is defying Cathbad really the way you want to play this? Didn't you learn anything the first time?"

Johan bristled. "Look, I'm thankful for what the Korda's done for me, but I'm doing my job *and* taking care of my own business. That's how I'm always going to play it." He looked to Austin. "We can have him back in under fifteen minutes if we go now."

Again Anki shook her head though said nothing more.

Austin looked at the viewer. Memory of Kaiya's return to a Korda host echoed, mixed with the knowledge of Cathbad's orders. They could be back before anyone noticed...

"Alright, but we do this my way."

Austin toyed with the silver ring Kaiya had slipped on his finger. She'd cried when he left; reassurances only went so far. Ignoring her plea to run away with her had been difficult. He'd barely rejected the temptation and instead promised to make things safe enough so they could be together. He wondered now if he'd ever be able to keep the promise.

Johan laid down in the bunk while he crouched near the hatch. They would expect them to use the ship, so going in without it made the most sense. He pulled the hood element over his head and face, effectively becoming invisible in the dimness of the cabin.

"Cathbad's going to shit bricks when he hears about this."

"He already has," Johan said. "Heard about it, that is. Not sure about the bricks."

Austin smiled despite his nerves. The ship hovered fifteen thousand feet over Mount Chokai, Japan. Memory of the AG ramming played over and over.

"You sure you're okay with this?" Anki asked him.

"I've got it, yeah. I'll be fine."

"And you're ready?"

"Yep."

"Okay... here goes."

The hatch opened to reveal early evening skies. Austin peered over the edge. Mount Chokai protruded from the earth as his marker. Returning with Ryota, he need only get to the mountain and go straight up for the rendezvous.

Johan checked his watch. "Give me two minutes from my signal. If you don't see him on the patio by then, go in and get him."

Anki looked in his direction from the command chair. "Make it back, okay? I don't want Kaiya hating me forever."

Austin smiled. "No worries. I'll be right back."

He stood at the very edge, hands on the ship's hull. The earth shone below in high resolution. For a moment he was fifteen again, feeling resentment at his mother's objection to him skydiving. His dad had okay'd it, but she wouldn't allow it.

"You can change your mind, Austin," Anki said once more.

"It's alright. I've got this."

With that, he tipped forward and fell into the gravity of the planet – his first real skydive.

He split the blue sky at terminal velocity, falling towards the mountain without effort. For one long minute he fell – time enough to imagine nothing had happened the way it had and that this was just another fun activity while on vacation in Hawaii; that four cities hadn't been destroyed by nukes he'd failed to stop and that his mind was as isolated as he remembered growing up. Best of all was imagining Kaiya waiting for him below.

As the earth loomed closer, he envisioned a sunny afternoon swimming by her side, lunch on the veranda, making love before dinnertime... until the vision shifted to a fiery mass swallowing the island – a nuclear bomb flown in a light plane and detonated over the southern end of Oahu. The Comannda would never stop until their ship was in their control or destroyed–

What the fuck – pull up PULL UP!

Individual trees and boulders on the mountain's peaks came into sudden focus. Intention engaged like steel gears and he arced down the side of the mountain in a powered curve that brought him up again to level flight.

Zone out again and you'll get yourself killed.

Shaken and embarrassed, he corrected altitude and barreled on towards Sendai City.

He passed over the industrial districts following a rail line until he spotted the sprawling hub of Sendai Station in the downtown district. The Hotel Metropolitan Sendai towered over the rail depot, gleaming white-gray in the gathering dusk. From two thousand feet, he stared down over the patio gardens of Ryota's fifth floor suite.

Johan signaled. *I'm going in.*

Austin dropped lower and cued intention. The patio's oversized fronds and fanned-out ferns created natural cover. In the far corner, he made out two people sitting in lawn chairs. If the boy rushed out, he had seconds only to manage those two and anyone else who came from the suite.

Time passed. Half a minute. He squinted to keep the sliding door to the suite in focus. A train pulled away from the station on its way south. One of the men on the veranda stood and stretched. The lights on the patio flickered on.

A minute. The yellow duck feeling returned.

"C'mon..."

He hovered, willing the boy to emerge. Coming up on two minutes... too long. On the verge of action, a bump from Johan: *I'm outside in the service parking lot. Grab me.*

A small figure dressed in blue ran around a truck to hide between it and a concrete wall. Austin swept down in a rush, touching the ground to scoop him up. The little guy wore pajamas and slippers and looked like he should be watching cartoons at home, not running for his life, controlled by another human being.

He unzipped the suit and allowed the boy to wrap around his torso like a monkey. He stretched the fabric to zip it closed again.

"Hang on."

They boosted up and outward then, lining up on the distant form of Mount Chokai. Its summit glowed in the last rays of the sun. Relief and excitement mingled at the thought of reuniting Ryota with his old self. A sense of accomplishment made the flight that much sweeter.

The feeling lasted exactly eight seconds.

Trap after all. Anki's on the move. AG's swarming. Get us down, now.

He dove, scanning as he went. Panic led the hunt for a safe path. Dusk contrasted with the lights of the city to make it harder to see what lay below. To his left, the unmistakable patterns of a golf course stood out. He closed the gap in a burst, passing over a hotel and eyeing the farthest edges of the course.

He set down near a stand of trees and burrowed a hole in the grass big enough to slip into. "In we go." He dropped in then pressed the earth to form a small cave. They slid further down into its darkness.

Austin couldn't help his anger. "If we get out of this one, I swear to God I'll never follow your half-assed plans again. By the Lord of the Wood, the Lady of the Stars, and Humpty Dumpty's broken ass, I swear it."

Ryota's voice was small in the darkness. "Anki's taken them for a chase but there are still ships searching the city. I'm giving Ryota his body now. Keep him calm. I'll send someone for you."

"Poor kid's going to be scarred for life. Probably doesn't know dreams from reality at this point."

"At least he'll have a lifetime to figure it out. Hang on. I'm going for it."

"Tell him it's going to be pitch black."

"Right."

Austin unzipped the suit and found the little boy's hand. Moments later it went slack, then jerked and the boy cried out.

"It's okay Ryota, you're okay. We're just hiding in the dark. Relax."

"Where are the bad men?" His little voice carried fear.

"Not here, Ryota, not here. They're looking for us but we'll be okay. We'll be just fine. Help is coming."

Help better be coming, he thought to himself.

Twenty minutes later, lawn sprinklers split the silence. The white noise became a symphony playing outside their hiding hole. Ryota lay in a ball in his lap. The moist earth soaked through to his pants but he didn't care. Waiting only made him more anxious.

Johan finally returned. *Get ready. Hatch will open at the hole.*

He barely had time to stand before reality split open above them to reveal the ship's interior. Anki had the ship at an angle to receive them. Johan stood there ready to help them up.

He rose with the boy in his arms and cleared the hole. Before landing on the ship's floor, he saw a golf cart rolling not twenty yards off.

"Close it, quick!"

It closed and Anki pulled the ship away. "What was it?" She looked at the screens. "Oh shit! How did I miss him?"

"I think someone's gonna have a helluva story to tell about that hole in the ground."

Before returning to Martin's in Velletri, they flew up to the Astra satellite to check on the blog. They found a new entry.

The angry king plots this night
Revenge colors morning light
Blooming fire in the city
So many lives, so much pity

"Oh god," Anki said.

"Which city?" Austin asked, frustrated. "Can't she do something?"

Johan set the laptop aside. "It's beyond her. She can't break ranks."

"I told you. I *told* you." Anki pulled the ship away and set a mark for Velletri. She didn't hide her displeasure. "When will you listen to me?"

• • •

The barn doors opened to receive them, pushed by the two guards. Standing just inside was Martin. He met them as they climbed out.

"Cathbad has ordered you separated. Johan, Anki, there's a car waiting for you. Austin, I've got coordinates and instructions for you. You'll take the craft with Bario here."

Johan glanced at the two guards. "And if we don't want to split up?"

The old druid shook his head in disappointment. Before he could speak, Anki left Johan's side to join him.

She looked at Johan with conviction. "We'll go."

When he didn't reply, she said to Austin. "It's time to get with the program before we really screw things up."

Chapter 27

All things come to him that waits - provided he knows what he is waiting for.
- Woodrow T. Wilson, 1856-1924, Twenty-eighth U.S. President

Austin hefted his duffle bag over his shoulder.

"Thanks, Niko."

"See you in the morning."

The beat-up station wagon pulled away in a u-turn. He watched until its taillights disappeared around a bend in the road. The night sky beckoned from behind a blanket of clouds, hidden but still expansive. Knowledge of life throughout the galaxies made the planet under his feet feel tiny. Remembering that alien species might be as devious as humans left him frightened for Earth. He fingered the ship's remote and thought about the blogger's message. If true, tomorrow would be a fucker of a day and it was again partly his fault. Guilt shadowed his every thought. It had to stop and soon.

He started up the stone walkway. The sprawling two-story villa sat amidst rolling olive orchards on the Greek island of Corfu. He counted four garage doors and at least three decks. A pool glowed in between shrubs.

At the door a portly, tan-skinned gentleman in his sixties appeared. Gus Apostolos welcomed him with a gravel baritone voice.

"Long time, my nephew from America. You look great. Come in, Tasia will take your things."

If Gus feared taking in one of the most wanted men in the world, he didn't let on. Despite his resemblance to a crime boss, his warmth was genuine and his vibe relaxed. A thin, dark-haired woman took his duffle bag and jacket and disappeared. They strolled into a home of white stucco and earth-tone tile.

"You're tired and hungry." He gestured down a hall. "There's something ready for you in the kitchen. Tasia will take you to your room when you're ready. There is a spa and sauna and a pool if you want them." He stopped and faced Austin. "I'm told a method for monitoring the web page has been found so the long trip up won't be needed. I need the remote. Scientists will arrive soon to continue studying the ship."

Austin gauged the man.

379

"It won't go anywhere, you have my word. They need to study it more."

Trust was possible. He handed him the remote.

"I have business tonight but we'll talk in the morning. Welcome. Be at peace and relax."

Austin devoured a plate of fish. He had to ask Tasia what kind.

"Mediterranean red-mullet. You never had?"

"Never had. Delicious."

He retired to the adjacent living room with a glass of wine and turned on the television. He couldn't help but tune into the news. Another airliner down, outside Detroit. Large bombs in Amsterdam and Los Angeles had killed more than four hundred people. *Our hometowns.* A new terrorist group had claimed responsibility. Pakistan's military had taken charge of the country, its intentions unclear. Tensions between Israel and both Iraq and Iran had flared to the point nuclear exchanges were feared.

He turned the television off. There was more but it was too much. Sitting at the tip of so much death made him sick with guilt. The High Comannda were pressuring the families to turn over the Change and return their ship.

He closed his eyes and worked hard to put down rising anger. Vividly, he imagined Bastion's severed head falling, slow motion, and him drop-kicking it into a blazing campfire by the sea. Instead there was nothing to do but wait. Anything else would risk losing the opportunities that lay ahead. That truth had been hard earned. Still, to have so much raw power at his fingertips and not use it to fight back grated against every instinct he had. He opened his eyes and thought of Maria. If she came through he might have a chance to stop the campaign of death.

He finished his wine and rinsed his glass in the kitchen. Tasia watched from a chair in the hallway. Probably in her late forties, as unreadable as stone except for her servitude. She reminded him of Williams at Shamrock but without the outgoing spirit.

"That's it for me."

She gave a small smile and led the way upstairs to his room before disappearing down the hall.

The room was more a small suite with couches, sink, and wine cooler. A slider led to an attached sun balcony. A PC and printer sat on a narrow desk. He couldn't shake the images of the bomb damage back home or of the ring of fire at Montevideo. More and more people dying. Because of him.

Again he thought of his dad.

He went to the cooler and poured another glass of wine with the notion of truly dulling the guilt and anxiety. Dad, dead or alive...? That he couldn't feel him at all hurt. Good guy or bad guy? To even have the thought was crushing. What the past held was a mystery. Anything was possible.

He drank half his glass in one lift, filled it again, and stepped out onto the balcony. A probing wind stirred an otherwise serene night. Rows of olive trees stretched away in the dark. A pair of headlights wound along a distant hill.

He tried to empty his mind and succeeded only in emptying his glass.

• • •

The thrum of engines below decks sounded like music, a powerful beat of physical freedom. Maria stood in the galley and poured a drink. Her guards kept watch outside as the sixty-four foot luxury trawler *Dionysios* left Port Alacati headed for the Aegean Sea.

She padded barefoot towards the couch and stopped to look out at the lights of the remote Alacati Resort. The dark waters and clouds overhead swallowed everything around the resort – it could have been a space station in a lonely patch of space and *Dionysios* a small shuttle departing. She suppressed profound relief at being clear of the Core but deep down her feet tingled. This very ship helped avoid what could have been an unpleasant outcome with Bastion.

Her encounter with the god Dionysus held lingering emotions that Bastion had alerted to. He'd labeled them subversive. She convinced him that when she had laid down to rest, her last thoughts were of leaving for home on her boat and that she remembered only the sexual experience with the Greek god. Purely a random dream. Any residual emotions were complex and beyond her control. She even managed to chide him for his paranoia.

She feared it had been one of those 'roles of your life' moments that if she hadn't given her all she wouldn't be on her way back home.

Under the dimmed cabin lights she curled on the couch and pulled a blanket over her lap. She sipped her wine and closed her eyes. The additional protection she'd ordered to ward off suspicion made conducting intrigue much harder. She managed to reach out and see how Samantha was doing. The old woman was fine, unmonitored and untouched. Adding to her concerns was the possibility that Bastion might not actually come. If so, all her posing and plotting would be for naught.

Her interaction with Bastion before leaving the Core would have him appearing in Mykonos for a lusty reunion. The fascination he still held for her would finally serve a useful purpose. She opened her eyes in response to a troubling thought: what if Bastion did not wait for her to return to Mykonos? A seven hour cruise... he might not be able to hold off. It would be just like him to yank open the door once unlocked and rendezvous by sea instead.

She reached out once more and conveyed a message for Samantha, modified for the circumstances. The autistic received it via the 'special place' she always looked to for inspiration in her writing. No matter the hour or present activity, she would drop everything to post to her blog.

She breathed deeply and raised her glass for a sip.

The druids would check the page. They had better be prepared to act. Fucking Bastion for nothing would really piss her off – worse if it happened while on her beloved *Dionysios*.

• • •

"It's unthinkable she would give us her position," Sean said, pacing the room. "We're talking one of the twelve."

"It's either a measure of her solidarity with us or it's a ruse," Cathbad said.

Fire flickered behind the glass insert of the woodstove, a magnet for his gaze. There was little else in the second story apartment to look at. Pizza cartons and wine bottles from the rural pub and pizzeria next door lay on the wicker coffee table. An ancient television's rabbit ears angled towards the front door, the set itself unplugged. They were south of Rome in a dingy apartment complex tucked amid the many small family orchards and vineyards. A chill braced the countryside and pressed through thin walls. He tipped his wineglass and drank deeply, engaged in the primal input of the physical.

Johan lay in one of the bedrooms working with bràthair to locate the 'god-like ship' departing 'the thanksgiving bird' en route to 'the party island'. They'd already located the estate described in the blog entry, a hilltop affair overlooking the northern sea inlet on Mykonos. Property records showed it belonged to a Greek shipping corporation.

The blog's latest suggestion that Maria might be intercepted by Bastion at sea required they try to find and track her ship somewhere between Turkey and the island.

"It could be a ruse, yes," Sean said. "But Clare read nothing of that."

Cathbad nodded slowly, a kind of shrug. "If she's sincere about wanting to remove Bastion, she needs to draw him out of the Core. I suspect we'll soon have a better feel of what she's up to."

Sean came around to face the old druid.

Cathbad looked up. "What?" he asked, then knew. He straightened in his chair. "No, no, I'm fine. Don't start with the nurse routine. I'm slowing down, what do you expect?"

"Worse than slowing. You shouldn't be here. A driver will take you back to Hastings for treatment."

"That is not my choice." He set the wine down and pulled his sweater close. "I'm tired, nothing more. Focus on what's important, Sean. Keep the bràthair on task, on their toes. I'll hold my own and go if and when I need to."

The creak of flooring signaled Johan's rising. He appeared from the hall looking worn.

"Found her." He sat at the couch and took up a bottle and glass. "I've trained two bràthair with a screen they can follow from as long as they stay quiet. Two at a time."

Cathbad didn't approve. "Relying on your new techniques is dangerous. You can't be sure they won't find them."

Johan paused mid-pour. "It's that or have them rounded up by riders. They've cordoned half-mile around the boat and are scanning miles further. Besides, it's not that different than the folding they've been doing. Better, I think."

Sean shook his head. "Great. Maria's reinforced and now she's covered. She's been made. Has to have been."

"Anything's possible." Johan set the bottle down and lifted his glass. "The riders around the boat are to be expected if he's coming. And yes, it may also be a trap. They've got an AG out looking around. Anything near her ship will be suspect, in the water or air. I'll go back and join the monitoring if you're uncomfortable with it. It's the best I can do. Otherwise, they may hide Bastion's approach too well and we'll miss the opportunity."

"There's a few satellites that touch that area," Sean said. "I'm checking what's available."

"That's fine but we need to monitor things up close right now. I trust Austin is ready to go?" Johan drank, painfully aware Cathbad was in bad shape and working hard to hide it. The old man would rather die part of the game than idle under treatment. He asked, "Friend, have you considered giving up that old shell in favor of a new one?"

Sean answered for him. "Won't do it, not his style. We've tried."

"You're feeding that thing more than you can afford to give. You're strong, but not that strong."

"So be it. You'll help me to Gwynvyd."

Johan didn't reply. If the old druid didn't sleep soon, the damage would compound and the drain would kill him. He had given too much to expire before the first results of the Conflict came.

Cathbad sighed, finally responding to their concern. He stood and asked Sean to keep on top of the satellite effort. He lumbered down the hall to the bedrooms to rest.

Johan sat back, glass in hand. "He's dying, alright."

"You're not going to let him move on when the time comes, are you?"

Again Johan didn't reply.

• • •

The first shades of dawn revealed bulky clouds on the march. Winds from the still-dark north pressed the tips of waves into spray. The *Dionysios* kept speed despite heavier seas, the engines' changing pitch an angry growl. Two guards stayed deck side with IR goggles scanning for anything the radar might miss. Three other guards took position on the bridge. Bastion's riders stayed on, spread out in a wide circular swath without attempts to hide. Nothing had been seen of the druids or Gerrit. Or of Bastion.

Maria stayed below deck and nibbled on cheese. The coup would occur in her other beloved space then, unless she'd already been made. His growing displeasure with her had been tempered only by allegiance to his obsession with her. If not for that lust, fixation, or whatever it had become, she probably would have long been deposed. To have it come down to an elimination round both scared and relieved her. Mastery of her hidden world was not without a constant effort. One way or another it would be over.

The captain called down to announce the lights of Mykonos.

The rest of the morning proved to be an exercise in rote. Her guards cleared the house and set the heat. A hot shower returned color to her face, now that of Despina Chara, former chief financial officer for Xene Global Shipping. Elias showed up at ten with groceries and started lunch.

By noon the circle of Bastion's riders had gone, leaving her own as sole guardians. Anti-climactic in one sense, the situation remained fluid. Bastion's unpredictability would no doubt be a factor in the plan. She had to be ready for it and so did the druids.

While eating she reviewed her encounter with Bastion. Had she successfully landed her lusty innuendo? Or had she misread him? Possible but unlikely. She'd used the most natural tact: to please him in exchange for continued status, an act of both desperation and submission. His references to replacing her had become more frequent and stinging of late, in exact response to her criticism of his plans. Status had not officially degraded but it seemed a matter of time, especially with Ganzai steering him. Pretense of a sexual remedy still made the most sense.

The evening's Council meeting would offer the opportunity to gauge him. If need be, the post-meeting lull would see a formal proposal for a nostalgic romp in the flesh. She minimally dispatched a message to Samantha, careful to preserve discretion. The priests had to be kept informed. Everything rode on their successful engagement of Bastion.

Lily pad is the likely place
The frog will chase
The evening's dream
Will enhance the scheme
The faithful will keep abreast
Via the lady's digest

The salad was fresh, the dressing Elias' own brand of magic. By the time she went on to the grilled lamb she knew the message had been posted.

"This is simply yummy, Elias. You are a culinary magician."

The middle-aged man Friday flushed with charming modesty.

"You are too kind, Ms. Chara."

• • •

The muted din of pigs and chickens. A small window high in the dirt wall. Several straw beds on the floor. Morning air thick with incense, a ward against evil spirits but more practically against the aroma of a densely populated clan fortress. Maria's heart shuddered in recognition. Fujian, late eighteen-fifties. Summertime in Bastion's favorite part of China during the bloody clan wars of the last dynasty. She hated the memories, hated his perfect recollection, and hated returning.

He knew this.

She took stock of her avatar. A young Asian woman's body, of family and not a servant judging by her clothing. She descended the steep stairs into the second floor living area and found it empty. Further down, to the ground floor kitchen with its brick stove and built-in tile cupboard. Firewood lay stacked to the side. This was one of Bastion's masterpieces, the detail so sensory as to make one believe it real. Despite the depth and complexity, an exit still felt readily available.

Outside, chickens pecked the narrow strip of earth that followed the bend of the fortress' circular construction. The central buildings of the courtyard rose on expertly cut granite. Everything except the perimeter rooftops lay in morning shade.

She followed a stone lane inward towards the temple where the meeting would take place. Lacking were the hundreds of people that would live here; far too much overhead for the purpose of a council meeting. Most of it was overdone already and that was concerning. The extra effort hinted at a special occasion.

She found the doors to the temple closed so she pushed on them.

Beyond them a gathering of Asians knelt before a raised platform with an altar. Candles flickered and incense wafted. She counted eleven of them with their backs to her.

All of them early? Her guard rose. They continued their stance, unmoving and unreadable. She felt obligated to kneel as well – absurd, but there it was. It was his game and she didn't want to stand out.

She took up position and knelt, wondering why Bastion would not be prominent as usual. The answer came when a Chinese warlord appeared behind the altar. It was Bastion, sporting Manchu facial hair and makeup.

I am the thirteenth.

Immediately she checked the exit and found it barred. She closed her eyes. A group effort, then.

Calm. Fiercely calm. Head down, secretly feeling for the gap.

386

"Maria de Oro, Sequence Three of Grecian Royalty. Stand!"

She raised her head to meet his gaze. He had known. Or had found out, maybe thanks to the druids. In any case, it had come to this. She was too powerful with too many secrets. Bastion would send her on.

When she stood, the others also stood and fanned out in a half moon to face her, their faces now their own. New to the group was burly Gerold Severin, the G1 administrator for Europe. He stared back without expression.

Bastion came around the alter.

"For almost two centuries you and I made good on this planet, Maria. Fifty years we spent in love. Always, we worked together. I supported your formal rise to Council, though you had been my thirteenth for years. And despite your weakening resolve to preserve our plans, I trusted you. I respected your differing opinions. I often followed your advice though I sometimes felt it contrary to our advancement."

He stepped off the platform and stood in front of her. "And this is how you reward me. Your desire for power is almost cliché."

"You're becoming ill, Bastion. You will destroy the only world we have."

"No." He shook his head. "No, Maria, I am not ill and I will not destroy the world. However, I cannot say the same about your world." He began to pace. "There is a beautiful young woman by the name of Ina Chen living in the Pearl River Delta region of southeastern China. She's just been taken hostage by a crime lord. Her mind is sharp and she is already plotting escape. Unfortunately, the crime lord is going to gouge her eyes out and make her his sex slave."

"You will have a hard time keeping me in that mesh. I hope you're all prepared for the fight."

Bastion walked the length of the gathered council. "My friends, your efforts to handle Maria will not be required, just as they are not right now. She will be placed in Ina Chen's body and held there. Volgograd rangers will oversee her punishment, a painful, purely physical existence before being killed." He looked at Maria, measuring reaction. "I've arranged for you to be collected by Eden, eventually." His expression changed to reflect something like sincere regret had it not been so perverted by the pallor of revenge. "I wish you had been truthful with me, I really do. We would have talked it through."

The floor of reality shimmered, threading fear into Maria's core. A horrible mind group approached, quick and sickening, full of evil and nail-strong intent. They were rangers but empowered in a strange way. Combined, they were more powerful. *Which team had he sent for her?*

She addressed the council. "This can happen to you. Volgograd's research will be your undoing. You'll regret this. You all will."

The last she heard was Bastion saying, "Somehow I doubt—" before the rangers stole her every thought and replaced them with their own.

• • •

Atop the roof of a bank outside of Rome, two square panels on pan-tilt mounts carried data traffic between identical panels miles away at the apartment and at the farm where the bràthair worked from. The pan mounts were radio controlled, ready to be repositioned to scramble the telltale line of sight configurations.

From the farm, shùil-equipped druids acted as bràthair and monitored Maria's Greek estate as well as Samantha Sigler's blog. Via the temporary wifi network, they passed imagery to those in the apartment. Sean ate breakfast and watched a laptop's screen. He watched as Maria swam morning laps in the pool.

Johan's voice sounded from the bedrooms. He was rousing Cathbad to join him. They came down the hall together.

"Something's happened to her," Johan said.

"Who?"

"Maria. I woke and felt it." He started to pace. "She's trapped."

Sean looked at the screen. "That's not Maria?"

"Can't be. Not anymore."

Sean ordered the farm evacuated and the bank's wifi panels repositioned. He turned to Johan.

"Failure is not an option. She's an incredible asset. We need to know for sure."

Johan parted the blinds and peered across the street at a villa with pale green walls and a terra cotta roof. From a second story balcony a woman shook a carpet clean with her face turned away from the dust. She finished, her expression one of self-contained, casual contentment; he remembered the feeling. Beyond the villa, olive trees ran in rows, dormant for the winter. It was the normal world, yet he felt like a visitor now.

He let the blinds snap closed. "I'll look for her. There's no other way."

"Clare will help in this," Cathbad said. "She has the strongest and most recent impressions of Maria. She will know how to find her."

• • •

Two miles from Vatican City, Anki took in the hotel auditorium from the back row and sighed. Attendance to the sold-out investor exposition had been crippled by the world crisis. It was difficult sitting there listening to talk of investment devices, especially in a business suit. She hadn't worn a skirt and heels since just after college.

Several seats over on her right, a German broker kept peripheral watch, wild with hopes for a chance at banging her. To her left and a row forward, a prim female independent investor from Copenhagen absorbed the session's presentation with impressive focus.

For Anki, the panel of speakers could not have been more dry and tedious. No spontaneity. No sense of the small gathering's mood. They worked through a PowerPoint slideshow with information that a week ago may have meant something. The chaos of the global markets had stolen their thunder and spirit. Only the host had any spark and that he tempered so as not to appear ridiculous compared to his panel.

One of the slides for a resort property showed a poolside sunbather in a bikini. That intensified the German broker's vibe, earning her a full-on glance. Ignoring him only twisted his spiraling obsession. She considered moving forward a few rows when her cell phone vibrated.

"Ms. Renate, I'm sorry but you are needed at the office. A driver is waiting at the taxi queue."

She eyed the hormonal broker. He looked over instantly, keyed to the slightest brush of meta.

"Thank you. I'll be right out."

• • •

Clare shook her head at the recording of Maria swimming.

"Obviously a cover. This one knows she's supposed to be someone important and is enjoying the role."

"Because she's really not."

"Yes. She's good for show, but that isn't Maria."

Clare faded quickly, leaving her daughter at the forefront as a courtesy. Anki had grown more comfortable with the duality and letting her mother surface. The wine helped.

389

Johan sighed. "So she's lost then. Bastion must have her."

"It would seem so," Cathbad said.

"Damn it. What now?"

Cathbad looked at the pair. "Anki, your mother spent time engaged with Maria. Join with Johan and go deep within her, see what you can find of Maria's essence. Then use it to find her. We have to know if she can be grabbed."

Anki plopped on the bed and scooted to make room for Johan.

He sat on the edge and studied her. "You're nervous."

"Yeah, well I've never done this."

"We just have to find more about Marie. A little survey, is all."

He laid down beside her. Eventually their calm breathing filled the room. A car passed by. Voices from outside the pub next door carried over. He wouldn't start until she was ready.

"Do you think we'll have to face Bastion?"

He shrugged. "If we do, then it will be the time for it. First we have to get a good feeling for Maria."

She slid her hand into his. "I love you, Johan." Saying it aloud was a validation, confirming all they'd felt together and while apart.

He faced her. "I know. And you know I love you, Anki."

"I do." She stayed in the cradle of his eyes, not wanting to leave. "We should start."

"I know." He smiled. "But you aren't ready yet."

With that, she was.

Familiar. Warm. Integrated. Intimate.

Johan and Anki lingered in the bliss of the joined space, their first time so perfectly and lucidly connected. All comfort and ease, he molded with her as if he'd been there all along. Thoughts entwined and mixed, shaping a shared perspective from their duality.

From the shade of surrounding thought, Clare emerged, a single light, small and subdued – used to being overlooked, careful not to shine; survival minded. She approached, gaining in size but dimming to compensate. Dozens of hair-thin probes unfurled, stretching outward, seeking communion. At contact, a flow began and they entered a new space defined by three instead of two.

Anki faded to a point just behind him, shifted to become an observer. He pushed forward into Clare and affronted all convention to slip between the structures that shielded her core. Blinded by the rush of foreign assemblies of thought, Anki shuddered and shielded herself in Johan's strength. Glimpses revealed molecular-scale representations of her mother's memory, piercing and overriding in their proximity. A single unit's intense loneliness stole her attention and nearly ripped her free. Johan pulled her in tighter in response.

He navigated by intuition, shifting perception gradually until he encountered memories tinged with Maria's feel. Those few already turned by Clare and Steffan lay exposed and familiar. The rest needed attention and interpretation. One after another Johan and Anki engaged them, untangling associations and repressed meaning until the granular experience of each memory lay bare.

Clare was right. Taking without regard underlay everything Maria did; it was what every Comannda believed their right. Humans were in fact the feed nourishing their version of mankind's Earth, their empire.

So fundamental was the realization that it proved staggering, threatening to stall their focus and effort. Johan shifted twice to achieve enough clarity to proceed. They continued to scavenge through memories imprinted by Maria, sharing interpretation duty until they uncovered a complex knot unlike any before. Had he not been so neutrally tuned and Anki not so sensitive, it would have been missed as intended. He drew it in and together they probed it.

As if stored in the darkest of holes, shaded to blend with the space between all other memories, the knot had been crafted to defy recognition. Detail lay just under the stealthy non-ness of the memory cluster. Latching onto any aspect of it was like picking up a lively worm with wet fingers. Somewhere in the knot, Maria kept a very personal sense of self. He tried continuously but could only manage strong impressions.

They emerged from the deep scan and relaxed in the shared space again. Johan played through the samplings of Maria, building a profile of vibration to use as their guide. He included Steffan's memories and his own latest sensation of Maria being trapped.

Is this really enough?

Agreement came. It would have to do.

We're ready then.

Together, they pushed forward into the wash of Saoghal.

Finding a match for the profile didn't take long. Centering on the vague, trapped feeling of Maria, he approached slowly, trying to understand what surrounded her. A dizzying array of expressions washed over in the natural chaos of Saoghal. Some part of it, some reflection, might be a trap. He worked with Clare to understand scope and scale, to track position and intention. Emotions and imagery lathered and mixed until slowly clarity emerged.

Maria was held alright, bound and muted in a frightening state of existence. Seen and felt as through a looking glass, she seemed to want to communicate. Suddenly their proximity was too much, as if they'd entered a tunnel without knowing it. The feeling was all the warning he had before a piercing jab shattered reality. Like the moment you kick yourself awake, the next moment saw a new dream world forming around him.

His last willful act was to set Anki and Clare free.

• • •

Anki slammed her elbow against the door frame and stifled a cry. She pulled on Johan's arm, helping Sean drag his body from the room. Sean's meta flow coursed to keep the heart and lungs pumping. Cathbad stood in the front doorway as they came down the hall.

"The driver's here. Be careful, Sean."

"*Teicheadh ort!* Go already!" He handed Anki the keys. "The blue Renault. Open the rear door and start the car. Remember, stay completely to yourself, do nothing in Raon."

Whatever had taken Johan sliced through the covering bràthair and retreated without being felt or seen. No wall of korjé descended, no hunters popped in the grid. It didn't make sense.

Outside on the stairs, Anki helped Cathbad down. "What happened?"

"I can't be sure. G2 are deploying to find his body, which means it must have been a strike from Saoghal. Bràthair are doing their best to protect us."

"You've sent for Austin?"

"Not yet. If Johan can't break free then it's too dangerous for Austin. If they swarm, the bràthair won't be able to shield him."

She wanted to ask, *"Then what about us?"* The past pummeled like a hammer, amplified now and ringing in her ears. She'd known joining with Johan would mean danger. It was happening now far worse than she could have ever imagined.

The stairs shook as Sean descended with Johan hefted over his shoulder.

"Hurry!" he called down.

They reached the driveway. The old druid said to Anki, "Clare is key to helping the Change. Stay safe, listen to the family, work with them." He softened, easing back from urgency. "No regrets."

He was right, of course. She nodded. "No regrets."

The driver came forward and guided Cathbad to a darkened sedan while Sean dumped Johan in the back seat of a blue compact and climbed in after him.

"Drive, Anki!"

• • •

The two cars left in separate directions under the scrutiny of the pub's bartender and his three patrons. They each shook their heads at the Mafioso.

Some things would never change.

• • •

"I'd hoped you'd screw up at some point but wasn't really sure you would," Jesus said. "Seeking Maria again was reckless."

Blue skies shimmered with depth around him. Sand flowed above the desert, carried by a wind that tossed the man's robe. It was Bastion-as-Jesus, a suitably perverse avatar selection. His presence burned as intense as the sun overhead. Johan cast out to the horizon in all directions. It was bone dry and nothing – no exit, no seam.

"The Empty Quarter," Bastion said, following his thoughts. "They call it that for a good reason. Nothing lives here. Nothing wants to. No one remembers anything out here, just as no one will remember you. They convinced you that you were a druid's son, yet here you are, abandoned to fend for yourself. Do you feel it now? The truth? You were used, Gerrit, made so dangerous that we have no choice but to send you on. They gambled with your life, knowing the odds."

The words cut deep when they shouldn't have. Mind games were to be expected, but here, in this space, it felt games were impossible, that only truth could exist. It was a mind fuck of a tweak employed to put him at a disadvantage. But why? The framework had to require an army of skill-adapted korjé working together to form and hold it. He remembered then. Maria had mentioned combining. It had to be that.

The wind gusted and sand stung his face. Cracked lips burned. Thirst pressed in. Leather armor pressed the sweaty robe to his chest.

A sand-infested linen loincloth etched his inner thighs. Definitely all distraction, meant to keep him from processing anything other than pain and discomfort.

"What did you do with Maria?" he asked Bastion.

"Nothing you'd approve of. Oh I know, I know. From your point of view, I understand why you wouldn't. You, the poster child for a new beginning in humanity's evolution. You, burning holes in the structures made sacred by the Creator, stepping through them like you know a better way."

"It's okay for you but not for me?"

"I am the leader of an ancient race given the responsibility of mankind's survival. You are not. Without the Comannda, humanity would have imploded and destroyed itself countless times over by now. Your problem is that you lack the history and the context of Comannda rule. Without it, you have no vision and no regard for the structures we've created. You're a sharpened tool, nothing more. An instrument of power wielded by the priests. They would use you and Austin to break down the system until it collapses under the weight of what keeps it together. You'd bring that kind of change if we let you. Rest assured, we will not."

He spoke to an unseen audience, his confidence high, much like the general in the clearing in Epping Forest. Unlike the clearing, this stage had been properly prepared: it lacked possibility. Change was an abstract and unactionable concept. Johan was a child again, helpless – the stuff of nightmares.

But he wasn't eight. He still had his core, most of his memory, and the ability to think. Pacing Bastion and paying attention to detail was the best strategy, even if the only strategy.

Bastion continued to rant. "You must know, Gerrit, of the incredible insights you've provided our most skilled rangers. Our units gained more effectiveness this past week than they have in decades prior. Thank you for calling us out to a higher game. I hadn't considered we could become this powerful or that we would ever need to."

Johan fueled the interaction, drawing it out for a chance to understand the framework. "What I really want to know is, what took you so long? With centuries to practice, I expected better. Hell, I just used a bit of creativity and intelligence and overpowered you all. Obviously you and your twit of an army didn't have much of either. How long before others come along and overthrow you altogether?"

It was the right mark to keep him talking. Refusing the bait to anger, the Comannda's leader calmly started defending his korjé. Such was Bastion's confidence that he offered Johan the time to pry and plot, knowing full well the design of his remarks. That was troubling in itself: he was sure Johan was stuck and stuck good.

Forming such a strong framework would require combining, which was a group effort. That meant there would be seams – one of the korjé represented the weakest link. He had only to find and overcome that one in order to tear an exit in the fabric. But pressing, shifting – all manners of flux and reorientation – yielded nothing, not so much as a ripple in the continuity of the dream.

Bastion paused. "I see you're realizing you've come to the end of your game, Gerrit. That's your 'bit of intelligence' working for you, isn't it? It tells you your 'bit of creativity' is no longer enough. It tells you that you're screwed, if you listen to it. There is no weakest link. That's not how it works."

The wind whipped sand in his face, shunting any reply.

Bastion chuckled. "Well, enough. I'm off to watch the capture of Austin and your girl and Cathbad and all the rest of the priests. So for now..." He nodded a goodbye.

Then Johan was alone, a stick figure in the sands of an endless desert, squinting against the sun.

Chapter 28

He who trusts secrets to a servant makes him his master.
- John Dryden, 1631-1700, British Poet, Dramatist

Cathbad cursed traffic, careful to keep to himself.

Tourists crossing the boulevard straggled well after the green light. His driver appeared bored despite a pair of municipal police officers on the corner just meters away. He knew only they might be stopped for questioning.

"Definitely looking for someone," Andre said casually. The number of police increased the closer they traveled towards St. Peter's Square. Tour busses edged the sidewalks to take on passengers with arms full of shopping bags. "Some kind of special event in the square, I'm guessing. News crews up there. Two of them, looks like."

Cathbad didn't like chattiness, especially when it implored a response.

"I've no idea." In fact he knew it was a prayer flash mob, aimed at soliciting God's intervention on behalf of the world. Ahead, the dome of the Basilica loomed in the hazy mid-afternoon sun.

The driver cracked his window. "Mm. Smell the coffee. What I wouldn't do for a cup right now." He looked in the side mirror. "Uh, rolling inspection. Motorbike." He glanced in the other mirror. "Two."

"Nice day for a ride." *Do nothing different.*

Traffic pulled ahead, allowing them to cross the intersection before the light changed red again. The two riders stopped while side traffic flowed across the boulevard. Some cars made the turn and tucked in behind them at odd angles, adding to the congestion.

"Should I plan to evade?"

"God no. Please relax, Andre." Bràthair would have to handle it, provided they were still covering. He didn't dare extend. His was a purely physical experience for the time being, the best cover.

"Of course, sir."

The light turned green and the riders maneuvered into the lanes again. Cathbad felt it nearby, the stealthy extension by bràthair as each rider neared.

They passed, scanning vehicles as they went.

The driver exhaled. "Nice day for a ride, yes."

Cathbad watched the motorcycles. "Change lanes when you have the opportunity. We'll go left at the square."

The crosswalks ahead cleared, allowing the flow to advance. The driver passed on two chances to move to the left because of police standing along the sidewalk. Cathbad approved. The druid glanced down a side street and spotted a police rider circling around for another pass. Traffic picked up again and then they saw the reason for the slowing – blue police cars lined the safety lanes leading to the square. Police stood in the street, now waving cars on, not allowing anyone to disembark. The news crews were being hassled by dark-suited officials.

The driver signaled and merged to the left lane, accelerating to follow the curve past the massive pillars guarding St. Peter's Square. Pigeons scattered when a gang of youths ran across the street and up the stone steps. The road led to an ornate four story building and veered left. Broad pedestrian stripes demarked an area to the right where gray steel gates blocked off a parking lot. The cathedral rose just beyond.

"Slow. Now go right, towards the gates," Cathbad advised. "Don't startle anyone. Good."

They cleared a river of pedestrians and approached the gate. Colorful uniformed guards paid every attention to their arrival. One approached the car. Cathbad rolled his window down and presented a card.

"Passaggio protetto, per favore. Comunica Padre Septimus. E 'di grande importanza."

The Swiss guard produced a pen and ran it over the card. The pen flashed green. He returned the card and waved them forward. "*Procedere direttamente al Palazzo del Tribunale!*"

"Oh mio," the driver said as they rolled through the gates and onto the grounds of Vatican City. Another guard halted them. Cathbad noted a dark blue armored van with viewports just inside the gates. Dogs were used to sniff the car while guards checked every part of it. They were finally waved on.

"Keep straight, towards the arch."

A guard there worked a radio and waved them through, as did a guard at the next arch. The Basilica's walls towered over them. Ahead, a bloom of color spilled from a building as papal guards formed a U-shape under an expansive red canopy.

"Park there, within their ranks."

Alongside their ceremonial sabers these guards also wore compact machine guns. As soon as the car stopped the doors flew open and Cathbad was whisked inside.

"Signore Esposito. I thought I'd never see you again."

The guards wheeled Cathbad into the offices of Danilo Moreno, the Cardinal Secretary of State. The narrow-faced official sat at a cherry wood desk, as passive as the Zuccari portrait of Pope Sixtus V on the wall behind him. His spectacles hung low on a pointed nose to accentuate eyes sharp as blades. The second most powerful man in the Vatican presented as civilized but otherwise unreadable. The druid stood and moved to a chair.

"I am not sure why you thought that, Cardinal, but I am no less pleased to see you. You look well."

Danilo nodded, also a dismissal to the guards. "You are aging gracefully, signore."

"Grazie." Waiting for the guards to leave, Cathbad looked to the painting of Sixtus V. "Ah, the great Sixtus, rebuilder of a church in shambles. Cleared Rome of brigands, rebuilt the city, refilled empty coffers through taxation, and restored the church's authority abroad." The office doors closed. He exhaled. "May I speak candidly?"

"Please do. Start by telling me what you have begun."

"Not I, Dani. The Change has come."

The cardinal pursed his lips. "Legend? You're acting on legend?"

"Prophecy, not legend. You must have heard what's happened."

Danilo laced his fingers and rested them on the desk. "I heard the unlikely rumor that the Korda were threatening to reveal secrets. Then the nuclear bombs went off. Then the terrorist campaign began. Now the world is in chaos. Moments ago, I learned the army launched helicopters from Viterbo and are scouring Rome for a terrorist cell targeting Vatican City. I'm told evacuation is necessary and that forces will need to search the Holy See end to end. That is what I've heard." He stared quietly. "Make this worth it, Cathbad. Tell me more about the Change."

Cathbad frowned. "I cannot accept you don't know of what's happened. Allegiance to the Comandanti brings more in the way of information than that."

Danilo did not ripple. Instead, he turned and gestured to the painting behind him.

"Sixtus helped the church survive. Against the designs of those you mention. He leveraged what he could to help preserve the integrity of the church and the spirit of God in man despite the occupation." He turned back. "Those efforts continue today. I need say nothing more. Trust or do not. Now, why have you come?"

"You agree that without our solidarity in those days things would have become much worse. But that was then, Danilo. The church has weakened and become complicit in the transgressions of the Comandanti. Inaction can be as much a stroke of approval as deeds. I question if you could even manage a coherent message of revelation, now."

"The authority of the church—"

"—is nothing if its people are in fear for their lives. As it is, a declaration describing the Comandanti would be an admission of centuries-long guilt of that inaction. You would only remove the last restraints from their plans and throw the world into chaos."

Danilo shook his head. "And what are you doing? Have you not noticed the world coming apart at the seams?"

Cathbad grunted. "The world had precious little in the way of seams before this began and you know it. I'm following the path to restore what ought to be. To sew new seams in stronger material."

Danilo nodded. "Yes yes, of course. The trackways. You're following the trackways, dragging everyone with you. Damn them if they don't like it. Who cares if the trackways lead to the end of what little remains?"

"The time has come, Dani. I cannot choose to ignore it any more than you can choose to abandon your beliefs. I need to know that I can count on you to help the Change."

The cardinal removed his glasses and set them down to rub his eyes. He withdrew, once again passive but Cathbad suspected holding back a storm beneath. "What is it you want from me? What can I do for them that you cannot?"

Cathbad hesitated. "'Them', Danilo?"

Their eyes caught. The cardinal looked away and slowly replaced his spectacles. When he looked back, it was with sadness.

"You had to know, Cathbad. Why did you come?"

The doors opened and meta-strong Swiss guards entered, followed by half a dozen priests of greater power. Cathbad made a last push to reach Johan but it ended in an arcing call of distress. The violent backlash of meta by those subduing him nearly knocked him free.

"Don't," Cardinal Moreno warned. "Don't do that again. Not if you ever want a chance at reaching heaven. The rules have changed, my friend. They have well and truly changed."

• • •

The whine of a helicopter's turbo shafts passing low overhead drowned out the television's report. Instructions scrolling across the screen prompted citizens to call 113 to report any unusual or suspicious individuals that might be related to the terrorist plot against the Vatican. The small bedroom smelled vaguely of cat, unwashed laundry, and the dissipating odor of human feces, all of which would soon be overpowered by the smell of parmigiana baking in the adjacent kitchen.

Sean sat beside an unconscious Johan and watched Anki and Cristina finish cleansing his body. The old woman helped pull oversized pants up over the bulky diaper while Anki stood on the bed and lifted at the waist.

"Franco! Get the wheelchair!" she called out.

Her nephew leapt to comply.

"We'll download his new metrics to a deck then wash his hair and dye it."

Sean dabbed his own cheeks with a wet towel. "Cristina, what of relief?"

The heart beat. Lungs rose and fell. He'd been running the life system for over two hours, refusing to let lesser experienced take over. Too much meta and korjé would notice – too little and the brain would starve of oxygen and suffer damage. He needed a break and soon it wouldn't matter who took over as long as they did. He was not trained for the sustained effort.

"Si, Terenzio is on his way, just over the river. Franco!" She turned to Anki. "I will download a new face for him. Have Franco help him into the chair."

"Okay." Anki looked at Sean. Only the faintest feeling indicated he was tied to Johan in any way. "Tell me *before* you wear out, Sean. Cristina can help."

He nodded. Seconds later he cringed.

"Sean! What?"

Eyes closed, he sorted through information. "No. No... *madre mia*, no..."

Anki knelt before him and gripped his knees. "What is it, Sean? What? What?"

"Cath. They've taken him, too. At the Vatican."

"No! Why would he go there?"

The shine of tears lined his eyes. At the door Cristina crossed herself and muttered in Italian.

Anki stood and backed away, afraid her panicked emotion would distract him from giving to Johan. Questions and fear had to wait. Instead she busied herself with putting shoes and socks on Johan, imagining his return. She wanted him ready to get up and walk with her. Franco appeared with the wheelchair and together they loaded him in it. She pressed her hand to Johan's chest just to feel the faint beat.

A bustle from the front of the house turned out to be Terenzio. He called for his aunt.

"In here, Terenzio!" Anki cried.

A tall, handsome fellow with a mop of dark hair came in and immediately put a hand on Johan's shoulder. He gestured to Sean, who visibly relaxed.

"Thank you. Anki?" He stood and left for the back screened porch. Anki followed.

He sat heavily on a padded wicker couch. Parakeets tweeted from a nearby cage. Rose trees lined the small backyard's fence. The thud and whine of another helicopter sounded in the distance. The news had reported twenty-one of them in the skies over Rome.

Anki leaned against a post. "We are at risk then."

"Of course. If he hasn't cut loose, they have a chance at his meta store. The families have been alerted. I've work to do."

She felt his fear but also the complexity of something stirring. "Maria must be found," she said. "Who càn I work with?"

"A moment, please."

Sean leaned back and rubbed his face, a new effort beginning. His vibe began to shift as he worked internally to forge a new identity – a disturbing feeling. Glitches and gaps signaled he'd become morphic. When he leaned forward again, the new meta arrangement was in place but still changing subtly, as if settling. He vibe was that of a stranger.

"Right now?" he asked. "No one."

"You're waiting to see how much of the Family falls."

His expression grew more severe. "The families are scattering, shifting. We are at our weakest. Bràthair are fewer. Later we will rejoin and grow strong again. You are a concern. You are not trained to shift."

"So if they break him—"

"We assume they will. They will have a strong imprint to find you with."

"Can't Clare take over and hide me?"

"No, she is bound to you. If they scan, it will be your essence that responds."

"Then what can I do?"

He hesitated. "I must do it for you. Subjugation. Binding with a new brain and body will alter your presence in Raon."

"Please! You have got to be kidding. We have to kill someone?"

"You and Clare are central to everything. And right now, you are our best chance at finding Johan and Maria."

She was repulsed and had to hug herself. "It cannot be someone innocent. I refuse to kill an innocent."

"No time." Sean's look said that he understood the unfairness of the situation. "And for Cathbad it is all a matter of time. Minutes, hours at most." He paused, gone distant. "We need to move. There is growing interest in this part of town and I don't believe in coincidence."

"So either way someone's going to lose their life. No other options?"

Things were desperate but thinking of knocking someone free made her sick. Sudden death, confusion – a waking and unexpected nightmare. Then there would be their family's nightmare; a loved one thought kidnapped or perhaps run off to do who knows what for no apparent reason. The uncertainty they'd feel... it turned her stomach.

"When do we have to do this?"

"Right away. Now."

"We bring Johan?"

"We leave him. No," he held up a hand at her protest. "We must leave him."

He headed inside.

Anki stood in the bathroom doorway and looked at the upturned face that was again unrecognizable. Johan's metrics were new, the face a stranger. She'd come to say her goodbye but couldn't. Terenzio dabbed at the dye trickling down Johan's face as Cristina massaged his hair. The old woman met her gaze and softened.

"You cannot see him in this," she gestured to his body. "Do not try. See him in your heart. That is where you will find him. And prepare yourself – if you see him again, it may not be in this. Be strong, signorina. He will need you no matter what."

She wanted to respond but words failed her. It was as if he'd died and no one would tell her.

"Go," Cristina waved with plastic gloves dark with dye. "Take some parmigiana with you. Franco makes the best parmigiana."

Low, filmy clouds perched over the sunlit beach like exotic gasses of another world. Sean and Anki drove along the seafront boulevard of Lido di Ostia, fifteen miles from the Vatican, looking for a target. She sat in the back seat behind tinted windows and scanned faces. The search for terrorists kept some people home but not all.

Sean shook his head. "Absolutely not."

Plagued by guilt, she had suggested an old woman sitting on an apartment balcony. The woman had less to lose having lived a longer life.

Sean was losing patience. "You need an agile body, not a fragile one." His intention to act rose. "We don't have time, Anki."

"I can't stand hunting like this. It's absolutely horrible."

They came upon a woman fishing her purse for car keys outside the Belvedere Century hotel. Anki panicked at Sean's sudden sharp vibe. The car slowed to a stop.

"Anki, prepare."

The woman stepped from the curb to unlock her car.

Anki started to protest but the world jerked to blackness, a shadowy non-ness that swallowed sensation. The next instant the sun blinded her and something fumbled from her hands. She caught her legs before they went out from under her. She stood outside in a world filled with new colors and unfamiliar smells. A purse hung from her shoulder. Car keys lay on the ground at her feet.

She shuddered at the physical essence now ringing through her soul. Skin so sensitive, her arms and legs thinner. She heard a whistle and saw Sean waving her over from the car. She took two or three steps before balance and gait resolved.

She climbed into the front seat and Sean drove off.

"You did very well, Anki."

"I– I didn't *do* anything." The voice was higher, more feminine and flexible. She didn't want to think of the magnitude of the theft just performed or her part in it. She resisted the urge to turn around.

"I'm dead now. I'm dead." Panic rose despite herself.

"No, Anki, you are alive. *It* is only a shell. The woman you replaced is being cared for on her way to Gwynvyd. Soon she will understand. She will be comforted beyond what we can imagine."

She wanted to believe him. Anything to keep the feeling of murder at bay. Still, she struggled with it. The smell of loosened bowels made her want to be sick. Sean cracked all four windows.

He looked over. "We need to drop it off. No disrespect, Anki, but there will be nothing of a burial or anything close to tradition."

"I understand." She did and it seared to her core. The body in the backseat that she'd cared for and lived in all her life would be discarded. The body she was in was now hers, stolen from another. Yes, she understood – nothing would ever resemble normal again.

She forced herself to open the purse to learn who had lost everything so that they might win.

· · ·

Father Keefe placed his hands on the coffin and bowed his head.

"God our creator and redeemer, by your power Christ conquered death and entered into glory. Confident of his victory and claiming his promises, we entrust Phillip to your mercy in the name of Jesus our Lord, who died and is alive and reigns with you, now and forever. Amen."

Edward stood as the six-person choir began a hymn, joined by the fifty or so gathered in the medieval church. Old Phillip Shaw's funeral was both an unavoidable obligation and a timely refuge from which he followed events in Rome. He prayed for the many souls departing or being captured. Segmentation helped stem the bleeding of ranks but the rate of the felling was far worse than he'd imagined possible. There was no sure way yet to know whether Cathbad's plans had backfired or were in play, or if he'd even had a plan. He prayed for either his safe return or graceful departure before they had use of his core. The thought of it made him shift further. Sad as it was, there was too much danger in staying even vaguely linked.

The Concord of Ascension would be enacted soon if Cathbad didn't break free. Leading the Runa Korda in the Conflict would be an honor but only if it were in a state of unity. Padrig and the others might contest his ascension, a grim prospect given the scattering. To have the family warring now would make things impossible.

The singing ended. Smoke wafted from a copper thurible as Father Keefe censed the coffin, commending Phillip's soul to rise to God. Edward knew for a fact it already had.

He bowed his head not to pray but to think. Details of the strike on Johan fit no pattern he'd ever seen. To have overridden him suggested they'd mastered combining. What more they might learn threatened everything.

Father Keefe finished the commendation and addressed the congregation. He then passed down the aisle with his three acolytes. The singing began again. Atop the coffin, an arrangement of flowers seemed to droop under the weight of an uncertain and troubled future.

Edward sighed. He should have paid more respect to the funeral, to his friend's memory, but there wasn't much choice. Phillip probably understood.

Twenty minutes later, an attendant filed out after turning down the lights over the altar. Edward sat alone in the church. Rain played against the stained glass windows. Somewhere in the churchyard a set of chimes pealed low and thoughtful in the wind. Inside, stillness pervaded so deep as to slow the heart. The church had always had that effect on him.

Edward closed his eyes and sought the edges of Gwynvyd. Its warmth and light lay just beyond the barrier that contained all of life in the universe. With all his might he stretched forward into it, only to feel infinity – and in that endlessness, his mortal limits.

A messenger came then, with a ghostly and quick delivery from the realm of Saoghal. Bràthair had found the transport depot in the Persian Gulf, along the coast of Qatar. They were following a tunnel in search of the base.

Decisions loomed suddenly, each with its own possible outcome. The trackways were vague, harder to sense. There were so many variables, so many possibilities. Soon he would have to choose.

Edward opened his eyes and stared at the figure of Jesus hanging on the cross. For an instant it was Austin's face he saw, suffering in pain.

Chapter 29

A man's subconscious self is not the ideal companion. It lurks for the greater part of his life in some dark den of its own, hidden away, and emerges only to taunt and deride and increase the misery of a miserable hour.
-P.G. Wodehouse, 1881 – 1975, British Novelist

A storm front stretched across the Aegean Sea and blew sheets of rain on the patio roof. Lightning flashed and thunder shook the villa's timbers. Tasia worked on preparing breakfast for Gus while Austin sat on the couch watching the news, a half-eaten bowl of cereal on the coffee table. On screen, the Pope made a special entreaty to all organizations with power – governments, corporations, militaries, terrorist groups, and gangs – to cease hostilities and work on behalf of all people to restore civility and order to the world.

Tasia clucked and shook her head.

"What?" he asked.

"Nothing," she said, stirring scrambled eggs. She nodded at the television. "I'm only thinking how sad."

Nothing... *right.* He suspected the housekeeper knew more than he did. Segmentation was one thing – information blackout was another. Johan hadn't reached out to him since Maria arrived at Mykonos. Gus would have to give him an update of substance. The truth, in any case.

A report began that covered the situation in Rome, including the Vatican bomb search. Seeing the brightly colored guards bearing machine guns seemed wrong, like court jesters readying for war. He felt like a fool himself, sitting on his hands not doing a damn thing to stop any of it. Holding back was taking its toll, adding to an already emotional morning.

Gus arrived for breakfast. He issued greetings to Austin and Tasia as he passed through the kitchen. Austin followed and leaned against the entry to the white-tiled breakfast nook. Gray light fell from a circular skylight in the ceiling. Windows looked out on a row of grape trellises with barren vine leaves fluttering in the wind. He studied the old druid and could tell he hadn't slept well, if at all.

"Good morning, Gus. I was–"

"Before you start, have a seat." He scooped eggs onto his toast and took a bite. He waited for Austin to sit. "You're right, I haven't told you what's happening and for good reason. The Korda is on the run. Scattering. Necessary when the Comandanti are hunting and hunting they are. They've captured Cathbad."

"*What?*"

"And Johan, too."

He anchored himself to the table and tried to absorb the implications. "Maria turned on them?"

"Possibly, or she was discovered. We have Johan's body. He's been severed from it. But Cathbad... they have him."

"Where?" Intention and potential swirled.

Gus held up a fork. "Settle yourself." He raised both brows in challenge until Austin nodded his understanding. "He was last seen entering Vatican City. No trace of him there now."

"They'll take him to their base. Bastion wants to see his prize. I need to know where it is. You know where it is, don't you?"

Gus returned his gaze. "You have a more immediate problem to deal with. Your shift training. It's time to use it." He drank his coffee. "Tasia will help you. Go now. You're taking twice the bràthair to shield until you shift."

Austin recalled the thousands of souls fleeing Montevideo, cast out of life, and all those lost in Istanbul, Johannesburg, and Miami. He thought of the billions of people lured into ignorance and compliance by systems that limited potential and preserved suffering. And now more death, a massive trending tied directly to him. Guilt fired anger again, accompanied by fear. Intention rose. He would kill Bastion, rescue Cathbad, and lay waste to the Comannda's core.

Gus shook his head at the rising vibe. "This is not the time for emotional indulgence. Either contain yourself or I'll have you drugged. It's hard enough to keep you off the radar as it is. Now focus, damn it. Go work with Tasia. We'll talk only after you're done."

• • •

The wind carried a river of hot sand around Johan's sitting form. Atop a dune, with hood drawn and eyes closed against the endless dry world, he wished for sleep, for a daydream, for any release from the punishment of the sameness surrounding him.

Instead, nothing changed.

Not the angle of the sun, the temperature, the degree of his thirst, the shape of the dunes, or the color of the cloudless sky. Nothing moved except the sand and wind, and even those he found ran in patterns. The landscape held no vibe, no echo of character other than his own. He was alone and isolated beyond anything he'd imagined possible, completely locked into a physical experience with no hope of escape.

No change.

No chance of sleep.

No relief.

It was the exact opposite of what he'd come to know. Imagination lacked, intuition failed, inspiration flat lined. He could no more leave for Saoghal than he could fly from the desert or cool the hot winds. Something had claimed his soul. Doubts formed about it being Bastion and his korjé, combined or not. It was the most complete state he'd ever experienced, unlike any dream or waking state in memory.

For the hundredth time he attempted to scour the edges of what passed as reality. As before, he found only what five senses could gather. It left him feeling plastic, an accessory for the scene. Purpose waned. Memory of the Conflict stirred him less and less. Time had stopped its march and left him to die.

He forced air across his vocal chords just to experience change. The mournful sound matched the useless feeling that had taken hold. Distantly he knew the apathetic state was a form of surrender. He stirred and opened his eyes, unwilling to give in. The sand flow mesmerized, encouraging inaction. He started to chant. Long, measured intonations to restore a sense of control. Should an opportunity come, he had to be empowered and sharp enough to act.

Distant dunes restored spatial clarity, reminding him of Raon and of his meta presence. Even in such a solidly crafted bubble, something of his meta had to exist. Knowledge of that existence proved an irrefutable reinforcement.

The chant morphed into a muttered declaration: "I am alive."

Silence followed. He drew out each word again.

"I. Am. *Alive.*"

The desert suddenly filled with the sense of another. From absence to singular otherness, the difference was unmistakable. He clambered to his feet and turned in a circle, scanning.

Nothing seen, yet the feeling remained. Someone was in the world with him.

He prepared to sit again when he saw a dark patch at the bottom of the dune. He descended, dashing sand in great leaps before falling and rolling several times. He approached a brown patch and caught a glimpse of a hooded face. Close in, the beard was unmistakably that of old Cathbad.

He fell to his knees and brushed sand away. "Cathbad!"

The old man opened his eyes, squinting. He frowned upon seeing Johan. "I'm coming to understand your gift, Gerrit."

"You are, huh?" Johan scooped sand away from his head and shoulders. "And what is it?"

"Your greatest gift," he spat sand, "is finding trouble."

Johan reached under to help lift Cathbad to a sitting position. "I thought you already knew."

"I'm sure of it now."

Johan finished clearing sand from Cathbad's legs and sat next to him. "Here to rescue me, are you?" At the druid's glance, he said, "You tried, didn't you? Yes, well nice thought anyway. Any idea where we are?"

"In the belly of a beast, it seems. I think we've been taken in by a dark horse."

"What do you mean?"

Cathbad shrugged and looked up at the dunes. "Bastion's managed an extraordinary advance with his korjé. He's taken the lead."

"Why did you come then?"

"Things are falling apart. Without you, the Words fail."

"Well, I can't do a damn thing here and now you're stuck, too."

"Yes. It feels quite absolute, doesn't it? " Cathbad paused. "Then all we can do is explore."

"There's nothing but desert and sky. Not a seam anywhere. I've tried and tried."

Cathbad shook his head. "I mean explore the beast, not the belly."

Johan looked downwind. His shadow fell predictably stark against the sunlit sand. Blue sky met dunes in a sloping line across the horizon. Cathbad was right, the holders of the dream were directly accessible by the very nature of their position of control. They could not ignore the pair despite the illusion of desolation. The challenge was to find the right message to ignite contact. Contact could lead to clues to their methods.

"No need to waste time with introductions. Either they'll be interested in also helping us or they won't be. We can only try."

"Given that, might we surmise they aren't?" Johan gestured to the dunes. "We're still here."

"We've not begun, have we?" His glance was sour. Hope did not like being stepped on.

Johan turned to him and bowed. "Then lead the way."

"No. I think you should. You're much better at arresting attention."

Johan managed a smile. "Of course. Being the Change and all. Well then, we start by filing a compliment." He faced the sun. Through squinted eyes, he focused on what he couldn't see. "Um, greetings captors and fellow sentients. We are humbled in your presence. Your mastery of Saoghal is complete and awe inspiring."

Cathbad grunted at the sarcasm in his tone.

It was pure defense, masking his fear. He set it aside and let seriousness settle in. Emotions rose, real feelings.

"I do not know why you've chosen to work with the Comannda or what else you may have done to the people of our planet, but I know you understand why I seek your counsel."

Sand blew in familiar patterns from the soulless wind. Nothing changed. He coughed in the sameness. Confidence glitched. Cathbad stared up at him.

He lowered his head. Truth would have to suffice.

"Until recently, I had assumed that people capable of reading minds and dream walking would tend to be of a higher moral fiber, that they would have somehow evolved beyond the primal flaws found in most men. Why I imagined standards so high I don't know. Maybe wishful thinking after watching technology evolve without people also evolving. I wanted to believe there was hope for us, that we had room to grow. Well, this is my wake up call. The human mind has been exploited like another technology. You're working with the Council and proving that humans are still quite capable of being flawed despite possessing such great knowledge."

The desert's vibe held nothing except his and Cathbad's meta pulse. Emotions carried away in the wind.

Johan turned from the sun to stare at his shadow. "While you sit behind the walls of this... this container and listen to me ramble, billions of souls are wrapped up in a play machine for the Comannda and its privileged minority. The Council has controlled its slaves for four millennia. Slaves like you. Now, with your effort, our world tips towards a new kind of hell." He stared at the horizon, at the line between sky and sand... and he *became* the seam there – pressed against the face of whoever was holding them. "Tell me you don't think there's a better way."

The edges of reality shimmered and he caught the first hint of others. Focus snapped back to the mundane heat and sun and drying wind. The horizon remained the same.

"You had something there," Cathbad called out.

He had. Or was given the thought he had. For a long time he stood, awaiting a response.

None came.

He shuffled back and sat down heavily.

"Not bad for a first try," Cathbad offered.

"Perhaps."

The desert continued to bake them. Heat lulled, slowing thoughts.

Was it imagination that he felt tired? He entertained the feeling and laid down with his back to the flowing sand. Whatever the reason, it felt good to imagine being close to falling asleep. So good.

He emerged from the darkness to a neck cramp. With his eyes still closed, he felt the sand beneath him and then, vividly, felt awkward – something was missing, the absence of it alarming.

His eyes flicked open. He realized what it was: the sand flow was gone. The wind had died. He pushed into a sitting position. Something else, too, bothered him.

Cathbad looked over. "Long nap. Did you dream?"

The *shadows*. He looked up and saw the sun hung at a new angle.

"What's the matter, man? What is it?"

Johan explained the unchanging nature of the world and the sudden change. And his unexpected sleep.

"That's progress. Maybe you did make an impact. Tell me, did you dream?"

Had he? He couldn't remember falling asleep, only waking from it.

"You should try to reach them again."

Johan looked past Cathbad to the top of the nearest dune. A single figure stood looking down. Tan like the desert, the sandman was soon joined by four others.

"No need. Looks like they're reaching out to us."

At the prompting of the sandmen, Johan and Cathbad climbed the dune and were rewarded with a view of a stone oasis floating over the valley between dunes. A path made of stepping stones led out to two monolith slabs that created the platform. The top slab hovered above the lower one to create shade. Raised stone benches surrounded a shallow pool set into the center. The tan figures sat and waited for the pair to join them.

"What's your reading?" Johan asked Cathbad as they took the path towards shade.

"None. You?"

"Not a ripple. This is all very primitive."

Under the stone roof, the temperature plummeted to a tropical feel. The druids pulled back their hoods and knelt at the pool without hesitation. They cupped cool water and drank until their biting thirst eased. Close up, the sandmen's features were plain and the result of indentations, not actual eyes or noses. One spoke, the mouth feature's movement merely symbolic, the voice paradoxically mellifluous.

"The Council are again jeopardizing balance with their imperfect approach to oversight. We recognize their approach as flawed and incongruous to the needs of our species. It is our task to act on behalf of the world's best interests. To that end, we have agreed to support Maria's plans with your group."

Cathbad sat back on his haunches and wiped his beard dry. "Who are you? How many?" he asked.

"You need only know we share the goal of removing the council and restoring Maria to power."

"She's still alive?" Johan asked.

"Yes."

Johan shared a glance with Cathbad before turning back. "If you want our trust, we need to know who we're dealing with and why."

"You want ideology and purpose. You want assurances. You will not receive that. Either join in achieving the agreed goal or forfeit your chances at resuming your lives. We have already made contact with your peers. The opportunity to act is now."

"Who have you contacted?" Cathbad asked.

"The one you trust most, of course. Edward."

Cathbad's eyes showed his concern.

Johan said, "The plan was to remove Bastion. You want the whole council gone? And Maria saved, I presume?"

"All the council except three gone, yes. We will save Maria."

"Uh huh. Okay." Johan said to Cathbad, "At this point do you see a choice? Because I don't."

"How do we proceed?" Cathbad asked the sand men.

"You will be facilitated. Let us discuss the details."

The two men shared an uncertain glance.

• • •

Mr. Lathrop walked into the lab where Soldado had set up shop and home. Styrofoam cups and food containers littered the surrounding tables.

"And?" he asked the hacker.

Soldado stared at the flickering stats of Booty as it massaged the algorithms driving Overseer's encryption sequences. So far five different encryption models had been found on the Comannda's global networks, suggesting a 'protection by segmentation' technique. Each model had been broken using the second version of Booty. By combining analysis data on all five models, they had located several network routes to the base. A sixth encryption model presented itself that looked nothing like the others. Booty2 was at the entrance to the Core, probing it for a way in.

"Still spaghetti, but at least the combiners on the distribution equations are latching on to some matches. The deterministic generator is adapting and making progress."

"Time?"

He threw up his hands. "Could be any second, could be hours." He didn't say days but it stood as being possible. "If I can think of anything to change I will, but based on what I see, this is the best approach there is."

Mr. Lathrop cleared a spot on the edge of a table and sat.

Soldado noticed his expression. "What is it?"

"They're in-country. Heading for Qatar."

"Why the fuck? They found the building? What happened to waiting for the network?"

"The family is scattering. Cathbad and Johan are captured."

"Oh Padre Pio... madre mia. Fuck a *duck*. What does that even mean?" He sat up in his chair. "And sending Austin in alone? Now who's gone crazy?"

"Not alone. With a team. Bràthair found the depot and a tunnel leading into the desert. It dead ends, though. They're jamming remote viewing past a certain point. The team is going to see what they can find out there first. If nothing, they'll have to make entry at the depot and see where it leads. So you have time still."

"They'd better not do anything without more intel. We need to monitor the networks, see what they're planning–"

"Exactly." Lathrop removed his glasses. "We need to get into the base's control network."

He expelled a breath. "Then we wait for Booty2. No one's gettin' into *that* castle without some keys."

"We'll wait as long as it takes them to find the best way in."

"I don't like it. Might as well walk them into a bear trap."

"The luxury of time just isn't ours."

· · ·

The road lay flat and straight alongside power lines feeding Pearl City. Wires between the massive skeletal towers hung like the clotheslines of giants. A tired Cessna Skymaster sat on the road surrounded by the gray-white Kuwaiti desert. A blindfolded pilot waited at the controls while a man sat watch in the co-pilot's seat.

Outside, a third man paced under the wing. Occasionally he stepped out and looked skyward, his white robe flowing in the morning wind.

He glanced at his watch and shook his head.

"Salam."

The man jumped at the voice and spun. "Jesus Christ! Give me a fucking heart attack."

"You knew I was coming, Javier. What the hell?"

"Whatever."

Austin stood at the open wedge of the cloaked ship's hatch. He'd never seen his former trainer caught so off guard.

The druid went to the side door of the Cessna and knocked twice. The man in the co-pilot's seat emerged with a duffle bag. Like Austin, the pair wore Kevlar armor and holstered weapons under their robes.

Austin shook his head. "Meng, are you sure you shifted? 'Cuz I still don't sense a trace of personality."

The Asian-turned-Arabian flipped him the bird.

"Let's go," Javier said and climbed in. "I'm sick of this robe."

They hung low over the desert a mile from the runways of Al Uleid airbase outside downtown Doha. Rows of aircraft lined the tarmac with the most prominent being five B2 bombers at one end. Ground crews worked around three of them.

Austin zoomed the camera to one of the black craft. "Arming teams?"

"Yeah," Javier said. "Sixteen units each."

"Nukes?"

Javier nodded.

"You're sure the beam won't accidentally set off the bombs?"

"That's what I'm told. Hopefully we won't have to intervene."

Austin zoomed out and rubbed his face. Just another of a number of scenarios requiring monitoring. The effort was taxing the fragmented Runa Korda. Preventing attacks on cities remained the highest priority, followed closely by taking out Bastion and protecting the Confrere.

"So Edward is in charge?"

Javier nodded. "He's regathering the Family."

"So soon?"

"It's the only way now. Too much on the line. Especially with this rig."

While at Corfu, Korda engineers had scoured the ship with better tools. They found and disabled a localized signal being broadcast. With a transmission radius of a mile, it was likely an anti-collision signal for other antigravity craft.

"There's the Orion," Javier said, pointing at a screen. An orange blip entering the map from the east was an electronic surveillance aircraft. "He'll scrub the skies for other AG craft using that signal. His orbit will keep us covered all the way to the gray zone." He checked the time. "4pm local. Be ready, I expect a go message any time now."

Austin breathed deeper. Time. He thought of Puerto Vallarta and his half hour with Kaiya. Thoughts of her mom followed. Guilt burned like the ring of fire at Montevideo. Anger rose.

Meng felt it. "Easy. Stay in your lane or you'll crash."

His early advice formed from the darkness... *or you will drown in the pain of loss and of memory.* He hadn't warned about rage.

"Sure."

"And there it is," Javier said, responding to an inner message. "Soldado's crack hasn't worked yet. Without network access we don't know what to expect. We'll get inside the gray zone and see what we can see. If we don't find access, we'll be looking at an operation at the depot."

Doha's skyline appeared as capacitors on a motherboard, rising tall in contrast to the barren land around them. Patches of dead grass along the roadways spoke of the failed attempt to transform the desert into something of an oasis. The only lasting change was the concrete and steel and that had little to do with the oasis theme. The theme of old, anyway.

He slowed at the strange-shaped building at the center of a large coastal compound. Meng stood behind them, watching the screens.

"Funky building alright. Looks like a shuriken. Easy access from the bay. High walls though," Austin said. "Not much around it except those fancy mansions to the south. How much you wanna bet Commanda owns them?"

"The driveway descends under the building. How wide is that?"

"At least seven meters," Meng answered.

"And the tunnel?" Javier asked.

"Bràthair estimate about the same."

"So worst case we fly straight in?" Austin said.

Javier laughed. "And I thought I was the crazy one. Bring up the tunnel."

"I don't give a shit how we go in. Just let me at 'em."

The tunnel's route set by bràthair showed as an overlay on screen. "Go ahead and follow this."

Austin took them two hundred miles south over desert before making a turn southwest.

"There's a junction building at the bend. Another tunnel connects to it from Jeddah on the west coast. They run bullet trains. Maglevs most likely although there are embedded rails, too."

Austin shook his head. "No wonder you never found it. This is bum fuck Egypt."

"You mean bum fuck Saudi Arabia. And yeah, the tunnels are a kilometer underground."

They bursted another thirty miles south and stopped at what the Bràthair called the gray zone. They simply couldn't sense anything beyond it. Exploring the perimeter found it to be almost three miles in diameter.

"Go ahead and run your junk." Javier told Austin.

"Alright. Like I said, this ultra-wideband radar is our best bet, but it's high powered shit. If they are scanning, we'll be advertising our location."

"Just scan and jam," Javier said. "We'll study the results later."

"So you wanna play whack a mole with them? I really wanna go in, too, but are you sure about this?"

"Got a better plan?"

"Well... there's other tunnels, right? If we press this now they could get stupid pissed. If we wait for Soldado, we may be able to just board a train and go straight in. You know, under cover."

Javier considered the input. "Problem is time–" He fell distant, listening. A light grew in his eyes. "Okay, kids. New data, new plan, and time is short. Punch these coordinates into your map." He rattled off the longitude and latitude, a position almost two hundred miles southeast of the gray zone.

"Empty desert," Austin said. "Nearest anything is a border crossing village and that's twelve miles away. No, wait. There's a military airstrip just three miles off. Thabhloten."

"Get us there. High altitude approach, over fifty K, then descend to ten on coordinates."

"Ten K?"

"Ten feet."

"Okay..." A minute later they arrived high over the desert. "What are we looking for?"

"Nothing. Just go in. Ten feet off the deck."

The ground rushed up to meet them. He spun the craft to get a visual. At the foot of a large dune, they were surrounded by a flat expanse of sand and other dunes.

"Hold here."

"Who's leading this detour?" Meng asked.

"They aren't saying, but it's got a taste of authority to it. High authority."

"I don't like it," Austin said. "Just sitting here."

"If we don't have company in one minute, we go down for a look."

"Into the sand? For what?"

"Backdoor. What else?"

"Backdoor or trap? Seriously, who's feeding us? And what about waiting for Soldado?"

"Relax. Things are happening. This is the right way."

He shook his head. "I don't like it."

A few seconds later, Javier gave the order to descend. "Pitch straight down and dig thirty feet before using the short-scan radar."

"You sure?"

"How else are we going to see what's there?"

"Okay. Down we go to signal the bad guys we're here."

He piloted the craft into the sands of the Rub' al Kali. The wrinkled kinetic field scooped the sand around the ship as it sunk down into the sandy ocean. At thirty feet he adjusted the settings of the radar and kicked it on. The return showed the underlying topology was anything but flat.

"There, see the ridge line?" Javier pointed. "The lighter shades beyond. That's what we want."

He steered towards what became a large crevice in the rock floor. Scanning it revealed a larger chamber where a perfectly symmetrical disc-shaped rock lined the floor at an angle.

"Looks like a huge plug," he said.

"That's exactly what it is. Meng, get the gear ready."

"Abandoned tunnel?"

"Construction tunnel. Used when they were building the base. Sealed off and we're told forgotten."

"Forgotten, huh? Better be. How are we gonna pop it?"

"They say knock. Really hard. And turn up audio."

Again he shook his head. "This better not be a fucking trap, man. Better. Not. Be." He parked the ship near the rock plug. A slight hum issued from the speakers, the sound of the sand vibrating against the field. "Scan shows two feet thick. How hard to I punch?"

"Hard enough to break that rock."

"Okay. If we pancake, I blame you. On three. One, two, *three*."

He snapped the disc fully forward then back in a quick motion. A thunderous crack sounded followed by a rumble. Fragments slammed onto a metal floor under the weight of the sand.

"Visual."

"Can't. Sand's in the way. I need to go in further."

"Go then."

He nudged the craft into the tunnel past the sand collapse. Low-light cameras revealed the perfect circular form of a tunnel and rails set in the floor. On the sides of the tunnel were recessed panels that might have been lights.

"See the seams? Looks like rings, twenty feet each. Steel? Maybe an alloy. Wonder who made them."

Meng set rifles and bags against the hull.

"Check for power readings, any electromagnetic fields at all. See if they've got eyes down here."

Austin shook his head. "If they do, they're closed right now."

"Good. Let's get moving. Augment visual with the radar. The angle will level out about a kilometer in. Take it carefully. There should be nothing ahead but I don't want surprises."

• • •

Bastion stared out from the observation lounge as it rose from the MILOPS levels to the SUPOPS levels. Control teams from all operations branches now worked under direct coordination from CoreOps. Overseer managed the presentation and prioritization of all data and communications.

The models and techniques being employed had been tested in small scenarios involving multinational theatres but this was the first time they had been utilized live on a global basis. It was an ambitious engagement made more challenging given the mass dispersion of the priests. They were weakened but also less predictable.

He looked at an overhead screen and chuckled. Behind him, some of the council clapped softly. The screen alternated between cameras following the progress of a gurney through the Core. Prone atop the gurney, dressed in a commoner's robe, was the leader of the Runa Korda.

"Ganzai, how about that? It pays to think outside the box, no?"

Ganzai smiled and raised his wine glass in salute. "Yes, it does."

"I think we'll rather enjoy the next few hours. Team One has learned the locations of key priests as well as some of their civilian conspirators. Their collaboration will finally cost them."

Markus asked, "And what of Gerrit and Cathbad? Team Three has been quiet."

"We'll not do a thing with Gerrit until we are certain of the technique. Combining got us this far with them, I want to be sure they don't slip through cracks made by our haste. For now their containment is more than sufficient progress."

He smiled at the screen showing the gurney in the lift. "He's arriving. More wine, everyone. Get a glass ready for old Cathbad, too. He may want to destroy us but we will remain civil."

Ganzai made a round to refill glasses. Bastion ordered the screens changed. Remote views appeared from G2 and G3 in pre-deployment readiness. Initial operations in five cities were set to begin, the targets of which not yet revealed by Bastion. The floor behind the council slid open and attendants rose with the gurney.

"Sit him over there." Bastion watched the men handle Cathbad into place. The old priest's head lolled forward. He walked over and tugged at the beard. "Fantastic. He's almost exactly what I'd imagined."

A message arrived via his neural link. He froze. "Oh really?"

He faced the council, all mirth dissolved. "The Korda have found the Qatar line and presumably the Jeddah line as well. Probably all of them. Overseer, close the feeder shafts and recall trains. Monitor the sites and prepare total destruct orders for all but the Duqm terminal. Have troops ready there. BaseOps, extend the mesh jammer, use whatever power is necessary. And *test* it. Highest alert condition for all rings. Cormac, have Team One readied. Deploy the guardians. Focus them on all outer ring entry points."

"You think they will enter one of the lines?"

"I think they will try. They may use the ship, somehow." He looked at Cathbad's sleeping face. "Notify G2 to be ready to suppress any reports of discovery of the terminals. And prepare dirty bombs for Jerusalem, Rome, and New York City. They want to keep playing, so play we will."

• • •

"Faster."

The tunnel had descended before leveling out as expected. Cruising at a hundred miles an hour through the narrow shaft, Austin relied more on the short-scan radar than the cameras.

"Any faster and I won't have time to correct. What about 'taking it carefully'?"

"They say it's clear. Extend the radar if you have to. We've got to reach the junction quickly."

"Your call." He increased the radar and accelerated to five hundred miles per hour. The darkened light panels and ring seams flickered by on screen. What Javier and the others were planning hadn't been shared yet. Whatever it was, at some point he would be free to go after Bastion and the council... whether Javier liked it or not. The certainty of his grip on the fabric of Raon calmed him. He would destroy those who had killed and hurt his family and the entire world. He sat at the very tip of history, ready to inflict long overdue retribution that was once thought impossible. The thought made his heart pound.

"We're into the gray zone. Careful."

Sure enough, Austin tried to extend from his body and nothing happened. The option was simply absent.

"Okay that's wicked bad. What the hell could be doing that?"

"We need to find out."

A change in the radar showed the junction ahead. He slowed as a break in the circular tunnel revealed a platform and beyond it a large hollowed out staging area with tracks and other platforms.

"Still no power readings. This bar's closed."

"Good. Go left, head for the far side. We're looking for a descending ramp with rails."

The lights of the ship pierced the darkness and reflected from the metal rails. It was easy to imagine train cars loaded with materials and some empty, awaiting return. Presumably others would carry workers or maybe they'd used robots...

"How old is this place?" he asked.

Javier looked to Meng.

"Its existence was first suggested in 1919, either to be built or already built. Confirmation it existed didn't come until 1937 but with no intel on where. There was never an industrial trail for materials or labor or even rumors of projects covering something this big."

An opening formed in the floor, the beginning of a ramp.

"Down?" He lined up on the ramp and followed it into another angled tunnel. "So it could have been here all along?" Austin asked. "Built by others? Aliens maybe?"

Meng shrugged. "Anything's possible."

"There may be clues," Javier said. "Already I see standard rail track gauge. Rather conventional and suggests mid-nineteenth century. The precision on the tunnel sections suggests fine milling techniques but nothing beyond their capabilities, even then. The metal composition could shed further light. Until I see more, it's hard to know."

The tunnel leveled out. "How far?"

"A stretch then a loading area. Not sure how far. Keep the radar up and halve the speed."

They shot through the tube until eventually arriving at the end of the line. Rail switches lined the space ahead, further suggesting human tech. Three inch tubing ran along the ceiling with spigots at intervals along the track.

"What were they filling up with?" Austin asked.

"With any luck, you'll see. Still no readings?"

"Nada."

"Alright. Grab a rifle and a kit. You and I are going for a walk. Meng will guard the shack."

Austin stood and traded places with Meng. The druid had skimmed most of what he knew about the controls.

"You good? No questions?"

"I'm good."

He hefted a bullpup design assault rifle with mounted laser guide and spotlight. "Whoa, this made of plastic?" It was lightweight, no more than three or four pounds, even with a full clip.

"Keep it off full auto," Javier said. "You'll eat a clip in just a couple seconds. Grab your kit. We'll use the goggles."

He inventoried the waist-mount bag. Three clips total for the rifle, four clips for the Glock, four quick-timer C4 door bangers, and one fuck-you-asshole slab of Semtex high explosive with a remote detonator. Two knives, an LED penlight, five smoke balls, a small med kit and the low-profile goggles rounded out his supplies.

"Are these thermal? Or night vision?"

"Both."

"No shit? Nice. You guys think of everything. But no beer. I could use a beer. Wait, what's this?" He held up what looked like a steampunk shower cap with wafer-like elements woven into a covering pattern.

"Nanofiber cap. Might save your brain. Put in on first."

It slid over his head and side flaps velcro'd together to cover his face.

"This is for you," Javier said, offering him the familiar light-bending fabric.

"What about you?"

"The best trick goes to the most talented prick. That would be you."

"Well thanks and fuck you, too, pal. What about the rifle?"

"Sling it, keep it inside. Hopefully with that suit and your voodoo we won't have to fire a round. If need be, I'll return fire first. Your safety is top tier priority so don't engage with guns unless your suit's been torn. No, it isn't bulletproof."

"I don't like you being exposed."

"Just put the thing on, will you? And quickly."

He played with the fabric until the insides were visible and he could stuff his legs in. It stretched easily over the body armor and boots as well as the rifle.

"Tell me this isn't alien tech."

"I don't think it is." Javier shuffled to the ship's door. "Meng, stay open to me. We stay linked the whole time. Austin, ready?"

"Ready."

"Pop the hatch."

A damp, cool air flowed in.

Austin asked the obvious. "Water?"

"Ten points for Mr. Crichlow. Now, no voodoo unless you have to. The idea is to keep to yourself and keep your energy up. Stay stealthy. Comprendè?"

"Ci, ci."

"Alright then." Javier climbed out and engaged his rifle's spotlight in feeder mode to enable night vision. "Kill the lights, Meng. Stay with me, Austin."

At the far end of the loading area a doorway opened into a hall. Javier led them to a utility room with a hatch set in the floor.

"Bingo. Intel's good so far."

He pulled a lever to unlock the hatch and hefted it open. Cold, moist air flowed upward. A ladder descended into blackness.

"You still trust the source?" Austin asked.

"Sometimes faith is all you have."

"I'm going first," Austin said. "Seriously, I'm fucking invisible."

"Invisible, not invincible. You still light up my goggles like a Christmas tree."

"Really?" A few seconds later Javier cussed. He'd formed a bubble to hide his heat.

"That's a neat trick but what is it costing you? Knock it off until you really need it."

Austin took to the ladder. "Where's this lead?"

"To water."

"That's some serious intel right there, pal. Good to know."

"Don't get punchy. I need you sharp. Watch for cameras, flooring plates, trip wires, everything."

"Got it."

"I'm right behind you."

The ladder took them thirty feet down a cored rock shaft before it let them out onto a horizontal passage. Smooth walls also indicated large-bore drilling but only a third of the diameter of the main construction tunnel. It lacked any of the improvements.

"Foot traffic only?"

"Seems like."

They walked along the passage using the rifle's feeder beam to guide their steps. Occasionally Javier switched to infrared to scan for power sources from cameras or other electric devices. Ahead a dim outline of the tunnel grew.

"Termination ahead. Light source. Stay behind me."

Thirty strides on, Javier slowed and then stopped to turn off his goggles. Light filtering into the tunnel created too bright a wash.

"What is it?" Austin asked, doing the same. His eyes adjusted. What looked like raw cave formations loomed ahead.

Javier gestured for Austin to stay. He walked forward to approach the edge of the tunnel.

"I've got a bad feeling about this," Austin whispered.

"Stop feeling then."

Javier crouch-walked to reach the edge. "Holy fuck."

"What?"

"Come see. Carefully."

Austin crouched beside him. "Daaamn."

Below them, hundreds of lights illuminated an underground reservoir stretching away into the distance. Floodlights along the bottom showed a depth of hundreds of feet. The water was so clear they could see individual rocks and into sinkholes that fed lower passages. Four columns of rock stood as if placed there by a race of giants to support the cavern. Smaller ones lay collapsed along the bottom.

"What the hell..."

"Ancient water. All that the region ever had, looks like. And look there," Javier pointed. "Past the second column." A cluster of lights hung from the cavern's ceiling. He pulled the rifle from his shoulder and used the scope. "It's the bottom of the Core."

Austin brought out his rifle and scoped in.

The structure protruding from the ceiling was huge. He resolved scale by spotting windows in the structure. A latticework cord hanging from it contained a pipe that descended into the water below. Probably a feeder for the Core's water supply.

"What do you think?" Javier asked.

He continued to scan the upper structure. "The lattice has a ladder."

"So there's an entrance."

"Has to be." Austin lowered his rifle.

"How do you feel?"

"Ready." He felt strong, capable, and connected to the potential around him. He wanted only the chance to destroy the council. Whatever it took. Anything between him and that act was going to have problems. "Ready to take care of business."

"Good, because this is the most business I've ever seen."

He thought about it. "I'd still like to know where all this information is coming from. Who's guiding us in and why."

"So would I. Segmentation, though. They are protecting the source."

"But do they even know the source?"

"No clue." He pointed to the Core. "You'll have to carry me over."

Austin estimated the distance, gauging the effort required. Not much, but once they made entry… reaching the Council would require downing many obstacles, the danger incalculable. For some reason he thought of Javier's son, Miguelito. He asked about him and received a sharp look.

It was there in the silence, in the glance, something Javier didn't want to slip, something he didn't want to even be. The druid looked away.

"Oh god. They got to him, didn't they? That's why you're here."

Javier walled up, containing whatever raged within.

The world tilted then, as realization struck. He pulled back the fabric to reveal his head. "Meng, too. They got to Marcel." Guilt found a new foothold and kicked viciously. "Oh my god. They back traced. Fuck. It's all my fault. Both—"

Javier pinned him with a stare. "Enough. Stop trippin' on things that aren't your doing. You didn't lead them. You didn't know. No one did. Don't you get it? There's only one thing to focus on now. We go up there and we get the council. We take off the motherfucking head. Whatever the cost. Whatever the price. That's our job."

The druid's intensity burned through the fog of loss and guilt, reigniting his own anger.

"That's better. Focus. You're what's left of the Change and this is our last chance. We're going to find them and end them. Now, are you ready to fly us over there?"

"I need to know the plan. We kill their bodies, they just land in others. What's going to stop them?"

Javier shook his head. "They won't tell me and I can't afford to know. *That's* all I know. This is the way sometimes, so get used to it. Now, are you ready?

"You're sure they have a plan?"

"That's all I'm sure of."

Austin looked across the distance to the Core. Faith had never been easy. Nothing about this was easy, though.

"Alright. Okay." He breathed deep. "Let's see where the trackways take us."

• • •

Lathrop didn't like him drinking it but the tequila helped. Soldado watched his crack program's failed efforts climb into the tens of millions. Sitting on his ass digesting burritos while Johan and Austin risked their lives fucked with his head something fierce. People were dying out there in numbers, losing their minds and all hope, and he had nothing to do but tap on a keyboard and run programs.

He caught himself. No, he'd modified the Booty algorithms three times to keep it hidden on the AI's network and was helping monitor for the worst kind of action orders. So it wasn't like he hadn't been doing *something*. The time in between, though, was what got to him. Limited updates from the Korda made it all worse. The gold juice helped keep the worried monkeys in his head quiet.

He tossed back a shot and followed the burn down his throat. On screen, a yellow square lit in the corner with the number one. Another unidentified packet type. They'd become more and more rare as they analyzed and documented traffic. Curious, he brought the detail up... and sat forward as he read.

"What the..."

A long sequence of numbers stared back at him. The packet had no transport details and wasn't categorized or even encrypted with any of the five known methods. He called for Lathrop. Twice. The second time became an urgent shout.

The scientist arrived at a run. "Did you break it?"

"No, no, look at this."

Mr. Lathrop peered at the screen. "Overseer found us?"

"Something has."

"Pack it up, we're out of here," Lathrop said, heading for the door.

Another yellow packet came in. "Wait," he said. "What the mother lovin' sam fuck is this?"

Lathrop returned to read.

IT'S THE ENCRYPTION SEED FOR THE CORE, FUCKEREDFACE

Lathrop stared. "What the hell–"

"Fuckeredface. SlotZero called me that," he said, looking up at the scientist. "Johan. Nobody else. Nobody."

"They're drawing you in. They have him and they're looking to draw us all in. We're moving out now," Lathrop said and disappeared down the hall.

He flipped back to the first packet. The sequence was long enough to be the seed.

Use it assbyte. Hurry up.

He shivered at the thought and ran his hands through his hair. They'd either found him or somehow Johan was breaking through.

He brought up the manual entry field and keyed in the sequence but didn't press Enter. Holding his breath, he waited for another message, another sign.

Nothing came.

"Fuck hell shit damn bitch whore. *Fuck!*"

Lathrop hollered to get moving.

Push it fucker, Austin needs you bad. Push the damn key.

The message came quickly, resolving in his mind after it arrived. It felt like Johan. Every bit like Johan. Johan in a squeeze.

"Fucking voodoo shit." His eyes flickered from the screen to the Enter key and back.

"It better be you, dude. It so better be you."

He pressed Enter and froze. His irises dilated and his heart beat.

Every dot turned green at once. The failure counter halted just shy of thirty one million.

Now get into their security shit. Don't fuck it up!

He slapped the table. "Fucking ghost in the machine, man. You are the ghost in the *machine!* Lathrop!"

• • •

Austin took a solo run across the reservoir to scout the base of the Core, heat dampened to avoid sensors. The structure was immense, as big as a football stadium. How far up did it go? What defenses might lie inside? Potential pounded in his veins along with fear. Keeping them both in check, he scouted for a full five minutes. In some of the upper windows he saw people in white uniforms working at consoles. Cameras pointed in every direction along the exterior. Getting them both in was going to be tricky alright.

He returned to brief Javier, whistling softly as he approached.

"What took you so long?"

He pulled back the fabric. "Checking things out. I don't think they're expecting us."

"That's the hope. What about cameras?"

"Tons of 'em but I think I found a safe route across the top of the cavern. We reach the Core and slide down and under to the access hatch. There's windows, though, and people in 'em."

"What about the hatch?"

"Gonna have to bend some bars to get in the latticework. I can do that once I disable the camera covering the hatch. Don't worry, I'll make it look like it failed."

"That's a lot of work up front. Carrying me around, too."

"Getting in isn't what I'm worried about. It's what happens after we're inside."

"Well I've got an idea. You might not like it, but at this point strategy is one of our only assets."

• • •

Javier soared high above the reservoir and darted among stalactites hanging from the cavern's ceiling. In just a few frantic seconds the lights from the Core neared. He stayed in the shadows, navigating until he reached its black walls. Palming the smooth surface, he slipped down eight stories, zig-zagging around lit windows to arrive at the bottom of the structure.

Avoiding the cameras pointing down at the latticework, he flew to a point just behind a solitary camera aimed at the entrance hatch. A second later, the camera fizzled and smoked. He latched onto the latticework with a firm grip. The metal bars parted abruptly, big enough for him to climb through and reach the ladder.

He was right, Austin did not like his idea at all. All the posturing and pretending was to make them think he was Austin. "That's like using you as a minesweeper. I don't like it. Think of another plan." There wasn't one, despite a few ideas Austin put forth. They would proceed with the impersonation, preserving stealth to the last possible moment.

He extended a hand upwards and the hatch shifted, groaned, then popped open into the room above. For a moment he imagined actually having the power Austin had. A shiver ran down his arms.

He waited several seconds, then flew up and disappeared inside.

• • •

The steel door inside the compression chamber was locked. An invisible Austin stepped back, guiding Javier by touch to stand aside. He tried to force it and managed only to bend the door. A second try wrenched the lock free.

The door swung outward and revealed a hallway filled with three gunmen in tactical gear. He stabbed the grid. Guttural cries filled the hallway. The gunmen fell to the floor.

"So much for stealth," he whispered to Javier.

"We knew it wouldn't last."

Beyond the rush of adrenaline, the big feeling raged again. Something else was in play—

—he rotated away from the door in time to miss the blast. Shrapnel ricocheted into the chamber. The explosion reverberated outward into the cavern. Smoke rolled from the open door.

He leaned against the wall. "You okay?"

"Yeah," Javier answered. "Turn around full circle."

Austin did.

"No tear in the suit. Let's move."

The big feeling loomed smaller but in waves, reflecting possible futures. As if surfing them, he waited for a lull then went into action.

Small fires lined the bloodied and blackened hallway. He pressed through the stench, passing two doors to reach the far end of the hall. It opened to an area with a bank of elevator doors and a staircase. He peered up an endless stairwell and found it clear as far as he could see. The elevators had LED lights over each door with numbers reading as high as 212.

He clicked his tongue to signal Javier to advance. He tapped an elevator door twice. Javier raised a hand and the elevator doors parted, seemingly at his command.

Austin stood in the elevator shafts. Red safety lights marked each floor and blurred into a single red line far above. Cables ran up two sides of each shaft. Conventional design, not very alien at all. To think men had built this structure underground in the 1900s still seemed incredible, almost implausible.

The opening tones of an overhead announcement echoed.

"Austin, I apologize for the impression you just received. Your arrival was anticipated and we do not want you harmed. I repeat, we do *not* want you harmed. The guards were there to make contact and guide you up. Unfortunately you struck them down and triggered their auto-destruct gear. The most important thing you need to know up front is that you do not understand the larger reality at hand. The fact is that the Korda wants the same thing we do, just on a different timeline and with different terms. Everybody knows you and Johan can be the bridge between the two factions. We understand that, even if the Korda does not want you to. We are willing to compromise and we think the other Korda families do, too. We need you to bring them to the table. Please, I ask that you join us for discussion so that you can make informed and educated decisions. No further bloodshed is required, I promise you. I cannot communicate with you from where you are. An elevator will descend momentarily, so please pick a floor and it will arrive there. We can talk then."

Smooth. Years of practice. Centuries. The brevity and frankness was powerful. He could almost forget the 747 aimed at the hospital.

He tugged Javier to bring him into the elevator shaft. He whispered, "They couldn't have booby-trapped all the floors."

"But they could have troops stationed at each."

"Only one way to find out. I can take care of them."

"Then let's go."

They rose up the shaft, flying past red floor indicators in a blur. Austin slowed after passing a couple dozen levels. Still no sign of the elevator car above. The massiveness of the base carried its own vibe. *Fuck it.* He chose a floor and forced the doors open.

A wide hallway crossed in front of them with non-descript white walls and gray seamless flooring and ceilings. He peered out and saw doors and intersecting hallways but no people. He tugged Javier to bring him out.

The overhead sounded again. "That's fine, Austin. I want to address one issue in particular first. I personally regret the actions that led to Kaiya's death. It was not our design but rather the result of field operations gone bad. We employ a vast array of professionals though sometimes it is just the human factor that becomes unpredictable. We can discuss the details later. The elevator will arrive in just a moment. In it will be Hannah, my very own great niece. Such is the trust that I place in who you are. She will be your personal escort. Do you have questions or any physical needs?"

"No," Javier answered simply.

The cables zipped into motion, lowering the car. Austin sought the grid, gathering potential. More and more came, energizing the very cells of his being. There was more to tap, limitless – under the hood, between the seams, an ocean of it just out of view. Why it was suddenly so available was concerning. Shying away from it, he took up position to the side of the door.

The cables slowed and the elevator car came into view. It stopped and its doors slid open.

A woman no older than Austin stood with arms at her side. Mid-length brown hair fell across her shoulders in stark contrast to her white uniform. Striking hazel eyes enhanced her beauty. She politely nodded to Javier, noticing his rifle. If she was afraid, she hid it well.

"I am Hannah. It is an honor to meet you, Mr. Bakken. Please be at ease. I am to take you to meet with the Council."

"Step to the far right please. No offense, I just need my breathing space."

"Of course."

Austin followed Javier into the elevator.

"Director's level," Hannah said. The doors closed and the car rose.

"Do you know where my father is?" Javier asked.

She shook her head no. "I offer my sympathies. I am not involved in operations."

Operations, Austin thought, Her tone and expression made her seem artificial, programmed, incapable of empathizing with the murdered and missing subjects of 'operations'. Surely a clue to life in the Core. Anger joined the dance in his head. All he needed was a shot at the council.

The elevator slowed. The doors opened onto a curving hallway. Hannah smiled briefly and walked ahead of them with the grace of a runway model. Perfect people.

They walked in silence without seeing another human being, down unremarkable hallways and past unmarked doorways. Small glowing dots revealed the material of the walls and floors had integrated display capability. If the goal was to get them lost, they would have turned all navigational indicators off. *They might succeed.* He had only a vague idea how to get back to the elevators.

"Have you ever been outside?" Javier asked to fill the silence.

"Topside? Yes. It is beautiful. I cherish going."

"Ever been to Hong Kong? Or east L.A.?"

She looked back. "No."

"Why aren't you afraid?"

"Afraid of what, Mr. Bakken?"

Javier pressed the rifle between her shoulder blades.

She stopped. "Afraid of you pulling the trigger? It would be unpleasant but other bodies are available." She turned to face him, dismissing the barrel pointed at her chest. "You know I've thought about you. About how you must be angry at the management of the species. Angry at the perceived deception and injustices inflicted upon humanity. You feel guilty for Uruguay and Miami and all the other death and suffering of the last several weeks. But deep down, most of all, you are angry that you don't know your father enough to know if he would work for the Comannda or not."

Austin heard the words and fought a sudden urge to cease the madness. He could start right here, symbolically, by blowing a hole in her chest. One down, thousands to go. The hidden ocean of potential suddenly raged, demanding that he rip free of moderation, of tolerance, of sequential and linear thought and decimate everything. The Comannda. Here, all around him. The source of all the greatest evils mankind had ever faced. The draw to destroy was so powerful, so right—

"Is something wrong, Mr. Bakken?"

Austin, Edward had said, sitting in the study at Shamrock. *Are you with us? Is something wrong?*

The memory of the manipulation shocked him, restoring focus. Hannah wanted him to snap, wanted him to expend energy.

"No, nothing's wrong," Javier said. "Just go. Keep moving."

"Are you sure that's what you want?"

In answer Austin spun her around and forced her down the hall. Aggression lingered like an unpleasant aftertaste. He needed to stay in control.

They walked in silence until the passage opened on a vaulted area with a black glass wall on the far side. A single door marred its surface. Four floors of railings looked down over the lobby-like area. Couches and end tables served those who might wait outside the door.

"The Council has asked that you first be updated on current affairs on the surface. The issues are important to the overall discussion." The door opened onto another elevator. "This will take you to the Directors' chambers for your briefing. The Council will see you immediately afterwards."

"You're not coming?"

"I am not allowed in the chambers."

Javier appraised her. "Do I look stupid?"

Hannah half-smiled. "It's not like that. There is no threat to you. If you open your mind and take in what they have to say, you'll understand the situation fully. Isn't that an important part of decision making?"

"You've heard the term 'brainwashing', yeah?"

She smiled fully. "Yes. Perhaps we all are brainwashed in our own way. I hope you choose wisely, Mr. Bakken. Be well." She turned and walked away.

Austin watched her go. For long moments he listened until her footsteps faded down the hall. Javier approached the open elevator. He tugged him back.

"I don't like it," he whispered to the druid. "Give me a minute."

His eyes were drawn to the black wall where it met the gray ceiling four floors up. He rose into the air and pressed both hands to the ceiling first, then to the black wall. His hands almost tingled. *There*. He could only think 'trackways'. The feeling of knowing where to go was unmistakable.

"Hey!" Javier called out.

Austin turned to see soldiers fanning out on all four floors, leaning over railings with rifles aimed at the druid. In just seconds, they had the lobby floor surrounded.

"No need to get excited, folks," Javier said, holding his hands up. "I don't want to hurt any of you."

"Enter the elevator so you can be briefed," the voice said. "You will not be harmed. If you don't, you will be considered a threat and eliminated. Please enter the elevator, now."

Austin stirred the grid, potential at the ready. A quick count showed over two dozen troops on three sides over four floors. He imagined the attack, a complex strike but with enough energy… he prepared to let it loose.

Javier said, "I'm interested in what the directors have to say. How about they come down here? Theses couches look comfy. Plenty of room to sit and talk."

Austin hesitated, wondering if Javier could talk his way out of it.

There was a pause then, a moment that drew too long. The next instant, gunfire roared – Javier's body jerked as rounds struck him all at once. Blood erupted, the rifle rounds passing through the Kevlar.

Austin screamed and slammed into the grid, slapping the soldiers against the walls, some still firing wildly. He sent a second wave, this time with piercing bolts that struck the soldiers' chests, force modeling through armor to shred their hearts and lungs. Some missed, severing arms or heads instead. Others missed altogether. One shouted, "Up there!" and swung his rifle around. Austin sheered his head off before he could fire. Quick grid punches silenced the few remaining threats. Gasps of the dying filled the otherwise silent halls. Torn sections of the fabric he wore rippled light to reveal his armor.

He steadied himself against a dizzy feeling. He'd struck them all down in just seconds *and it felt good.* It wasn't good, it wasn't okay to feel that way... but he couldn't shake it. He descended to the fallen form of Javier.

So many armor-piercing rounds had made short work of the Kevlar cap and body armor. Blood flowed onto the gray floors. Part of his left eye hung from its broken socket bone. His face was covered in blood and breathing was raspy and shallow.

"They can see you," the druid managed.

"I know." He shook his head. "I fucked up. I hesitated–"

"Don't whine. Go get 'em. Don't wait..."

He went still then, his breathing gone. The force that had been Javier dissipated.

"Austin, there is so much you don't know," the voice said. "You are on a suicide mission with no chance of success. This can still stop now. I don't have to send in troops if you just enter the elevator and come up to the conference room. Set aside your rage and open your mind. There is no need to waste your gifts. I would hate to kill you but will if you make it necessary."

The sounds of shuffling feet echoed in the hallways.

Don't wait...

He rose to the high corner of the glass wall and released a barrage of intention. Shards of glass broke away from the wall in a sudden stream, ricocheting off the ceiling and falling to the floor. A rough indentation formed in the wall and became wider and deeper as he kept up the effort.

"No, Austin. Stop that." The voice echoed in the halls. "Stop or we'll be forced to open fire."

Troops began to file in again, rifles trained on him. He lashed out, crushing them to the floor. For the next several seconds, he alternated between drilling and killing, pacing himself until the first light poured from a small hole. The bodies lay in stacks by the time he bore the hole open enough to enter.

A control room full of people stared up at him in alarm. Clear glass walls separated additional control rooms situated in a wide circle around a central black glass core. A rapt audience of dozens faced him.

A uniformed man stood. His was the face behind the voice.

"Alright, last chance, Austin. Things do not have to get worse. The chaos on the surface can be quelled with your cooperation. Join us to draft the solution or die here and now. Be someone who makes a difference or someone who fails. It's your call."

It didn't take meta to see they'd been caught unprepared.

Good.

He surged towards the black glass core.

• • •

On the fifth floor in a closed wing of the Volgograd State Medical University in southwest Russia, four men and two women lay asleep in beds connected to IVs and EKG-type monitors. The room's blackout curtains kept it dim.

A door opened and a nurse pushed a cart into the room. If the patients had been awake, they would have realized she was a full ten minutes early for the changing of their IVs. She visited each bed. Upon each patient's throat she placed what appeared to be a square of pastry.

When done, she opened the curtains. Afternoon light poured in. For long moments she stared out the window at the busy thoroughfare, at the bustle of everyday life. As if called by name, she turned to face the row of beds.

"I am ready with Team Two."

She sat then, in a chair beneath the window, and waited.

• • •

Bastion leaned on the glass panel, ignoring strained requests from the others to move the lounge towards safety. His fingers hovered over two colored areas, one green, one orange.

"Hurry, Xuet!"

Austin approached, a floating specter belonging in the dream mesh rather than here. Even Ganzai stepped back.

The orange button turned to green.

"Sorry, Tomov." He touched the panel to activate the field.

Overseer's synth voice announced activation. "CONTAINMENT COMPLETE."

"In theory," Nora said as she joined the others in returning to the window.

Austin's expression changed. He cast about and found the invisible edges with growing panic.

Bastion regained composure. "See, it's done."

The field had been defined to encompass the directors' conference room, not the control room Austin had bored into. Xuet successfully relocated the field just in time. Unfortunately, Director Tomov and his crew were stuck inside its boundaries and might be the first casualties of Austin's desperation. He opened a channel to the room.

"Austin, you'll be held until you calm down. You don't trust us and that's understandable. The gaps in your knowledge of the truth are severe but not insurmountable. There is someone whom I think is best suited to help fill you in. Someone you know and can trust."

The black glass turned transparent. A wave of surprise rose from the control rooms. Apparently the Council did not reveal itself to anyone.

"Austin, I believe you recognize this man?"

• • •

Austin flew to within feet of the glass and pressed a hand to the field.

His dad stood behind the glass in a white uniform.

It couldn't be him.

No. They'd taken over his body. Subjugated him.

That wasn't his dad. *He* was long gone.

"Son, I know this is a shock but it's incredibly important that you listen to me. Really listen. Don't act, don't react. Just listen."

It was exactly what he would say. His mannerisms, too, were familiar. His presence filled his senses.

He blinked away tears that wanted to form. It had been a possibility, but seeing him now forced a painful reality. He fought to keep a mission perspective. The man next to his dad had to be Bastion. Beyond them, Cathbad sat propped in a chair as if dead or asleep. He counted two guards which left the remaining eleven as the Council.

"Austin, nothing I can say in the next few minutes will justify the nukes in your mind but there is a larger narrative at work that goes far beyond your current understanding. Trust me on that for now. What you have accomplished so far in the service of the Runa Korda is amazing. It's astounding and I'm proud of your choices *knowing what you know.* But it is absolutely imperative that you stand down long enough to hear the entire truth. You've only been given parts of it and have been steered according to a specific agenda."

"And you haven't?" He forced a laugh and turned away from the glass, unable to handle the conflicting thoughts. Why hadn't he reached out to him? Why hadn't he shared more earlier? How could anything truly justify killing hundreds of thousands of people? Or making the world the mess it was? More than anything he wanted his dad to be acting under duress, not as a spokesperson for the Comannda. If not that, then he wanted him to be an imposter, an agent. Not his father.

He turned and stabbed a finger at Bastion. "You shot my friend down when you thought it was me. You weren't able to capture me so you went for the kill. Now you've got me and for what? Brainwashing? Forget it. Playing gods and making the world the way it is will never be okay, no matter how comfortable a life you offer me. And I'll be damned if I'm going to let you study me. I will not become a template for a human weapon factory."

"Austin," his father began. "You've been–"

"Just shut up. Who you were to me was based on a lie. You are not human now, if you ever were. You are Comannda. That's your choice, your problem. Not mine."

He turned away as if to reinforce the disconnection. A gap of some twenty feet separated him and the floor director. Four others remained seated and watched without fear.

He lifted the director clear into the air and positioned him so they were face to face. Speaking low, he said, "Director, I'm going to bust out of this bubble or die trying. I promise you that if it's the latter, you're coming with me. Now, how do I disable it?"

"The field?" He shook his head. "You can't. Your best bet is to calm down and talk with us. Seriously. Get the whole picture."

He tightened his grip. "They'll let you die. Help me and I'll see that you live."

"I'll live in any case and you know it. I'm just afraid you're going to screw up my leave. I've already had to reschedule my island trip thanks to the Miami incident."

The remark set him back in amazement. The director saw it.

"Look," he said. "You're something special. You know it, everybody does. But you've been flogging around, pissing off management. You want to make a difference? Stop being a tool. Open your mind. Pay attention to what you're going to hear. You don't know the larger truths. They matter. The world is a much different place than what you've been programmed to believe. Judge and decide after you know more."

Austin shook his head and put the man down. "You're just fucking sick. What larger truth justifies nuking entire cities? Or keeping a planet suffering for thousands of years? What can you possibly tell me to justify any of that?"

Director Tomov put his hands up in defense. "The nukes, I can't speak to. I hate the idea, personally. I've got friends who'd get sent on. Too many beautiful places would be ruined for a long time. Keeping people in the dark, that's another story. Without our efforts, without containment, mankind would descend into madness in just a few generations. Civilizations would crumble. They're just too primitive, still. Too close to being animals. If you listen and learn, you'll know it's true. Not everyone is made like you and I. Humanity needs the framework they exist in right now. The Korda are dangerous and their leaders know just how much so and why."

Austin felt a glitch, a change of indistinct origin. He pressed outward but the field held tight. Listening to the director was maddening – both for the disgust and the interest it generated. How much bullshit and how much truth? Were Edward and Sean ignorant of bigger truths? How would civilization behave given access to the experience of shared consciousness? Would it truly be destructive? Had Cathbad played him? The Comannda wanted him to believe so. Still, nothing justified keeping people diseased and dying from cancers and hunger. Nothing.

He lowered himself to the floor and raised potential. He walked over to a young woman at a console. All eyes followed.

"What's your name?"

"Log448." At his look, she corrected, "Logistics 448."

"Your name, girl. Your *name*."

She looked down and then briefly at the director. "Nadine."

"How long have you been working for these people, Nadine?"

"All my life." Again his look prompted her. "Since July 2nd, 1923."

Bastion cut in. "Austin, I'd like to focus on–"

"I don't give a shit what you'd like, Bastion."

Nadine screamed then, a brief but intense burst before she fell from her chair to the floor. Blood flowed from her ears and nose.

"What the fuck–"

The other three also cried out before falling over, lifeless. Director Tomov shook his head.

Bastion's voice took on new emotion. "This is not the time for power plays, Austin, nor for prolonged negotiation. You say you are a truth seeker, but the truth can only be found if you open your mind here and now. What the Korda has shown you is a version of reality, their version. Filtered, redacted to suit their needs. Cathbad is awake now and is wisely prepared to speak the truth. If you can't accept it, if you refuse to understand, then you will be destroyed."

Austin rose into the air to peer into the glass.

Bastion helped the old druid to his feet and spoke to him briefly before returning to the window with him. Cathbad's look was weary. His voice filled the room, familiar but strained.

"Austin. It's true. I withheld information from you. The Comannda in charge today are not the same as those that started the repression back then. The truth is, we have more in common with them than I wanted you to know."

"Nice try, Bastion. A sock puppet would have been more convincing."

Cathbad's hand went up. "No Austin, don't discount me. If I sound a puppet it's because I had so completely held your trust before while I lied." He began to slowly pace along the window, gesturing as he spoke. "I led a campaign to achieve goals that in the final analysis are the same as theirs. Why? Because I don't agree with their methods. You suspected it. I steered you from it as I have all the rest. There is much more but it's not important now. They have the upper hand. The Conflict is over. It was never meant to be."

"Bastion, this is a crock of shit and you know it. I may be new but—"

Cathbad held up a hand again to emphasize. "*No*, son. Set aside your bluster and feel the trackways. They will lead you to the truth." He stopped near one of the Council women. "Listen to what your father has to say. Work with him. Be prepared to help lead the change that lies ahead. The moment for that is very close, now. With your help, it can be achieved."

Floating above the control room, he was struck by the surreality of everything. Once again he felt split, but not just down the middle. Now he was split into jagged pieces, weighted by realities that could be, might be, once were, and maybe never were. He fought the rise of panic. There had to be a message within Cathbad's message. Was there one?

"What about J86 and all the nukes? And the wars and disease? What exactly is the goal, Cathbad? How is humanity supposed to evolve under these conditions?"

"All good questions." The old druid paced towards Bastion again. "There are truths that extend far beyond your current references. You cannot imagine what makes up life and what happens beyond it. Give your father and I time to bring you up to speed, with the truth. Only then will it make sense."

"Bullshit. I don't believe this."

Cathbad nodded. "Of course you don't. Because you trusted me. Again, I'm sorry for the betrayal. You were destined to be steered and it was my intention to do it right. To do it my way. Listen to me, Austin. As I created you, you are dangerous. If you refuse us now, you will be destroyed. The same for Johan. I urge you to consider my advice seriously. With your help, we can end the Conflict, end all division, and start down the aligned path of the ancient trackways."

Bastion put a hand on Cathbad's shoulder. "It is difficult for you Austin, but give us time and you will understand what—"

The druid spun suddenly. From his hand a series of lengths of silver extended to form a long blade, swinging in an arch at Bastion. In the same instant both guards fired defensively.

The sword passed through Bastion's neck, lopping the Comannda's head free just as Cathbad's torso exploded onto the window. Between the blood and gore Austin saw his father dive at the glass control panel before he, too, was shot through. Beyond his pain was a look of pride leveled at Austin. He toppled from view.

The field dropped.

Kill them all now now now! Johan's voice shouted from within his skull. *No time no time do it do it do it now now now!*

Austin pressed hard – slamming the grid forward into the glass Core. A wall of shards tore into the High Council, shredding flesh in explosions of blood and fabric. He bared his teeth and grabbed the field of glass as one to grate back and forth across the room, grinding flesh and bone in blender-like fashion. Death filled the space and left nothing to receive his anger.

He refocused his rage. The glass between control rooms burst outward like buckshot. Director Tomov's head exploded and his chest burst open, spilling organs in a splash of red and pink. Waves of quantum flux billowed, tearing apart people and machinery. Electrical flashes and fires erupted and screams filled the air. The Comannda were to die, had to. The ceiling bowed upward and cracked while the floor dipped and fragmented under the storm of raw physical pressure.

The field may come up again! Keep moving!

He shot back through the opening in the wall. From below guards opened fire as others ducked and ran. He pressed them into the floor. The walls lit with red alert symbols and images identified him. He bolted down the way Hannah had brought them in, shouting obscenities, remembering the souls of Montevideo. Bodies flew, smeared like flies against the white walls. Revenge flowed from their blood. He threw his voice into the killing waves, amplified to haunt their entrance to eternity. He felt like a demon and it felt right – so, so right.

"How do you like power now? How does death feel to you?"

At every corner he pile-drived those fleeing into one gruesome end after another. They weren't human, they were *Comannda*. Stolen bodies, selfish souls – more alien to man than any extraterrestrial race. Soldiers appeared and fired rounds that he sent whirling back at them. He flattened some of the men and shredded others. Hatred for the Comannda boiled over until he felt it physically. His face blushed and contorted. Intention swelled in intensity, the ocean of potential at his fingertips. He would show them what it meant to destroy.

Johan managed a distant communiqué: *Stop it man, you're losing it! You're losing control! We're free! Get out! Watch the walls, Soldado will guide you out. Just get out! Get out before you lose it!*

The warning hit him like a tap amidst a thousand punches but he held on to it, knowing vaguely he was not fully in control. On the wall a yellow Pac Man appeared, chomping at blue dots. To see the video game graphics interrupted the rage and returned a sense of self. *Soldado…* He followed the blue dots, racing ahead of Pac Man, knocking down troops instead of destroying them. Left, right, another left then the hall intersected with the curving hallway. Down a ways stood a bank of elevators. Blue flashing arrows pointed down and game ghosts disappeared as if following them. He clenched both fists and split the doors open to expose a dark elevator shaft.

The draw to rise up the shaft and destroy the base felt like a welcome heat in the chill of night. He could do it. The potential was there, all there, and so were the reasons. Millions of them.

"God *damn* this shit!" he shouted and shook his hands as if they'd been burnt.

He leapt forward into the shaft and descended instead.

Chapter 30

There are intangible realities which float near us, formless and without words; realities which no one has thought out, and which are excluded for lack of interpreters.
-Natalie Clifford Barney

Storm clouds dumped rain in the murky dusk, forming mud in the trenches. Bursts from a tripod-mounted machine guns drowned out the cries of the wounded. Orders shouted were lost to all but the nearest soldiers. A breach had occurred and grenades were expected.

Johan stood on a trench ladder and saw the improbable – two men midfield, grappling in hand to hand combat. A wall of soldiers rose from the enemy trenches and filled the sky with thrown charges.

"Change!" Johan shouted and blinding light stole the moment.

High winds buffeted the two men struggling on a skyscraper's wide ledge. Gray clouds wrapped the sky and cold air chilled them to the bone. Below on a broken window-washer's rig, eight of the Council stood helplessly, three having been released according to the sand men's plan.

Cathbad throttled Bastion's throat and banged his head against the stone wall. Bastion kneed Cathbad in a bid for control. Overhead, a pitch-dark cloud descended and coalesced into a band of black birds that swarmed over Cathbad.

Again Johan shouted for change but the scene did not. He leaned into it and formed a hand the size of a bus. He batted a swath of the birds away and took both men in his grasp, tossing them across the city—

—and stole into a pickup truck speeding along a dusty road. Sun-baked earth and browned weeds stretched out in every direction. Cathbad turned and nodded in approval at the tied and gagged bodies stacked in the back. Bastion's murderous eyes peered through the window at the two men. Somewhere ahead a border crossing with a single hut loomed.

"You've got it locked in?" Cathbad asked.

"I've got it in mind, if that's what you mean. God knows if it'll be there or not."

The race to find Eden and deliver the Council was on. Johan grimaced at pressure from the hunters. A pothole jarred the truck. The resulting bounce threatened control. He fought the sliding pitch of the back end against unnatural forces.

443

The road suddenly curved and rocks appeared alongside it.
"Bastards!"

He pulled the wheel and willed the truck to follow. Tires narrowly
missed rock. The landscape rose ahead, a sudden hill that grew
impossibly steep.

"Change it up," Cathbad advised.

The truck began to fold into geometric squares until it collapsed
into a single matchbook-sized cube cart-wheeling on the dirt. It slowed
and caught the edge of a rock and bounced in the air. When it landed,
the train's engine strained, vibrating the floor. Johan leaned from the
open window to assess the approaching tunnel. Thirty, maybe forty
seconds away. He glanced back at the car where the Council was held
then ducked back in at the sight of single-engine fighters lining up to
strafe. Metal popped as their rounds made their mark.

A fighter released a bomb that struck near the tracks and rocked
the trailing cars. Johan doubled their weight to keep them on the rails.
Another bomb fell, then another. Both missed but still tipped the cars.
Each time he countered with the needed weight, slowing the train. The
korjé pressed many distinct fronts, coordinating in an overwhelming
collage of creativity. Distractions grew – children ran onto the rails and
were struck, sections of rails disappeared requiring his instant
attention, black widow spiders dropped from the ceiling, and the floor
superheated as if on fire. While limited to the world he'd created, they
were taking advantage of their numbers to tweak it and distract him.

"Damn!"

The engine ducked into the tunnel just as a bomb hit the third car
back. The explosion sheared the car's walls outward which struck the
tunnel's entrance. A thunderous report filled the tunnel and the train
shuddered when the linkage broke between the cars. The engine and
second car shot down the tunnel line alone.

A dim bulb in the cabin revealed Cathbad's worried face.

"Keep it focused, man!" he shouted.

Johan peered out again. The light at the end of the tunnel grew
impossibly bright, as if a giant flashlight had been placed at the
entrance. The train rocketed towards it.

"Is that it?" Cathbad asked.

"I don't know!" Vague shapes swam in the light. He prepared to
release the Council.

The train shot from the tunnel into bright sunlight and the lurch of
freefall. Johan saw blue ocean out one window, sheer cliffs from the

other. Rails gone, the engine tilted and fell towards a rocky shore far below. He grabbed the window frame as he rose in microgravity.

"This is *not* Eden!" Cathbad shouted.

Johan pushed off from the side of the cabin and shifted, just clearing the mothership before it blinked into hyperspace. His tethered cargo recoiled behind him – Cathbad in a suit, the Council stuffed into a life-support crate. Billions of stars peered at them from every direction, distant but infinitely present. Silence pervaded.

Via a tinny comm link, Cathbad asked, "Where are they?"

"Fighting my ghost on the ship. At least for the moment. Think Eden. We need to attract it."

"Aye. I'm doing my best."

Warning lights in the helmet's rim lit and an AI announced a possible collision imminent. Johan spun in time to see the mothership return, fresh from hyperspace.

"At this rate, we won't see Eden," Cathbad said.

It was all too familiar, too easy for them to wedge in and push or pull the scene. Something drastic might give them the time needed for Eden to approach.

He burrowed deep and found what he wanted. The next shift brought them to a market in Barcelona. Crowds gathered to watch street vendors perform. Laughter rose above the din from a group of men outside a pub.

Johan walked with an old woman and pushed an old man in a wheelchair. The old man's head bobbed and drool rolled from his mouth. In his lap was a ceramic cremations jar. The old woman raised her brows and looked around.

Johan smiled. "Catherine, what a delightful dress. Purple is your color."

Cathbad wobbled alongside, awkward in heels. He ignored the jab and the garb and looked around. "The weave... amazing. Truly amazing."

Johan nodded at the compliment though he owed the technique to the sand men.

The throng jostled them as they passed under the arches of the market. Fruits, vegetables, fish, and meats of all kind lay on display. The memory of La Boqueria Mercat proved a beautiful setting to become lost in. The most impressive aspect, though, was the meta flowing out of each and every person – so authentic it formed several layers of group minds. At the edges of the dream, multiple observers dwelled with depths that felt alien. Almost certainly Mu. In the crowd were korjé, out-classed but still searching.

Cathbad stopped to sample a morsel of bread. The aged Bastion slumped and made a gurgling sound.

Johan leaned in for a piece of bread. "Heavenly, isn't it?"

Cathbad nodded. "But I'd rather have some good news."

There was none, yet, other than the freedom of movement. Or the illusion of it.

"I rather think we're being toyed with." Johan tried the bread. "They may have a way of keeping Eden away."

Cathbad scowled his old woman face. "Where are the sand men? I'm still not sure I trust them."

The sand men's betrayal of Bastion was not in question. What they might do after a successful coup was.

"If they fail to take out teams one and two, we have a problem. And if their intent is to double-cross us... well, it won't be long before we know."

Cathbad shook his head. "I don't like to gamble."

A group of merchant sailors buffeted the crowd, searching. Another three entered the market through the arched entrance. Johan moved on to the busy fish vendor and joined a hodge-podge that served as a waiting line.

The sailors were converging on their position.

"This is getting old," Johan said. "Either they're smarter now or they've got someone stronger at their back. Catherine, something more drastic is in order. Brace yourself. I've been toying with an idea and now's as good time as any to try it."

"Oh Lord."

Colors in the dream shifted hue, sounds pitched higher, and time slowed. A driving sense of déjà vu struck then, the moments of which aligned like gear teeth... he'd formed this energy before, had been in the market when he did, and had faced the unknown outcome before. The wet tip of intuition held the answer to what would come next yet still a fog obscured the future. He took it as a sign. Primed and focused, he pushed the energy to manifest further.

The market suddenly splintered, second and third dimensions fragmenting in a confusing array. He cried out, the sound lost in a crush of imagery and noise. Voices shouted among a cacophony of whispers. A background silence held the cries of millions. Agony and ecstasy rang like two bells in a darkness with a hidden light no man would ever see. Near felt far away. Familiar felt strange. Right was also wrong, and evil had expressions that ranged to the divine. He struggled and shifted to retain control but couldn't. The maelstrom he'd unleashed was more than him, more than he could conceive. There was no withdrawal, no avenue of retreat.

Layers upon layers of imagery exploded in flickering contention for dominance. Each tick of thought popped random experience. Rejection. Ponderance. Arrival. Displacement. Negation. Demand. Each stuck like a pin in an endless stream of punctures.

The beginning of it fell away, as did any expectation of an end. No sides nor safety. No height nor depth. All meaning arrived and departed at once. Chaos reigned. His sense of the others faded and one of sheer crisis took its place.

He'd gone too far, grown too sure of himself. He'd lost the others and been caught again—

"No." A whisper close but distant. The concept of speech pierced the madness with a sense of time. He pulled the voice around him like a safety blanket.

"What have I done?"

"Shhh."

The chaos continued unabated until it seemed he would lose himself after all. He had loved his childhood kaleidoscopes, had stared into them for hours, but this was a perversion of the beauty of randomness, a recipe of creation serving up a demented and disassembled reality. How anything remained *cohesive* in the universe – meta, soul, individualism, thoughts, let alone the rigidity of Raon... how did meaning form from the vast mix of infinite possibility? Who was *responsible*? A more pressing question rose: where was the pristine beauty and order of Saoghal? It was as if he'd struck a crack and fell through. He clung to the ebb of emotional response like a floating device.

"Impulsive and dangerous, dreamer. You create ripples in all that is."

Pale sun-yellow face with black eyes. He internalized the pang of understanding. It was the Mu with him, there in the field of –

"Not Mu."

Meaning flickered in the chaos, glimpses that became messages. No, not the Mu. The Mu belonged to a confederation, to the Owners – one of a vast collection of species.

"The Pure. We are free."

The Pure didn't belong to anyone – they were Outside. The Owners had claimed entire galaxies but the Pure had escaped their control.

"What is this?"

Beyond the mesh, beyond the Last Seam lay the raw stuff of reality, the ingredients of Saoghal. From here, in the wash of what felt like God's own mind, the alien race thrived and watched all that manifested. They observed life forms fish for meaning, divine for secrets, and contend for authority. From here, they had sensed Johan's affect and grew interested.

"Dreamer, you have broken free. Fortunate we saw. Soon Faction will act."

"Who are they? What do they want?"

Answers formed. Layers of structures represented the bureaucracy of the many Factions, the most advanced species from hundreds of galaxies. Together they tended worlds for the Owners. Who or what the Owners were wasn't clear, but their place at the head of the confederation was.

Earth was a new world, its life having been groomed. Saoghal was only a container for mankind, a kind of womb for their collective consciousness. The Comannda had been grown to facilitate controls and safeguards that would ultimately allow Earth to be pressed into the folds of the confederation. The Korda was another growth for greater control. The ying and the yang, both by design.

"Plans long drawn. You, dreamer, are dangerous to them. Young and powerful. Unpredictable."

Then he felt it, the approach of something massive, a form that displaced chaos. He shied away as did the Pure. The giant mass flowed, creating a distinct sense of locality amid the disarray. A sense of otherness arrived with it, something full of malice.

The Pure drew him in and away, surrounding him in darkness like an embrace. Silence bloomed, it's silky absence comforting as continuity and identity reformed. Something intimate occurred, the nature of which he couldn't fathom and felt only as an afterthought when he emerged in the virgin expanse of Saoghal. Cathbad and the Council materialized once more under his control.

Pawns, placed back on the chessboard.

Madness! What the hell was that? Cathbad asked. *Where did you go? What did you see?*

I'm not sure. Not what I'd planned. The space had been unreal, so basic and fundamental that it might have encompassed Eden as well as

Saoghal and Raon. He hoped not Eden. Heaven ought not be accessible by alien beings. To be adept in that space would put him on par with the Factions, at least.

Cathbad bristled. *Change this, we're exposed.*

Bastion and the Council pried and pulled in the effort to escape, sometimes savagely. Otherwise he felt alone – no korjé, no aliens, and no God. If the Factions could monitor him, they did so quietly. Across a distance that challenged perception, mankind's consciousness burbled like a stream, undulating and flowing towards an uncertain future. He cast in the other directions and felt unlimited expanse.

This is safe as anywhere to wait. No need to draw attention with elaborate creation. I trust we're here for a reason.

Cathbad disagreed. *Saoghal is a container, you just proved that. They'll scan and find us. Something, add something to shield us.*

Cathbad's worry alone made waves. Johan settled in to pace the existence of the realm. After the chaos, Saoghal's fabric became apparent. He entered the now-seen weave, lacing through and saturating it like the space between DNA helixes. He became an antenna, sensitive to the footprint of approaching meta. A web, and he the spider tending it.

You have something ready if they intrude? Cathbad asked.

Aye. In a dash.

The old druid offered an affirmative vibe, impressed and appeased. *Ten souls floating free. Nine with expiration dates long past. We shouldn't have much of a wait.*

One would think.

Pond-smooth moments passed. Cathbad broke the surface. *I've always felt there are others, in and beyond our galaxy and this or other realms. I'm left with the certainty now. Do me a favor. See if you can reach them. Be smart about it. See if there is a species that will intervene fairly, with universal justice and morality. Find someone to help. If not spiritually, then at least physically. Free the nations from their grip. Take down the ivory towers. Give man a chance to evolve.*

Didn't you try before? To reach out and find them? Didn't Pons?

Aye, but we're not you. I feel the trackways now. They tell me you might succeed.

If the Pure were what they said they were…

I wish I could see those trackways.

You will, when it's most important that you do. Be open to what's around you. They're inlaid in every moment, in every situation. The strong ones stand out, thick with potential. Learn to read them, learn well the path they speak and they will serve you.

Johan drifted in the memory of the pale yellow face with its black eyes and slitted nose. The first visions of apocalyptic fire had come true. They had been trying to guide him and had just protected him from whatever was hunting in the chaos. He would try contact again when it felt right. Learning to sense the trackways, even possible futures, would be invaluable. If the Faction held sway over both the Comannda and the Korda, the future would be filled with as much conflict as anything seen so far. He wanted to believe some in the Comannda wanted to rule in a more civilized way, and if so, learning of the Faction might create a bridge between the groups. Maybe even help form an Earth faction to defend itself from the Owners. There was no way of knowing yet.

Time passed and again Cathbad surfaced, this time with a softer vibe. *I am not sure what you have in mind, but it truly is my time to go. I feel it as a certainty.*

Johan didn't respond.

The trackways have led here. A safe passage to Gwynvyd is all I ask. I'll deliver the Council myself. I've felt your binding technique. I can do it.

The Council pried in odd ways, still trying for release. Johan pressed them into silence. Saoghal lay timeless around them, rich with unformed potential. A soul could get used to the peace.

Cathbad sighed. *Too long I've been in this world. I don't want another's body. I don't want to extend. I want to go home. It's time.*

He felt a movement, then. A stirring. Johan cast out but found nothing of meta.

What is it? Cathbad asked.

The stirring came again, this time recognizable and totally unexpected: a wind. Something from Raon, felt in Saoghal. Indeed it was wind, stirring to rise and fall as natural as any wind on Earth.

Eden? Cathbad's hope stirred its own kind of wind.

A scent carried in, that of ancient forests and wet bog lands. Johan continued to cast around but failed to find the source. A bird cried from a great distance. Then a drum beat; faintly in the rise of the wind, louder as it fell.

Bodrán. The war drums. Cathbad manifested a younger self. Leather armor laid across a barrel chest. He wore a brown beard braided with palm reeds. Muscular arms bulged with the paint of a clan. Gone was the aged face. He stood as a young warrior in the time before Awakening.

Johan cringed at the impression he made in the mesh. *What are you doing?*

More drums sounded and then a wail of bagpipes joined in a sweeping march song. The darkness of Saoghal split and white light poured across his sense net. Nothing of meta – it was pure Eden, where human finality met the beginnings of eternity. A dirt path formed. Green bog-moss and vivid lichens grew outward from it. Rain fell in shimmering drops from unseen trees. Welcome shouts crossed the span, familiar voices from ages past.

Cathbad pulled his gaze from the portal. In his right hand he bore a sword and in his left he gripped long hair attached to the head of Bastion. Embodied within it were the souls of the council.

I am called. The rest is for you to see through, Gerrit. Go with the Lord of the Wood. Follow the Lady of the Stars, lad. Trust in yourself. The world has a chance now, that much I know. Just don't let the families split.

In the shimmering space between them was the need for Johan to release him.

Are you sure? The question was more for himself than for the druid.

Aye, lad. You're made for this. Trust in that.

Cathbad lifted the severed head high. *Ní síocháin go saoirse! No peace 'til freedom!* He turned and ran along the path until the light enveloped him.

The release happened of its own, as natural as death and with the same pain of loss. In the emptiness the drums subsided and the calls faded. For long moments, the peace and beauty of the light glowed, as if waiting to heal his pain. The rain drops fell like tears. Johan felt the tug of indecision when two figures emerged from the light upon the path.

Mother. Father.

Johan manifested as himself and took steps closer.

In their eyes was pride and love and no small amount of longing. The draw of Gwynvyd draped itself around him. He held his place and shared their gaze. The sense of belonging made the distance between them painful. Choice lay bare, untethered to any concept or obligation. A few more steps would lead to the embrace of his parents and to the fact of peace and untold adventure beyond. Earth and humanity would continue without him, as ever. The scales of decision tipped heavily towards taking those steps.

As an anchor hitting bay waters, Anki's intentions splayed across memory, rooting him to the spot. *I want to try with you, to push the change forward. As far as it can go.*

That spirit still owned his soul. It called him back, calmed the fire of impulse, and dipped the scales in reverse. What lay before him was timeless and inevitable, best he knew. Gwynvyd and his parents would wait. They looked on with renewed pride as he made his decision.

I cannot yet. There is too much left to do.

With a final nod of approval, they turned and walked back into the light. The portal withdrew its vision and sealed itself, leaving blackness in its wake. The wind blew for a time as if keeping him company then faded into the eternal night of Saoghal.

He had never felt so alone.

• • •

Terenzio reached up and advanced the song on his phone. Again he reprimanded himself for not removing the annoying song from his playlist. The clock ticked closer to two-thirty. Another long overnight session with the stiff. Little Simon, the last feline of the litter not yet adopted out, lay curled on the guy's chest. Not the warmest spot around but it wasn't moving, either.

While glad for his gift of endurance with the life system, the work was far from glamorous. He eyed the face of his 'cousin from America'. Had to be someone important. Auntie Cristina wouldn't say if he was involved in the so-called terrorist hunt but it seemed likely. As long as they didn't bust in on them, he didn't care. Thoughts of achieving station in New York or Los Angeles made the long night easier to endure.

The kitty woke and raised its head, alerted to something.

Terenzio paused the player to listen. He stood and went to the window to peer towards the street. Seeing and feeling nothing, he turned back and jumped. The stiff was staring back at him, petting Simon. A shadow of meta emerged and he knew he'd been violated. He stopped the life flow.

"Man, why'd you pull that?"

"Relax," Johan sat up, careful with the kitten. "I just wanted to see who was taking care of the 'stiff' while I was gone. Thank you. Most seriously."

"Yeah, okay. I gotta get Aunt Cristina. Stay put." He strode from the room, put off by having been snuck up on. Embarrassment leaked like water from a burlap bag.

Johan petted the critter in his lap. "I am a bit stiff, actually." He chuckled. "Time to catch up with Austin, hm? Make sure the sand men backed off like they said they would."

The kitten purred and closed its eyes and so did he.

Chapter 31

There are two kinds of people: those who say to God, "Thy will be done," and
those to whom God says, "All right, then, have it your way."
- C.S. Lewis

The whir of steel cables, the blur of red shaft lights, and the shadows of the cars coming up at him made the descent a treacherous, sensory experience. Elevator doors opened and gunfire erupted from above and below. Rounds struck, sometimes pushing him off balance. He dodged into other shafts, weaving to avoid threats.

He flew past an open elevator door only to see a trooper leap into the shaft, firing an automatic weapon. A round struck his shoulder and nano-fiber cap to slap his head at an angle. Dots burst in his vision and he shouted in pain. His rifle clipped a cable guide and spun him wildly. He recovered only to take another round in the leg. He couldn't focus well enough to act. Frustration took hold and—

"Fucking stop!"

He froze mid-air and deployed a bubble as he had while over Tokyo. The free falling troop smacked into the quantum brick wall. Two floors down, muzzle flashes lit the shaft. He flung the dead troop at them. Flashes from above grew brighter as more soldiers leapt into the shafts and fired.

"Mother *fucks!*"

Down he went, nudging the kamikazes into the walls or cables. The bubble failed and he let it go. Two yellow lights at the bottom of the shaft glowed faintly. He concentrated on them and burst downward, slowing at the last second to land on his feet. He stepped between the shafts to avoid bodies punching into concrete. One after another they exploded in blood and bared bone.

With an effort, he formed another shield and tore open an elevator door. A barrage of gunfire erupted from a room full of guards. He spun out of the way, losing the shield, and was almost crushed by another falling troop. Blood sprayed his cap and through the eye holes to speckle his eyelids. He pressed himself into a corner of the shaft. In that moment, the reality of exhaustion dawned. The endless supply of potential had gone dry, almost as if revoked.

More rounds punched through the closed elevator doors. They were fishing for him.

"God damn it." He stuck his hand in his vest pocket and pulled out the Semtex slab and detonator. He readied the detonator before sending the explosives out the open elevator door and high over their heads.

The first shouts were his signal. He gathered himself and once more turtled with a thick shield and pressed the detonator button. The explosion flashed in silence as sound waves, metal, and concrete bounded off his shell, pinning him in his corner.

The shield fell and a headache took its place. The air tasted of acrid chemicals and death. He listened but heard nothing but the echo of the blast in the caverns below. Carefully, he stepped around the mangled remains of elevator doors and over bloodied concrete blocks to see the hole blown in the floor and ceiling. Torn bodies lined the walls of the room. The disturbed waters of the reservoir cast light and shadows on the carnage around him.

He stumbled and caught himself near the edge. Peering over, he saw the waves and chunks of concrete at the bottom.

That was close. Sorry about Javier. I wasn't sure you'd make it, either.

Johan's presence felt good. "Did you get them?"

Yes, I got them. And yes, Cathbad has gone on.

He shuddered in relief. It had been worth it.

"And my dad?"

I'm sorry. Javier was seen passing on but I don't know about your dad. He wasn't visible to me when I was set loose. I'll try to find out, though, I promise.

The room seemed to dim at the news. Not again... he needed to know, needed closure or hope. "Maria's back in charge?"

Don't know yet. You have a minute at most. Soldado's messing with the elevators but they're coming down the stairs now.

"What about the meta scrambler?"

Never mind that. Get back to Meng. You're more important. Can you do it?

He was exhausted but not completely. The bullet to the skull cap had started an ache that was getting worse, adding to the issue of focus. Dots framed his peripheral vision. He wondered what internal bleeding of the brain felt like.

"Yeah, I can get there."

The clang of a door and boots on stairs startled him.

Get gone then.

"Going."

Clearing the cavern, he made his way back through the circular shafts up to the utility room and into the hall. The goggles still worked but glitched every time he looked too far up. He used the rifle's feeder beam again, this time with the rifle's safety off. Old-fashioned firepower would have to augment his defense.

He opened the door to the loading area and was met with silence. He turned up the feeder beam and scanned the entire space and saw nothing. He waited for Meng to crack the hatch. Johan's presence had faded abruptly, making him wonder what was happening in the world.

"Um... hello?"

Walking along the wall towards the main tunnel, he wondered if Meng leaving was related to Johan's leaving, too. Closer to the tunnel, sounds echoed faintly at first, then grew until it was clear something was coming from the direction of the base.

"Johan, you wanna tell me what's going on?" he muttered while running to the edge of the tunnel.

A light grew with the sound.

"Ah fuck."

He bolted back towards the door, half running, half flying. The approaching train spoiled his night vision so he turned it off. Looking back, he saw the cylindrical car arrive in the loading space. It turned just as he reached the doorway, flooding him in light.

A loud clank sounded – the door locking. Rows of overhead lights suddenly glowed as power was routed to the wing.

Panic sent him gathering potential. Still exhausted, his mind resisted. He fished for a C4 door banger from his kit and pressed it to the door, triggering the timer. It went off with a flash and deafening pop. A pull on the handle showed the lock still engaged.

"Damn it."

A hiss sounded from the train car and its door opened. Troops fanned out, their rifle beams flickering in his direction.

He flew then, fast and to the right. Gunfire followed him, with a round striking his lower thigh. He shouted in pain and immediately raised the rifle to return fire, pissed off more than scared until he actually heard the rounds slicing the air near his head. The rifle spit out a stream of bullets at the troops. He circled around to put the car between them. The tunnel was close so he darted into it, heading towards the exit. The tunnel lights were now lit, creating a dizzying peripheral effect as he flew. The spots in his vision grew bigger and began to pulse in time with the pain in his head. Only a few hundred yards later, focus gave way and he fell to the tunnel floor, skidding to a stop.

Hang on, help is coming.

Johan's message only vaguely registered. Completely spent, he saw the train's lights enter the tunnel and begin to accelerate towards him. The grid had gone solid, dry of potential, as unyielding as it had been growing up.

"Get my core, man. I don't want to leave yet. Kaiya needs me."

The lights grew blinding, becoming the white field in his first out of body experience. He couldn't leave now, couldn't avoid the impact. The pain would have to be endured–

A booming crash reverberated in his skull and the lights died. Sparks and flames receded at high speed as the train reversed down the tunnel with a screeching report – pushed by the cloaked ship.

You can keep your core. I've got enough on my hands.

"Jesus Christ," he breathed. "I can't keep doing this."

Soldado's been cut off from the network and they're about to bomb your only exit. Get clear now.

Moments later, space split open to reveal the dim interior of the ship. Arabian Meng waved him in.

"Let's go, inside."

He managed to stand and clamber into the ship. The hatch closed and Meng flew on. He fell into the seat and strapped himself in, ignoring the throbbing headache. "Who's in charge?"

"Of them? No telling. They know we're here. I wrecked another car near the exit."

He prepared the ultra-wideband radar, setting it for maximum power but not turning it on.

Sortie of F15's scrambled out of Khalid are headed your way. Set up for air to ground. Get the hell out of there.

"Okay, okay," he said. "Meng, let me have the controls."

"You sure?"

"Yes. Hang on."

He engaged the radar and adjusted settings to focus on the end of the tunnel. The train car wreckage showed clearly. "Shields up." Eyeballing it, he slid the disc forward and shot down the tunnel.

"Damn, man."

Speed indications read mach 1.2.

"I got it."

He slowed at the last second and rammed into the debris, driving it into the sand and against broken fragments of the rock wall plug. The train car's framework crumpled until it fell behind them. They passed into the sandy outer chamber.

Ground forces arriving topside. Maybe laser spotters.

Austin expanded the radar. A staggered line of blips indicating incoming aircraft.

Go, full throttle. Get out now.

He set the angle to clear the chamber. Just as he slid the disc forward, all readings stuttered and shifted. Thermal readings glowed brightly, making the screens a mess. A missile had struck – and they were still in the chamber. He adjusted the angle once more but additional missiles exploded, one after another, bouncing the craft around.

"Damn it!" The screens were a confusing mess.

Beam weapon! They're firing into the sand. Get out of there!

"I'm *trying*," he said, but again found his trajectory forced into the rock. He killed the thermal layer of the readout to make the axis gridlines easier to see. He tweaked the stick and jimmied the disc until the ship rose shot out of the chamber. He slapped it fully forward and blue sky filled the screen. The blips receded from the radar.

"They tried to seal us in," Meng said.

"They almost did."

Austin took the ship out of the region. To the east, dusk pressed on the western shores of India. Coastal lights glowed in miniature.

"What next?" he asked.

"You lay down. Ignore this. You rest, nothing else."

"What?"

"Edward's orders. You need to rest and recharge. We're headed to Iran. If I need you, I will ask."

Despite the action that followed over Iran and Israel, Austin did fall asleep. He dreamt of a long and treacherous camel ride across the desert, ending at an oasis where Kaiya waited. When he went to kiss her, she became another woman, one he didn't recognize until she spoke.

"Been waiting for you," Maria said.

• • •

Sirens sounded across the rural countryside. Morning air carried the smells of the lagoon into the kitchen where the woman sat. The

457

side door was open but blocked by one of the two guards not dead or gone mad. Tense to the point of shaking, he stood with weapon ready in his blood-spattered clothing. The other of Xian Shung's men stood at the arch to the living room in a similar state. Both kept their backs to the woman wrapped in the blanket. Both were terrified of the power pouring from her.

The sirens grew louder. Somewhere in the house a clock rang the hour.

The woman reached up to touch the swollen sockets where eyes once rolled. Infection created pockets of pus that pressed against the severed optic nerve. She rode the pain.

At first she couldn't believe they had left. Released, she acted savagely and without reserve, sure a mistake had been made. The little wench became the powerful witch and drove twenty-two men to kill one another. The bodies of Xian Shung and his mistresses adorned the upstairs bedroom where she had artfully arrayed them in death. The revenge was shallow, localized. Bastion was who she wanted retribution from yet he was also strangely absent. Team Three said only that she would be kept isolated until situations stabilized.

Vans belonging to the local police kicked up gravel upon arrival. Bodies on the front steps would confirm the caller's report. The two guards turned against their will and took aim at one another from across the kitchen. The two shots sounded as one and they fell to the floor, the last witnesses.

She pulled the blanket tighter and followed the police in their discovery of the compound's horrors.

Chapter 32

Revolution, in order to be creative, cannot do without either a moral
or metaphysical rule to balance the insanity of history.
- Albert Camus, 1913-1960, French Existential Writer

Johan stepped from the train onto the sunny platform at Murcia in the southeast of Spain. Near the station entrance a man in a yellow and blue windbreaker turned and began walking. Johan followed him to the parking lot. They climbed into a red Citroen C4 and set off on the highway for the Spanish coast.

They rode in silence as the city fell behind and the hills of the Baetic mountains rose around them. Johan used his phone to finish reading the article in the Mirror Online about the British playwright, Harold Hughes, who'd been among those arrested in a child pornography sting. His lawyer issued a statement indicating his client had been framed as retribution for not paying out to a blackmail threat.

Marco looked over. "As I said, uncommon awareness."

He put his phone away. "Some would call it freakish, now."

"Not that bad, I hope."

"Not exactly bad. But freakish, yes."

"Maybe later you can show me what you mean."

"Maybe. Is she there?"

Marco nodded. "Soldado, too."

A patrol SUV with Guardia Civil markings passed them. The untrained sweep of meta told the same story as Italian police forces had. Spanish peacekeepers were on edge in the wake of what the media was calling *los Dias de Diablo*, the Days of the Devil. Not far from the truth, considering what Bastion had launched. The domino effect would take months if not years to stabilize – provided a truce with Maria held.

While a central power vacuum never appeared to form, the Comannda faltered in the days following the ingress at the Core. A period of obvious command and control issues resulted in frozen or exposed operations, dangling intelligence structures, and the triggering of sometimes violent self-sealing mechanisms throughout the ranks of Groups Two and Three. In a sense, the Comannda experienced a Scattering of their own; the first ever recorded.

"How's Samantha?" Johan asked.

"She's got a green thumb now with those plants on her sill. That was a nice gesture. She's loving them. Otherwise nothing new."

Five days prior, the blog produced a clear message indicating the return of Maria to a state of grace at the controls of the Comannda. What it lacked was an indication of intent.

"Neutrality is difficult in times like this." He watched the passing hills.

"Anything pressing you?"

Johan shook his head. "Only the korjé, searching still. Nothing of the others." He looked to Marco. "Any word on Austin's dad?"

"No, nothing."

"We'll have to work on that."

Three cars lined the driveway at the house in Bolnuevo. Marco and Johan entered the front room to the sound of light applause. Soldado, Sean, and Rachel stood along with a smaller woman whose aura was veiled but still unmistakable. The stranger came forward and slipped into Johan's embrace. He pressed his lips to her head, thankful for Anki's presence.

She looked up. "Holding in there?"

"Yes. You?"

She shrugged. "Knowledge is a hurtful thing."

"If we'd known that before, would we have not tried?"

She stared back, holding on to her reply. There had been no choice. "I'm told there's a surprise in store for me this evening. At this point, I absolutely hate surprises."

"No clue what it is?"

"No, just that it's something big." She didn't admit to being scared but didn't have to.

Sean greeted him with a handshake. "I told her not to worry but she won't listen to me. Is Austin going to make it?"

"Not likely. He's still holed up with Kaiya in the ship, responding to only the biggest emergencies. I'm trying not to bother them."

Anki said, "I'd say they've earned as much quiet as we can offer."

Soldado came over and hugged both Johan and Anki. "Good to see you, hombre. Close call."

"No shit. Thanks for everything."

"Wish I'd done more. Totem busted my game."

Johan nodded. The encryption sequencing had changed across all Comannda networks.

"There's still a small chance my Booty2 survived somewhere on their net. If so, I might hear back from it in time."

"Here's to hoping."

"Okay, okay, let's go people," Rachel called from the kitchen. "This food isn't going to make itself and I sure as hell am not doing it alone."

The group spent the afternoon putting together dinner. Rachel and Anki ran the kitchen and had Marco and Johan grating cheese and chopping vegetables. Sean sat at the table and shared with Johan in recounting their recent and narrow successes.

Maria's conspiracy threaded through key areas of the Comannda. Vital to her plans were the three Volgograd research teams. With six members each, they had worked toward and recently achieved a state the Korda referred to as *dùnadh*, or joining – something the Korda had previously been unable to achieve. When joined, the korjé became exponentially more capable in Saoghal and presumably in Raon. Team three was the most powerful, with team one being the weakest.

Second team had contained Maria while third team had captured Johan and later held Cathbad. It was team three that had sworn secret allegiance to Maria. They insured second team's bodies were killed to free Maria and then helped Austin and Johan with the Council itself.

The risks of Johan joining the dùnadh had been great and were still cause for concern. He'd had little choice at the time, but in joining with team three he shared himself on deep levels. Identity, core desires and fears, and techniques had been laid bare equally by all seven. Liabilities were born at the same time new understanding bloomed. What that meant for the future wasn't clear but the exchange allowed both sides to reach their immediate goals.

"Do they know you learned the method of dùnadh?" Rachel asked.

Johan shrugged. "I'm guessing yes. Joined like that, everything flows. It's all laid bare."

"So what's next?" Soldado asked.

"We work on strengthening our Confrere and rebuilding the families," Sean answered. "We'll see what Maria's plans are. Many of the new geopolitical structures remain in place. I suspect System Seven has begun, like it or not. We face the Conflict as long as the world is still hostage."

"What about the Mu?" Soldado asked. "Did they help Austin with the AG ship?"

"We're still not sure. Whoever he was in contact with warned that the Mu weren't all they claimed to be. It could have been a Mu whistleblower or it could be another race."

Johan didn't mention the Pure or the Owners and the Factions they controlled galaxies with. Until he was able to verify what he'd experienced, there was no sense in complicating things.

As if sensing an omission, Sean said to Johan, "I'll want to spend some time with you recollecting your capture and release, if you don't mind."

"Of course."

"I don't know about everyone else, but all this is making me very, very hungry," Rachel said. "Can I get some help setting the table?"

Dinner and drinks carried them past nightfall and out onto the deck. Stars overhead lent the gathering a timelessness and purpose that was unmistakable. Johan leaned against the railing with his back to town. He'd noticed four times the number of guards as before and more in a neighboring house down the hill. Bràthair folded the night air in a wide ring. Expectation raised the hairs on his neck.

Sean joined him. "Figured it out?"

"Someone important arriving?"

"Can't put anything past you."

"But who?" Johan asked.

Sean nodded towards the headlights on the road. "You'll see."

A black sedan rolled up the drive. It stopped and two passengers emerged from the back seat. An older man dressed in black looked up and waved. The other was a younger man. Together they headed for the entry.

Sean announced the guests' arrival as they stepped out onto the deck. "Please welcome our patron and respected friend, Father Eduardo Apodaca."

The white collar was missing but the look was complete. Edward appeared and felt like a veteran clergyman. "Beautiful night for a party. Good to see you all again. I'd like to introduce my old friend, Steffan Lawrence."

Anki sat up and held the arms of her chair. Her vibe shifted and it was Clare that stood and stared.

Edward smiled. "I believe you remember Steffan, Ms. Clare."

She hurried to him and fell into his arms. For a moment it was apparent to all that mother and father and daughter shared the loving embrace. Soft applause mixed with congratulations.

Edward went to stand with Johan.

"Father Eduardo. Have you come to receive my confession?"

Edward smiled. "Thank you for the hard work in training our bràthair. It might have been months or longer before they figured out dùnadh."

"Oh, I don't think it would have taken more than a few encounters with their teams to get the feel for it."

"If they survived, that is. I also wanted to hear directly from you on Cathbad's leaving." Edward made himself available.

"I see."

He summoned the memory and set the scene for them both. It played out as it had, complete with his own decision to stay on.

Edward nodded, his gratitude powerful in the moments following.

"Have you found anything of Austin's father?" Edward asked.

"I was going to ask the same of you. He had to have fled or been taken after being shot."

"Contact with Maria?"

"None."

"Be careful there."

"Oh, I know." Johan turned to the railing and looked out at the coast. "Let me ask, have you ever thought maybe the Runa Korda and the Comannda are part of something bigger?"

Edward joined him. "What do you mean?"

"I don't know. Like two chopsticks, being used to accomplish one goal."

"I rather think they are at odds, don't you?"

"Unless there is something greater working the sticks."

Edward studied him. "What else happened out there?"

Johan looked over. "I'm just thinking big picture. Do you suppose we would realize it if we were being played?"

"You could drive yourself nuts imagining things."

Johan chuckled then shared his encounter with the Pure.

Edward took it all in and responded with a frown. "If true, this changes things. The Mu wouldn't be just observers, they would be guards, agents of a Faction."

"Which explains the warning Austin received about the Mu."

"But who helped him?"

"I don't know."

"That space, it needs to be explored. Work together with dùnadh to better understand it."

"It's literally chaos. I'm not sure taking them there is a good idea."

"You made it okay."

"No, I fell down the Rabbit Hole and someone lifted me out. I'll get back to you on that. There may be a way to do it safely." He sipped his drink. Maybe the Pure would help. "So why else are you here?"

Edward turned to receive a glass from Rachel. "Gracias. Would you believe to thank you for being who you are and for doing all that you've done?"

"I might."

"Actually there is one more surprise for Anki. Or rather, Clare."

"You've found her a new host."

Edward nodded. "Should be here within the hour."

"How will it affect Anki? Clare's been there her entire life."

"The absence will no doubt be substantial but we think so will the freedom. Duality has its own burdens. She'll need you."

"I'm there."

"I know. Time for a toast." He turned to the group and gathered their attention. He spoke to them but also to the thousands of Korda who would receive the Words and someday, perhaps the world.

"Despite the recent and ongoing horrors and tragedies, tonight we have reason for gratitude and hope. Our understanding of reality has expanded, offering the opportunity to create a better framework for the rise of all of mankind. The long journey towards disassembling the ruling empire has reached its most challenging and intriguing miles. We have found the Change and replaced the most hostile Comannda leaders. I cannot imagine a better indication that we have followed the right trackways to the future we desire. You all have my sincere thanks for making it so." He raised his glass. "To Johan, Austin, and Anki. To Cathbad, Javier, and to Mug. To all those lost and whose fate is yet unknown. To surprises and friends to share them with. To long life, and to change!"

Chapter 33

To know how to disguise is the knowledge of kings.
- Cardinal De Richelieu, 1585 – 1642, French Statesman

Doreen König stood in the kitchen rinsing breakfast dishes and listening to news on the radio. Her husband Karl had just left for the hardware store to pick up supplies to repair the drooping roof on the hencoop. She suppressed mild anxiety at his absence and focused on the news.

Out the window, the morning's snow lay stark against the blackened timbers of George and Faiga's barn. Memories of that night still frightened her. At some point it would be torn down. The sooner the better.

She put a mixing bowl in the dishwasher. A pair of headlights on the lane caught her eye. A gray Land Rover slowed at the Bergmann's drive, came to a stop, then turned in. She saw only a driver.

"Oh dear."

She toweled her hands and quickly went to the side of the refrigerator to unclip a piece of paper. She carried it with her to the den where she found Karl's binoculars. Back in the kitchen, she turned off the lights and raised the glasses to spy on the visitor.

At first he just sat there, parked next to the house, staring at the barn. There wasn't enough light to see his face clearly. She glanced down at the sketch though she really didn't need to. The face it portrayed had already been burned into her mind.

The car door opened and the man emerged. He stood for a moment and then turned to look in her direction. No, directly *at* her. She shivered and put the glasses down, relieved. At least it wasn't *him*.

The man walked towards the barn a few steps and again stopped, as if unsure. She used the glasses to watch him, lost in the wondering of who he was. He turned towards the house then and came upon the front porch. He rang the bell. With no answer, he knocked on the door.

Nothing about him felt dangerous. It seemed possible it was a friend who had not heard. She decided it would be worth it to go and talk to the man. If she hurried, she could be back before Karl returned.

Knowing she'd gone over to meet a stranger at the Bergmann's would anger him no end.

• • •

She came out finally, donned in boots and a winter coat, responding to his manipulation. She was worried the Butcher of Rotterdam was back to finish the job. What exactly had happened he couldn't tell and worry demanded he get the full story. George and Faiga weren't home and hadn't been by the feel of it.

Since the night he'd left, he hadn't dared to reach out for fear of bringing harm their way. In truth, he'd also been afraid of what he might learn if he did. His love and regard for them made not knowing a gnawing thing that he had to resolve. Coming to visit under a ruse would allow him to know.

He turned to his car as if to leave and acted surprised when he saw the woman approach.

"Hello."

She nodded. "You're looking for the Bergmanns?"

"I am. George and Faiga?"

"I'm Doreen, their neighbor." She accepted his offered handshake.

"Are they on vacation?"

"Who are you, may I ask?"

He introduced himself as Ben Roth, a reverse mortgage specialist.

"I see. Well, they aren't on vacation and they won't be needing your services. They've moved to a care home. The place is for sale."

"Ah, a care home." He turned to look at the barn. "That looks recent. What happened? Everyone okay?"

"Yes, no one was hurt. Arson, they say."

She had a story involving intrigue and the Butcher and needed just a nudge from him to feel comfortable telling it. From her thoughts he knew the gist of it without asking. They'd had the murderer in their home and later, when the barn burned, they attributed it to him. It burned his soul to think of Faiga thinking of him that way.

There was no helping it. He imagined finding Faiga to explain things and having the Korda repair George's mind but knew it wasn't a reasonable thought. They were near their own natural end, in the world they knew. He had to fight the impulse to change it.

He thanked Doreen and left her company before she could get started talking. He returned to the warmth of the rental. With a final glance at the barn and house, he turned around and headed back down the drive to the lane.

Chapter 34

We have inherited the past; we can create the future.
- Source unknown

Austin and Kaiya walked along the path near the giraffe exhibit. The catcalls of the red apes they'd just left made Austin smile. He squeezed Kaiya's hand and adjusted his shades.

"What? What are they saying?"

"Just be glad you aren't in their cage."

His meta skills were improving with the second stage of training. Kaiya's training was underway, too, and Edward had ordered round the clock covering services from the dùnadh-enhanced bràthair for both of them. Her new body was a suicide recovery, though the wrist wounds had been repaired. It was as close to her old body as she could have asked.

He steered them towards the rear of the park. It was busy for a Wednesday in January, despite the blustery wind and chill in the air. The bombings terrorizing the nation had stopped and people were eager to take back the norm. Groups of school children swarmed the pathways and clung to the rails and fences of the exhibits. The previous night's rains left the zoo's shaded pathways damp and the smells fresh and poignant.

The animals all alerted to his presence and seemed to be following his progress in different ways. Some managed to extend their meta, some passively tracked his, keen on its difference from those in the crowd. A lion roared nearby. Austin felt its unhappy protest, part demand and part interest. Not all the animals resented their captivity but the lions certainly did.

She sipped her soda from a straw. "What do you want to do after this?"

"I'm open. What are you thinking?"

"I'm thinkin' Long Beach."

"La Palapa." The restaurant they'd first met in.

"Of course."

Kaiya's biocat program had her looking very nearly her old self, something Edward didn't want them to do. She shrugged it off, knowing they were protected. Their day in LA wasn't exactly about recapturing the old days but it had some of that feel. Returning to their roots had an undeniable grounding effect.

They neared their destination and the crowd grew thick around the exhibit. Already he heard the vocalizing. Kids and chaperones created a sea of humanity with behavior not unlike the animals they'd come to see. They managed to squeeze in along the rail directly across from the rock house that staff had penned the chimpanzee's "penthouse". The males were in motion, apparently agitated for no reason.

He spotted a female atop the penthouse holding onto her young chimp. The little one was standing and uncharacteristically scanning the crowds.

"There, the little one on top."

Kaiya smiled. "Aww. Is she looking for you?"

He did his own passive scan. Satisfied there was no threat, he extended across the distance to Darcy. She jumped up and down on contact and her mother kept hold of her to contain her. She looked directly at him, pointing and patting her shoulders, as excited as any kid. Their meta mixed and Darcy vocalized to emphasize the message that she had gotten better and that she had grown.

He resonated love back to her.

The little chimp danced and hollered and turned to hug her momma. The older chimp glanced over and emoted a deep maternal gratitude. The alpha male hollered and beat his chest. The other males joined to create a racket.

Being upstaged was never a pleasant experience for a male.

They took lunch at La Palapa and browsed the simple memories of their past, marveling at what had once passed as trials and tribulations. Cramming for finals, a missed job opportunity, a late rent payment... they sat silent for a while and let it sink in. The terrors and wonders of the last several months had carved new lines of appreciation for life and for the unknown.

A sympathy had also formed for the bulk of humanity that lived in the fish bowl, barely interested in what was beyond it. They agreed that in some ways ignorance was bliss but also knew a comparative analysis would easily favor meta-awareness. So much of mental illness was actually the result of unfiltered input causing neurotic reactions. The change had to continue. People had to make sense of their connectedness.

"That's what it's all about, really." Austin stirred his tea. "Accessing the gestalt that's been kept locked up. Taking it back and unifying around it."

"Philanthropy shouldn't be as treacherous as this."

He managed a chuckle. "You aren't kidding. Damned Robin Hoods, all of us."

"What do you most want to do? What do you want to see change?" she asked.

"All of it." He half-grinned. "Really, that's tough to answer. Part of me would say the medicines, free energy, cleaning the food supply. Control of those keep the structures of power in place. Clean up government. Economics could be reworked and quickly. The new tech would render so much suffering obsolete. Out with greed, in with our highest ideals. Another part of me says break down the barriers to meta awareness first. If people knew how connected we really are, we could face the challenges together. Leverage resources to improve all of humanity's experience. It would change the world. I understand that might be a bit naïve, but it depends on how we do it." He drank his tea and watched a waiter seat a couple at a nearby table. "I can't help but think of all the people who worked against odds to make a difference. History's filled with heroes who tried. They scratched at the surface without knowing how thick the truth was."

"Or how serious the consequences would be for trying."

"Exactly."

He again thought of Yuni and his dad and Javier and all the people lost around the world. Guilt pinged his core with a familiar ring. They had not been able to visit her mother's grave, though memories of her funeral had been provided. Word of his father had not yet surfaced though Johan would continue searching. His fate weighed most heavily but he suppressed it out of regard for Kaiya's actual loss.

She wadded up the paper cover of her straw. "I'm just glad we have a better chance. Seems the idea of karmic balance really is a facet of nature and not only on the micro scale. It's just taken a while to swing back this way."

"Karma needs force to operate. The transfer of power."

"You and Johan are part of that now."

"We all need to be." He sighed. He was failing at keeping his mood up. Instead of encouraging her, she was striving to prop him up in the moment.

Kaiya looked out the window at the beach. Down a ways, crowds gathered at a kite competition. The loops and dips and the effort by those on the ground revealed the sport that it was.

"Hey," she said. "Let's take a walk."

They strolled the sand at surf's edge and watched the kites ahead. The wind ran steady and brisk off the water and buffeted the nylon constructs. The flyers were talented, their acrobatics well-practiced.

A local radio station's van was out with its mast up and their event canopy looked ready to tear away in the wind. The DJ acted as master of ceremonies for the competition. Kids on their father's shoulders waved at the kites dancing in the sky.

"So answer me this," Kaiya said, putting her arm through his. "Why didn't you ever tell me about the wind and the out of body experiences?"

"Really? C'mon. What would you have thought?"

She considered it. "Yeah, I guess you're right. I probably would have wondered about you. The UFO stuff was bad enough."

"Which is exactly what I didn't want. Hell, I didn't want to wonder about myself."

"Now look at you. Telekinetic talent. First contact. Someday you'll be famous."

"Don't hold your breath. And first contact wasn't me."

"Don't be so negative. You're one of the first. It's amazing." They walked in silence for a bit before she asked, "Has anyone mentioned your mom?"

"My mom? What about her?"

"She reached out to you in the dream, didn't she?"

"Maybe. It sure felt like it."

"It was her, I'm sure of it."

He slowed. "Why do you say that?"

She looked up at him. "I had a dream last night about Mac Payant. He said there was something that you needed to know."

"What?"

"That the accident that killed her wasn't an accident."

"And my dad knew that?"

She nodded. "He had gotten mixed up with something that he wasn't supposed to. Her death was their response. He knew you would have been next."

"Fuck." He stopped and stared out past the waves. "*Fuck.*" It explained all the shit he'd received from him over the years. He'd been trying to steer him clear of trouble, despite his affiliation. A new layer of guilt formed around the irony. On its heels came a more anger at the Comannda and the system it had created.

Kaiya faced him, hands on his stomach. "Wait. Don't lose yourself in it. Please, listen. Your mom appeared in the dream, too. She thanked me and told me to tell you she loves you. She also said your dad isn't dead."

A mixed thrill shot through him, lifting his hopes. In the next instant he faltered, wondering if her dream had been another manipulation by the Korda to keep him positive. Kaiya followed his thoughts.

"I don't think it was Edward's doing, I really don't. I can't say why, it's just there, in my gut. I think it was your mom, Austin. I felt her love for your dad and I felt her longing for him."

"Does she know he worked for them? Did she know?"

Kaiya's face showed her sadness. "I wish I knew, babe, I really do. Either way, it's important to know he chose you over them. Every time. That helps, right?"

"There's no guarantee he still will, is there? Or that he's who I think he is." He realized his tone had been biting. "I'm sorry."

"No, there isn't a guarantee and not knowing makes it hard, but at least he's not passed on. He still has a chance. There is still hope and you'd better not lose it."

He walked on, not wanting to draw attention. The wind tossed their hair and made the kites dance overhead. It seemed secrets would always haunt him, that truths would never be fully exposed. His dad was a mystery and it hurt knowing what he did. Hope was hard to feel.

She patted his stomach. "You wanna be cruel?"

"What?"

She looked up. "The wind, silly."

"Ah. Too risky." It wasn't exactly true but it was an effective deflection. The day's semblance of a normal life felt so good that exercising his telekinetics felt freakish.

"C'mon, I don't mean bending, I mean reach out to the wind. Do it like you did when you were a kid. Try for me, I'm curious. You need to shake this funk."

He hesitated, not ready to give up the emotions swirling about.

"You said it seemed intelligent somehow. Who knows what that really means? And when was the last time you tried?"

He looked down, then away to the ocean's horizon. The ancient trackways Cathbad spoke of seemed to run through everything, throughout time. He had to get better at spotting them. This felt like one. When he looked back at her, it was with a mix of gratitude and respect for her and for the universe at once.

"Years, actually."

"It can't hurt, I don't think."

They retreated to a spot some distance from the competition where she sat and he laid down, ankles crossed.

"Post-lunch sleepies. I might fall asleep."

She nudged his ribs with her knee. "I'll keep you awake."

He closed his eyes and for a jarring moment was thirteen again, on the roof with the same wind and the same need to calm it down. He cleared his mental deck and settled, centering on the present. After a bit he formed the earth and the Schoolhouse Rock winds. The imagery returned, as familiar as the first time.

"Alright, here comes."

The calm feeling arrived, though whether from memory or not he couldn't tell. He formed the gloved hand and focused on the billowing winds. Slowly he lowered it. The cartoon winds compressed, leaving room for only a little to pass. The calm feeling pervaded then, not memory at all, and nothing of his doing. He felt it echo from Kaiya in a saturating vibe. Validation tingled like tiny bells in his soul.

The wind gradually fell, bubbling up but then falling softer until the groan of the crowd was heard. He bottomed out in the peaceful shallows and stayed there. What it meant, how it could be, and why him were currents only, questions he had no answers for and knew he wasn't meant to, yet. Without effort, without touching the quantum foam, he joined with the wind in the agreement of stillness and peace. It did suggest some kind of intelligence, some level of awareness from whatever force governed the wind's flow. Two, then three minutes passed. After five, the DJ on the PA announced a break.

More time passed with barely a hint of a breeze. The sun warmed his face. He opened his eyes and with an effort pulled himself to a sitting position. His muscles felt like they had been marinated in the calm. He took a deep breath. And another. He wiggled his feet to get his heart rate back up.

She smiled at him.

"Alrighty then." He thought of his mother and father and all the things they had done for him. He owed it to them to keep trying, to keep learning.

"Nice job, babe," Kaiya said. She watched his face and waited for it. Over the next minute, the winds gradually returned until pendants on a nearby pole flapped again. Her eyes glistened.

A small cheer went up as the first kite leapt back into the sky.

He smiled at her. "How about that."